The Code of the Hills

The Code of
the Hills

An Ozarks Mystery

NANCY ALLEN

WITNESS
IMPULSE
An Imprint of HarperCollinsPublishers

THE CODE OF THE HILLS. Copyright © 2014 by Nancy Allen. All rights reserved under International and Pan-American Copyright Conventions. By payment of the required fees, you have been granted the nonexclusive, nontransferable right to access and read the text of this e-book on screen. No part of this text may be reproduced, transmitted, decompiled, reverse-engineered, or stored in or introduced into any information storage and retrieval system, in any form or by any means, whether electronic or mechanical, now known or hereinafter invented, without the express written permission of HarperCollins e-books.

EPub Edition April 2014 ISBN: 9780062325945

Print Edition ISBN: 9780062325952

HB 06.10.2024

To the center of my universe:
Randy, Ben, and Martha

Let the woman learn in silence with all
    subjection.
But I suffer not a woman to teach, nor to
    usurp authority
over the man, but to be in silence.

1 TIMOTHY 2:11–12

Prologue

Tiffany picked up the tiny pink plastic brush and ran it through the Barbie's silky hair. Smoothing the blond hairdo with her hand, she turned the new doll around to closely inspect every detail of its face and figure. She'd never owned a new Barbie before, just had to make do with cast-off dolls her older sisters passed down: old Barbies with missing clothes and limbs and ragged hair.

This doll was a Christmas gift, but it had to be a secret, because Tiffany's daddy wouldn't like it. Daddy didn't hold with Christmas; he said it was a waste of money. When it came to presents and such, they kept their mouths shut if they knew what was good for them.

But the PTA ladies from Tiffany's school delivered a basket on Christmas Eve, when Daddy was out. Mom wouldn't have been allowed to open the door to them if he was home, because Daddy and Uncle Al didn't like people snooping around.

So when they spied the new Barbie in the box sitting on top of the canned goods, her mom told her to grab it and get it out of sight, because Daddy would take it back to the store and swap it for money if it was still in its plastic box.

Tiffany got it out in the nick of time, right before Tiffany's daddy and Al came home with a bottle. The men sat on the front steps, drinking and laughing until the liquor ran out. Then the fighting started, and Daddy beat Al up pretty good. Storming from the house with his face dripping blood, Al yelled about getting even. Mom said the commotion was likely to bring the police down on them. Then Daddy said he'd teach her a lesson about back-sassing.

Tiffany ran upstairs so she wouldn't have to watch it. She took the Barbie to bed with her and stuck it under her T-shirt for safekeeping.

The next afternoon, on Christmas Day, Tiffany hid with her new Barbie, whispering secrets into her plastic ear. Huddled against the tattered back of the couch, she heard heavy footsteps stride through the living room. Tiffany froze, hardly daring to breathe, as her dad stomped into the kitchen.

The feet returned to the living room. She could see his scuffed toes when she peeked under the couch.

"Where the hell is Charlene?" he demanded.

Tiffany's mom called from the kitchen. "She's out back. What do you want her for?"

"I want a rubdown."

"She don't like to," her mom responded in a hoarse

whisper, tiptoeing into the room. The silence that followed was terrible. Tiffany could imagine the expression on his face. When he said, "I ain't gonna tell you again," her mom went to the kitchen window and called for Charlene.

Charlene came inside. When he took her to the bedroom and shut the door, she didn't put up a fight. It was just as well. Charlene would have to do it anyway, and she'd buy trouble if she made a fuss. Still, noises came from behind the door. Tiffany stuck her fingers in her ears and hid her face on her knees. She could stay right in that spot and no one would know she was there. She wouldn't make a sound.

Chapter One

THE RINGING WOKE Elsie from a restless sleep. She rolled over on her side, registering a nagging headache, a terrible thirst, and a sense of chagrin. Dear God, she thought, I'll never drink again.

Fumbling for the phone on her bedside table, she checked the caller ID: PRIVATE. "Forget it," she said, and rolled back over.

She closed her eyes and tried to drift off again, but her thirst wouldn't let her rest. Soda, she thought. It might jump-start her recovery.

Groaning, she tossed off her quilt and trudged into the kitchen. Opening the refrigerator door, she pushed aside a jar of Hellmann's to reach for her medicine: the box containing shiny silver cans of Diet Coke.

With a sigh of relief, she pulled one from the box and popped the top. It slid down her throat tasting like the nectar of the gods, and she gulped gratefully.

Making her way to the living room, Elsie thought she'd check to see whether she'd made the morning news. Reporters from the local TV stations had been at the courthouse when the jury returned its guilty verdict in the felony assault trial she'd won the night before. She squinted at the digital clock on her cable box: 8:46 A.M. She'd missed it; the morning news ran at eight o'clock on Saturday.

Well, hell, she thought. Looking around, she surveyed the damage that a week of neglect had wreaked in her apartment. Though she couldn't see clearly without her contact lenses, it was easy to make out the dirty coffee cups, the congealed pizza on the coffee table, and the stacks of files and wadded sheets of discarded arguments for the prosecution littering the floor. *Maybe I'll clean up today,* she told herself, adding, *later.* She was too tired to contemplate labor. The hangover was an unwelcome reminder that thirty-one was not twenty-one. She felt as old as the hills.

Elsie headed to the bathroom in search of her glasses. Digging through a drawer of jumbled cosmetics, she was conscious of the bitter taste that the Diet Coke failed to wash away. The taste brought back memories of the prior night, and she grimaced at the thought. After the jury had returned its guilty verdict in her hard-fought trial, she had joined a group of cops at Baldknobbers bar. Flush with victory, she led the pack in rounds of beer, downing one Corona after another.

What began as uproarious fun had taken a downhill turn when her boyfriend, Noah Strong, a patrolman for the Barton, Missouri, Police Department, copped an attitude. She'd been going out with him for nearly a year, had always nursed a weakness for a pretty face, and Noah's was certainly a pleasure to gaze upon. At six-foot-four, with golden hair and blue eyes, he was every red-blooded midwestern girl's wet dream. His blinding white smile could melt butter—that is, when he chose to turn it on. He'd shown a tendency in recent months to become moody.

While Elsie and her trial witnesses—Detective Bob Ashlock and county deputies Joe Franks and Kyle Wistrom—were bellied up to the bar rehashing the evidence, Noah wandered over to the pool table. She was not inclined to follow; this was her party, after all. She and Ashlock crowed as they recounted his testimony to the deputies.

Elsie said, "In cross-ex, defendant's attorney tried to take the hide off Ash, but it can't be done."

"What'd he say?" asked Franks.

Ashlock waved a hand in dismissal, but Elsie merrily gave the account. "He tried to make out that Ash tampered with the tape of the defendant's admission."

"You're shitting me. Who is the guy?"

"Someone from a defense firm in Springfield. A St. Louis guy." Elsie took another swig from her bottle. "So Ash said, 'I would never tamper with evidence. But maybe the police do that kind of thing where you're from.'"

"Wish I'd seen it," said Franks. "Did the lawyer have one of those St. Louis accents?"

Ashlock said, "Well, he sure didn't sound like an Ozarks boy."

When Elsie twisted around on her bar stool to check on Noah, she saw him giving a woman from the crime lab way too much help with her pool cue.

"Uh-oh," she said, "looks like I need to check out the competition." Deputy Franks snickered. Though she and Noah had been an item for some time, Elsie knew that he still had a reputation as a ladies' man.

She slid off her bar stool and headed over, concentrating to walk a straight line. As she approached, Noah and his pool partner hastily parted, the woman fleeing to the other side of the pool table. Elsie slipped an arm around Noah's waist and asked, "Am I going to have to get in a catfight over you?"

He glanced away, defensively. "I'm just playing pool."

"Looks like you're playing," she said. She lifted her beer bottle to her lips and drained it.

He bent over the pool table and knocked a striped ball into a pocket. "You could've come over here, hung out with me, instead of holding court at the bar." Indicating her empty bottle, he added, "You're getting pretty shit-faced."

"Well, yeah," she responded, stung. "That's why I came. I'm trying to relax." She noted that Noah's pool partner had joined a group at a table by the door but continued to glance over at Noah. "Hey, baby, who's your little friend?" she said to him. "She's checking you out."

Noah tossed the pool cue on the table. "That's it." He snatched his jacket from a nearby chair and left in a huff. Elsie watched him go, surprised by his sensitivity. Surely she was the one with the right to have her nose out of joint.

Stumbling a little, she returned to the bar, where Franks had a fresh beer waiting for her. "My hero," she said with a forced laugh, trying to keep her game face intact as she swilled it down.

After that, her recall became fuzzy. She knew the party ended when she slipped on a slick spot on her way to the restroom and landed on her back on the dirty barroom floor. Her tumble earned her a hasty departure and a ride home from Ashlock.

Now, cringing at the recollection, she wished she hadn't played the drunken fool with Bob Ashlock there.

Ashlock was an old-fashioned law-and-order pro, a straight arrow. He was powerfully built, like a boxer, and conveyed authority with his erect military posture, no-nonsense manner, and the jut of his square Irish jaw. Juries loved him, and she liked and respected him immensely. Not forty yet, he had already served as Chief of Detectives for the Barton P.D. for nearly eight years, following a stellar decade on patrol. In her four years in the Prosecutor's Office, his careful investigative work and ease on the witness stand had turned the tide for her in many cases.

As she sat on her couch, wondering what she would say when she encountered Ashlock at the courthouse, and contemplating how long Noah would pout, her cell phone rang. "Leave me alone," she muttered, even as she grabbed her purse and fumbled to answer.

"Hello," she said without enthusiasm, wondering what inconsiderate oaf would call a working girl before nine o'clock on a Saturday morning.

"Elsie, it's Madeleine. I've been trying to reach you."

No, no, no, no. An early morning call from her boss, Madeleine Thompson, was not likely to be good news. She slumped down on the couch and squeezed her eyes shut. "Hey, Madeleine, what can I do for you?"

"Will you be coming into work today?"

Elsie was speechless for a moment. "Madeleine, it's Saturday."

"I know what day it is. Did you plan on coming in?"

"Well, no, I didn't," she said. She heard an apologetic note in her voice, and hated herself for it. "I just finished up the jury trial on that assault case last night. I've been burning the midnight oil all week. I thought I'd take it easy today."

"Is that right? I've been over here at the courthouse since eight o'clock. I'm working on the Taney case. Do you know who Taney is?"

"Sure. He's the guy who was messing with his daughters. The new incest case."

"That's the one." Madeleine's tone grew friendlier. "I need a second chair on this case, I think. I made a commitment to the voters in McCown County to aggressively pursue these abuse cases. Everyone says you have a real gift for handling young witnesses and developing rapport with children. Elsie, I want to bring you on board to assist me."

"Great." She sat up straight on the couch, feeling a

twinge of excitement; she certainly believed in locking up sex offenders. It was the reason she'd decided on law school in the first place. And she wasn't above appreciating that the Taney case had already sparked media attention. It would be high profile, and she was flattered to be chosen to assist. If her boss had expressed an interest in the outcome of the trial she won yesterday, she would be even more flattered.

"The preliminary hearing is next week," Madeleine said, "but we have a witness interview scheduled at ten o'clock. Can you be here in thirty minutes?"

"Sure, thirty minutes is no problem," Elsie replied, and then added, "I got a guilty verdict last night. The jury recommended twenty years."

"Oh. Too bad you didn't get more prison time. Well, see you in half an hour."

When the call was over, Elsie stared at the phone in her hand. "Bitch." She shuffled to the bathroom and had picked up her toothbrush when she was struck by a recollection that nearly made her drop it. She didn't have her car. It was in the parking lot of Baldknobbers.

BY THE TIME the taxi delivered her to the courthouse, thirty minutes had long since expired. She paid the driver, slammed the taxi door and sped down the sidewalk to the old courthouse in the center of the Barton town square. Nestled in the Ozark hills, Barton was the county seat, and its courthouse was a local jewel. Built on classical lines, with a low dome over a rotunda, the white stone courthouse had been the pride of McCown County since its construction in 1905. Other counties in the Ozarks had opted to move to new court facilities in recent years to deal with challenges of modern technology and security, but McCown County refused to budge.

The stubborn insistence on maintaining the old courthouse was emblematic of the character of the town. Barton was a community largely untouched by the progress of the twenty-first century. Founded by poor farmers eking a hard living from the rocky soil of the Ozark hills, Barton had short brushes with industry for periods of relative prosperity: mining in the 1800s was followed by the railroad, and when the lead and zinc mines tapped out and rail travel slowed, the torch passed to a paper cup factory that settled in Barton in the 1950s—because of the cheap local labor force, it was said. But in the 1980s the plant relocated to Mexico, leaving McCown County where it had begun: a community of rural hill people, as suspicious of government intervention as the moonshiners from whom they descended, wary of politics in general and liberals in particular.

The character of the community made Elsie's job as prosecutor easier in some ways, harder in others. While McCown County jurors were law-and-order enthusiasts as a rule, they also clung to stubborn notions that became stumbling blocks in the courtroom. They would not credit testimony from a state's witness who used drugs, and they were hard on women who imbibed in barrooms or dressed provocatively. McCown County jurors also balked at prosecutions against seemingly upstanding members of the community, believing that the business-man's son, the churchgoer, or the hardworking farmer could not be guilty of a criminal charge. And always, they rejected the word of an outsider.

Fumbling with the big courthouse key, Elsie slipped inside, bypassed the elevator, and ran up two flights of worn marble steps to the county prosecutor's main office. When she entered Madeleine's office, she was breathing hard. Her boss greeted her with a look of disapproval. "You look terrible. What took you so long?"

"Car trouble," Elsie replied. The one thing that could make her rotten mood worse was hearing how terrible she looked. She dropped into a chair facing Madeleine, who sat behind her impossibly tidy desk. "Is the witness here yet?"

"No, and I don't expect him for a minute. Here," she said, tossing a slim file across her desk, "you'll need to review this quickly before he gets here." As Elsie reached for the file, Madeleine stood up and pulled a bejeweled key chain from her handbag. She was exqui-sitely dressed in a winter white suit with a pearl brooch, not a hair of her smartly bobbed head out of place. Mad-eleine had been a beauty in her day, Elsie knew from the glamour shots in her office; but as she entered middle age, she had permitted a plastic surgeon to tinker with her face, and with her Botox-injected forehead, collagen lips, and eyebrows pulled up a bit too high, she'd devel-oped a scary look.

Elsie looked at her with surprise. "Where are you going?"

Madeleine paused just long enough to give her an imperious glance. "I have a meeting. I'm having brunch with the president of the Rotary. We're planning a fundraiser for the Girls' Club."

"But what about our case preparation?"

"You need to get to work on it." Madeleine pulled on a pair of expensive tan leather gloves, picked up the Burberry trench coat draped over a chair and gave it a shake. "Call me this afternoon and tell me how it's going. I want to hear about the witness. But don't interrupt me at this meeting." Then she swept out of the room.

Elsie had never really liked her boss, but now Madeleine dropped even lower in her estimation. Madeleine Thompson had obtained her political position through a gubernatorial appointment, which the prior governor bestowed out of gratitude to her husband, a generous longtime supporter. As a young attorney in the 1980s, Madeleine was the first woman to practice law in McCown County and showed great promise, taking on criminal appointments and representing them with panache. But then she'd married the local John Deere distributor. In rural Missouri, the only person with more money than the John Deere distributor was the man with two dealerships. Madeleine's husband had three. She quit practicing.

When middle age progressed and she tired of being a social matron, Madeleine wanted to toy with politics, and found her opportunity when the current state prosecutor was appointed to an opening on the circuit bench. The governor at the time, a young man with little experience and even less legal background, gladly handed the position to her and considered the political debt to her husband paid in full.

Madeleine clearly enjoyed the spotlight, and the job of prosecutor certainly provided the attention she wanted; but she was not work brittle, and her trial skills were rusty. So she tended to take high-profile cases for herself and plead them cheaply, which appalled Elsie. Is this what Madeleine had planned for the Taney case?

After her boss's exit, Elsie walked down the hallway to her office, acutely aware of how quiet the building was on a Saturday morning. She settled into her padded chair, rubbing her forehead and wishing she had some Advil. She wished, too, that Noah would call and clear the air; their spat was hanging over her like a dark cloud. She checked her phone just in case, but there were no texts or calls.

She shook her head to clear it. *I've got more to do than think about his bullshit*, she reminded herself.

Resolutely, Elsie pulled her chair to her desk and reviewed the file. There wasn't much to it: an incident report from a police officer made reference to a juvenile court file, which was not duplicated for confidentiality reasons. From the police report she learned that Kris Taney lived at a residence in Barton with a wife and a girlfriend, had three minor daughters with his wife and an infant son by the girlfriend. She checked his DOB: he was thirty-six years old. He had an older brother, Al Taney, who had cooperated with the police when they interrogated him as a witness.

She studied Al Taney's affidavit in preparation for the interview. His statement contained allegations capable of setting her hair on fire. He claimed that his brother regularly had relations with two of his young daughters, maybe all three; and that he also had a sexual relationship with the girlfriend he kept on the premises.

Al Taney had told police that Kris was also involved in the production and distribution of controlled substances, but the police hadn't found any evidence of illegal drug activity on the property when they took Kris Taney into custody. The report noted that Al's face was battered and bruised; when the reporting officer asked about his injuries, he attributed them to his brother. Al had stated that Kris was dangerous and told the police they needed to step in before something terrible happened.

Elsie checked the language of the criminal complaint that Madeleine had prepared and filed: it said the rapes occurred "at some time within the past five years." She circled the language with a red pen. That would never stand up; they needed a date of offense. She'd have to pin Al Taney down when she talked to him, and amend the complaint before the preliminary hearing.

She checked her watch, frowning; it was way past ten. Al Taney was supposed to ring the bell that sounded in the Prosecutor's Office when he arrived at the courthouse, and there was no way she could have missed him. You could hear that bell in the next county. She reread the file, pulled out a clean legal pad and jotted down questions to ask him.

Engrossed in her work, she lost track of time. After preparing several pages of interview questions and an outline of the reports, she remembered to check the clock. It was nearly noon. This guy wasn't showing up.

Well, she thought, if Mohammed won't come to the mountain, and gathered up the file with her notepad. She had Al Taney's address. She'd just pay him a visit.

But first she had to get her damned car.

Chapter Two

ELSIE'S GRAY 2001 Ford Escort waited for her right where she'd left it in the parking lot of Baldknobbers bar, several blocks from the courthouse. It sat under a weathered painting on the side of the bar, depicting a grinning hillbilly smoking a corncob pipe. It was a historically inaccurate image; the Baldknobbers, Elsie knew, had been a secret band of vigilantes living in the Ozark hills over a century ago who covered their heads with scary-looking bags to hide their identities. They purportedly organized to fight lawlessness in the Ozarks, meeting on the bald knob of a hill to don their horned masks, turn their clothes inside out, and warn off pig thieves and other wrongdoers with the threat of a flogging with hickory sticks. Predictably, the men who claimed to combat lawlessness became the problem as the Baldknobbers' acts of vigilante justice escalated to murder. Elsie sincerely hoped she wasn't descended from them, but there was no telling.

She shut herself inside the car in a hurry. The January wind blew cold, and she'd lacked the presence of mind that morning to bring a scarf or gloves. The Ford started right up; though Elsie often fantasized about driving something red and sleek and foreign, her car was as dependable as clockwork.

Dependable though it was, the Ford was too old to feature GPS, and her phone sometimes proved unreliable for navigation, so she kept a city map torn from an old phone book in the glove box. She took it out and studied it for a minute, searching for the unfamiliar address. It was on the wrong side of the tracks, sure enough, but she didn't feel too apprehensive about making a visit at this hour of the day. She had her county ID, and anyway, she wasn't the timid type. She got her bearings and drove out of the parking lot headed north.

Now that she was on the road, the gnawing feeling in Elsie's stomach captured her attention. She hadn't eaten all day, but was reluctant to lose her momentum. The McDonald's down the road presented a solution, and she pulled into the drive-through lane.

"I'll have a cheeseburger and a forty-two-ounce Diet Coke," she told the voice inside the speaker box.

"Do you want fries with that?" the box inquired.

"No," Elsie said, then amended that. "Oh, what the heck. Yes, I'll have a small fry. The size that comes in the little bag." It was justified—she needed some grease and salt to fortify her.

She ate while she drove, keeping a sharp eye out as she searched for her witness's neighborhood. Barton was not a big town, but she wasn't familiar with this area. She pulled up in front of 985 North High Street.

It was a peeling white American foursquare that had once been stately but clearly had suffered neglect and fallen into disrepair, and at some point was chopped into apartment units. Elsie pulled her county badge out of her purse, shoved the purse under the front seat, and grabbed her file. Taking care to lock the car, she thrust her keys in her pants pocket. She felt a little flutter of nerves; she considered herself a plucky gal, but something about this tumbledown house conjured up an image from an Alfred Hitchcock movie. Hopefully, her witness would not channel Norman Bates.

Screwing up her courage, she headed for the door, nearly tripping on the cracked pavement path. She had to step carefully toward the sagging porch, where a jumble of makeshift mailboxes hung beside the door. She studied them, trying to determine which one might belong to her witness. The boxes bore peeling layers of Scotch tape and hand-scrawled names, signs that the tenants did not stay at this High Street residence for long.

She finally made out the name Taney on the mailbox for apartment 1B. In the building's entryway and found a door marked 1B in black marker, gave the door a decisive rap and waited. No response. She knocked again, and waited again, to no avail. She counted to ten, then knocked a third time. Then a small commotion behind her, the rattle of a doorknob and angry murmurs.

Hearing a harsh voice whisper "Hush your mouth," Elsie whirled around as the door across the hall opened briefly and the occupant of Apt. 1A peeked out at her. "Can you help me?" she began, but the door closed as quickly as it had opened.

Stepping across, she knocked briskly. When she got no response, she called through the door: "I don't want to bother you, but I need to talk to your neighbor. Can you tell me who lives across from you? Please open the door."

She heard a hushed exchange within, followed by silence. After another moment, the door opened again and a woman stood in the doorway, glaring at her suspiciously.

"Well, hello," Elsie said in her friendliest tone. "I'm so sorry to trouble you on this awfully cold day, but I have an appointment with Mr. Taney, and I'm having trouble reaching him. Do you know him?"

The woman looked at her as if she'd inquired after the devil. "What do you want him for?" she asked, an unmasked note of dread in her voice. Her face was skeletal, with an unhealthy pallor, and her long dark hair was lank. The smell of mildew in the woman's apartment hit Elsie like a fist. "He's not in here," she added, though Elsie had not asked.

"Al Taney is a witness in a court case next week," she said, "and I want to talk to him. See, I'm an attorney at the Prosecutor's Office; this is my badge." She offered her ID to the neighbor for her inspection. The woman took it and gazed at it for a long minute. When she looked up at Elsie, her expression was less hostile.

"So it's Al you're looking for. You're not here for Kris."

"No," Elsie assured her. "Kris Taney is the defendant.

I'm looking for Al; he's the witness for the prosecution. I want to run through some facts that Al will cover in his testimony next week."

"Well, Al won't give no testimony," the woman said as she handed Elsie back her ID, "because he's gone."

"I know; I knocked and knocked, but he didn't answer. Would you have any idea when he might return?"

"He ain't gonna return, because he done gone."

"I don't suppose you have a phone number where I could reach Mr. Taney?" Elsie ventured. The police reports had not listed a phone contact for him.

The woman's laugh was a short hoot low in her throat. "Al ain't got no phone. He's gone." She shut the door in Elsie's face.

Elsie stared blankly at the door. It was covered with old white paint, cracked and peeled like an alligator's hide; a sure sign of lead paint, her mother had taught her. This was a house where important matters were neglected. She turned on her heel and walked back to the car.

She settled into the driver's seat and fished her phone out of her bag. Man oh man, this was a call she didn't want to make. She took a breath, held it, and blew it out. Then she called Madeleine, to tell her that she couldn't find the star witness.

Madeleine's casual reaction surprised her. "Oh, well, if he's not there, he's not there. We'll have to get somebody else. What other witnesses did we subpoena for the hearing next week?" Elsie could almost see her shrug.

"That's just the problem, Madeleine," she said, pressing on. "We need Al Taney to make our case at the preliminary hearing. The only other witness we've called is the Social Services worker, and she can't testify about the elements of the offense because she wasn't there."

After only a brief pause Madeleine said, "We'll just have to use the social worker. She can testify about the allegations that were made to her."

"No, she can't; that's hearsay. The judge won't let her testify about what someone told her."

"Well, then," Madeleine said impatiently, "we'll introduce her report."

"But we can't, Madeleine; that's hearsay, too. The judge won't make a probable cause finding based on that." Elsie silently cursed the governor for appointing a lawyer whose trial experience had been cut short decades ago.

"Well, we'll figure something out by Wednesday. Look, I'm at the hairdresser and I've got to get off. I'll see you at the office Monday morning." Then Madeline ended the call without waiting for her response.

Elsie sat back and rubbed her temples. That was it, then. She started the car and drove home, looking forward to her warm apartment. She was weary and bone-tired, and more than anything, wanted to wrap up in a quilt and stretch out on her sofa.

Chapter Three

ELSIE'S APARTMENT WAS small and snug, just as she liked it. The living room window looked out onto a school-yard and the Ozark hills rising in the distance. The cozy kitchen was filled by her grandmother's red and gray linoleum kitchen table and chairs, while the bedroom barely accommodated the double bed and dresser from her childhood. The rooms were sparsely furnished with an eclectic mix of old and new: she had purchased a green velvet couch and easy chair for her living room, and a flat-screen television with all the bells and whistles, but the remaining pieces were hand-me-down odds and ends, blond and maple furniture that relatives no longer wanted.

By nine o'clock her wish for a quiet Saturday evening on the couch was finally coming true. Dressed in a soft flannel nightshirt and her old blue terry-cloth robe, she curled up under a patchwork quilt. Her hair, damp from a hot shower, smelled of coconut shampoo. The television remote was at hand, resting on the coffee table next to a bag of Lay's potato chips and a dish of Hershey's Kisses. She drank from a tall glass of iced tea, holding an open copy of *The National Enquirer* on her lap. Underneath that was the Taney file.

She turned the pages of the tabloid, idly reading, too distracted to pass judgment on the fashion mistakes at the Golden Globes. She still hadn't heard from Noah, and the resounding silence troubled her. She picked up her cell phone and toyed with it; she could dial his number and put an end to the wait but rebelled against the idea. Noah was the offender, she thought, and so he should be the one to initiate the call. She just wished he'd hurry up and do it.

Elsie turned on the screen and checked her texts, just in case. A new message had escaped her notice, from Ashlock: *You okay?*

The question made her face flush, reminding her of his grip as he pulled her to her feet the night before. She hit Reply, but stared at the phone, wondering whether she owed him a lengthy explanation. After a moment, she responded, *Fine! Thanks!* and hit Send.

Setting the phone and gossip rag down, she took a swig of tea and began to examine the Taney file. As she read, digesting the case, her focus narrowed and her personal concerns faded. The file didn't reflect a thoroughly investigated case, and she realized that the three sex charges against Kris Taney had been filed prematurely. The allegations didn't sound fabricated; everything rang true, but it all seemed incomplete. Madeleine had rushed to file before the case was ready, and that could lead to disaster. If their errant witness—the mysterious Al Taney—failed to appear and testify at the preliminary hearing on Thursday, the case would be dismissed and Kris Taney would walk free. The rape and incest charges would disappear like smoke. And she couldn't let that happen again.

She examined the notes she'd made at the courthouse that morning. At the top: *FIND AL TANEY.* Underneath: police interviews—daughters, wife, girlfriend—in that order. She needed specific recollections of acts by the defendant that constituted sexual assault and child abuse, and they had to pin those acts to dates and places. Shuffling through the pages of the reports, she checked the social worker's statement again, to see if the woman heard the allegations in the daughters' own words, which the report confirmed.

Elsie wondered what event precipitated the accusations against the father, since the report didn't reference any particular family crisis. As a prosecutor who had handled many of these cases, she knew that a strict code of silence generally accompanied a family history of abuse, and something must have happened to crack it. She knew all too well the ways in which terrible wrongs could be hidden from the world.

Elsie had first learned about the tragedy of incest in seventh grade, when a friend from school, Angela Choate, accused her stepfather of sexual abuse. Angela had confided in her mother, who reported it to the police. The stepfather was charged with statutory rape, and the local paper followed the case with breathless fascination because he was a prominent businessman, a big shot in the Shriners and the Chamber of Commerce. But ultimately the case crumbled. Angela became a reluctant witness, traumatized by the media attention and the stress of public testimony. Her mother filed for divorce, moved with her daughter to Kansas City, and the charge against the stepfather was reduced to misdemeanor assault.

Elsie never saw Angela again. But during her junior year of college at the University of Missouri, her mother had called with tragic news she'd heard at church—that Angela was dead, of an apparent suicide. It was whispered in Barton that the stepfather had remarried and was abusing the teenage daughter of his new wife. The theory was floated that when word reached Angela, she'd blamed herself.

Though it had been years since Elsie thought about Angela, the news sent her into a deep funk. There weren't many girls who grew up and left Barton, and remembering Angela as a quiet but intelligent classmate, she'd hoped her old friend had found happiness after leaving Barton. Stricken and angry, thinking about Angela's suicide, and sick to death of the secrets kept in towns like Barton, Elsie had gotten drunk on cheap wine at the Heidelberg bar across the street from campus, stumbled home, and slept through her morning classes the next day. But as she lay numb on the worn sofa of her student apartment, she'd had what she felt qualified as an epiphany, given the aimlessness of her college life till then: she had a calling. She would go to law school so she could fight to protect children like Angela, trapped in abusive homes. For real change to happen, abusers like Angela's stepfather had to be penalized.

Now, concentrating on the Taney case, Elsie scribbled another note: *Check old police reports for domestic disturbance calls on Kris Taney.* Then, after a moment's thought, she added: *Talk to daughter's teachers—did they see or hear anything that corroborates the charges?* She wondered if anyone had made a mandated reporter call. A Missouri statute required teachers to report signs and allegations of abuse to Social Services. She looked again at the language of the three-count complaint that bore Madeleine's signature and realized it would never stand up. Taney might be the worst kind of child molester, but they'd have to flesh out the case and amend the language of the charge to make it fly.

Her spurt of productivity was interrupted by the buzz of the cell phone. Elsie snatched it up and looked at the caller ID; Noah, at last. She wondered how she should sound. Mad? Hurt? Forgiving?

The phone buzzed again and she quickly answered, lest he give up.

"Hey," she said, keeping her tone noncommittal.

"Hey, there," he replied.

There was a pause, one she was determined not to break. Finally, he spoke.

"How you feeling?"

The question irritated her; she did not intend to serve up any hangover angst for his entertainment.

Tersely, she said, "I'm okay. A little tired. I worked today."

"I thought you'd be laid out all day, after last night."

She decided to grab the bull by the horns. "Yeah, about last night. What was the matter with you? Why on earth did you run off like that?"

She heard him sigh into the phone. "I got pissed off."

"I could see that."

The phone was silent for a long moment, before Noah said, "You want to know why?"

She was starting to simmer, but she said, "Sure. Tell me."

"I didn't see you all week, not one damn time, because you were all tied up. Then we finally meet up at Bald-knobbers, and all you wanted to do was talk shop with your witnesses."

Pressing her cold tea glass against her forehead, she said, "Noah, I was in trial for a week. I have to come down after it's over." When he didn't respond, she added, "You know what I'm talking about."

"Yeah," he admitted. "How'd you get home? Did you drive?"

"No. Ashlock drove me home," she said, intentionally omitting the circumstances.

"That's good. That you didn't drive." After a pregnant pause, he said, "Sorry I wasn't there to do it."

At the word "Sorry," the tension in Elsie's chest began to ease. "Okay."

"Really, I am. I think I must have been kind of drunk, to go off like that."

"Well, that makes two of us," she offered, as a concession.

"And you know that you don't have to worry about Paige."

She didn't follow. "What?"

"The woman I was playing pool with: Paige. She works at the crime lab."

"Oh, yeah. Her."

Switching topics, he said, "I wish I wasn't working tomorrow, but I'm pulling the second shift."

"Yeah, I figured."

"So I guess I won't see you till Monday."

"Monday?" she repeated. "What are we doing Monday?"

"I'm set to testify at the courthouse. I'll come and see what you're up to. We'll get a bite to eat later on."

Her mood lightened at the prospect. She was tired of eating alone. And they could catch up on some other activities that she'd been missing.

"Okay," she said with enthusiasm. "I'd really like that."

"See you Monday, then," he said.

Once they hung up, she tossed her phone on the table. She was a sucker, she knew. But it was hard to hold a grudge against a man who looked like he could be in movies.

Sometimes Elsie thought that when it came to romance, she had been born under an unlucky star. She wondered, and not for the first time, how she managed to reach the ripe old age of thirty-one without even coming close to a walk down the aisle. Once she stumbled through her awkward adolescence and moved beyond those years of nearsighted angst and acne, she attracted her share of attention from men; she'd been told she was very attractive, and she knew that she had a winning smile and a shining mane of blond hair. Maybe she was built more like an hourglass than a waif, but she found that a buxom girl had plenty of appeal to the opposite sex. Nonetheless, she was still waiting to be lucky in love.

Lots of things came easy to Elsie: academics were a breeze, public speaking was natural, and she could make people laugh. But beneath a veneer of confidence, she battled self-doubt. Was she good enough to ensure that the guilty were convicted? Were her instincts keen enough, was her courtroom advocacy convincing? And on the personal side, did she lack some essential quality men looked for in a mate? Because it seemed to her that finding the right man was like hunting for treasure without a map.

Admittedly, she had a long history of targeting the wrong guy; from high school, when she chased after the star of the basketball team and ignored the star debater who pined for her, through her undergraduate years, partying with frat boys. And in law school, she'd bypassed the quiet scholars in the law library to lounge with a flashy guy in the student bar association office. It never quite worked out.

Four years ago, when she'd returned to her hometown, Elsie had resolved to forget about romance altogether, to keep her nose to the grindstone and hone her professional skills. Barton didn't offer a generous population of eligible partners anyway. Most men were married, and none of the few singles who remained could be considered a diamond in the rough.

So she wasn't looking for love when Noah came on the scene. She'd heard some buzz about him from the courthouse clerks: a new cop was in town, fresh from the farm country in the Missouri Bootheel but looking like he stepped off the movie screen. Elsie didn't credit the reports until she saw him in the flesh, when he appeared as a witness in a liquor store burglary. Putting Noah on the stand, she had the chance to engage with him, and sparks flew. She'd always felt most confident when she was in the courtroom, and with him on the stand calling her ma'am and answering every question with a lopsided grin, the electricity was so hot, she had trouble remembering the direct examination questions she'd prepared. While the defense attorney cross-examined Noah, Elsie sat at her counsel table with her legs tightly crossed and couldn't stop herself from eye-fucking him between his answers.

They went out for drinks that night. Charmed by his easy "aw shucks" manner and his sheer physical magnificence, she eagerly went home with him and tumbled into his bed that night. He ate her like ice cream, and she thought: this is it.

But she had learned a lot about Noah since then. A man who'd initially appeared simply perfect was, like everyone, neither simple nor perfect. She could overlook some of his shortcomings, but after passing the milestone of her thirtieth birthday, and then her thirty-first, she began to worry a little. Maybe she was just marking time with Noah; and time was slipping away. Thirty-one years might be regarded as youthful in some places, but in the Ozarks a woman past thirty was over the hill.

Satisfied by the phone call, Elsie peeled the foil from a Hershey's Kiss. At least Noah Strong looked like a treasure. And she was still hungry for romance. "I think you're on probation, Noah," she said aloud. "We'll see how you behave on Monday."

Chapter Four

ELSIE GENERALLY MET Monday mornings with dismay, but she was up before the sun today. She felt like her old self again and was anticipating her date night with pleasure. She liked the idea of starting the week on a bright note, she thought as she showered briskly, shaving her legs with smooth strokes. Standing before the foggy bathroom mirror, she applied her makeup with care and chose a brighter shade of lipstick than usual.

After pulling on a pair of slim wool pants and buttoning a tight-cropped blazer over a shiny blue camisole, she checked herself in the mirror. She looked more like a television version of a prosecutor than the real thing, but that suited her just fine; she didn't want to look dowdy next to that good-looking man. Balancing on the edge of her bed, she grimaced as she pulled on boots with painfully high heels. They killed her feet, but she examined herself with satisfaction: they looked really good. They'd set her back only forty-two bucks at Shoe Carnival. She could find a bargain like nobody's business.

Leaning against the kitchen counter, she ate half a banana and washed it down with Diet Coke. There was no time for the coffeemaker; she'd get a cup at work. She didn't want to risk missing Noah when he dropped by to see her. He might have an early court appearance, and she wanted to nail down their plans for the evening.

As she drove her Ford Escort to the courthouse, even the traffic lights accommodated her. It was so early that she thought she might be the first one in the office, but her friend Breeon Johnson already sat behind her desk, checking her e-mail. Elsie stuck her head in the door of Bree's office.

"'Morning, Bree."

"Hey, 'morning to you. How did it go on Friday?"

"Guilty. They gave him twenty years."

"That's great. You did good, honey. The case was falling apart on Thursday."

"Oh, yes it was." Elsie leaned against the door frame, struggling out of her winter coat. "So what did you do this weekend?"

"Laundry. Sound glamorous?" Breeon was fiercely devoted to her dual roles as mother and prosecutor. A native of St. Louis, she'd moved to the Ozarks after law school, determined to make a go of her law school marriage. The marriage didn't work out, but it produced her daughter, Taylor. Breeon's grit was a quality that served her well, working as the only African-American attorney in a community that still ran largely on the "good ole boy" system.

Like most of southwest Missouri, McCown County had not yet embraced the notion of women in positions of influence or leadership. With the exception of Madeleine Thompson, no women held political office in the city or county; certainly, they did not sit on the bench. To find a woman circuit or associate circuit judge, it was necessary to drive 120 miles in a northerly direction, halfway to St. Louis.

As women practicing criminal law in the Ozarks, both Elsie and Bree had to battle for respect; but without question, Bree's struggles outnumbered her own. Just several months before, a visiting attorney from Purdy, Missouri, had tossed a file at Bree and told her to make his copies and scare up a cup of coffee. While Elsie stammered in indignation, Bree wasted no time telling the man he could shove that file up his fat white ass.

"What about your weekend?" Bree inquired. "What did you do to celebrate? Did you have some fun?"

"Yeah, I guess. I went to the old Baldknobbers."

"Oh, don't tell me that." Breeon shook her head in disgust. "Why did you go to that old dive?"

"The cops wanted to go there, to get a drink after the trial."

"Ugh. That place is nasty."

A memory of her tumble flashed through Elsie's head. "I'll never go back. I swear."

"Liar," Breeon said, and they both laughed.

"I'm going to get you out there one of these days," Elsie said.

Bree pushed her chair away from her desk with a

skeptical look at her. "I'd do a lot for you, baby girl. But I draw the line at risking my neck in that cracker box."

Elsie took a step inside the small office and said in a hushed voice, "Hey, something else happened over the weekend. Madeleine brought me in on the Taney case."

"That's cool. Good for you." Bree's enthusiasm was sincere; she and Elsie were the only female assistant prosecutors on the staff of seven lawyers, and they worked hard to support each other. "What's up with that guy, anyway? Standard pervert? Addict? Crazy?"

"Sounds pretty standard from the brother's statement. Just another hillbilly who thinks he's entitled to nail his daughters."

"You sure the brother isn't doing it? Wasn't he the one who snitched him out?"

"Yeah, the brother went to the police and made the report. Hey, how do you know so much about it?"

"I was in Judge Carter's court when they brought Taney in, appointed the public defender, and set a preliminary hearing. Judge Carter was chatty, and I got the inside scoop."

"He's not too chatty with me," she said, shifting her weight from one foot to the other to keep the circulation moving in her aching toes. "I gotta tell you, Bree, I'm worried about the case. There hasn't been enough investigative work."

"What's missing?"

"The daughters' statements. There isn't anything in the file that's in their own words. I don't like that."

"Is Madeleine worried?"

Elsie glanced over her shoulder. "Hell, no. She's just afraid the case will interfere with her many pressing social engagements."

Bree shrugged and picked up her coffee cup. "Well, she's first chair, right? This is her case, not yours, and if she's not worried, you're not worried. It's not in your hands, Ms. Second Chair. You're the errand girl. You get the coffee."

"Okay." Everything Bree told her was true, but it troubled Elsie anyway. "I still can't believe she brought me in."

"Why not? You're damned good."

"But she can't stand me."

Bree waved a hand in dismissal. "That's an exaggeration, don't you think?"

"I don't. I'm serious. She acts like I'm a leper. A leper who wants a bite of her sandwich."

Bree laughed. "You nailed it. She thinks you want her whole sandwich."

"Huh?"

"You're a threat, honey. She's got to run for office next year, and a bright young thing like you—a local girl—you could beat her. You're a better trial attorney than she is, that's for sure."

"Who'd know? She never takes a case to trial." Elsie rubbed her nose, thinking. "But you're a dynamo in court, Bree. Why isn't she mean to you?"

"Oh, baby. I'm no threat. I'm not electable in this county."

Elsie nodded, conceding the point without argument. Bree continued, "A black woman on the ballot in

McCown County? The city fathers would get out the torches and pitchforks. But hey, I'd probably get the black vote."

Elsie's response was an apologetic shrug. The town of Barton boasted no diversity; people of color made up only two percent of the population.

As Elsie turned to go, Bree asked, "How are you and your boy toy?"

She paused in the doorway. "Okay. He's coming by today."

"Lucky you."

Elsie sighed. Bree had counseled her before on her taste in men, said she should be more concerned with brain mass and less with muscle mass. "I don't want to hear it."

"You know what I think."

"I know."

"You can do better."

"So you've told me," she said over her shoulder, heading to her office.

The weekly court calendar lay on her desk, and she checked to see if she was assigned to Associate Circuit Court. Mercifully, she wasn't. Monday would be a catch-up day for her: no traffic cases to negotiate, no misdemeanors to try, no preliminary hearings in felony cases. For once, her appointment book looked like a clean slate.

So she sat at her desk and waited. Noah might testify in any of the associate divisions; he didn't say what kind of case it was, but it was likely to be a traffic matter, maybe a DWI arrest. All manner of criminal cases were ongoing in the courtrooms on the third floor on Monday. She knew he wouldn't be in Circuit Court because there were no jury trials set.

She caught up on a stack of correspondence she'd neglected the week before. She ignored all incoming calls when she was in trial, so now she listened to her voice mail and noted calls that she'd return and those she would blow off. She checked her e-mail, and when she was done, checked the time: nine-thirty. Maybe she'd be better off covering one of the courts, after all. The morning was creeping by on feet of lead.

After idly browsing the news updates on Yahoo, Elsie decided to go down to the basement to buy a cup of coffee at the courthouse coffee shop. She stuck her head in the reception area on her way out. "Stacie, I'm going to the coffee shop."

"Right." The receptionist was a cute local girl with limited enthusiasm for her job. Attorneys generally didn't report their whereabouts to the administrative staff, which suited Stacie very well indeed. Studying her reflection in the shiny brass county seal that hung behind her desk, she pinched an errant clump of mascara from her lashes.

"If anyone comes looking for me," Elsie added, "they can find me down there."

"Okay." Stacie, still examining her makeup, didn't take her eyes from the brass seal.

"Noah is coming by. You can tell him where I am." To the woman's back, she added, "I've got my cell with me, too."

She sauntered down the stairs and peered into the coffee shop, but found no uniformed law enforcement professionals passing the time. Ordering her coffee to go, she rode the elevator to the third floor, thinking she'd see what was happening in Associate Circuit Court. There was an associate courtroom in three of the four corners, and she made the rounds of the courts, keeping her eyes peeled for a familiar tall figure in blue.

Unable to find Noah on the third floor, she cruised the Circuit Court rooms on the second floor, but without success. It was fifteen minutes before eleven when Elsie returned to her office. As she passed by the receptionist's desk, Stacie called after her and said, "Somebody was looking for you. There's a note on your desk."

How did I miss him? she wondered. A single message lay on her desk; she snatched it up. *See me ASAP. Madeleine.*

The door to Madeleine's office was securely shut; she didn't pretend to have a welcoming open door policy. When Elsie knocked, a moment passed before she was invited to enter.

Madeleine sat behind her desk drinking coffee from a china cup. A bright lipstick mark stained the gold rim. Elsie wondered whose job it was to wash those cups each day; she was certain her boss didn't do any kitchen patrol duty.

"Sit down," Madeleine said. "Did you have a chance to look at the Taney case?"

"Yes, I've gone over it pretty thoroughly," she replied. "It needs a lot of work."

"Like what?"

"For starters, we need witness statements from the daughters—all three of them. We need corroboration from the mom, too. It'd be a hell of a note if she tells a different story than they do. And what's up with this girlfriend? Is she living under the same roof with them, like Sarah and Hagar and Abraham?"

Madeleine's face was blank. Elsie guessed she didn't understand the Old Testament reference. Madeleine asked, "What else?"

"So far, you've charged a couple of counts of statutory rape and a count of incest based on the defendant's brother's statements. We need to amend the complaint. I'm betting that once you do your witness interviews, they'll reveal other incidents of criminal behavior. At least we know Mom wasn't an active participant in all this behavior."

"How do we know that?"

With effort, Elsie kept her eyes from rolling. She doesn't know anything, she thought. "If she participated in the abuse, Social Services would have taken protective custody. She's cooperating with the prosecution, so the Children's Division didn't take the girls away."

"Hmm," Madeleine said, a nettled look on her face. She picked up a newspaper and unfolded it.

Elsie persisted. "Check and see whether Social Services obtained medical exams on the girls. If they didn't, we'll want to. If nothing else, we can show that someone took their virginity, and that will corroborate their testimony, even if there's no way scientifically to show that it was the defendant."

Madeleine looked up from her newspaper. Elsie noted that one of her eyebrows was higher than the other. "Why not?" Madeleine asked.

"Because too much time has passed since the last sexual assault. He's been in jail since right after Christmas, right? There's only a seventy-two-hour window of time to get a sample from the victims for DNA analysis of the sperm. If they do a rape kit now and get a swab for DNA testing, it won't show defendant's DNA."

"Oh. Forget it, then."

"Forget what?"

"The medical exams."

"Madeleine, we need some medical evidence. The jury will wonder why no one checked them out."

"Okay. But no DNA testing. No need to confuse the jury."

Though she was nervous about the ramifications of her boss's decision, Elsie pressed on. "Check records at the P.D. and the school to see if we can find outcry evidence. But the most important thing is to talk to those girls."

"Any other recommendations?" Focused on the paper again, Madeleine didn't look up.

"No. Well, I take that back. Yes. We have to prepare the witnesses more carefully in this kind of case than any other prosecution. Kid witnesses are hard, Madeleine. They're intimidated by the courtroom and by the defendant. Hell, we're setting them against their own father; they're bound to have mixed feelings, even in a case like this."

Madeleine rattled the page of the newspaper. Elsie edged up the volume of her voice a notch. "I think juries want to convict child molesters, but they like the certainty of scientific evidence, and we can't give them that. The Taney case is a swearing match. So we better be sure it's a good one."

Madeleine gazed at Elsie over the paper, her face impassive. "This isn't my first time handling a case with children."

"I know."

"I am very concerned about protecting children. Deeply concerned."

"I know," Elsie repeated. "I've heard you say that." She swallowed the urge to add, *I've heard you say it on TV. Never in a courtroom.*

"Is that it?"

"Get someone good to work this up," Elsie said earnestly. "This is not a case for on-the-job training. Get Bob Ashlock, if you can."

"Well," Madeleine said, pushing her chair back slightly, "the preliminary hearing is Wednesday, isn't it? We have our work cut out for us."

"Madeleine, about the prelim, you've got to subpoena some backup witnesses in case you can't locate the defendant's brother in time. You need to have Charlene or Kristy or Tiffany ready to take the stand."

Madeleine's smooth forehead wrinkled a fraction. "Who?"

Elsie tried to keep impatience from creeping into her

voice. "The victims, Madeleine. Taney's daughters. Their names are Charlene, Kristy, and Tiffany."

"Oh. Right. We'll need to think about that." There was a pause, followed by an uncomfortable silence, which was broken when Madeleine said, "Okay, then. I guess that's all."

"Right. Here are the notes I made on the case. Talk to you later." Placing a copy of her notes on Madeleine's desk, Elsie walked out, feeling troubled. Madeleine hadn't specified her role; did she want her to run with the ball, or sit back and watch? She knew that a case of this type required special handling or it would fall apart before it had even begun.

She needed to be careful. She couldn't let Madeleine lead her down that path again. Even after four years she shuddered whenever she thought of Patrice Moore.

Elsie had come to the McCown County Prosecutor's Office, fresh from law school and ready to realize her ambition of becoming the Ozarks' avenging angel. In her third week on the job, Madeleine had sent her into court to dismiss a sodomy charge, with the explanation that the witness had recanted. "I'd do it myself," Madeline told her, "but I'm all tied up. Just tell the judge we're dropping the charge due to problems with the state's witness."

Elsie, who at that point had handled nothing other than traffic arraignments, did as she was told. But she had a sick feeling in her gut when she read the charge: the victim was nine years old. As the defendant was brought before the judge, she saw the look that passed between him and his wife. Turning in her chair, Elsie spotted the child, a plump third grader with wispy blond hair, huddled in the courtroom, her posture a mix of resignation and misery.

Shaking, Elsie had stood before the judge, who dismissed the case. The defendant's shackles were removed and he left the courtroom with his wife and child. She opened the file, madly flipping through the pages, then stopped when she saw a handwritten confession, signed by the defendant, admitting he had been anally sodomizing the child for some time.

Elsie had flown from the courtroom, desperate to show Madeleine the file, and camped at her office door until she finally returned.

As she explained that a terrible mistake had been made, Madeleine regarded her with an impatient look. Then she calmly said, "It's been decided. It's out of our hands. The defense attorney took the child's deposition, and he got it under oath. She said she made it up."

"She was coerced, don't you see? They made her say that. Good God, Madeleine, look at this: he confessed. In his own hand. It's signed."

"The case is unwinnable. She's given conflicting accounts. The jury won't believe her, it's a waste of time."

Madeleine walked away, her departure a clear dismissal. Elsie had tried to broach the topic the next day, but with the same results. She had never mentioned it to Madeleine again. But the image of the girl slumped in the courtroom, her eyes dull, was a picture she was sure she'd carry for life. She'd let that child down, sealed her fate. *Never again*, she had vowed.

Now, back at her office, she toiled over paperwork, checking the front door twice to see if anyone was waiting outside. She plopped back into her chair with a scowl; Noah's tardiness was beginning to seriously rankle. Spinning in her chair to face the computer screen, she checked her e-mail: seventeen messages, but none from him. Next, she checked her texts and incoming calls: nothing. She shot him a quick text: *Where are you?* Then she stared at the silent phone as she ate a cup of blueberry yogurt at her desk and washed it down with Diet Coke.

By mid-afternoon her temper was flaring; it looked like he wasn't coming by, after all. When she stalked to the third floor courtrooms, activity had settled into an afternoon lull. Not much was going on, and nothing was set after three o'clock. She knew there was no other explanation: he hadn't come to see her, and he hadn't called to cancel.

Hell, hell, hell, she thought. Her spirits fell, and she trudged painfully back to her office, ruing her decision to wear boots with freaky high heels. A glimpse of an officer on the stairs raised her hopes for an instant, but when he turned toward her, Elsie's hopes were dashed. It wasn't Noah.

She had experienced her share of disappointments, but this stung. She felt deflated. What kind of idiot was she, letting him stand her up like this? What self-respecting grown woman would tolerate it?

By the end of the day she sat at her desk in a funk, leafing through an old copy of *Missouri Lawyers Weekly*. Shortly before five, as she turned in her chair and stared out the window, the phone rang. She jumped, hastily grabbing the receiver.

"This is Elsie Arnold," she said.

"Honey, it's Mom. How's your day?"

"Oh, Mom," she said, lowering her voice. "Not so good."

"What's the matter?"

"Nothing," she lied. "Really, it's no big thing. Just stupid stuff."

"Is that boss being mean? Did a judge bawl you out in court?"

"No, nothing like that." She checked the time again: five on the dot. Noah had blown her off. She swiveled in her chair. It was dark outside, and she saw her own reflection in the window.

"Mom, am I fat?"

"Don't be silly. You are a beautiful girl."

"That's not what I asked you."

"Well, you're not a toothpick, if that's what you mean. But you know what your grandfather used to say."

"Oh God, Mother, please."

"Your grandfather always said men like a girl who's got some meat on her."

"Mother, he was born in 1920. He lived through the Great Depression. Look, I've got to go."

"Is this about a man? I could give you some good advice if you'll just talk to me. Tell me what's the matter."

"I don't really want to go into it." She switched the phone to her other ear, bracing herself; her mother was very free with her advice.

"You know, it's not what they look like, it's how they treat you that counts."

She rolled her eyes. "You're talking like I'm an eighth grader." Her mother had spent the past forty years teaching middle school English, and Elsie suspected she would always regard her as a member of that age group.

"Any girl can get married if she sets her standards low enough," Marge Arnold advised.

"Thanks, Mom. That's helpful."

"What I'm trying to say," Marge continued, "is that you shouldn't set your standards low."

"I think I zeroed in on that." She glanced at the clock. "Look, I've got to get back to work. Thanks for calling, though."

"Come over for supper tonight. Dad wants to see you."

"Can't make it, Mom."

"I'm making chicken and rice. I bet you haven't had a thing to eat all day."

Elsie sighed into the phone. "With a can of cream of mushroom, I bet."

"Cream of celery."

"And Minute rice?"

"Yes, with Minute rice," Marge said, affronted. "You don't need to take that tone. You've loved it since you were a little girl."

"I know, Mom. Thanks for the invite, but I really am tied up. I'm still catching up from last week."

"All right, then. I love you, baby."

Elsie's heart tugged. "I love you, too, Mom. Tell Dad hi."

When she got off the phone, she felt a little better, much to her surprise. But she had blood in her eye for Noah.

Your probation is hereby revoked, shithead, she thought.

Chapter Five

EARLY TUESDAY MORNING the Taney sisters emerged from the old white house on High Street and started down the steps to the cracked front walk. Charlene, a thin fifteen-year-old, led the way, pulling her worn nylon jacket tightly around her. The wind whipped her long brown hair into her face. She pushed it back with an impatient gesture, revealing her pointed chin and sharp jaw.

Following behind, Kristy stepped carefully down the icy steps. At twelve, she was nearly as tall as her sister Charlene, her dark hair the same shade, but Kristy's features were softer, her face rounder, a pronounced dimple in her chin.

Tiffany, a child of six, maneuvered the slick steps with difficulty, stumbling before she made it safely to the cement sidewalk. Her hooded coat revealed tendrils of red hair that curled in unruly waves. Looking around in the cold morning air, Tiffany froze, gazing up in delight.

Fat snowflakes drifted from the gray sky, and Tiffany twirled around, arms upraised to catch them. Her brown coat, recently purchased from the Disabled American Veterans' thrift shop, was much too big for her, with sleeves that hung well below her fingertips. She waved the oversized sleeves in the cold air, her bare fingers reaching for the sky.

Charlene tugged the loose shoulder of Tiffany's coat. "Come on, crazy thing. If you want me to walk you to school, we got to get a move on." When Tiffany didn't respond immediately, Charlene gave her a little shove. "You don't want to miss school breakfast, do you?"

Tiffany fell into step with her sisters. The girls walked three abreast down the narrow street, because the sidewalk was so broken it was sure to trip them up. They jumped to avoid frozen puddles along the rutted curb. Tiffany's long sleeves flapped at her side.

A frost-covered beer can appeared in Kristy's path and she kicked it. It skittered up the road ahead of her, and she ran after it and kicked it again, using the instep of her foot. Kristy chased the can, leaving her sisters behind.

Charlene thrust her bare fists deep into the pockets of her old jacket. She nudged Tiffany with her elbow. "What they having for breakfast at your school today, you think?"

Tiffany answered with a shrug.

"Bet it's cinnamon rolls," Charlene said. "Wouldn't that be something? Cinnamon rolls and milk."

Tiffany smiled but didn't reply.

Charlene continued. "Everything good at school? Teacher nice?"

Tiffany nodded, still smiling, studying the snowflakes that clung to the fabric of her coat.

"How about the kids in your class? Are they being nice?" Charlene regarded the child with fierce affection. She took a cold hand from her pocket and pulled Tiffany to her side. "Anybody don't treat you nice, you tell them your big sister will come looking for them. Tell them I'll pop a cap in they ass."

Tiffany covered her mouth with shock and delight. Kristy turned on the pair, abandoning her pursuit of the Old Milwaukee can. With a hard look, she said, "I heard that. You cussing again."

"Am not."

"I heard it. You got a filthy mouth. I'll tell."

"Who you gonna tell? Daddy's in jail. Ha."

"I'll tell Uncle Al. Or Roy."

"Aw, go kick your stinking can."

The elementary schoolyard came into view. Charlene walked Tiffany through the chain-link fence and dropped a kiss on the top of her tousled head.

"You remember what I said."

Tiffany watched as her older sisters walked away. She whispered, "Slap a cat in your ass," and then covered her mouth with the long sleeve of her coat.

DONITA TANEY WATCHED her daughters from the window. The dirty glass allowed only a hazy view. If snow was falling outside, Donita couldn't see it.

She was glad they'd found that warm coat for Tiffany

at the DAV thrift shop. Winter was hard this year. She wished she had a better coat for Char. Seemed like Char got the short end often as not.

Char was tough, though. Whatever got dished out, thrown her way, Char could take it. And Charlene hadn't had to suffer anything that Donita hadn't been through herself. She survived. Her girls would too.

Donita needed a cigarette. She must've been smoking too much lately; the urge for tobacco felt more like a compulsion than a nagging desire. A crumpled cigarette pack sat by the ashtray and she rifled through it with hope, but it was empty. Someone had taken her last smoke.

"Char," she muttered through her teeth. With Kris locked up, it had to be Charlene taking her smokes. Kristy only smoked once in a while and Tiffany hadn't started yet.

She weighed her options. She wasn't inclined to walk to the Lo-Cut Market this early; it was cold as all get-out outside. Besides, she was almost broke. "I'll teach her to take the last one," she said as she poked through the ashtray, looking for a butt to relight. They'd all been burned down to the filter, save one. Donita sighed with satisfaction as she plucked up a wrinkled butt that had been stubbed out with a good third of the cigarette remaining.

Moving into the kitchen, she turned an electric burner on high and lit the cigarette off the coil on the kitchen stove. She took a grateful drag but grimaced as she examined it between her fingers. A relit cigarette never tasted as good on the second go-around.

What was the matter with her daughter, stubbing

out a cigarette with almost half of it left? It was wasteful. Donita's daddy had smoked unfiltered cigarettes, Camels when he could get them, hand-rolled sometimes. He used to say you was to smoke them till you could smell the flesh burning.

As Donita eased into a kitchen chair, taking care not to put her weight on the wobbly leg, she spied a whole sheet of paper under the table. With a grunt, she bent over to pick it up, thinking, I have to pick up after everybody around here.

It looked like a homework paper, so she supposed it must belong to Kristy, but the page bore Charlene's name in the upper right corner. Surprising; Charlene didn't bother much with schoolwork. Donita couldn't fault her for it: you plant corn, you get corn, as her mama used to say. She hadn't been too interested in school herself. She'd sit in the back of the class, daydreaming while the teacher talked.

After school, Donita and her sister would take the long way home, walking by the Dari Sweet where the boys hung out. Kris Taney was generally there, smoking and shouting at the passersby. He was the baddest boy in town. Mean as a snake.

So when he started sniffing after Donita, it took her by surprise. At the time, she thought it was a compliment, a distinction, having a tough like Kris chase after her.

She wasn't much older than Charlene when she turned up pregnant. They got married pretty quick after that. It was funny to think how glad she was back then, to cast her lot with Kris Taney. She thought she was lucky to get out of her daddy's house.

From the frying pan into the fire.

Donita blew the smoke out with a sober expression. She didn't like to think about her daddy, not even with him long dead and buried in Arkansas. She was glad when he died, shameful as it was to admit it. Part of her would always hate him. She wasn't sure how old she was the first time she'd had to take care of her daddy, but she was just a little thing. He made her do it with her hand, at first. Sometimes he'd rub up against her in bed. Before long he said she was ready to be a woman.

It was god-awful, that's a fact. But when she went to her mother that night, Mama refused to give comfort or solace. Donita would never forget the closed look on her mother's face, the set of her jaw as her mother disentangled herself from her frantic grip.

"You don't know what he done, Mama."

"I don't want to hear it. Go to bed."

"You got to stop him." Donita clutched at her mother's dress, but the woman held her off.

"'Wives submit to your husband, as to the *Lord*.' Bible says. Daddy's the boss of this house. Now you get to bed."

"I got to tell you what he done."

Donita's mother snatched her by the upper arm and hissed in her ear, "You don't never tell. Nobody. Never."

She remembered that her mother had relented a little after that, possibly at the stricken look on her face. Mama patted her arm and whispered, "Don't you think about it,

Donita. Think about something else." Grimly she'd advised, "Think about heaven."

Donita had followed her mother's orders. She never told a soul, and she tried to think about something else when he came to her.

It was advice she passed on to her daughters. Char had been nine years old when Kris started in on her. Donita knew that for a fact, because she was pregnant with Tiffany, about ready to pop, when it happened the first time. She should have seen it coming. She'd seen the look in his eye as he watched Char. He'd corner her behind the sofa or run a hand up her thigh.

But Charlene put up a fight, that was for sure, hollering and carrying on till Donita came running, holding her belly with both hands. He had Charlene pinned on the bed—the marriage bed they'd made their babies in. Charlene was fighting like a bobcat, trying to scratch his face. He was too drunk to catch her wrists.

Donita tried to help her girl. She grabbed Kris's shoulder, said he didn't know what he was doing, he had to stop. He reared back and kicked her in the stomach so hard, she went flying against the wall. Huddled in pain, she clutched her middle, scared she'd lose the baby. Looking up, she could see that he'd done it. He was going at it with Charlene under him.

She couldn't watch. Crawling out of the room on all fours, Donita lay on the carpet in the hallway, waiting for it to end. *It's just because I'm so fat with this baby*, she told herself. *He don't want me with my belly this way. After the baby, he'll leave her alone.*

Of course, she was wrong. It happened again, regardless of her protests. And by the time he started up with Kristy, the girl knew better than to resist. Donita felt her failure, carried it around her neck like the oxen's yoke.

She taught them her mother's lesson: that it had to be kept secret, that it was just something men did, and that it must be kept within the family circle, never to be spoken of to others.

"Think about something else," she'd whisper to her girls. "Think about something nice." She didn't tell them to think about heaven. She parted with her mother's example on that score. Donita wasn't too certain that she could count on the existence of a heaven, or that she would get in if there was one.

But she was a better mother than her own, she believed. She never pushed them away when they wanted to come to her. She would comfort them. Give them some sugar. Share a cigarette, give a squeeze.

She would stroke Charlene's back as the girl shuddered. "Think about ice cream," Donita would urge.

But Char didn't cry no more. Not for a long time.

Donita stubbed out the cigarette in the sink. Things would get better. She would see to it.

Chapter Six

On Tuesday, in Associate Division 3, Elsie spent the morning trying traffic cases and negotiating plea bargains with defense attorneys. She had to exercise control to keep from snapping at the lawyers. She was morose, still smarting from Noah's failure to appear the day before.

The afternoon docket was devoted to preliminary hearings in felony cases. Sitting at the courtroom counsel table, she studied a witness statement intently, and scribbled direct examination questions on her yellow legal pad. She had a three o'clock preliminary hearing in a first degree robbery case, for which she was thoroughly prepared; she had conducted phone interviews of the convenience store witnesses on Monday night, after her dinner date didn't show up. Checking her watch, she gauged the amount of time she had before her witnesses appeared.

Moses Carter, judge of Associate Division 3, was still

in chambers, which suited Elsie just fine. Judge Carter was not fond of her, though not because of her courtroom performance or demeanor. She'd had the misfortune of walking in on the judge enjoying the charms of a municipal clerk at the county Christmas party a year ago, and since that time he'd refused to look her in the eye.

The party had begun as a quiet affair, centered around a bowl of Hawaiian punch mixed with ginger ale and a platter of stale sugar cookies. Courthouse personnel, looking ragged from the demands of the holidays, chatted listlessly. Elsie was gearing up to make her getaway.

But after a rascal in the county commissioners' office added a bottle of Everclear to the punch bowl, the party took off. Crusty clerics melted into belles, and courthouse stalwarts who hadn't cracked a smile in years roared with hilarity. Elsie, partaking of the spiked punch bowl, decided it would be good fun to take off her bra and wave it like a flag. But when she stepped into a utility closet to disrobe, she stumbled onto Judge Carter, reaching a climax in the arms of a woman who was not his wife.

Since then her relationship with the judge had been severely strained.

Worse, he tended to rule against her, given the opportunity. As a result, she always prepared her cases with particular care when appearing in Associate Division 3.

Elsie toyed with the idea of going downstairs for a Diet Coke, but she'd had one with lunch and she was trying to cut down on aspartame. She couldn't remember just what the sweetener's bad properties were, but the evils were formidable, she knew. She'd sworn off diet drinks entirely on New Year's Day. When her abstinence plan didn't last twenty-four hours, she revised her resolution to a single serving per day, and tried to stick to that. Sometimes she succeeded, sometimes she didn't. Work days were tough. Gotta have some kind of reward system, she thought. Since her love life was stalled, she would substitute chemicals for romance. She dug four quarters from her briefcase and ran down three flights of stairs for a can of solace.

When she returned to the Division 3 courtroom, the chairs were only sparsely occupied, mostly by the remainder of the afternoon traffic docket. A man facing revocation of his probation due to a new DWI charge brought his wife and baby in a bid for sympathy. The child cried, a lusty wail that made it difficult to hear anything being said in court.

Judge Carter sat at the bench, a slight man in his forties with a head of prematurely gray hair. He gave his bailiff, Eldon, a meaningful look over his glasses. The portly bailiff rose from his chair with an effort, walked over to the young mother and told her she'd have to take the baby outside.

The witnesses from the Jiffy Go store waited on the front row. Elsie patted her first witness on the shoulder as she walked to the counsel table.

The judge asked, "Ms. Arnold, are you representing the prosecution in *State v. Bradley*?" He looked at a spot somewhere above her head.

"Yes, your honor," she replied.

"Are you ready to proceed?"

"I am, your honor," she said.

The judge inquired, "Is the defendant here with his attorney?" The public defender stood and prepared to come forward.

The wail of the baby echoed in the rotunda outside the courtroom door. Judge Carter paused, frowning, and said, "I'm sorry to inconvenience the parties, but I'd like to take up a probation violation first."

"That's fine, your honor," Elsie said smoothly, though inwardly she was disgruntled. The delay would make her day that much longer: another complaint to add to her growing list. She gathered her papers together and moved to the empty jury box, where she took a seat.

Breeon represented the Prosecutor's Office in the probation hearing. Addressing the court, she announced she would present evidence that the party had been driving drunk, in violation of his probation. She asked the bailiff if he would call her witness out in the hallway.

"Sure," the bailiff said. "Who do you need?"

"Officer Strong."

Elsie's head jerked up as the bailiff opened the door and shouted for Noah. He entered the courtroom and strode up to the bench. Noah had the distinctive tread of a uniformed officer when he walked: the squeak of the leather boots, the heft of the belt, supporting holster and sidearm, ammunition and flashlight, radio and baton. He raised his hand as he swore an oath to tell the truth, and sat ramrod straight in the witness chair.

He did look fine in that uniform. Elsie stared at him as she might eyeball a sideshow freak. When he returned her look and flashed a smile in her direction, she looked away with a twist of her head, seething. She had no intention of engaging him. *Ain't giving you a come hither look from the jury box, Officer No-Show,* she thought.

She fiddled with her papers and tapped her pen, composing her face into lines of total disregard for the officer testifying in court. If he could forget he made a commitment to see her on Monday, she would forget he was in the room. She would make him pay for his offense. She looked at her files, the judge, the light fixtures overhead, her nails: anywhere but the witness stand.

Bree's direct exam of Strong was brief, as was the cross. When the accused took the stand in his own defense, Bree moved in to grill him over his misdeeds.

Out of the corner of her eye Elsie watched Noah approach the jury box. Leaning over the rail, he whispered, "How's it going, Elsie?"

She shrugged, still not looking at him. "Fine. I guess."

He rested his arms on the railing. "Nice to see you." He smiled, relaxed, as if he had nothing to apologize for.

"Oh, yeah," she said with scorn. "Nice surprise."

"What do you mean? I told you I had a case today."

She shook her head and hissed, "It's Tuesday. You said you'd see me Monday."

"No," he whispered, "I wouldn't have said that. I have two cases set for today: Tuesday."

Frowning, she didn't respond. She was trying to remember. *Could he have said Tuesday?*

"Aw, come on. Don't tell me you're mad at me for testifying on Tuesday instead of Monday. I don't put the date on the subpoena, I just show up," he added in a teasing tone.

"Hell yes I'm mad," she whispered. "I don't know why I'm even speaking to you."

He bent his head to her ear and whispered, "Elsie, honey, you're making a big mistake. You mixed it up. Do you really think I'd blow off a chance to finally be with you?"

Judge Carter interrupted the exchange; she nearly jumped when he snapped, "We're ready for you, Miss Arnold. Call your first witness."

Flustered, she picked up her file and walked to the counsel table. Pulling out her handwritten examination questions, she said: "If it please the court, the state calls Maria Rodriguez to the witness stand." The store clerk came forward, and after being sworn, sat in the witness box. Elsie smiled at her, gave her a second to get settled, and said, "Please state your name."

Elsie got her head into the game, regained her composure, and proceeded through direct examination without a hitch. Convenience store employees didn't always make good witnesses, but this woman was a dream. Mrs. Rodriguez identified the defendant in court without hesitation, spoke clearly, and described the gun he'd pointed at her in minute detail. Moreover, the Jiffy Go had a video recording of the robbery, and the corporate office sent the correct witness (for once) to establish the chain of custody for the tape. All in all, the hearing went very well indeed, but she wasn't totally focused on the outcome; she was still distracted by the encounter with Noah Strong. She kept going back to the phone conversation on Saturday night: exactly what had he said?

After the defendant's attorney finished his cross-examination, the judge found probable cause to believe that the defendant committed the offense charged, and decreed that the defendant would be bound over for trial in the Circuit Court.

Elsie breathed a sigh of relief. She spoke with her witnesses briefly and thanked them for coming, then sat back at the counsel table. She wanted to wrap this up quickly so she could get back to her office. She needed to think: could he have actually said Tuesday instead of Monday? She'd been totally wiped out when he called.

Or maybe he just said the wrong day, accidentally. Said Monday instead of Tuesday, without realizing it. Anyone could make a mistake, she reflected, and she felt herself softening, her resolve to be done with Noah melting like butter in a skillet.

I'm a schmuck, she thought, shaking her head at her own foolishness, but knowing she'd give him a chance to make it up to her. A schmuck and a fool, she added while scrawling a quick note in the file about the chain of custody witness from Jiffy Go. As she wrote, someone put a hand on her shoulder, and she spun around with a forgiving heart.

"Hi!" she said. Then she saw that it was Detective Ashlock.

Elsie felt the heat rise in her face. "Oh, Ashlock," she sighed, "I owe you one."

He shook his head with a dismissive gesture. "Don't mention it."

"Really, I do," she insisted. "And Ash, I am so, so, so embarrassed."

He leaned against the railing that separated the gallery from the counsel table. "I mean it, Elsie; don't give it another thought." With a smile he added, "I got your back."

The remark flustered her. She looked down at her file and shuffled her papers. "What brings you over here today?"

"I'm presenting a search warrant across the hall, but the judge is tied up for another twenty minutes, so I'm waiting around. Thought you might want to go for coffee."

"Oh, Ash, thanks," she said, shaking her head, "but it's way too late for coffee."

"I'd buy you a cold pop, then."

"Sounds good, but I don't have time. I need to check in with Madeleine to see what she wants me to do for tomorrow's preliminary hearing in the Taney case." She stood, picking up her file. "I gotta get downstairs. But really," dropping her voice to a whisper, "thanks. For last Friday. Really."

She cruised through the halls, looking in vain for Noah. When she finally arrived at Madeleine's office, she found the door closed, as always. Elsie knocked; no response. Sticking her head in the cubicle of Madeleine's private secretary, Nedra, she asked whether Madeleine was around.

Nedra thought a minute. "She left around two."

"When will she be back?"

"Don't know. She said she might be back today, and she might not be."

It wouldn't help to get mad, but her blood pressure spiked. She decided to find the file and see whether additional subpoenas had been issued for the next day's hearing. The electronic file was essentially empty, so she looked in the main file cabinet for the paper file. It was checked out.

Back at the secretary's desk, she asked, "Nedra, have you seen the Taney file?"

Nedra didn't have to think. "Nope."

"Does Madeleine have it?"

"Probably."

With growing frustration, she tried Madeleine's office again, pounding on the door with her fist, twisting the knob. No luck. She thought that Madeleine had to have the file with her; she must be getting the case ready for tomorrow's hearing. Elsie wished Madeleine would include her in the process. Frowning, she headed back to sit at her desk and stew, then saw Noah standing in the doorway of her office at the end of the hallway.

"There you are," he said.

Her frown disappeared. "What are you doing?"

"Waiting for you. We're getting some supper, aren't we?"

Elsie lit up like a lightning bug, in spite of herself. "Come on in and sit down while I get my paperwork in order. It's almost five; when the clock strikes, we can hit the floor running."

He took her by the hand, urging, "Grab your coat and

let's go. If we don't leave now, there'll be a big line at Little Hong Kong, and I won't make it back to work on time. I want some of that cashew chicken like they make over in Springfield."

She hesitated, checking the clock. "Oh, Noah, I don't know; we're not supposed to leave before five."

"Come *on*," he said. "You know you love cashew chicken. How come you have to be the last one to clock out every night? Let's go; we'll act like we're talking about a case." He grasped her upper arm and gave it a little squeeze as he bent down and spoke softly in her ear. "Very important business."

Elsie relented. "Oh, all right." She'd worked late Monday night, worked Saturday, worked every night the week before, when she was in trial. If Madeleine could ditch the office early, why couldn't she? "But we need to be subtle about it," she warned.

"Definitely," he agreed.

As they exited the Prosecutor's Office, he pinched her backside, and she shrieked with surprise. She looked over her shoulder to see if anyone had heard, and saw Stacie shaking her head.

Chapter Seven

ON WEDNESDAY MORNING the Prosecutor's Office buzzed with activity. Breeon battled a young defense attorney outside her office door, refusing to reduce a felony assault to a misdemeanor in clear and colorful language. The administrative staff sat at their computers, and Stacie already had a line of county citizens with problems and complaints.

Elsie was running late. That morning, Noah awoke in a randy mood, and she was disposed to accommodate him. As a result, she was walking bowlegged as she hurried through the office, but she believed it was a price worth paying.

Passing by Nedra's desk, she noted that Madeleine's secretary was three deep in local reporters. It was Nedra's job to handle the press and juggle media requests. Spying cameras from both of the local TV stations as she headed down the narrow hallway, Elsie ducked her head to disguise her glee. They had to be covering the Taney case. Seeing her face on television always provided a deliciously guilty pleasure.

She needed to talk to Nedra about the morning court schedule, but she didn't like to bother her while the reporters were around. She decided to check her e-mail first and enjoy the coffee she'd picked up at the Kinfolks Café on the way to work. Kinfolks boasted the strongest coffee in town, and though she had to spend precious minutes to run in and get it, she wanted a cup of good coffee in anticipation of her big day in court. While she was a loyal patron of the chummy little coffee shop at the courthouse, their coffee was a rank, watery brew parceled out in tiny white foam plastic cups.

The sight of her desk brought her up short. A familiar manila file had been laid atop the scattered mess of papers she left the day before. A stapled set of her handwritten notes sat beside it, with a single sheet of paper on top. It read: *I have a Dr.'s appointment. You'll need to handle this. Madeleine.*

"Fuck me," Elsie said, panic rising in her chest. This was the kind of scenario she confronted in nightmares sometimes, the anxiety dream where she showed up in court totally unprepared, missing important clothing items. The difference, of course, was that she wasn't dreaming. She was horribly, terribly awake, and the consequences were real. If she appeared for the preliminary hearing with no witnesses to support the charge, the judge would dismiss the case, and a child molester would be set loose.

Elsie snatched up the Taney file and ran back down the hall to Nedra's desk, where the secretary was deep in discussion with a reporter for the city newspaper. "Nedra," she panted. "Gotta talk to you."

"I'm busy," Nedra said, without a glance in her direction.

"It's really, really important," she insisted.

Nedra looked at her impatiently; nobody interfered with press relations in the Prosecutor's Office. Elsie made a frantic gesture behind the reporter's back, and Nedra got the message; she followed as Elsie dodged into a nearby conference room.

"Nedra," Elsie said, clutching her arm, "where the hell is Madeleine? The Taney preliminary is in one hour, and I've got a note saying she won't be here."

"She said she had an appointment. She said you could handle it. She said you know more about the case than she does, at this point." Nedra edged toward the door, but Elsie stopped her.

"Nobody told me," she said.

"Madeleine gave me the file and told me to put it on your desk yesterday, when she got back from her meetings." Nedra's tone betrayed her desire to return to the demands of her own job.

"No one told me yesterday. I didn't have the file yesterday; I was looking for it, I couldn't find it."

Nedra threw her hands up. "I put the file on your desk when I left at five o'clock. Madeleine came in at five and told me to."

Elsie snapped, "What are you talking about," then

stopped. She'd left work before five last night. She and Noah fled just a few minutes early, but her departure had set her up for disaster.

Leaning against the wall for support, she moaned. "Oh man, Nedra, are you sure she's not coming in this morning?"

"Absolutely positive."

"Can I reach her on her cell?"

Nedra shook her head. "She left instructions that she was not to be disturbed under any circumstances." She paused, then added in a whisper, "She's at her gynecologist."

Grasping for a crisis extreme enough to justify this desertion, Elsie asked, "Is it an emergency? Is she sick?"

"No," Nedra hissed, obviously offended. "It's her annual exam."

"You are kidding me. Nedra, we don't have the witnesses we need for preliminary; the case will be dismissed. I have to get in touch with her."

"Well, she did say that if you weren't confident enough to proceed on your own, get it continued. Until Friday. She has some room on her calendar Friday morning."

"Friday!" she wailed, but Nedra moved on down the hall.

Back at her desk, Elsie flipped through the file. Nothing had been done or added since she first reviewed it on Saturday. She checked the return copies of the subpoenas; as she feared, they were not updated. One subpoena was issued for Al Taney, and the other had been served on Tina Peroni, a social worker whose testimony would serve no purpose at the preliminary hearing.

Shutting the door, returning to her chair, she willed herself to calm down and think. The blood pounded in her temples. She was used to flying solo but was supposed to be second chair on Taney. It was the job of the first chair—Madeleine—to take the lead and ensure that catastrophe was averted. The role of second chair was to provide support.

The prospect of appearing alone at the preliminary hearing, when the state was clearly unprepared, terrified her. The state would lose; the judge would be furious; and the victims, the press, and the public at large would lay the blame at her feet.

She shut her eyes and tried to breathe slowly. A knock sounded at the door. Stacie called, "Your witness is here."

Elsie's heart jumped. "Which one?"

"Tina Peroni from Social Services."

Well, of course it was Tina. Al Taney was gone with the wind; she reckoned it was more likely to see Paris Hilton walk through the office door, toting a little dog in a fancy handbag, than Kris Taney's elusive brother.

She told Stacie she'd be right out and sat quietly for a moment. Reaching for the phone, she dialed the Detective Division of the Barton Police Department. When the line picked up, she said, "Connect me with Detective Ashlock, please."

After waiting for a second, she heard his voice: "Ashlock here."

Those words came through the line like a chorus of angels.

"Oh, Ash, it's Elsie, and I'm in a terrible bind. You got a minute?"

"Sure, Elsie. I'm heading to a meeting, but I can talk for a minute. What's up?"

"Madeleine dumped the Taney case on me, and I have a preliminary hearing in thirty minutes, and I've got no witness. The place is crawling with press. I don't know what to do. Don't have a clue." She was so relieved to confide in him, she nearly cried.

The detective's voice was warm and calm as he spoke into her ear. "Elsie, I'd be glad to help, but if you don't have a case, how are you going to come up with one in thirty minutes? Is there a witness that needs to be picked up? Can I get a patrolman to round somebody up for you?"

On a pad in front of her, she drew frantic circles. "I don't think we can find the witness on time. It's the defendant's brother. He skipped a meeting with us on Saturday, and I couldn't find him at his address."

"What's up with this guy? Isn't he the one who blew the whistle on the situation?"

"Yeah. It looks like he changed his mind about cooperating with us."

"That's no good. Can you get a continuance while we look for him?" Ashlock suggested.

"I don't know. Madeleine said I should continue it for Friday, but Kris Taney is incarcerated. The judge won't be sympathetic to a request for a continuance; we're not supposed to drag our feet when the defendant's sitting in jail. Shit, Ash, this case is in Judge Carter's court; you know he can't stand the sight of me."

They were both quiet for a moment. Ashlock swore under his breath. "Elsie, I've got a meeting with the police chief in about five minutes." Her hopes sank as he continued, "I'll check in on you as soon as I get out of there."

Shaking her head, she said, "Thanks anyway, Ash; thanks for listening. Sorry to bug you. I'll handle it."

A feeling of doom enveloped her as she hung up. She felt like she was battling a forest fire alone, with one gunny sack. With an effort, she rose from her chair and opened the door to the hall, calling out for her other witness.

"Stacie, where's Tina Peroni?"

"Right here," answered Tina, rounding the corner of the hallway. "I'd like a chance to run through the questions before I testify."

"Come in and sit down, Tina," she said, closing the door behind her. Tina settled in a chair across from her desk. Elsie had a high opinion of Tina and considered her a friend. After twenty years in social work, Tina had not succumbed to burnout. She was dedicated and savvy, and made a good appearance on the stand, too, with her articulate speech, trendy glasses, and relaxed manner.

Elsie asked, "How much contact have you had with the defendant in this case?"

"With Taney? Never met him. I did some interviews in the case after he was arrested." She pulled notes out of a folder and referred to them. "They assigned me to the family on December twenty-ninth. He was already in jail."

"So you can't provide any firsthand accounts of Taney's abuse of his children?"

"Well, no. Obviously."

Tapping a pen on her desktop, Elsie considered her options. As she suspected, Tina's testimony could not provide admissible evidence against Taney at the hearing. The rules of evidence required direct proof, and since Taney's brother was AWOL, she needed to go to the heart of the matter.

Elsie asked, "Can you set up interviews between Detective Ashlock and Kris Taney's daughters and wife this week?"

"Certainly. What's up?"

"I'm trying to salvage this case. We're about to fumble the ball." She made a face. "Sorry about the football analogy. It's just that I'm working around policemen all the time."

Tina laughed. "Hey, I like football. I'm a Steelers fan."

Elsie gave her a look. "Good Lord, Tina. That's an East Coast team."

"I'm not a local, my hillbilly friend."

"Oh, Tina. No one would mistake you for an Ozarks native."

"Because I'm gay? Or because I have a full set of teeth?"

A knock sounded; the door opened and Detective Ashlock stuck his head in. "Ladies, how can I help?"

She had never been so glad to see anyone in her life. Beaming, she jumped up and ushered him in. "Damn, you're fast."

He laughed. "It's handy to have the police station across the street."

"What about the chief?" she asked.

"I told him there's an emergency at the courthouse. It sounds like there surely is."

Elsie offered her seat, but Ashlock refused, leaning against the file cabinet instead.

"What did you all allege in the felony complaint?" he asked.

"Count one is statutory rape in the first degree; that's Kristy, she's under the age of fourteen," Elsie replied, pulling out the sheet of paper. "Then Madeleine charged statutory rape in the second degree for count two. That's for his sexual intercourse with Charlene; since she's fifteen, it's a less serious felony offense."

Looking up from the page, she said, "You know he must have had sex with Charlene when she was younger. If I could talk to her, she could pinpoint some times that her father had sex with her before she turned fourteen."

"What's the third charge?" he asked.

"The third charge is a count of incest, having sexual intercourse with his blood descendant. But incest is only a Class D felony. We'd be much better off dumping the incest charge and filing more specific counts of activity under the first degree statutory rape statute, because the penalty is higher."

Tina asked, "What's the penalty for incest?"

"Well, it's Class D, so the most time he can get for that is four years. But the maximum penalty for statutory rape in the first degree is life imprisonment."

"Life," repeated Tina with awe. "That's tough shit."

"Damn straight," Elsie nodded. "This is Missouri, hon." Indicating the criminal complaint, she said, "I've got to get this complaint cleaned up. It's a mess."

Ashlock walked over to Elsie's desk, bending over her shoulder as they examined the language of the charge together. Even through her desperation, she was acutely aware of his proximity as he took the pen from her hand and made notations on the paper, underlining portions of each of the three counts against Taney.

"You need your victims here for preliminary," he said. "You should have them on the stand, regardless of whether we can run down Taney's brother." He handed the pen back to her.

"How quickly can you take witness statements of the Taney women?" she asked.

He took time to consider the options. "Do you want them on video?"

"No, just basic Q and A on audiotape, with your clerical staff making a transcript. And making it *fast*. How soon can we get that accomplished?"

"When do you need it?" Ashlock asked.

Elsie checked her watch. "In about five minutes."

A LOCAL TV cameraman trained his lens on Elsie and Tina as they walked toward the courtroom. If her knees were inclined to wobble, Elsie thought, they'd be shaking now. She knew her motion for continuance would be met with disapproval, and the stakes were high. Just about as high as they could be.

If Judge Carter overruled her motion for continuance and ordered her to proceed, she couldn't. She didn't have a witness. The judge would dismiss the charge against Taney, and he would be released.

And then he would go home. She could never let that happen again.

The defendant and his attorney were already sitting at the counsel table when she approached. She cut her eyes at Kris Taney, curious to get a first look. He was a barrel-chested man in his mid-thirties, maybe a head taller than her, with long, unkempt ginger hair and a florid complexion. Despite being attired in the standard county jail orange jumpsuit, he reeked with the odor of a man who had not bathed for a long while. The stink was so strong, she had to fight the urge to cover her nose as she walked over to Taney's court-appointed attorney, Josh Nixon, and served him with a copy of her motion for continuance.

"What's this?" Nixon asked.

"Got an evidentiary delay. Sorry, the motion's not too detailed; I had to knock it out at the last minute. Madeleine's out of pocket, and she wants it reset for Friday. Are you good with that? It's only a couple of days."

Nixon turned to his client, but Taney's eyes were glued to Elsie, surveying her with a dubious squint. Nixon placed the motion where Taney could see it and told Elsie, "No way. We're not agreeing to a continuance; my client has been locked up for nearly two weeks, waiting for this hearing. Do you have a case or not?"

The door to Judge Carter's chambers opened and he

entered the courtroom. Everyone rose to their feet with the exception of Kris Taney, who remained in his seat even as his attorney tugged at the sleeve of his orange county jail scrubs.

Judge Carter murmured, "Be seated," from the bench. Rustling could be heard as people in the gallery settled onto the curved oak benches.

"Ms. Arnold, is the state ready to proceed?"

Elsie stood again and steeled herself to face the music. "Your honor, we've had an unexpected delay. I'm presenting a motion for continuance on behalf of Madeleine Thompson."

"Where is Ms. Thompson and why isn't she presenting her own motion?"

"She had a conflict this morning. An unavoidable conflict."

Irritation etched the judge's face as he briefly scanned the motion Elsie handed to him. "Since Ms. Thompson sent you to appear on her behalf, Ms. Arnold, I propose that you proceed."

"Your honor, this is Madeleine's case."

"Then she ought to be up here today, handling it. What is the conflict? Is she appearing in another court? We could reschedule the preliminary hearing after lunch."

Oh, shit. "She's not in another court. Your honor."

The judge frowned. "Then what's the nature of the delay?"

Elsie scratched the hair at the back of her neck. "Medical."

Judge Carter fiddled with his gavel for a moment.

"Ms. Arnold, I want you to proceed with your evidence. Call your first witness."

"I can't, your honor," she said, flushing pink with mortification. "A witness failed to appear, even though he was served with a subpoena."

The judge barked, "Call another witness, then. Surely you had more than one witness to appear for a preliminary hearing in a three-count felony complaint."

Lord, you'd think so, Elsie mused, her heart rate increasing. Aloud she said, "I have to have this continuance, Judge Carter. I don't need much additional time: just a few days. I have to obtain the testimony of a crucial witness."

The judge sat back in his chair. "Is defendant out on bond?"

She winced inwardly; the question was a bad sign for the prosecution, because the judge clearly knew the answer. Taney was attired in the orange garb of a county inmate.

"No, your honor," she said as Nixon chimed in, "No judge, he is not."

Judge Carter opened the file and studied the charge. "I'm not in favor of a continuance request by the state," he said in a forbidding tone. "I'm inclined to believe that if the state isn't ready, they shouldn't file the charge."

Her stomach twisting, Elsie was poised to argue the point, when Nixon jumped to his feet as if on cue and launched into a litany of objections and protests: that the prosecution was violating defendant's rights; that if the state didn't have their case ready they should not have filed the charge; that the state was oppressing defendant by imposing a high bond amount that kept him behind bars. He pounded his fist on the table as he proclaimed that Elsie Arnold was personally violating the defendant's Fifth, Sixth, and Eighth Amendment rights.

When he paused for breath, she said, "Your honor, if it please the court," but the judge lifted a hand to silence her.

"I've made my decision," he said. He picked up a fountain pen and prepared to write. "As a courtesy to Ms. Thompson, I'll grant the motion for continuance."

Elsie exhaled and her shoulders relaxed.

"But I'm releasing Mr. Taney on his own recognizance. I don't believe in holding the accused when the state is responsible for delays."

She gasped, and shot a quick look at the defense table. Taney stared at her, then broke into an expression that couldn't truly be called a smile; it was a hostile grimace of gritted teeth, like the rictus of a graveyard skull. A chill went through her. She said, "Judge Carter, I object; defendant is a flight risk, he should not be let out ROR. The defense hasn't even made that request."

"Your honor," Josh Nixon countered, "I'd like to request that the defendant be released on his own recognizance."

"Granted."

"Wait!" Elsie cried. The judge looked at her, shocked. She couldn't remember the last time they'd made eye contact. She scooted around her counsel table and marched up to the bench.

"Judge, it would be destructive—devastating—to the case if you release the defendant today. I implore you." She grabbed the wooden edge of his raised bench as she said, in a passionate whisper, "Judge Carter, he's got nowhere to go; nowhere but home. Think of the effect it will have on the state's case if he shows up there."

Nixon, who joined her at the bench, said, "The judge has already ruled."

Elsie didn't look his way. "Judge Carter, these witnesses are children. *Children*. Look at the charge."

The judge opened the file and toyed with the paper. "A charge is just that, without proof. Court is adjourned."

Chapter Eight

ELSIE WATCHED IN horror as the judge tossed the file to his clerk and walked to his chambers, opened the door, and shut it behind him without a backward look.

Nixon shot her a smug glance and said, "You know, at the Public Defender's Office, they call you 'Miss Missouri from Hell.' Guess you're just having an off day."

Actually, she did *not* know that. As she struggled to compose a fitting retort, Nixon turned his back to her and spoke quietly to his client.

Taney asked, "This is it, right?" His voice was a rumbling bass, thick with the accent of the Ozark hills. "They got to let me go now."

"No!" Elsie cried. She ran to Judge Carter's chamber door. Without stopping to debate the propriety of her action, she banged on the door with her fist.

"Judge Carter," she called, "we gotta talk."

No sound came from the other side of the door. She

knocked again, louder this time. "Judge Carter, open the door. Please. You have to reconsider your ruling."

Nixon, joining her at the door, hissed, "What the hell do you think you're doing?"

"I'm appealing his decision," she said. Her heart beat so fast that her face was scarlet. When the judge still refused to acknowledge her knock, she tried the knob; it was unlocked. She twisted it and pushed the door open.

Judge Carter stood by a coat rack, fighting with the zipper on his black robe. He gaped at the attorneys with disbelief. "You can't just barge in here."

Elsie stood her ground. "Judge Carter, you've got to rethink this. Taney is too dangerous to cut loose."

"Too dangerous how?" The judge continued to jerk at his zipper; it was caught in the black fabric. "Has he killed anybody?"

"No."

"Does he have a felony record? For assault?"

She cleared her throat. "Well, no. No felonies that showed up on the rap sheet. But there's a bunch of arrests for assault on his wife, domestic disturbance calls."

"All dropped," Nixon chimed in.

"And?" The zipper finally gave, and the judge pulled the robe off and hung it on a hook. Running his fingers through his hair, he took a seat behind his desk. "That's not uncommon. Particularly with this class of people." He appeared to mull it over for a moment, then shook his head. "No. I've ruled."

Elsie planted both hands flat on his desk, so he couldn't avoid looking at her.

"Judge Carter, please. Change it."

"What?"

"Your ruling. Change it." When Nixon tried to interject, she cut him off. "You're the judge. You can make a ruling and think better of it."

The judge glared at her in silence.

She continued, "Judge, you know what he's going to do. He's going to go terrorize his family and shut them up."

"Your honor," Nixon protested, "the state is mounting baseless accusations; this is entirely speculative."

The judge regarded Elsie with a sour face. "Ms. Arnold, you're out of order—" he began, but she interrupted.

"If I'm right, if he goes out there and hurts them, somebody will have to shoulder the blame."

The judge looked away. She leaned in, eager to reinforce her point. "Did you see all the press out there? They will know it was you, Judge Carter, who cut him loose, when the state begged you to keep him in jail. Who will the press hang up to dry?"

Nixon interjected, "The judge has already ruled, Ms. Arnold."

Elsie kept her eyes glued on the judge's face. "You never make anyone mad when you lock up a child molester."

"Alleged! Alleged!" Nixon cried.

"Oh, yeah. Right," she said dryly. "I was speaking generally."

"Ms. Arnold," Judge Carter said, "back off, before I

call Eldon in here to throw you out." She took a step back, knowing she'd gone too far. The judge leaned away from her in his chair, adding, "You have no right to come tearing into my office, harassing me. You should show the same respect in chambers that's required in court. This borders on contempt."

Patch it up, she told herself fearfully. "Judge Carter, I'm sorry, I really am; please accept my apology. I didn't mean to offend, I swear. But," she went on, moving in again, in spite of herself, "I am so scared for those Taney kids. The youngest girl is just six."

A family photograph in a silver frame sat on the judge's desk. Glancing at it, she said, "About your daughter's age."

Judge Carter sat for a long moment. "Let me see the rap sheet," he said. She rummaged in the file, thankful it was still in her grasp. He studied it in silence, then said, "Twenty-four hours. I'm giving you twenty-four hours."

"Yesss," Elsie breathed.

"I object, Judge; this is unfair to my client—" Nixon began, but the judge waved his protest away.

"Oh, come on, Nixon," he said. "Twenty-four more hours in lockup just means your man will get a couple more free meals. Courtesy of McCown County." Into the phone, the judge said to his bailiff, "Eldon, I've changed my ruling. Take Taney back to the county jail." He set the phone in its cradle and pointed at Elsie. "Twenty-four hours, Ms. Arnold. If the state isn't ready to proceed at that time, I'll dismiss the charge."

"You bet, Judge. Thank you so much. We'll be ready."

With that, Elsie beat a hasty retreat back into the courtroom, with Nixon close behind.

The bailiff was struggling with Taney, who cursed and fought Eldon's attempt to return him to the jail. "Judge cut me loose. Get me out of these goddamned cuffs, you old fucker."

Elsie watched as Nixon tried to intercede, explaining that the judge had reset the preliminary hearing for the next day. "I'll come see you over at the jail and explain; we'll talk about tomorrow's hearing," he said. She heard the attorney add, in a low voice, "Listen, you have to take a shower before you come back to court. You stink. You'll make a bad impression on the judge."

Taney turned on him with a scowl. "You mean that judge that just fucked me over? That judge better worry about the impression he makes on me. I could kick his scrawny ass if I wanted, I guarantee you."

The defense attorney stared at Taney, at a loss for words. Elsie could hear Taney as he leaned in close to Nixon and added, "And I ain't going nowhere near them jailhouse showers. You know what they going to do to me in there?" Taney reached out with his cuffed hands and grabbed his attorney's wrist. He squeezed it, hard, and the lawyer winced. "What done happened back there? Why ain't you getting me out of here?"

As the defense attorney wrested his hand from Taney's grasp, a neatly dressed man in rayon pants and a yellow sweater came up and placed his hand on Taney's shoulder. He said, "Just want you to know I'm here for you."

Taney's mood changed instantly. "Thanks, man," he said in an ingratiating tone. "Means a lot to have you on my side. People been lying about me."

"I seen what you're going through. You're not alone."

The bailiff interrupted the dialogue. With a deputy as reinforcement, Eldon took Taney by the arm and led him from the courtroom. Before he walked through the door, Taney said loudly to no one in particular, "I got my rights. That whore won't bring me down. A man's got rights." He marched through the door, shaking his long red hair back from his face, his chin high.

The courtroom was silent for a second then gave way to a buzz of startled reaction. Elsie sighed with relief as she put her file back together. She glanced at Nixon, tempted to needle him. With a droll expression, she leaned over and tugged the defense attorney's sleeve. "Did you draw the short straw?"

Nixon appeared to be in no mood for banter. "I could ask you the same question. Where's your star witness? And what happened to the big cheese? My office said that Madeleine was handling this case personally. It's high profile."

Elsie wasn't well acquainted with Josh Nixon, but clearly, he took his job seriously. He was a new addition to the Public Defender's Office. The courthouse sages said that he graduated in the top ranks of his law school class, but took a job in the Public Defender's Office because of his crippling student debt. A new law forgave student loans for lawyers who served ten years in the public interest.

Though he seemed to be a tough opponent, she thought she might try to wrestle a concession from him. With a shrug, she proposed, "I don't suppose you'd be interested in waiving preliminary tomorrow."

He laughed in disbelief and shook his head. "You're pretty slick. Why would I waive when you just confessed to the judge that you don't have a case?"

She ignored the question and gave him her most winning smile. "Do you want to stipulate to testimony? I could make an offer of proof to you by tomorrow morning."

"My dear Ms. Arnold, you are going to have to produce a live body tomorrow, and drag it up on the witness stand, and make it talk."

"Hey," she said, deliberately casual, "I was just trying to save you some work."

Josh shook his head and walked off, calling to the man in the yellow sweater, but before the lawyer walked out the courtroom door, he turned again to look at her. Josh was an attractive guy, with casually tousled hair and clothes he wore with a careless air. Actually, she kind of liked his style, or lack of it. She pondered for a second what he would be like in the sack, then she caught herself and resolutely turned away. Any alliance between a prosecutor and a public defender was fraught with a hundred complications. There was no point in toying with defense counsel. No point at all.

Picking up her files with a sigh of resignation, a thin sheet of paper fluttered out and slid onto the floor.

Stooping over to snatch it up, she looked at the page in

confusion. It was not a part of the Taney file; she had gone through the file from front to back, several times.

The page she held was torn from a Bible, and two verses had been marked with a yellow highlighter. She read:

> *They are gossips, slanderers, God-haters, haughty, arrogant, boastful, inventors of evil, disobedient to their parents, foolish, faithless, heartless, and ruthless. Although they know God's just requirement— that those who practice such things deserve to die—they not only do these things but even applaud others who practice them.*

Jerking her head around, she looked to see who'd left the paper for her to find, but the courtroom had emptied out. If the text was in fact intended for her, the messenger had fled.

Maybe it wasn't for me, she thought. Could be a mistake.

Maybe it's a joke.

She looked at the page again, and the garish yellow marks on the paper gave her a chill.

Chapter Nine

——————————————————————

THE GRAY AFTERNOON sky spit snow as Elsie, Tina, and Bob Ashlock made their way up the sidewalk to the dilapidated white house on High Street. At a front window, a hand briefly pulled aside a patterned bedsheet that served as a curtain and then let it drop.

Still fired up from her close call in court, Elsie led the way, anxious to begin the interview. "I can't believe the woman I talked to last Saturday was the defendant's wife," she lamented. "I was knocking on the wrong door. I feel so stupid. Why didn't I ask her who she was?"

Tina clutched her coat against the frigid wind. "Yeah, why didn't you?"

Ashlock jumped to Elsie's defense. "You're not a cop; it's not your job to investigate." As they reached the door, he held it open and asked, "Tina, what happened to Taney's girlfriend and her baby?"

Tina shook her head. "You mean JoLee. She's not cooperating with us. Refuses to talk about Kris Taney. I don't know if she's afraid of him or loyal to him."

"Did they take protective custody?"

"Yeah, they took her kid away. Her baby's in foster care, and JoLee's back home with her family. We're supervising her visitation, but things aren't progressing very fast. She says she wants to get her kid back, though."

Ashlock asked, "But Donita Taney still has custody of her girls?"

"Donita cooperated with Social Services; JoLee refused. That's the litmus test in these cases. Some mothers want to protect the kids, others want to protect their man."

They entered the old house and Ashlock pounded on the door to 1A, the apartment Elsie had assumed was Al Taney's neighbor, but in fact belonged to Al's brother Kris. A child opened the door and peeked out, a small girl with a round face and wavy strawberry hair. Tina knelt and spoke to her.

"You're Tiffany, aren't you?" The child nodded. "I'm Tina, and I've been to your house before. Do you remember me?" Another nod, but the girl ducked her head, shy before the strangers. "May we come in? We need to talk to your mother and your sisters."

Tiffany scooted aside, clutching a Barbie doll to her chest as if she feared it might be snatched from her. They entered the main room of the apartment, and Elsie recognized the dark-haired woman she'd met days before. The woman sat on an old couch against the far wall of the room. The upholstery was in tatters, with threadbare towels covering the cushions. She stared at them like a deer caught in the headlights and did not rise to greet them.

Ashlock approached Mrs. Taney and addressed her in an authoritative voice, a marked contrast from Tina's warm tone. "I'm Detective Bob Ashlock with the Barton Police Department. Are you Donita Taney?" Mrs. Taney responded with a quick nod. He continued, "Ms. Peroni told you we'd be recording witness statements today, correct?"

Donita Taney nodded again, eyeing the visitors warily. She reached for a pack of menthol cigarettes on a side table and lit one with a kitchen match, pulling the dirty ashtray closer. Her hand trembled slightly.

Ashlock said, "We want to ask some questions of you and your three daughters." He surveyed her impassively. "That all right with you?"

She didn't answer immediately, looking toward the window as if something outside required her attention. Smoke curled up from the lit end of the cigarette. Finally she blew out a cloud of smoke and said, "Sure. Whatever."

Ashlock gestured toward the back of the apartment. "Okay if I set up in the kitchen?" Mrs. Taney nodded, and he headed through the doorway into a connecting room where a kitchen table was visible.

Standing alone in the room with Mrs. Taney, Elsie knew she needed to break the ice. Her relationship with the mother of the victims could ultimately decide her case. Putting on a smile, she stepped toward Donita and extended her hand. "It's nice to see you again, Mrs. Taney. I'm Elsie Arnold from the Prosecutor's Office. I was here last Saturday, actually."

"I remember you."

"Mind if I sit?" It looked like she was not going to be invited to make herself comfortable.

"Sure, go ahead."

A weather-beaten plastic chair, designed to be used outdoors in summertime, sat in a corner. Elsie dragged it across the floor and set it near Mrs. Taney. "There now," she said in a confiding way, "we can get a little better acquainted. May I call you Donita?"

"Okay."

While she spoke, Elsie furtively inspected the room. The floor was covered with a stained remnant of orange shag carpet, spotted with burn holes and matted with hair. Overhead, the ceiling was bowed in places, and areas of missing plaster revealed the lattice boards underneath. A couple of pieces of broken furniture occupied the floor space, but she noted that there were no electronics of any kind in the room, not even a television or telephone. Two naked Barbies with ragged hair, one with a missing leg, were the only toys in the place.

The odor of mildew hung in the air, mingled with an even worse odor. Plastic grocery bags filled with garbage were propped up beside the kitchen doorway, a clue to the stench. Elsie fought her inclination to pass judgment, but she couldn't understand why the woman sitting beside her would raise her children in squalor.

She smiled at Donita, taking care not to react to her surroundings. "Tell me how many children you have," she prompted.

"Three. There's Charlene and Kristy and Tiffany. Char

just turned fifteen, Kristy is twelve, and Tiffany is my baby. She's six." As Donita rattled off the information, she seemed nervous rather than hostile. She tapped her cigarette in the ashtray, rolling it repeatedly, as if she needed something to do with her hands.

"Tiffany is the little girl who answered the door today," Elsie said. Tiffany had slipped out with Tina Peroni, and the other girls had not yet made an appearance. "She is just precious; what a pretty girl. Where did she get that curly hair?"

"Oh, the other girls has straight hair like me, but Tiffany's got that curly red hair like Kris."

The defendant's name hung in the air like a dangling spider. Leaning toward the older woman, Elsie nodded.

"It's a big job raising three girls alone, I bet."

Donita Taney nodded.

Elsie ventured, "But it must be a relief to have your husband in jail."

Donita finally looked at her. "You got no idea."

Elsie clucked sympathetically. "Oh, I get it."

Donita leaned forward, her eyes boring directly into Elsie's face. She dropped her voice, as if they might be overheard. "I mean it. You got no idea. You don't know nothing about what it's like."

The woman's intensity was unnerving. Elsie met her gaze, unflinching, but she bore down so hard with her pen that it bled onto her hand. Looking down at the legal pad and the mess she made, she muttered, "Oh, shit."

She said to Donita, "Beg your pardon, but look what I've done. If I don't wash this ink off, I'm going to get it all over everywhere." Standing, she asked, "Could you point out the restroom?"

Donita looked unwilling. "Toilet's not working."

"I don't need to go," Elsie said in a whisper. Begging for a restroom pass was embarrassing, but she wanted a break from Donita as much as she needed to wash off the ink. "I just need to rinse my hand off."

Donita shrugged. Pointing, she said, "Through there."

Elsie followed the direction of Donita's finger. When she opened the door, an overwhelming fecal stench assaulted her. Though the toilet lid was down, it was clear that the nonfunctioning toilet was being used by the household.

She stood uncertainly, her first instinct to flee the room. Determined to overcome her skittishness, she shut the door and approached the sink. It was grimy, coated with gray scum. A battered sliver of soap rested by the faucet; she let it be. Turning on the cold water, she scrubbed at the ink staining her fingers. As she rubbed her hands under the water, a cockroach walked up the side of the sink and scampered across the surface.

Jumping back from the sink with horror, she shook the water from her hands and wiped the excess on her clothes. There was no towel on the towel rack, not that she would have touched it anyway. Her skin crawled as she turned the faucet off with her sleeve.

Shaken, she returned to Donita in the front room. Taking her seat in the plastic chair, she cleared her throat and said, "Okay, now where were we?"

She rummaged in her purse for a different pen, and

studied her legal pad. Blocking the vision of the bathroom from her head, Elsie plowed on: "I have to ask: were you aware that your husband was committing sexual acts with your daughters?"

"No," Donita said, looking away. "Didn't know nothing. Never."

"Yes you did, Mom." Elsie and Donita both looked up as a dark-haired teen entered the room. The girl joined her mother on the couch, plucked a cigarette from the pack and lit it. "You said we wasn't gonna bullshit about it no more."

"You ain't going to smoke all them, Char," Donita said. "We just gone through that yesterday. I had to go to the plasma center to get extra money this week, and it's about gone." The girl ignored her, inhaling deeply and blowing the smoke through her nostrils.

Elsie smiled at the girl, anxious to establish rapport. "So you're Charlene. I'm Elsie Arnold, from the Prosecutor's Office. Great to meet you." She scooted the chair closer to the couch. "I want you to know that I'm your ally in this process. As the prosecutor, I'll be with you in court every step of the way. When you are called to the witness stand to testify, I'll be the one asking the questions; and when your father's defense attorney asks you questions, I'll be right there, ready to jump up and holler if he gets out of line." She paused, smiling again, hoping to prompt a response. But Donita and Charlene just stared at her, their faces blank.

Elsie tried again. "I think it's a wonderful thing that you all found the courage to speak up. Did something that happened make you decide to come out with the facts of Mr. Taney's abuse?"

Charlene turned to her mother with a quizzical look. Donita studied the filter of the cigarette she held.

"It's time," she said, regarded Charlene for a bare second, then looked away. "That's all."

Elsie looked from Donita to her daughter. She wanted to dig deeper and was considering how to begin when Charlene said, "Toilet still broke?"

Donita nodded. With a sidelong glance at Elsie, she said, "I'm gonna tell the landlord. When he comes for the rent."

"What the hell am I supposed to do till then?" Charlene said, raising her voice.

Her mother glared at her. "Go to the gas station."

Charlene snorted. "I'm going in the sink."

Oh, dear God, Elsie thought. She kept her face impassive, but it was a challenge.

A door slammed in back, and Tina entered with little Tiffany following behind. Tina announced that Ashlock was ready to begin and sent Tiffany up the back stairs to fetch her other sister, Kristy. Tina turned to Charlene then, who was stretching her thin legs over the arm of the couch. "Charlene, are you ready to talk to the detective?"

Charlene said, "Why not?" and hopped off the couch. Elsie, Tina, and Charlene walked to the kitchen and joined Ashlock at the table; Donita remained in the front room. A pocket door in the wall could be pulled out to separate the two rooms, which Tina did, at Ashlock's direction, shutting Donita out.

At the kitchen table, a plastic bag with a loaf of white bread was pushed to one side. Some dishes were stacked in a strainer on an old sink. Elsie observed with surprise that the sink was a duplicate of the one in her mother's kitchen: a wide berth of cast iron covered in heavy porcelain, with a porcelain splash guard and two ancient faucets. It was probably original to the house, as her mother's was. However, this sink was stained and pitted, unlike her mother's, which was regularly scrubbed with Comet cleanser to keep it white.

Ashlock started by asking Charlene about her relationship with her father.

"Just what all you want to know?" asked Charlene. Her voice had a lilt, a flirtatious tone, as she cocked her head in Ashlock's direction and took a puff from the cigarette. She blew the smoke in a thin plume at his face. "What you going to give me if I talk to you?"

She laughed at Ashlock teasingly. He regarded her silently, waiting. Elsie felt acid rise in her throat. It didn't take a mind reader to figure out how the girl learned to play cat and mouse games with adult men.

When Ashlock didn't respond, Charlene shrugged and dropped her bantering tone. "He always treated me bad. He never liked me. It was Kristy he liked best, I guess. He got worse when he started seeing JoLee, though. Lots worse. Because it was like he could only be nice to her. Treated the rest of us like shit."

"Tell us about that."

Elsie braced herself. Hearing children relate their sordid experiences was a devastating part of her job.

"What do you want to know?" Charlene asked.

"How he treated you," Ashlock replied in a soothing tone.

"Well," she said, crossing her arms on the table and resting her chin on top, "we had to do anything he'd say. I mean anything. You couldn't never talk back to him, neither."

"That doesn't sound so unusual."

She snorted, and regarded Ashlock with a knowing expression. "I don't think everybody else was having to do what all we was up to. And we couldn't say nothing back. He'd even whip JoLee for back-sassing. And he liked her."

"What was JoLee's connection to your family?"

Blandly, she replied, "She's Dad's girlfriend."

"How do you know that?

She snorted. "Be hard to miss it. But even when she came along, he still made me take care of him."

"What do you mean?"

"You know."

"Charlene, could you be specific? What exactly did he do?"

Charlene laughed and looked away. "One time, he pooped in my mouth."

Elsie, who had been listening intently, reeled if she had been struck a blow. She had handled many sex cases and was no stranger to the abuses children suffered, but that particular act came as a shock. Tears pricked her eyes and she blinked them back.

"He made me eat it."

"Oh, Jesus Christ," Elsie said, and started to rise from the table. Ashlock grasped her arm, and she got her horror under control. She sat back down, eyes glued to Charlene.

"He did it 'cause I cussed. He said he'd learn me not to cuss." She looked defiantly at Ashlock. "Didn't work."

Elsie listened as Charlene related other offenses and described sex acts with her father in a flat, matter-of-fact voice, stopping at one point to get a fresh cigarette. Ashlock and Elsie watched the girl light the kitchen match by scraping her thumbnail on the tip. She lit the cigarette and French-inhaled the smoke.

Elsie exchanged a look with Ashlock. When she saw her profound sadness mirrored in his eyes, she placed her hand over his.

WHILE ASHLOCK WAS questioning Charlene, Tiffany slipped back into the front room where Donita sat. In stocking feet, she crawled up next to her mother on the ragged sofa. Donita studied the child for a moment and then whispered, "You scared? You scared of that man? Policeman?"

Tiffany shook her head.

"Oh," said Donita, "you're scared about Daddy. Worried Daddy's coming back."

Tiffany nodded and burrowed into her mother's bony chest. Donita sighed and gathered the child into her arms. Stroking the girl's back, she bent over her head and spoke softly.

"Don't you worry. We're getting rid of Daddy. Mama's fixing it."

She rocked the little girl back and forth, silently at first.

"Think nice things," she whispered. After a quiet moment, she began tapping her foot and softly, in barely a whisper, began to sing.

"She'll be comin' 'round the mountain when she comes, when she comes . . . "

Tiffany closed her eyes and relaxed in her mother's arms as Donita sang the words of the old folk song with a nasal twang. The girl was almost asleep when Donita finished the fourth verse, with a sly grin that showed the brown stains on her teeth:

> *"We will kill the old red rooster, kill the old*
> *   red rooster,*
> *We will kill the old red rooster when she*
> *   comes."*

Donita gazed down at her youngest child and smoothed the girl's tangled hair as she sang.

Chapter Ten

THE SWORN STATEMENTS of Donita, Charlene, and Kristy Taney were paper-clipped together in a file folder on the counsel table. Next to the folder was the state's copy of the amended felony complaint against Kris Taney, signed by Elsie Arnold, Assistant Prosecuting Attorney. The new complaint alleged that Taney committed five felony counts of statutory rape in the first degree against his two eldest daughters.

The courtroom was quiet. Elsie stood near the witness stand, ready to begin, adrenaline pumping and nerves on edge. In a case involving child witnesses, anything could happen, and she needed to be ready to roll with the punches. She felt faintly nauseous. She swallowed and focused on her witness, intent.

Judge Carter looked somber as he sat at the bench. Josh Nixon leaned back in his seat with his left hand gripping the back of his client's chair.

Kris Taney's eyes were glued to the witness stand, where his daughter Kristy sat. Kristy's dark hair was pulled back from her forehead with a rubber band. She looked forlorn in the witness box, her chin shaking, her hands clutching the sides of the wooden chair and hanging on as if her life depended on it.

Elsie leaned against the corner of the empty jury box and addressed Kristy.

"Kristy," she said in an encouraging voice, "I'd like you to think back to the twenty-fifth of November of last year, Thanksgiving Day. How old were you on that date?"

"Twelve," said Kristy, eyeing her father fearfully.

Got to pull her focus away from Taney, Elsie thought as she moved closer to the witness stand.

"Kristy," she repeated. The girl transferred her gaze to Elsie, who gave a reassuring nod and a hint of a wink. Once she had Kristy's full attention, Elsie continued: "Do you remember what happened last Thanksgiving?"

"Yes."

"Can you tell what you recall?"

Kristy was silent for a minute. "We ate. Mom got a chicken. But Dad got mad after supper. I don't remember why."

The child paused again. With a twinge of anxiety, Elsie thought, Keep talking, Kristy; if I try to lead you, Nixon will jump out of his chair.

Willing her to continue, she asked, "What happened when your dad got mad?"

"I tried to leave. I didn't want to be around. I knew he'd get mean. He always does when he's mad." Josh

Nixon rose from his seat, and the girl stopped speaking, looking at the defense attorney.

"Objection."

"Overruled," said Judge Carter, holding up a hand to silence Nixon. The judge's eyes never left the witness.

"Go on, Kristy," Elsie said, praying that she would get the necessary revelations out of the girl without making the child fall apart.

"He caught me going out the door. He grabbed me and made me come back in."

She prompted gently: "Then what happened?"

"He said I done bad because I didn't mind. I was sneaking out. He said I had to learn that he was boss."

"Then what?"

"He took me to his bedroom. He didn't even shut the door." She paused. "He put his thing in me."

Here we go, Elsie thought; this is it. Delicately, as though she handled a fragment of spun glass, she moved closer, asking softly, "Exactly what did he do?"

Kristy hung her head and didn't answer. Elsie's heart twisted; it was a horrific thing, forcing a child to speak aloud in public about her sexual violation. Resolutely, she took a breath and straightened, pushing her reluctance aside. It had to be done; if she could not make Kristy speak the words, the law would not protect the child.

"Kristy," Elsie said carefully, "are you saying that he put his penis in you?"

"Objection—leading," said Nixon.

"Overruled," said the judge.

Fabulous, Elsie thought, flashing an appreciative look

in Judge Carter's direction, because her question had in fact been leading. Kristy was silent until Elsie said, "Kristy, you may answer."

"Yeah. His penis."

"Where did he put it?"

"You know. Sex. My vagina."

"Where did that happen," Elsie continued.

"Our house. The front bedroom."

We're almost there, she thought. Just nail down venue, and we're done. With a nod, she asked, "Where was your house located?"

"Where it is now. 985 High Street."

"Is that in Barton, McCown County, Missouri?"

"Yes."

Oh, thank God, she did it. She wanted to collapse in her chair; it had been a nail-biter, guiding Kristy through the elements of count five.

She said to the judge, "No further questions, your honor."

The judge looked at the defense attorney. "Mr. Nixon?"

Elsie sat in her chair at the counsel table, but every muscle in her body tightened as she anticipated what Nixon would do to Kristy on cross-examination. She had seen children massacred on the witness stand by defense attorneys, a hideous thing to watch. The only advocate Kristy had, the sole person who could protect her from the onslaught, was her. She tensed, ready to pounce if Nixon made a misstep.

Nixon stood and buttoned his jacket. "Kristy," he said in a neutral voice, "who all saw this act you say happened on Thanksgiving?"

"Everybody."

"Everybody!" he said in disbelief. "Your sisters?"

"Yes."

"Your mother?"

"Yeah."

"Who else?"

Kristy faltered a little as she said, "JoLee. And I think Uncle Al. He might've left."

Nixon paused a moment for effect, and then he said, "You mean to tell us that your father had sex with you in a house full of people and nobody did a thing."

"Nope."

Elsie shifted uncomfortably in her seat. She saw that he was controlling the girl's responses, but he had not yet asked a question that called for an objection.

"Your mother didn't stop him."

"No."

"Five other people in that house and no one tried to save you."

Kristy was silent for a long moment. "No," she said finally.

Nixon scratched his head. "Why not?"

The girl stared at him, struggling to put the explanation in words.

"They couldn't do nothing."

"For God's sake, why not?" He shook his head, incredulous.

"They wasn't supposed to. He's the boss. We got to do what he says."

Elsie kept her face neutral, with an effort. Kristy had hit

the nail on the head. How many times had she heard victims explain that they were powerless to protest against the abuse, or confront the man of the house? She'd lost count.

"Your own mother—in that house—didn't lift a finger to help you." Nixon's look and tone conveyed skepticism.

Kristy shook her head. "She says it's no good to try. She says it would just make things worse if she'd try to stop him."

He paused to digest the answer, made a note on the pad, tossed his pen. Sitting beside his client again, he leaned back in his chair and said, "It's been a long time since Thanksgiving. Who did you tell about this?"

"I just told everybody in here."

"No, no, I mean before the case, who'd you tell? A special friend?"

"No."

"School nurse?"

She shook her head.

Elsie scribbled a note to herself: Nixon was trying to ascertain whether the state would produce outcry evidence at trial. Sadly, she suspected there was none.

"Teacher at school? Favorite teacher?"

"No. We wasn't supposed to tell *anybody.*"

A smile flitted across Kris Taney's face as he sat in his orange jail jumpsuit and watched his daughter.

The judge appeared to have heard quite enough. "Mr. Nixon?"

"Your honor?"

"Have you completed your cross-examination of this witness?"

Elsie looked up at the judge with surprise. Judge Carter was trying to cut off the cross-examination. He was going to bat for her witness. Her stomach unknotted a trifle. Having this particular judge on her side was a novel experience. She prayed it would last.

"Well?" the judge said to Nixon.

Nixon paused and reflected. Elsie fancied she could see him debating the merits of further inquiry versus the perils of badgering a child witness in front of the press. He bent toward his client to murmur the obligatory question: *Is there anything further that you want me to ask?* Taney shrugged.

Nixon shook his head. "Nothing further."

Judge Carter pointed his pen at Elsie. "Redirect?"

"No, your honor."

"Call your next witness."

Elsie turned and peered through the glass panels of the courtroom door. Charlene was on the bench outside, waiting her turn to testify. When the girls had arrived at the courthouse that morning, Kristy suffered such a fit of nerves that Elsie feared she would balk and refuse to enter the courtroom. It took forty-five minutes and the combined efforts of Tina and herself to settle her down, so she'd decided to lead off with Kristy as her first witness.

And when they arrived at the courtroom and Elsie had instructed Donita and Charlene to wait in the hallway while Kristy testified, they pitched another fit. Donita linked an arm with each daughter and hissed, "No. No splitting up."

With exaggerated patience, Elsie said, "You need to be out here with Charlene, to wait until she's called to the stand."

"We're all going in together. No splitting up."

"Donita, they can't. There's a rule against witnesses being in the courtroom, except when they testify. When Kristy is in there, Charlene's in the hall; when Kristy is done, you'll sit out here with her while Charlene testifies."

"Them girls can't go up against their daddy alone. You don't know him. We got to be together."

"This is the way it is. It's the rule." She gave them a smile that she hoped was reassuring. "But I'll be in the courtroom with you. Everything is going to be just fine."

It had been one hell of a morning; but with Kristy off the stand, Elsie hoped the hardest part was behind her.

"Your honor, the state calls Charlene Taney to the witness stand."

The bailiff walked to the door and opened it wide enough to poke his head through. "Charlene Taney," he bellowed so loudly that it made Elsie jump.

The girl approached the stand with a swagger. Elsie's heart went out to her; Charlene was a girl who balanced a chip on her shoulder. She walked up to Charlene and placed her hand on the girl's arm. "Walk up to the judge; he'll give you the oath to tell the truth." She had to speak up because Kris Taney and his lawyer were engaged in a lengthy exchange at the defense table. "After you're sworn, you'll take that seat up there, right by Judge Carter."

Charlene stood briefly before Judge Carter to be sworn, and took the seat as directed. Elsie approached for

her examination, a little nettled that the defense continued to talk audibly between themselves.

"Please state your name."

"Charlene Taney."

She smiled at Charlene, hoping to set her at ease.

"Charlene, how old are you?"

"Fifteen."

"When is your birthday?"

"December the sixth."

"Charlene, I'd like to direct your attention to—" Elsie
said, preparing to launch into her direct examination
when Josh Nixon jumped to his feet and exclaimed:

"I'd like to ask leave to voir dire this witness."

Elsie whirled on him with a flash of irritation at the
interruption. "What?" she snapped.

"Ms. Arnold!" the judge interjected. "This is my
courtroom, thank you. Mr. Nixon, what's the subject of
your inquiry?"

"We need to establish that the witness understands
the meaning of the oath."

Elsie gaped at the judge. "Judge, she just testified that
she's fifteen years old. The state is not obliged to demonstrate that a minor of fifteen understands the oath; she's
already been sworn."

"This request is crucial to the defense, your honor."

Her heart rate increased as she cried, "I object! The
state objects! Why is this crucial? Her younger sister,
Kristy, just testified; she's twelve, and the defense didn't
feel the burning need to quibble about the oath with her."

Leaning back in his chair, the judge turned his head toward the defense attorney.

"Mr. Nixon?"

"The examination may reveal a problem with this particular witness. I repeat my request."

The judge shot a sidelong glance at Charlene, who appeared genuinely confused. Elsie was confused as well; she didn't know what Nixon had up his sleeve, and that scared her.

Judge Carter shook his head but said, "I'll allow it. Proceed."

Elsie took her seat as Nixon approached the witness stand. "Charlene Taney, do you understand the significance of the oath to tell the truth?"

"Huh?"

Biting the inside of her cheek to keep from groaning out loud, Elsie leaned forward in her chair, eyes locked on Charlene, willing her to answer appropriately.

"The oath, Ms. Taney. You have sworn to tell the truth. Do you know what that means?"

Charlene's jaw locked. "Yep," she said through clenched teeth.

"Do you know the difference between the truth and a lie?"

"Uh-huh."

"Are you a truthful person?"

Charlene's eyes shifted. "Yeah."

"Have you ever told a lie?"

Elsie's heart hammered; it was a trick question, there

was no good answer. "Objection," she cried, but the judge waved her down.

"Overruled."

Nixon leaned back against the side of the jury box. "What do you say, Ms. Taney? Have you ever told a lie?"

Charlene took on a hunted look. She glanced at her father, then back at Nixon.

The pause dragged on. Elsie couldn't stay in her seat; she jumped up and said, "Your honor, this is ridiculous. Clearly, the defense is using this voir dire to badger and intimidate the witness. I object to the line of questioning and ask the court to cut it off."

The judge said, "Ms. Arnold—" but she continued.

"The witness has testified that she understands the oath."

"Sit down, Ms. Arnold." Reluctantly, Elsie obeyed, but her heart was beating so hard that she could almost see it pounding through the fabric of her jacket. She could feel the control over her case slipping away; Nixon was setting her witness up. I gotta stop him, she thought, growing frantic, though she struggled to remain outwardly composed.

To Charlene, the judge said, "Answer the question, Miss Taney."

Charlene fixed a brazen glare at Nixon. "Never."

"Never what?"

"Ain't never told a lie."

Nixon smiled. "Well, that's surprising. Amazing. Not even a little white lie."

"Nope."

"What about at school?"

Charlene's face hardened. She didn't reply.

Nervously, Elsie twisted her pen. *He's got something, but I can't fight it until I know what it is.*

Nixon persisted. "Didn't you get in trouble at school for lying?"

The girl's shoulders clenched and she stared at the carpet.

"Didn't you accuse someone of touching you? Isn't that right?"

Shit, shit, shit, Elsie thought, her stomach sinking.

When Charlene didn't respond, Nixon moved in closer and raised the volume of his voice. "Didn't you accuse boys of touching you? And it was all made up, a lie? What about telling the truth that time?"

Charlene jumped from her chair so suddenly that it took Elsie a moment to react. The girl vaulted over the witness stand and was out of the courtroom like a shot.

Elsie followed, chasing her through the courthouse hallway, shouting, "Charlene, stop! Come back!"

A highway patrolman who was standing nearby reached out and grabbed Charlene by the arm as she flew past him. As he restrained the girl, she fought him blindly like a cornered animal. Elsie caught up to them and reached out to Charlene, but the girl slapped her hand away.

"Charlene, settle down. You can't run off like this."

"He called me a liar."

Though Elsie was nearly panting from agitation, she kept her voice calm.

"Sweetheart, it's all right; just come back and explain to the judge that you understand the oath, and you're telling the truth in court."

"Can't. They say I'm a liar."

"Charlene, everyone, everybody on earth, has told a lie sometime; that's like a trick question, the lawyer was trying to trip you up."

Charlene quit struggling, and Elsie took her by the hand. To the trooper, she said, "Thanks, Sergeant Crocker, I've got it from here." As the patrolman walked off, she put an arm around Charlene and spoke earnestly.

"Charlene, come on back and testify, just like we practiced. This is so important; we've got to get back in there and get the job done."

"I ain't never going back in there."

"Come on, Charlene, please." Elsie gave her arm a tug, but Charlene snatched it away.

"I said I ain't going back, and I'm not gonna. And that is the *truth*." She spat the final word.

"Charlene!"

They both froze. Donita walked toward them and Charlene turned to face her mother. They were the same height, and stood nose-to-nose.

Donita raised her hand, and with it she grasped the nape of Charlene's neck and pushed the girl to the side of the hallway. Elsie didn't follow. She watched as Donita spoke fiercely into the girl's ear. Charlene's head bowed, and after a time she nodded.

Donita gave her a shove in Elsie's direction. "You go do as you're told."

Charlene shot a resentful look at Elsie. Sullen, she turned and walked back to the courtroom.

Elsie followed, eyes on the back of the girl's head. Is this it? She wondered. Have I lost it already?

Looking into the courtroom through the glass door, she saw Taney twist in his seat to stare down Charlene as the girl returned to the courtroom.

Elsie's bulldog instinct came to her in a rush; her chin jerked up and she regarded the defendant through narrowed eyes. She strode back to court with a determined step.

Chapter Eleven

———————————————

ELSIE CAUGHT UP to Charlene and tried to put a supportive arm around her shoulders as they walked through the
courtroom, but the girl shook her off and raced back to
the witness stand so quickly that it looked like she was
eager to return. Striding up to the bench, Elsie poised
herself to make things right with Judge Carter, expecting
him to be unhappy with her.

"Your honor, I apologize for the delay—" she began,
but he cut her off.

"No need," he said with a wave. "These cases are
highly charged. Miss Taney," and with a benevolent nod
at Charlene added, "I'll take over the inquiry regarding
the oath." Then he said to the girl, "Do you understand—"

Nixon, who had been reclining in his seat at the counsel table, leapt from his chair.

"Your honor, I'd appreciate it if you'd let me continue
with the examination."

"I'd appreciate it if you'd sit back down."

With delight, Elsie noted that the judge now withheld eye contact from the defense. So the worm has turned, she thought. *Yee haw*. Her earlier suspicions were confirmed; Judge Carter was on her side. Feeling a lightness in her chest, she stifled the urge to smile. When the judge stepped in to tie the defense attorney's hands, it made for a much fairer fight between a grown attorney and a slip of a girl.

Judge Carter turned back to Charlene. With a diffident expression, he asked whether she understood the import of the oath to tell the truth. Squaring her jaw, the girl said she did.

"Raise your hand," he instructed, and she swore to tell the truth.

The judge looked at Elsie and said, "The state may proceed."

She walked up to the witness stand, feeling guardedly confident. "Let's start again, Charlene. Please state your full name."

Charlene proceeded through the direct examination, laying out the facts of the offenses she'd described to Elsie and Ashlock at the Taneys' apartment the day before, and providing all the facts necessary to support the elements of counts one through four of the felony complaint against Kris Taney.

When Elsie was done, Nixon launched into his cross, but the judge held him back from battering the witness or opening matters outside of the scope of direct examination. She marveled at the change in Judge Carter's demeanor; whether it was the product of his personal sympathies or the presence of the local media, she didn't care. She was just happy to be the fair haired child in his courtroom when she really needed it.

Nixon finally concluded. The judge asked Elsie, "Will you be calling any more witnesses today?"

"No, your honor," she answered. She had no intention of putting Donita Taney on the stand that day. As a witness, Donita needed a lot of work, and she didn't want to give the defense a crack at her yet.

Smiling sympathetically at Charlene, the judge told the girl she could step down. When he announced his finding, Elsie kept a straight face, but inside she was jubilant, setting off Roman candles. She recorded the judge's words in the prosecutor's file:

> *Defendant Taney appears in court with attorney Josh Nixon. Preliminary hearing held. Court finds probable cause. Defendant bound over to Circuit Court for arraignment.*

"Court is adjourned," the judge said.

When she turned around to catch Tina Peroni's eye, she saw Madeleine peering through the door into the courtroom. Elsie bristled; if she dared to barge in and take the credit for the hearing, there would be a bloodletting. When Madeleine saw Elsie looking in her direction, she disappeared.

You'd better run, she thought. I've got a score to settle with you, bitch.

She was distracted from her irritation by Josh Nixon. He walked over the prosecution table and said, "I'm going to subpoena that girl's permanent record from her school. I'll destroy her."

Blood flooded Elsie's face. "You won't get it. I'll fight it. And you won't 'destroy' her, anyhow. Hard to shake a story like this one."

"We'll have an evidentiary hearing downstairs. About her behavior at school."

"Not relevant," she snapped. She had to protect Charlene; four of the five criminal counts depended on the girl.

"Wait till we get those records."

"FERPA. Ever hear of that statute? She's got privacy rights."

"Well, my client has rights. Parental rights. And right to confrontation. Sixth Amendment rights."

Elsie wanted to punch Nixon. "Well, I guess we'll just see about that."

"I guess we will."

She tried to think of another retort, but Tina tugged at her sleeve.

"Can I take the girls downstairs?" she asked.

"Sure. I'll walk you out."

The cameras were rolling as she exited the courtroom flanked by Taney's daughters. She pretended not to notice the press. *Don't look into the camera*, she reminded herself. As she guided the girls toward the stairway, a nice-looking male television reporter wearing an alarming amount of orange pancake makeup stuck a microphone in her face and said, "Can you tell us what additional evidence you'll have at trial?"

"I can't comment on a pending prosecution, sorry," Elsie said with what she hoped was a dazzling smile.

"Are you aware that Taney is calling in a parents' rights group to come to his aid?"

She was stunned for a second; she was not aware of that. What group would want to be associated with a dirt bag like Kris Taney? She repeated automatically, "Can't comment, like I said. Sorry."

The reporter turned on his heel when he saw the defendant leaving the courtroom. Taney had extra security today, and his attorney was sticking close by him; Elsie figured Nixon was glad to have the photo op. Kris Taney looked positively explosive.

"Mr. Taney," said the reporter, "do you deny the allegations?"

Josh Nixon fielded the question. "My client will enter a plea of Not Guilty to all counts at his arraignment on Friday."

The reporter pulled the mic back to follow up. "What is the basis of the defense you'll be presenting?"

As she descended the stairs, Elsie heard Nixon declare that the charges had been falsely made by Taney's daughters at the urging of their mother, due to a marital dispute. Right, Nixon; that's what they all say, she thought scornfully.

"We'll establish that the testimony of Charlene Taney, in particular, is totally untrustworthy," Nixon said. "I'm also happy to announce that my client has the backing of Our Earthly Fathers, a support group for men going through the ups and downs of marital dissolution proceedings."

Nixon was clearly warming up in the limelight. "This isn't a novel situation, really. Bitter people in a broken marriage use the children to hurt each other. What's frightening is when you see the Prosecutor's Office sucked into the game. It looks like Ms. Arnold is siding with the women's accusations as some kind of knee-jerk feminist response." Nixon gestured dramatically, pointing directly at Elsie on the staircase.

Her jaw dropped as she heard Nixon's statement to the reporter. Her blood was still up from the hearing, as well as their fight over Charlene. She stopped and spun around on the stairs. *How dare he trash me in front of the cameras?* "Tina," she said, "please take the girls on downstairs."

As she bounded back up the stairs, "Hey, Nixon," she said through the railings, "good thing you're a criminal lawyer. Your grasp of family law ain't so hot."

Nixon gaped at her. "The prosecution cannot comment."

But Elsie was mad, and she didn't stop. "Since when do 'parental rights' include rape and abuse?"

Nixon barked, "My client denies those charges. Arnold, you are out of line. You are violating your ethical duty."

Kris Taney weighed in, his face scarlet: "Hey, bitch—you got the wrong guy."

Nixon turned to his client, ordering him to shut up,

but Taney didn't follow his advice. He stood unmoving in ankle cuffs and handcuffs, demanding, "What about her? She don't know when to shut up."

Turning on Elsie with a snarl, he added, "Somebody ought to shut your mouth." He spat at her, the spittle spattering the shoulder of her jacket. His eyes wild, he roared, "Why ain't you talked to my brother? Him and Donita is the ones what ought to be locked up. Ain't you figured out that they're just trying to get me out of the way?"

The bailiff interrupted the altercation. "Get this man back to the jail. Get a move on, Taney."

The deputies attempted to pull him in the direction of the jail, but Taney refused to go voluntarily and had to be dragged. The bailiff and deputies pulled the big man down the hall as he bellowed insults against them, Elsie, and the accusation. She stood frozen while the cameras rolled. The lawmen, with much effort, managed to maneuver the struggling man into the hallway leading to the jail, and his shouts became fainter.

Staring after him, Elsie began to shake. In four years as a prosecutor she had been shouted down, cursed, and insulted. Being spit upon, though, was an entirely new experience. A filthy assault. Demeaning. She felt utterly humiliated. She struggled to snap out of it but heat pricked her nose and she knew she was in danger of crying right in the middle of the courthouse.

Wheeling around, she wanted to flee, but was surrounded by strangers, reporters, and onlookers, regarding her curiously. And the camera was trained on her face. *Act like you're okay. Pretend it doesn't matter*, she told herself.

The hallway now quiet, the reporter with the orange face strolled up and stuck the microphone in her face.

"Ms. Arnold, do you have a reaction to the altercation that took place here?"

Elsie just shook her head, blinking rapidly to keep the tears back. For once, she had nothing to say.

Chapter Twelve

As she walked down the stairs to the courthouse coffee shop, Elsie pulled off her suit jacket and rolled it into a ball, taking care to avoid touching Taney's spittle. She longed to escape to her office and lock herself inside. The hearing and the aftermath in the hallway had sucked all the sap out of her. However, she had an obligation to her witnesses. She had to make sure they'd survived the hearing intact.

When she walked into the tiny coffee shop, Tina waved from the corner table, where she sat with the Taneys.

Forcing a smile, Elsie joined them. "Phew," she said, leaning on a plastic chair back, "it's been an exciting day, huh? What can I get you guys?"

Donita shook her head. "Nothing. Got no money."

She dismissed the objection with a shake of her head. "It's on me. Girls, come on up to the counter with me."

Kristy and Tiffany jumped out of their seats. Refusing to meet Elsie's eye, Charlene rose, too. Elsie led them to the counter, where she ordered a round of Cokes and chips.

Charlene grabbed a bag of Doritos from the display, but Kristy and Tiffany hesitated, examining the selections, fingering one and then another.

"Order up, ladies," Elsie urged, affecting a cheery tone. But the girls lingered.

"It all looks so good," Kristy said. "I can't make up my mind."

Impatience formed a knot in Elsie's chest as she silently willed them to pick something and sit down. But looking into their faces, she chastised herself. The girls needed to recover from the hearing, just as she did. *Let them have a damned minute to pick their chips.*

Finally, Kristy plucked a bag of Lay's from the display. As Elsie handed Tiffany her cup of Coke, she asked if she wanted some chips, too. Tiffany didn't respond.

"Me and Tiffany can share," Charlene said, taking Tiffany's hand.

They returned to the round table and crowded their six chairs into a circle. As Elsie pulled the paper wrapper from her straw, her hand shook. *Pull yourself together,* she told herself.

Congratulating the girls on their good work in court, she began to explain the next steps: the case would be assigned to Circuit Court and placed on the trial docket.

During her explanation, Tiffany stuck her finger in her nose and commenced to dig. Kristy's hand shot out and slapped Tiffany on the side of the head.

"Stop it. That's nasty," Kristy said.

Charlene grabbed Kristy's hair and twisted it. "Don't you be mean to her, you stinking bitch."

Donita snatched Charlene's upper arm, pulling her away from Kristy with an iron grip. In a low voice she hissed, "You'uns all cut it out right now."

Charlene turned on her mother. "I won't have her hitting Tiffany."

"I mean it. I've about had it with you today."

Picking up Charlene's Coke, Donita took a long drink through the straw. "Hey," Charlene protested, but her mother stared her down.

"Lord, that's good," Donita said as she set the cup down.

Tina asked her how the family was holding up and Donita said, "Pretty good, I reckon. But I got to tell you about the WIC."

Tina nodded. "The nutrition program."

"Yeah. Now that Tiffany is in school, they won't give me the WIC no more. I need it."

"Tiffany is over five. You're not eligible."

"That don't make no sense. It's for women and children, and that's us. She needs more eats now that she's getting big."

"Donita, you don't qualify anymore," Tina told her again. "You'll have to get by with your food stamp account."

As the two women talked, Elsie leaned across the table and said, "Charlene, I need to know what happened at school, what the defense attorney was talking about."

Charlene ignored her, pulled Tiffany's chair a little closer to hers and smoothed her sister's strawberry hair behind her ear.

Elsie persisted in a quiet voice. "I'm not trying to be nosy; it's not that. But I have to know what the attorney is talking about, so I can protect you, and we can try to shut him down."

Charlene didn't answer. She was talking to Tiffany, close to the child's ear, speaking in almost a whisper. Elsie strained to make out what she was telling the little girl.

She heard her say, "Just do it when you're alone. Or in the toilet."

Tiffany nodded.

Charlene offered her a chip from the bag, and Tiffany took one. Then Charlene smiled indulgently and said, "Honest to God, Tiff, it ain't no big thing. Everybody picks their nose."

BEFORE TINA ESCORTED Donita and her daughters through the side exit of the courthouse, Elsie pulled Charlene aside, in a final attempt.

"Charlene, please. It's important that you tell me what happened to you at school that time."

"Ain't important to me."

Charlene tried to walk away, but Elsie put a restraining hand on her arm. "They'll use it as ammunition against you, don't you see? I have to be in the know, so I can fight it."

Tiffany inched up to them. Charlene lifted her sister's hair and tickled the back of her neck. "Spider on you," she whispered.

Looking up, Tiffany swatted at Charlene's hand. But she was smiling.

Frowning, Elsie said, "Charlene, we're going to have to discuss it sooner or later."

"Maybe later." She gave Elsie a hard look. "Maybe never."

Elsie watched as Tina walked Donita and her daughters to the parking lot, then slowly climbed the stairs back to the second floor. When she returned to her office, Josh Nixon was waiting for her, slouching comfortably in the chair facing her desk, drinking coffee from a plastic cup.

"Oh yeah, great," she said irritably. "Make yourself at home. Totally."

"I will, thanks."

Elsie displayed her befouled jacket, then wadded it back into a ball. After throwing it into a corner, she asked, "Don't suppose I can bill your office for that?"

Nixon just laughed.

Flopping into her chair, she swiveled around and put her feet up on the air-conditioning unit. "What the hell are you doing here?"

"I want discovery."

She looked at him with disbelief. "You'll get it. After the arraignment in Circuit Court."

"I need access to the prosecutor's file today. I want to read those witness statements before I go talk to Taney at the jail."

"You aren't entitled to discovery until after the felony charge is filed in Circuit Court. That's Friday. That's when you can see our file."

He surveyed her silently for a moment. "You know, Elsie, I'm trying to save you from yourself."

She blinked. He was really yanking her chain. "How's that?"

"I know you're mad at my client right now; he just spit on you. But you need to take a step back from this thing." He set his coffee down and leaned toward her with a look of sincerity. "You're getting tricked into playing the heavy in a simple domestic relations case. Really. Mom gets the girls to claim that Dad's a molester, and everything goes her way. Nobody will stop to ask what kind of scene Mom's into. Oldest trick in the book."

"'Oldest trick in the book,'" she mimicked back. "Defend your criminal case by saying the girls are bold-faced liars, set up by Mom to take down dear old Dad."

Josh picked up the coffee cup, raised it in a toast. "I'm just telling you. Trying to help."

She responded with a dismissive flip of her hand. She started reorganizing her papers in the accordion file bearing the name TANEY.

Nixon was okay, as defense attorneys went. And prosecutors and public defenders had a sort of kinship. As opposite sides of the same coin, they were both overworked and underpaid, and embroiled in the attempt to bring reason and justice to terrible crimes.

She wanted to get along with him, if she could. It was helpful to have friendly relations with opposing counsel;

it meant that fighting would be confined to the court-room, not deteriorate into personal animosity. But being friendly did not mean she would give an inch where the case was concerned. She was not opening her file to Nixon until Friday.

He persisted, saying, "Your star witness is a liar. Little Miss Charlene. Her record at school will prove it."

"Your defense is so farfetched. What would motivate the girl to go through all this courtroom torture if it wasn't true?"

"Mommy dearest."

"Oh, Lord."

"I'm serious."

Elsie set her file down. "Problem with your theory that Mom concocted this plot: I don't think you under-stand this woman's situation. She is the most powerless person imaginable. She's got no weapons in her arsenal."

"She's got a boyfriend."

"Please."

"She's got a boyfriend and he put her up to it."

"Would you get out of here?"

Nixon rose from the chair. "It's not too late to stop it from going any further. You'll be the one with egg on your face when this whole thing blows up."

"Well," she said wryly, "I'll have the pleasure of seeing you carried off the field on the shoulders of Taney and the Earthly Fathers."

Nixon shook his head. "You know, I like you. I'm trying to help you out."

"Yeah, right."

"Elsie?" Tina Peroni called from the hallway.

"In here," she answered.

Tina stuck her head in the door.

Nixon nodded with mock gravity. "I'll show myself out."

As he moved to the door, Elsie said, "I know you have to take whatever garbage they tell you and try to make the jury believe it. But Nixon, don't try to sell it to me."

He turned and sighed. "Can't wait for you to meet the boyfriend. Bet she really traded up."

Chapter Thirteen

"OH, TINA, PLEASE DON'T," Elsie begged as the social worker pulled her blue Volkswagen beetle into the parking lot of Baldknobbers bar.

Tina was perplexed. "Why not? I thought you liked this place. I'm always hearing some wild tale about the prosecutors and the cops at Baldknobbers."

Elsie shook her head. "That's just it. I was here last Friday and got pretty shit-faced. Fell on my butt. I'm still mortified."

Tina put an arm around Elsie's shoulder and peered at her over the top of her specs. "You do understand that you are not the first person who ever had too much to drink at a bar."

"I know, but it's embarrassing."

Tina got out of the car, walked around to Elsie's side and opened her car door.

"Come on. I'll buy you a burger. Let's go beard the lion in his den."

Groaning, Elsie hauled herself out of the car. She was being silly. Nobody at Baldknobbers cared about last Friday. It was ancient history. As she neared the front door, she spied a red Camaro occupying two parking spots: Noah's car. She felt a twinge of guilt; she hadn't called to touch base since Wednesday morning, when the Taney case blew up. Surely he'd understand that she was consumed by work.

The two women walked inside and paused for a moment to check the place out. Baldknobbers was an old dive, the kind of bar that covered the windows so the light of day could never shine in. It had a working jukebox, which would obligingly play a tune for a quarter; of course, the musical selections were sadly out of date. The smell of frying hamburger mingled with cigarette smoke. Baldknobbers was permitted by city ordinance to have smoking on the premises only so long as it had more revenue from liquor sales than food sales, and the owners were careful to keep that ratio in line.

Tina looked for a table while Elsie scoured the room for Noah. Tina tugged at her arm and pointed out a booth by the kitchen. As Elsie followed, she spied him.

He was at the pool table. His back was to her and he was in his civvies, but she'd know him if he was dressed for Halloween. The light overhead glinted on his hair, and his back and shoulders in a red flannel shirt looked good enough to eat. Just as her face broke into a welcoming smile, she recognized the woman next to him: Paige. From the crime lab. Paige glimpsed her and did a double take, then had the nerve to give her the hairy eyeball.

Elsie lifted her chin with a jerk. Marching up to Noah, she tapped him on the shoulder. "Hey, there," she said.

He grazed her cheek with a kiss. "Hey. Stranger."

She didn't rise to the bait; she had nothing to apologize for. "What's up?"

"Playing pool. Me and Paige." He bent over the table and studied the eight ball.

Elsie pressed her lips together, reflecting that she was experiencing déjà vu. Hadn't they had this very encounter less than a week ago? As she shot a glance at his pool partner, she saw Paige smirk. Elsie turned on her heel. "Have fun," she said without a backward look.

As she scooted into the booth across from Tina, the barmaid, Dixie, came up to the table. "Now what can I get for you ladies?" she asked.

I want gin, Elsie thought. Tanqueray.

"What kind of wine do you have by the glass?" Tina asked.

"Box," Dixie answered.

Tina looked at Elsie to see whether someone was pulling her leg. But Elsie was focused on her own order: *Bombay. Beefeater. It would be medicinal.*

"I'll have a Bud Lite," said Tina. "Thanks."

The smell of the grill reminded Elsie that she hadn't eaten all day. Sighing, she said, "I better have a cheeseburger." With a sidelong glance at the pool table, she added, "With onion."

"You want a beer, honey?"

She struggled with her response. "I want a Coke. A real Coke, not diet." She didn't want to get all ginned up while Noah acted the pool hustler with Paige. No telling what she might do or say.

Dixie jotted it down. "Sounds like a party," she said, and gave the table a quick swipe with a rag before she walked off.

While Elsie made a stack of the cardboard coaster squares, she kept a stoic face. She vowed she would not turn her head to check on Noah and Paige. *Not gonna do it.*

Tina got down to business. "How do you think the case looks?"

Elsie grimaced. "Could be better. But incest cases are tough; that's the way it always goes. Tangled family relationships, family secrets, busting that code of silence." Leaning back, she looked at Tina. "How on earth did you get them to talk in the first place?"

"Funny thing. We'd smelled a rat over at the Taneys' for years, but no one would admit to it. Donita always said everything was fine."

"And this time?"

Tina rubbed her nose reflectively. "I'm not sure, exactly. After the brother made the police report and I was called in, they were all ready to talk about it. Charlene, Kristy, Mom, all three of them."

"What about Tiffany?"

"No. Not Tiffany. How are you going to get Tiffany to testify for you?"

When Detective Ashlock had tried to take Tiffany's statement on Wednesday, he could not cajole her into uttering a single word. Tina took over but didn't achieve any better results. Even when they picked up the broken dolls in the room and played with the child, she would not speak. Taking Tiffany by the hand, Elsie began to question her, but when she asked the child about her father, Tiffany hid her face on her knees and wouldn't look up until she backed off.

When they asked Donita about Tiffany's silence, the mother feigned ignorance, said she didn't understand what they meant because Tiffany talked to her all the time. "A chatterbox," her mother called her. Tiffany had smiled and climbed onto her mother's lap.

"I'm at a loss," Elsie said. "Why do you think Tiffany won't talk around us?" She heard a peal of laughter from the pool table then. *Don't look don't look don't look,* she told herself.

Tina said, "Could be she's a little addled. Or maybe the kid has been ordered to keep the abuse a secret for so long that she opts to be mute outside of the family, just to play it safe."

Elsie thought that made sense. "We'll never get her on the stand," she said, shaking her head. "I'll bet you never get a statement from her for the Social Services file. Good thing the other girls are willing to talk."

She leaned across the table and continued in a low voice. "But I've got to find out what the deal is with Charlene and those accusations at school. Do you know what the defense attorney is talking about? Because I'll need to suck the poison on that."

As Tina shook her head, a cheer erupted from the crowd now gathered around the pool table. Elsie started to turn toward the noise, then caught herself. Deliberately, she stirred her Coke with the straw and asked Tina, "How's work?"

"Swamped."

"Worse than usual?"

"January's always a big month for abuse and neglect referrals."

Elsie took a gulp of Coke. "Why's that?"

"Winter is hard, hardest on poor people. Everybody's cooped up together in the cold, they start drinking, doing drugs; things get ugly. God, we see a lot of it in McCown County."

"Yep," she agreed. She had seen evidence of that.

Tina leaned back in the booth, shaking her head sadly. "We've got one of the highest rates of child abuse in the state. Higher than St. Louis or Kansas City."

"Who's highest?"

"Greene County, just a stone's throw from here."

"That's Springfield," Elsie said, adding, "Queen City of the Ozarks."

"We're right behind them. The other hot spot is the Bootheel."

Elsie frowned, trying to make sense of the numbers. "I don't understand why southern Missouri has more child abuse than the urban areas in the state."

"Well, there's meth. And poverty. And domestic violence, all tied up with patriarchy. The idea that wives and daughters are chattel." Tina leaned across the table, staring intently through her glasses. "In the hill country, people have hung onto some misguided notions of what they have the right to do with their children." When Elsie didn't respond, Tina added, with a sigh, "You crazy hillbillies."

"Hey. Watch it. My people settled this state."

"Impressive."

"It's true. Came here in a wagon in the 1820s."

Tina gave her a wicked grin. "Are you bragging or complaining?"

"So if you think it's such a sewer here in Missouri, how did you end up here? You're from Michigan, right?"

Tina said, "In my youth, I wanted to save the world through print media. So I decided to go to the best journalism school I could afford."

Elsie made a cocky face. "That would be Mizzou."

"Yeah, really. Imagine my surprise: the first J school in the world was in Columbia, Mo."

"So then what? You realized journalism is a dying profession?"

"Not exactly. I had a sociology professor who convinced me to check out the social work program. That maybe I could save the world one family at a time."

"How's that working out?"

Tina laughed. "Depends on when you ask me. Some days I wish I had stayed with the news."

Dixie arrived with the food and drink. Elsie squirted mustard and ketchup on her burger, arranged the red onion neatly atop the meat patty, and took a hearty bite. Tina sipped from the beer bottle and asked, "About the case: what are you going to do with the mother?"

Elsie swallowed. "She's a can of worms. I have to use

her, no way around it. She can corroborate Charlene and Kristy, and I need that. We don't have any physical evidence; you know how incest cases are."

Tina nodded. "People don't get it, unless they've seen it from the law enforcement perspective."

"Lord, no. A prosecution like Taney is the toughest case to make. We've got no DNA evidence, because the report is invariably made weeks or months after the fact. We've got no disinterested eyewitnesses, because the crime is committed in secret. We've got no forensic evidence to offer, like blood or hair or prints, because the defendant lives with the victim, so of course his fingerprints are in the home."

Tearing into the bag of chips that accompanied the burger, Elsie shook her head ruefully. "Our main evidence is the word of a traumatized child, and the only supporting evidence we can hope for is the corroboration of family members, people who'll say, 'This is what I saw.' So I'll put Donita on the stand. The jury will hate her, though."

"Will the jury associate Donita with Taney?"

"Well, the fact that Donita is cooperating with the police and the prosecution helps, but her prior complicity with her husband is a problem. The jury will wonder why Donita would stand by and let Kris Taney do those things." Elsie sighed and rattled the ice cubes in her glass. "I can't fathom it myself. What happened to the maternal instinct? Where was the enraged mother bear that fights to protect her cub?"

"It's not that unusual," said Tina. "You see it all the

time in my line of work. She was afraid of him. Dependent upon him. You should have seen her when I first talked to her about him. Shaking, looking over her shoulder, like he might appear at any moment and jump on her. Honestly, I think he scares the shit out of her. Got to give her some credit for cooperating with us now."

"Is that why the girls are still at home? I know you could've taken protective custody when the case broke."

Tina took another pull on the beer bottle. "Sure we could've. And then what? Where we going to put them? We're going begging for foster care in McCown County. And institutional care is not a happy ending, I promise."

Elsie had to acknowledge that Tina was right. Foster homes in McCown County were scarce as hens' teeth. Because of that, the juvenile judge was adamant about keeping children with family members, if it was a workable solution at all.

Tina leaned in close to Elsie and said in a hushed voice, "You're too young to remember, but they used to let any asshole in the county be a foster parent. Any shithead who signed on the line. Then, after that case north of Branson happened, everything changed."

"You mean where the foster parents beat the baby to death?"

Tina nodded. "Our judge is very careful about farming them out now. He wants to keep families intact. Blood relatives."

Elsie took another bite. "Damn, this case is sure enough full of crazy shit. What's up with this 'Our Earthly Fathers' thing?"

"Another caseworker was telling me something about that group lately, but this is the first time I've encountered them in the flesh."

"Well," Elsie said, "I'm not going to borrow any trouble about it. Looks like it's just one or two guys."

Tina said, "I wouldn't discount them altogether. They made for trouble in a case a while back, where the wife had a restraining order. They showed up in a group with the husband when he contested it. Shook the woman up so much, she backed off."

"Why didn't I hear about that?"

"It was the next county over, I think."

The cheeseburger was reduced to crumbs aside a wilted lettuce leaf on the oval stoneware plate. Dixie popped by to pick it up. "Your drinks okay?"

Tina asked for an iced tea, while Elsie ordered another Coke. When the drinks arrived, Elsie drank hers slowly, focusing on her friend, taking care to avoid looking around the bar. She was not going to indulge another fit of pique from Noah. Ignoring him would do him good.

Apparently he had other ideas. Glancing toward the other side of the room, Tina told her, "Somebody's trying to catch your eye, I think."

Elsie tied a paper napkin into a knot and smoothed it down. "That right?"

"I'm serious; it's some fine-looking guy. Won't you even take a peek?"

"Nope. Tell me about your wedding plans."

"Joanie and I are having the ceremony in March. The pastor at your parents' church is going to preside."

"He's pretty cool," Elsie said.

"It's the only church in town that welcomed us," Tina confided, and went on to describe floral arrangements and punch recipes until Elsie broke in to announce a bathroom break.

Heading to the ladies' room, she took care to stay out of Noah's path. She peed quickly, dashed soap and water on her hands, and checked her appearance for a split second. When she opened the door, Noah was waiting for her.

She paused for a moment, flustered, then conjured a careless smile, mouthed a silent *Hi* and moved to scoot past him.

Noah blocked her and took her arm. "Hey, Elsie, what's up?"

"Nothing."

"Aren't you even going to come over and see me?"

"You're staying pretty busy."

In the narrow path leading to the men's room, a gray-haired patron grew impatient. "You lovers is blocking the shithouse door," the old salt barked. Blushing, Elsie pushed by him and hurried back to her table.

Scooting into the booth across from Tina, she said. "Sorry about that. Where were we?"

"They're playing your song," Tina said, and sure enough, Elsie heard the opening strains of a familiar melody. "Your cheatin' heart," Hank Williams crooned. Oh, great, she thought. Perfect.

Tina nodded. "Your fave, right? You told me one time he was a natural poet."

"Well, he did have a grasp of the human condition," Elsie said. Maybe she would have a beer. It wasn't natural, listening to Hank without a drink.

Tina picked up the tab. "My treat," she said. "Back in a minute."

As Tina walked off, Elsie caught sight of an angry-looking redneck making his way toward her. The man walked straight up to the table and placed his hands on it, then leaned in toward her and said, "Your name's Arnold, right?" It was not a friendly greeting.

"It is," she said levelly. He looked like a rough character. He was medium height, and his sleeveless sweatshirt revealed a fondness for body building and body art. His brown hair was as long as hers, braided into a tight plait that hung down the middle of his back. The bill of his ball cap was pulled down so low that it nearly covered his eyes. When he spoke again, Elsie saw that one of his front teeth was missing.

"I come over here to tell you," he said, his eyes squinting under the bill of his cap, "you're a goddamned bitch."

Elsie's cortisol spiked as she realized she'd landed in yet another altercation. Hoping to discourage it, she shifted in the booth to put her back to the man.

"I'm talking to you," he said, his voice growing louder as he became more agitated. "You're the fucking bitch who put my brother away last year for DWI third and you're a lying whore."

"I'm not talking to you about this," Elsie said, but he was scaring her. Her eyes darted to the pool table, but Noah was nowhere to be seen.

"I'd like to know what kind of person puts people in jail for drinking, then comes to a bar."

"I'm not drinking," she said curtly, thankful that on this occasion no telltale glass or bottle sat before her. But her heart hammered in her chest. Family members of defendants sometimes wanted to challenge the prosecutor, but it generally happened in the courtroom, where the bailiff could keep matters under control. In a barroom, she was vulnerable and exposed, but it wouldn't do to let him know she was afraid. She put her hands in her lap, and though her expression was nonchalant, her body trembled as she waited for the tirade to end.

"Don't want to talk now? You don't want to talk to me?" He got right up in her face. From the terrible stench of stale liquor, he must have been drinking all day. "You're the reason he's doing time. I think I'm gonna whup your ass."

Then in a blurred instant he was gone, swung backward over a table and onto the floor. She watched in shock as Noah jerked him up off the floor by the front of his sweatshirt and said, "Outside, dirtbag."

"This got nothing to do with you," the man choked out as he struggled to escape Noah's grasp. Noah grabbed his pigtail and used it as additional leverage to usher the man to the door.

She stared after them, relief washing over her. "Dear God," she said softly.

Tina ran to her side, saying, "What the hell was that?" Sliding into the booth, she reached out and took Elsie's hand, while Dixie bustled up to get the lowdown.

Elsie's heart rate was returning to normal when the front door opened and Noah walked back in. He came up to the table and said, "He's cuffed outside. Do you want me to take him in?"

For a moment she didn't answer, her thoughts focused on the man standing in front of her rather than the one handcuffed outside. She looked around the bar; Paige was nowhere to be seen.

Clearing her throat, she said, "No, I don't think so. He mostly just talked ugly to me."

Noah cut his eyes at her. "That oughta be a capital offense." He squatted down so they were at eye level. In a teasing tone, he said, "Elsie, you get in a lot of trouble in this bar, you know that?"

She grimaced. "Lord, it seems that way, doesn't it? You'd think I was doing it on purpose. Looking for thrills." Gratified by his coming to her rescue, she was finished ignoring him. "Thanks, Noah. Thanks for jumping in."

He laughed, adorably shamefaced now that his adrenaline had abated. "It shouldn't have gotten that far. I was outside taking a piss. Bad timing."

"No, I'd say it was perfect timing. You saved my ass. Which he was determined to whup."

Noah shook his head. "Nobody's fucking with you when I'm around."

"Well, I'm grateful."

Tina's phone buzzed, and she slipped away to take the call. Noah scooted into the booth beside Elsie. They were both quiet for a moment as he studied the laminate tabletop. When he looked up, he gazed at her with an expression that made the blood rush to her pelvis.

"You know what, Elsie? You need someone to take care of you." Rising from the booth, he said, "Get your coat. I'm taking you home."

At that moment, the words were music to her ears. When he held out his hand, she didn't hesitate. She clung to it like a life preserver.

Chapter Fourteen

ELSIE REPORTED TO Division 2 of Circuit Court on Friday morning, her spirits improved after a night of deep sleep pillowed on Noah's shoulder. It was criminal day in Judge Rountree's court, so she was responsible for representing the Prosecutor's Office on all matters coming before the court.

Typically, the judge would first handle the felony arraignments, where defendants entered their initial pleas of Not Guilty after hearing the charge read. The judge would then place the case on the criminal jury docket. Elsie's only job would be reciting the state's bond recommendation.

Several cases were scheduled for the entry of a guilty plea to the charges, and Judge Rountree would examine those defendants closely to assure that the plea was knowing and voluntary. Elsie would relate the terms of the plea bargain and summarize the evidence against the defendant. If the judge accepted the plea, he would order a presentence investigation to be conducted by the Office of Probation and Parole.

Two men were scheduled to be sentenced for armed robbery of a liquor store. She knew that one of the defendants had a shot at probation, because the Prosecutor's Office was standing silent on the issue, under the terms of the plea bargain. But the other was likely to be sent to the Department of Corrections to do time.

As defense lawyers straggled in, Elsie surveyed the files the secretaries pulled, arranging them in order. Some lawyers walked in with clients who were out on bond, while others were solo, waiting for their clients to be brought over from the county jail. A few consulted Elsie, anxious to see their spot on the morning docket.

"Damn," complained Roger Hancock, a middle-aged lawyer who specialized in DWIs. "Look at that, they've got me dead-ass last. Push me to the front, Elsie honey, won't you? I've got to get out of here; I'm set in three different courtrooms this morning."

Elsie usually bristled at the condescending tone he used with her, but she was in an accommodating mood.

"No problem," she said, feeling magnanimous as she set his file on top.

The bailiff Merle Lindquist, a cantankerous old coot in a suit so old it threatened to come back in style, came blustering up.

"Elsie, do I have to pick up that Kris Taney for you today?"

"I don't know, Merle," she said mildly. "Somebody's got to do it."

"Well, miss, you and me got to get something straight. I am not touching him if he doesn't get cleaned up. That Kris Taney is the dirtiest stinkin' man I've seen in forty-three years working at the courthouse."

"Merle, you're barking up the wrong tree. I'm not in charge of his hygiene."

Ordinarily, fussing with the old bailiff about matters outside of her control could drive her over the edge. Today she just smiled, unruffled, and patted his sleeve.

"Why don't you pull rank on somebody?" she suggested with a wink. "Get some young guy to do it."

"Why doesn't he just stay in his cell?" Merle grumbled.

"Due process, Merle," she explained with a shake of the head. "We can't deprive Mr. Taney of his liberty without due process of law. He gets to hear the charges against him."

The court reporter entered and settled in her seat. Elsie checked her watch; it was almost showtime. Judge Rountree was never late.

A cluster of citizens walking into the courtroom caught her eye. She watched them idly as they filed in and took their seats. The group was largely male, easily identifiable as buttoned-up Christian evangelicals, sporting church clothes and televangelist haircuts. The few women in their company wore modest ankle-length dresses, their long hair pinned up on the back of their heads. It looked like a time machine had zapped them from the

1950s into the twenty-first century. Maybe they're here to see Taney get his just deserts, she thought hopefully. She would be glad to have a support group behind her. Like MADD, but against child molesters.

Judge Rountree entered through the chamber door, and old Merle shouted, "All rise! The Circuit Court of McCown County, Missouri, is now in session, Judge Rountree presiding."

The judge sat at the bench, looked out at the assembled crowd, and invited them to be seated.

Elsie always enjoyed appearing in Rountree's courtroom. The judge, a man in his late sixties, had thinning white hair and knees that were due for a replacement. He spoke in a slow Missouri drawl, thought deliberately, and moved painfully. But though he was near retirement and showing signs of age, he was still sharp as a tack; he knew more law than all the younger judges put together, and there was no fairer jurist in the state of Missouri.

"Miss Arnold," the judge said with his customary courtesy, "what matter shall we take up first?"

She called out the name of the defendant represented by the DWI lawyer who begged to go first. The judge arraigned the client, and his attorney scooted out of court in a hurry.

"Next?" asked Judge Rountree.

"We need to arraign Kris Taney, your honor," she said. "I see his lawyer in the courtroom."

Josh Nixon stood and came forward. "Judge, my client needs to be brought over from the county jail."

The bailiff rolled his eyes but stopped short of uttering a groan. Judge Rountree asked, "Mr. Nixon, isn't your client the fellow who caused a disturbance yesterday?"

Nixon nodded. "There was some trouble, yes."

Elsie almost snorted; only a massive exercise of self-control kept her in her seat. She had a suit headed for the dry cleaners that could illustrate some of the trouble Taney had caused the day before.

Rountree swiveled in his chair and addressed the bailiff. "Merle, what do you propose? Are you getting some help from the county to walk that fellow over here?"

Merle walked over and leaned on the bench. "Judge, maybe the jailer ought to bring him. Seems like he's a threat. I could make the call."

The judge chuckled. "Merle, I'm afraid the day you or I ask for a younger man to do our job, that's the day they'll tell us to move along."

The bailiff looked sullen, like a child who had been ordered to wash the dishes.

"Tell you what, Merle," the judge continued. "You call old Wantuck at the jail and tell him you're coming. Tell him I want two extra men for Taney. Tell him I'm asking as a favor, and I'll be by later to thank him personally."

The bailiff looked only half satisfied, but he headed off to do as he was told. The judge asked Elsie to call the next case.

"Judge," said a man at the back of the courtroom, "I need a word with you."

Curious, Elsie turned around to see what was up. The man who spoke was one of the church people. He stood, clutching a leather-bound Bible with gold lettering stamped on the front. It took her a minute to place him as the man who had shown up at the preliminary hearing in support of Taney. Oh, great, she thought.

Other judges would have cut short any attempt at interruption, but Judge Rountree's native courtesy extended to everyone who entered his courtroom.

"We're handling our criminal docket this morning," the judge said. "What is it that you want to tell me?"

"We're here about the Taney case. We want to make sure fathers got rights in Missouri," the man said. "I'm Martin Webster, and I represent Our Earthly Fathers. We come together when false claims are made against the head of the household." The man fumbled in his Bible. "I got one of our pamphlets right here."

Judge Rountree digested the statement. "I see."

Webster held the pamphlet aloft. "Can I bring this up for you to look at?"

"That won't be necessary," the judge said.

"It has a lot of facts about our mission, and our jail-house ministry, too."

The judge adjusted his eyeglasses. "Are you with the Promise Keepers?"

"No, we're not connected, but we sure do support the sacrament of marriage, like they do. We're local, a part of the Westside Apostolic Pentecostal Church. I got some church members with me today. You want them to stand up?"

"No. Please. We're arraigning Kris Taney in this court today," Judge Rountree explained. "I'll read the felony complaint to him and he'll enter a plea of Not Guilty. His case will be placed on the criminal trial docket. There will be no testimony, no other activity today. You will have no occasion to address the court about his case this morning, sir."

"That's okay. We're here to watch. We got our eye on the government. On *her*," and the man pointed at Elsie.

Oh, that's just swell, she thought.

The judge rose on his arthritic knees and struck his gavel for the benefit of the assembly.

"Ms. Arnold is a fine young woman. She represents the state in an exemplary way. Anyone who attempts to harass her in this courtroom will be held in contempt."

Elsie flashed him a grateful look. My hero, she thought. No wonder he was her favorite judge.

After a few moments two deputies ushered Taney into the courtroom, with the bailiff following at a safe distance. When Elsie saw Taney enter through the glass doorway, she did a double take; someone had given him a makeover. He had showered and shaved, and his tangled mane of reddish brown hair was gone; he had buzzed his head before coming to court. While he was still a far cry from a Christian evangelical poster child, Taney looked significantly more respectable and mainstream than he had twenty-four hours before.

The arraignment took place without incident. Taney did not speak. His attorney waived the formal reading of the charges and entered a plea of Not Guilty on his client's behalf. Elsie was sorry that the charges in the felony information were not read aloud; she thought Taney's new church friends would benefit from hearing the exact nature of the charges.

The docket concluded easily enough. Four defendants were arraigned, other defendants entered guilty pleas, and the two robbers were sentenced for their crimes. One man was sent away to be incarcerated for twenty years, but even that pronouncement produced no drama; the defendant, a hard-boiled persistent offender who had done time in several states, looked relieved that the sentence wasn't longer.

While Elsie represented the state's interests, she couldn't keep her mind off of Taney's cheering section. Even after Taney returned to jail, they remained in the courtroom, where she fancied they watched her every move. Why don't they just go home? she wondered impatiently. Granted, the courtroom was a public forum, but it wasn't a circus. Why were they hanging around?

After they'd exhausted the files and disposed of all court matters, court was adjourned for the morning. Elsie sat and scribbled in her files, but out of the corner of her eye she watched the Taney supporters; they still sat at the back of the room. Nearly everyone else had filed out. She grew increasingly nervous, and decided to get the hell out of there before someone spat on her again. Or threatened to whup her ass.

Hastily gathering her files together, she dashed for the door. The evangelical following rose when she did, and followed her out into the rotunda. In haste to return to the safety of her office, Elsie tripped over her own feet and had to catch herself to keep from falling. She heard one of the women snicker at her stumble. When she reached the door to the Prosecutor's Office and slipped inside, her heart beat like a drum. As she passed into the reception area, she stopped to catch her breath, leaning against the counter. She didn't understand why these people would target her. Didn't they realize she wore the white hat?

Stacie looked up from her computer. "Who are those people?" she asked.

"My fellow citizens," Elsie said, then amended her answer. "My critics, actually. They are my critics." But Stacie had already lost interest and was back at her computer screen.

After dropping the files off with Nedra, Elsie limped to her office and sank into her chair. She checked the clock; it was nearly lunchtime. Well, she thought, maybe she should fortify herself with food. She would see if Breeon was free. Bree was always good with advice; maybe she could help her get a handle on the cyclone she was currently trapped in. She picked up her phone and made a date with Bree to eat Mexican, leaving without delay to beat the lunch crowd.

"I'll drive," Elsie offered as they headed down the stairs. "I cleaned the trash out of my car last week, because it nearly gave my dad a heart attack when he saw that I was just throwing empty soda cans in the floor of the passenger seat."

"You make a bigger mess than my daughter," Bree told her, and they were laughing as they headed to the parking lot.

"Hey," said Bree, pointing at Elsie's car in the lot reserved for courthouse employees, "what's that on your antenna?"

"What are you talking about?" Elsie asked, but then she saw it, too. A chicken head impaled on the car antenna stood at attention like a faithful watchman. It looked comical, like a rubber chicken, except that as she drew closer it became apparent it was the real thing, dribbling a slow stream of gore down the metal pole that held it. And it wasn't the only one. Chicken heads were stuck into the door handles and under the windshield wipers, smearing the car with entrails and chicken blood.

Elsie was speechless. Her vision tunneled as she stood gaping at the mess, and for a moment she felt like she might pass out.

Breeon said, "Who's pissed off at you, Elsie?"

Shuddering at the sight of the chicken heads, she tried to remain composed. "Everyone, I think. Everyone in town. The list is long."

Bree said, "Well, it looks like somebody who's got a grudge against you is working at the poultry processing plant."

Elsie reached for a door handle, then recoiled. Tears stung her eyes and panic bounced in her chest as she tried to divine the reason for the vandalism.

"What do you think I should do?" she asked Bree, tension giving her voice a tremor. "Should I call the Barton P.D.?"

"Hell yes." Breeon turned to gaze at the back of the courthouse, where it adjoined the county jail. "It's a shame there's no security camera back here. The jail blocks the view from the courthouse, or else someone might have caught them in the act."

Elsie was dialing Noah's number with an unsteady hand. She let it ring nine times before she gave up. "He's on patrol," she said, as much for her own benefit as Bree's.

She next tried the Detective Division and got through to Patsy. "Let me talk to Ashlock, Patsy," she said.

"Honey, he's in a meeting with Vernon Wantuck, over from the county jail. They got the door shut." In a doubtful tone, she added, "Want me to break in?"

"No," Elsie said, turning away so she wouldn't have to look at the blood-spattered vehicle. "No, just connect me with the front desk downstairs. I need to report a crime."

Chapter Fifteen

THE MENTAL PICTURE of the chicken heads was still locked in Elsie's head when the clock in her office reached four-twenty. Thankful that she was only forty minutes away from the end of a crazy week, she swiveled in her office chair while Bree made a list on a legal pad.

"What else?" asked Bree.

Elsie rubbed her eyes. "Oh," she mumbled, "bread."

"Nah, I've got some."

"Milk."

"I already put that down."

"Cereal."

"That's good. I need that. Fruit Loops for Taylor, Raisin Bran for me."

Elsie was in no mood to ponder Breeon's grocery needs. She was edgy and distracted, still wondering which adversary made a mess of her car. Her contact with the Barton Police Department earlier that day had done nothing to allay her concerns. The woman who took her report over the phone didn't anticipate a speedy resolution.

"Why do you need my help with your grocery list?" she groused.

"I don't. I'm just killing time." Bree stretched in her chair. "I'm cutting out of here in a minute. I need to leave early. Cover for me if anyone comes looking."

"Okay. I'll say you're in the evidence room at the police department; no one would check that out." She watched as Bree folded her list into a square and dropped it in her purse. "Where are you headed?"

"Taylor has a home game at four-thirty. Sixth grade varsity," Breeon said with pride.

Elsie nodded approvingly, roused a fraction from her gloom. "That's great. I'm glad you'll get to see her play."

"I promised I wouldn't miss this one. I love to see those girls play. And," she added, as she dug in her purse for her car keys, "I'm keeping an eye on that damned coach."

"How come?"

When Bree looked up from her purse, she had a glint in her eye. "She's a screamer. Chews those babies out like they're playing pro basketball. Last week a girl spilled her water bottle on the court. You'd have thought the child took a piss, the way that woman carried on."

Elsie's eyes widened. "Oh Lord, I get it. The coach sounds just like Abby Lee."

Bree gave her a doubtful look. "Who?"

"Abby Lee. On *Dance Moms*."

Breeon groaned, rising from her chair. "Sweet Jesus, don't tell me you're watching more reality TV."

"Oh, Bree, it's so fabulous. You've got to watch it. You need to see those moms fight."

Bree pulled on her winter coat, a tailored camel hair from Talbot's. It was a shade too big, passed down from her sister, a lawyer with a big St. Louis firm. "You've got a taste for trash, girl. When I came in, you were on that TMZ Web site. I caught you in the act."

Embarrassed, Elsie blushed a little. She had in fact been browsing TMZ online, checking to see who'd been arrested lately in Hollywood. She needed to blank her head out, to escape into a mindless pursuit to recover from the Taney case and the chicken heads.

"A TV star just got arrested in Hollywood for domestic assault on his girlfriend," she said, trying to entice Bree into a show of interest. "I'll tell you who it is, if you want to know."

"Don't care," said Bree, heading for the door.

Elsie studied the story on the computer screen. "Why would a big star stoop to hitting a woman?"

"Why would any man do it? Why do men knock women around? But it happens all the time, honey."

She nodded, thinking. "It's a sick exercise of power."

"Of dominion," Breeon agreed.

"Okay, so why would that woman in Hollywood put up with it? With being slapped around?"

"She's got some issues. Just like your Mrs. Taney."

"Donita Taney is dirt poor. Uneducated." After a pause, Elsie added, "Ugly. But this woman on TMZ is gorgeous. Rich. I don't get it. Why would a woman stand for abuse if she had other alternatives?" As Bree paused in the doorway, pulling on her gloves, Elsie added, "You know what my mother says."

"What?"

"Ever since I was a girl, my mother taught me: a man who hits a woman doesn't get a second chance. Period."

Bree said, "Your mom is a wise woman. Hey, I'm out of here."

Nodding, Elsie reached for her computer mouse, but before she could research more Hollywood tragedies, the phone rang. Glancing at the caller ID as she picked up, she read, "Unknown."

"Elsie Arnold," she said.

"Well, hello there, Elsie Arnold," a voice said through the receiver with a smug drawl.

She couldn't quite place the caller, though he sounded familiar. She didn't like his tone, though, and she was in no mood to fool around with jokers or guessing games.

In a brisk, businesslike voice, she responded, "May I ask who's calling?"

" 'May I ask,' " the caller piped in falsetto. Laughing, he said, "That's real purty." The voice lowered deep in its register. "We need to talk, little lady."

Elsie sat straight up in her chair. "Who the hell are you calling 'little lady'? Do you know who you're talking to? Harass me over the phone and I'll file a criminal charge."

She didn't get the opportunity to elaborate on the threat. The phone clicked and the line went dead.

Hanging up the receiver, she studied the phone in silence. The man's thick dialect was an accent she'd encountered recently. When she made the connection, she shook her head; she must be slipping, she should've recognized the voice immediately.

The man on the phone sounded distinctly like Kris Taney.

What are they doing over there at the county jail, letting him call me on the phone? She shouldn't have any contact with him whatsoever, except through his attorney. It was for his own benefit, to protect his rights.

Moreover, she didn't want to have any contact with him. His voice on the phone was creepy, even creepier than when he shouted at her in the hallway of the courthouse. He made her skin crawl. She didn't want to be alone with him, ever, not even on a phone line.

She was obligated to notify his attorney about the call. And she needed to alert the county jail. Elsie reached for the phone, ready to dial, when she paused. Maybe she'd call Bob Ashlock first. He would have good insight on the phone privileges and policies of inmates in lockup. He understood the legal impropriety of a phone call from a defendant to a prosecutor. He'd have some good advice.

She picked up the phone and dialed the Detective Division of the Barton City P.D. When Patsy, the longtime receptionist at the division, answered, Elsie didn't stop to make small talk.

"Put me through to Ashlock, please."

"Is this Elsie?" Patsy asked in her cracked voice. "You just missed him, honey."

Disappointment made a fist in her stomach. "Where'd he go?"

"Over to the county jail. He's taking a statement. There's an inmate over there wanting to snitch out his buddy."

"Great! Patsy, that's just great. Call him and tell him I'll meet him over there." She hung up abruptly, grabbed her coat and ran for the door.

ELSIE HAD TO walk briskly to keep up with Ashlock as they strode the narrow green hallway leading to the administrative offices of the McCown County jail. He wore a no-nonsense expression as he pushed the security buzzer for admittance; when he didn't gain entry immediately, he pressed it with the heel of his hand until the jailer in the office hastened to let them in.

"Where's Vernon?" Ashlock demanded of the deputy who served as assistant to the head jailer, Vernon Wantuck.

"He's upstairs." the young man said. "With the sheriff," he added, as if the information would impress the detective. "Do you'uns have an appointment?"

"Nope. You get on the phone and tell him to get down here straightaway. I've got some questions for Vernon, about how he's running his show here."

"Who's down here raising a ruckus? Ashlock?" boomed a voice behind him.

Elsie turned to see the jailer slowly approaching. Vernon Wantuck was a huge man; he could have easily qualified as a contestant on *The Biggest Loser* had he been interested in weight reduction, which he wasn't. She scooted against the wall to give him room to pass.

"Got a bone to pick with you, Vernon," Ashlock said.

"We better get to the bottom of it, I reckon."

Wantuck shuffled through the door to his private office and grunted as he settled his girth into his chair. The jailer gestured toward a pair of chairs across from his desk, upholstered in dingy woven fabric. As Elsie settled into the seat, it gave off a smell of dirty underwear.

Ashlock got down to business. "Why are you letting the inmates harass people on your phones?"

"Well, that's easy. I ain't."

She exchanged a glance with Ashlock, and turned to the jailer with a skeptical expression.

Vernon continued, "What big idea got hold of you all? You think they got cell phones? Because I don't let them have no cell phones."

"No, that's not it," Elsie said. "Vernon, they're making calls on the pay phones here."

"Sure they do."

"And I think you need to know that an inmate called me at the prosecutor's office from inside the jail."

"Didn't happen. Ashlock, you ought to know the policy, even if she don't. They can use the phone lines in the jail to call their bondsman, their lawyer, their immediate family. That's it. Period." The man placed his meaty hand on his desktop, to rock his chair back and forth. "Why are you riding me? How come the Prosecutor's Office wants to kick my ass?" He winked at Elsie, laughing, and said, "Was it that old broad they got in charge? She send you to do her dirty work, little sis?"

Elsie broke in, an impatient edge to her voice. "Kris

Taney. He got to a phone somehow, and called me this afternoon. I recognized his voice."

The jailer threw his head back and laughed out loud, a reaction that made his belly shake like Santa Claus. "Now I got you. *Taney.* I seen you on TV last week, sis, talking about that case. You look good on camera," he said, looking her up and down, "but I'll be goddamned if you don't look even better in person. Well, this is starting to make some sense to me now, yes sir. You're the little cutie that's got Ashlock here running around like Prince Valiant." He laughed again, delighted with the comparison he'd created. "Just like Prince fucking Valiant in the funny papers."

Ashlock sat in the sagging chair, unamused. "Watch how you talk in front of Ms. Arnold, Vernon," he said.

"Now that's what I'm talking about. You're going on like you're sniffing her drawers."

Ashlock was on his feet in an instant. "One more word," he said with gravity, "and I'm gonna have to teach you some manners. And it's been a long day. But I'll do it."

"Well," the jailer continued, dropping the leer, "you wasted your time coming over here. Taney ain't calling nobody."

"It was his voice," Elsie insisted.

"Maybe it was an impersonator act. Like they do in the Branson shows, in them big theaters at Table Rock Lake. Elvis. The Beatles. Marilyn Monroe. Maybe one of them Branson impersonators got on the phone and done an impression of him, huh? All's I know is, it wasn't Taney."

"How can you be so sure?" she persisted.

"Taney got no privileges. He's trouble. I don't let him mix with the population. He ain't nowhere near a phone."

Ashlock shook his head. "I should've thought to ask this first. How do your phones come up on caller ID?"

"McCown County jail."

"But what about the pay phones? The ones the inmates use to talk to their attorneys and families?"

"Same thing. McCown County jail. Gives people on the other end a heads-up. Good for security."

Ashlock and Elsie exchanged glances. "Did you dial Star 69?" he asked her.

"Yeah. It came up 'pay phone.'"

Ashlock looked contrite. "Well, doggone," he said. Rising from his chair, he offered the jailer his right hand. "Guess I came tearing in here like a dang fool. Somebody's doing a number on us."

"Who?" Wantuck asked.

"We'll figure it out," Ashlock said, signaling his departure with a wave. He held the door open for Elsie, and as they left the jail a moment later and walked into the winter evening, they both inhaled the cold air gratefully.

"Sorry about that back there," he said, bunching his shoulders against the cold.

"*You're* sorry?" she exclaimed in disbelief. "I'm the one who's sorry, leading you on a wild goose chase. I could've cleared it up with a phone call."

"Wantuck wouldn't return your phone call on a bet. Sometimes, people who work around the criminal element forget how to behave. Wantuck gets the big head, being in charge of inmates. Makes him think he's king."

Elsie turned so the cold wind was at her back. "Really, I'm sorry to drag you into this. I don't think my head's been working right, ever since my car got vandalized."

Ashlock's brows came together. "Somebody key your car?"

"No, shit, I wish that was all it was. Somebody made a hell of a mess on it. I filed a report, though. Then I had to clean the damn mess up." Shivering, she said, "I'm freezing, Ash. I've got to go."

"I'll walk you to your car."

"It's just across the lot."

"I'll walk you anyway."

"Oh, Ash. You are such an old-fashioned guy. Don't you think I can make it there by myself?"

Shaking her head, she walked down the sidewalk toward her car. When she opened the car door she glanced back at the jail and saw that Ashlock was leaning against a concrete pillar, watching her.

Chapter Sixteen

A COLD DRIZZLE pelted the front windows of the old brick house where Elsie's parents lived. The room where the Arnolds spent most of their time was a parlor on the first floor, a spacious room looking out on the front yard. Beneath the windows, hot water rattled in the coils of a cast-iron radiator as it battled the frigid weather.

Marge Arnold, Elsie's mother, sat in her easy chair, grading papers. A potion of grape juice and apple cider vinegar sat in a juice glass nearby; Marge needed to bring her high cholesterol down, but she scoffed at pharmaceutical remedies. Elsie stretched out on the sofa in sweat pants and a worn University of Missouri sweat shirt. She hugged a sofa pillow to her chest.

"Oh, Mom, good God, what a week," she groaned, reaching for an Oreo from a stack of cookies on the coffee table.

Marge shook her head as she made checkmarks with

a red pen. Looking over the top of her spectacles, she regarded her daughter with a keen eye. She listened intently as Elsie recounted the events of the past week: the struggles with the Taney case, the defection of Madeleine, the difficulty of putting the hearing together under the gun, and Taney's personal attack upon her. She didn't leave out the chicken heads or Taney's evangelical support group, or the pigtailed character's confrontation at Baldknobbers. As Elsie talked, she felt her anxiety abate. Unburdening herself to her mother eased the load that had been weighing her down.

"Baby, I've always told you that you can do anything you put your mind to," her mother said, "but I confess that I'm worried about your job right now. This Taney case is putting you at risk."

"I don't know about that. It's making me crazy, that's all."

"Is it a good case?"

"It's a can of worms. The oldest daughter ran out of the prelim, and now I've got to unravel some veracity problem with her. And the middle sister flipped out before the hearing. The youngest sister doesn't talk at all. And the mother's a piece of work; I don't know what's up with her." As Elsie talked, she pulled a bright crocheted afghan from the back of the couch and wrapped it around her.

"Isn't this supposed to be Mrs. Thompson's case?"

"Yep."

"Then let her fix it. I don't understand why you always have to work these sex cases."

"Mother. That's why I became a prosecutor."

"But this case, Elsie, the facts in this case are so terrible." Marge rubbed her eyes behind her spectacles. "I can't bear to think about what that vile man put those girls through."

"I know. And I can't *stop* thinking about it. It's like I'm hauling around a maggoty bag of trash all the time."

The women sat in silence for a moment, until Marge sighed and said, "You have to wonder why."

"Why what?"

"Why he would do such terrible things. So hard to understand."

Elsie sat up, still wrapped in the afghan. "Not my job. I don't have to understand him."

As if Elsie hadn't spoken, Marge went on. "He may have been a victim of abuse, too. Those patterns get passed down. Someone is violated as a child and they do it to the next generation."

"Don't care." Elsie's dander was rising. "Let the defense attorney worry about whether Kris Taney had a miserable childhood. He's an adult now, he had a choice. And he chose to rape his children."

"I know. You're right, honey."

"I have the responsibility—the duty," she said, her voice growing strident, "because I view it as a personal duty, to see to it that he is held accountable for what he did to those girls. I don't have to be his therapist."

"You're right. I'm on your team, Elsie. And I may not have it right, anyway. The things this man did: it's more perverse than sex."

"Rape isn't about sex. It's about power."

"Well, I think that's it. He was showing his family he had power over them. Power to do anything he chose."

Elsie lay down again, satisfied that she and her mother were on the same wavelength. She shut her eyes when she heard Marge say, "When a person has too much power over other folks, things get twisted. That's the problem with that whole 'men are the head' family structure. Gives them too much feeling of entitlement."

"Daddy's not like that."

"I wouldn't have married him if he was."

Marge leaned over to the couch and pressed her hand to Elsie's forehead, as if checking for a fever. "So what are you going to do about all this? It doesn't sound like you're getting enough support from your office. Could you turn to someone with more experience? I know that Thompson woman couldn't shoot fish in a barrel."

"Mother, I am not punting the Taney case. And I'm not crying around to someone else, like I'm incompetent. I've been at this for four years."

"You've always been stubborn. Ever since you were a little girl." Marge made scratches in red ink. "Why don't you move back home for a while? Just sleep in your old room."

Elsie put a sofa pillow over her face. A moment of silence passed.

"Now you're being ridiculous," Marge said.

The air grew stuffy under the pillow, and Elsie tossed it on the floor.

Marge said, "Well then, stay here this weekend. Just till Monday morning."

"I can't. Noah's off tomorrow. We're going to the movies."

"Oh. Him."

Marge regarded Elsie in silence for a long moment, peering over the top of her reading glasses. Elsie turned on her side on the couch, and asked, "Do we have any Little Debbie Snack Cakes?"

Marge looked back to the papers on her lap. "We should have a box of oatmeal crème pies, unless your daddy ate them all."

Elsie went to the kitchen and rummaged through the cabinets; to her delight, the box she sought was still half full. Tearing the plastic wrapper with her teeth, she returned to the living room.

Marge was waiting for her. "The problem with you, Elsie, is you want a fellow who looks like a movie star. You are always going after Brad Pitt."

"Mother. I am not going after Brad Pitt. Lord, Mom, Brad Pitt is old. He's almost as old as Dad."

"Brad Pitt is from the Ozarks."

"What does that have to do with anything?" Elsie asked as she pulled the oatmeal pie into two pieces.

"My point is, what you need, Elsie, is a man with a good heart. Someone who loves you and takes care of you."

"Noah takes care of me," Elsie said, with a hint of devilment.

Marge looked away. "I don't want to hear any more of that," she said adamantly. "In the hills, that's called starting the honeymoon early."

Elsie couldn't help but laugh. "Mom, you've got a nugget of wisdom to cover every situation."

Marge's mouth twitched with a smile she could not conceal. "How about this idea: just stay here tonight. I'll make a pot roast. With mashed potatoes and cooked carrots. And gravy."

"Mom, you're like a broken record. 'Sleep here, stay here, eat here.' You're going to make me fat. I've gained weight this winter as it is."

"Honey, you need to put on some weight in wintertime. It keeps you warm, keeps you from getting sick."

Elsie decided to give in. What would it hurt to stay overnight? During the past week she'd slept poorly; she always slept better at home. The old brick house was a haven. She felt safe in her parent's house, felt that she could relax and let her guard down. She relented.

"Oh, that's just great," Marge said, nodding with satisfaction. "And tomorrow we can all go to church."

Aw, shit. Elsie pulled the afghan up to her chin and drifted off to sleep on the sofa.

Chapter Seventeen

ON SUNDAY MORNING George Arnold drove the short distance to Walnut Street Christian Church in a shiny 2007 Buick sedan. Marge sat next to him in front, pleased as the Cheshire cat to have Elsie along for the trip.

Elsie rode in the backseat, a little nettled at spending her Sunday morning in church rather than in the pursuit of leisure. Moreover, she was not thrilled with her attire. Because she had not planned to stay over, she was obligated to find something to wear from the choices that hung in the closet of her old bedroom at home, a funny mix of garments from days past. She finally donned an old Christmas frock for want of a better option, but she felt more than a little out of season in a red dress with spangles. Hell's bells, she thought, it's January, and I look like I'm in the Merry Christmas Pageant.

"I look so stupid in this dress," she complained.

"You look like the prettiest girl in Barton," her father assured her, winking at her in the rearview mirror.

"Honey, you could have gone through my closet to see if I had something you'd rather wear," Marge said.

Elsie sat up straight. "Are you trying to say I'm fat?" she asked indignantly.

Her mother crowed, unoffended, "I most certainly am not. I think you are perfect. And as for me, I'm proud to be fat. I've worked hard at it."

Elsie's dissatisfaction lingered. "Why do we have to go to church today? This will waste my whole morning. I've got stuff I have to do. Errands." She crossed her spangled arms over her chest and stared out the window, looking more like a spoiled kid than a professional adult.

George said, "There's a new member in the congregation. An engineer. Nice guy. Never been married."

"No, no, no, no," said Elsie.

"Now, Elsie, we just want you to say hello."

"Is this what dragging me to church is about? I already told Mom, I have a date tonight. With Noah," Elsie said.

"If you're going to date a policeman, I wish it was that nice Detective Ashlock," said Marge. "I've been thinking that he would be a good match for you."

"Bob Ashlock?" Elsie exclaimed, shocked. "Mother, stop it."

"He's just your type," her mother insisted. "That he-man type you like."

"Mother, he is a friend."

"Daddy and I were friends," Marge said, nodding at George.

"Nah," George said, keeping his eyes on the road. "Men just play along with that friend routine so we can get you in the sack."

"George! You didn't dare talk that way when we were dating. My daddy would've got out the shotgun. 'Code of the hills,'" Marge said with an expressive nod.

"Spare me the goddamned code of the goddamned hills," Elsie muttered.

"What, honey?" Marge asked.

"Nothing. But Ashlock," Elsie continued, "he's almost forty, for God's sake."

"Forty is young," George said as he pulled into the church parking lot. "I'd say this engineer is about forty."

Marge twisted in her seat, fighting the shoulder harness to get a good look at Elsie. "Honey, we just want to see you settled. You'll be thirty-two on your next birthday. Don't you want to be a mother someday?"

"This engineer is a Missouri boy," said George. "Grew up in Springfield. Nice family."

Elsie let out an aggrieved sigh and fell silent.

The Arnolds walked into the church, a Georgian structure built of red brick, boasting a tall steeple and beautiful arched windows. The hallway leading to the sanctuary was crowded, and Elsie followed a woman ahead of her too closely, stepping onto the back of the woman's shoe and causing her to stumble. The unfortunate woman was Tina Peroni.

"Elsie? Are you trying to kill me?" Tina asked, bending over to pull up the leather that folded under her heel.

She took in Elsie's holiday attire and exclaimed, "That's quite a festive frock you're wearing."

"Oh, shut up."

"What are you doing here? How did Ma and Pa talk you into coming to church?"

"Hog-tied me. Want to sit with us?"

"I'm on my way out. We went to the early service."

"No," Elsie said in disbelief.

"Yes, sleepyhead. I'm glad I ran into you, though. Donita wants to see you."

"Donita Taney?"

"How many Donitas do you know? Yes, Donita Taney." Tina slid past people in the narrow hall to reach the exit. As she opened the door to depart, she added, "When she was in to get her food stamps, she said she had something for you."

"Huh. Well, I'll tell Madeleine tomorrow morning. It's her case. Technically."

"You do that." Tina waved and headed for the parking lot.

ELSIE'S MIND WANDERED during the sermon. The preacher talked about the Epiphany, and the journey of the three Wise Men to discover the Christ child. Tell me something real. Something I can use, she thought.

To occupy herself, she picked up the pew Bible and riffled through the wafer-thin pages, browsing the Book of Genesis. When she caught sight of the Sodom heading, curiosity made her pause. This should make interesting reading, she thought. In Sunday school class the teachers had always skipped over the story of Sodom and Gomorrah.

Elsie scanned the story of Lot, scowling at the description of his offer to sacrifice his virgin daughters to an angry mob. As she read on, she came to verses that made her stop, shake her head and read again. She never realized that the story of Lot had an incest twist.

> 30. *And Lot went up out of Zoar, and dwelt in the mountain, and his two daughters with him; for he feared to dwell in Zoar: and he dwelt in a cave, he and his two daughters.*
> 31. *And the firstborn said unto the younger, "Our father is old, and there is not a man in the earth to come in unto us after the manner of all the earth:*
> 32. *" Come, let us make our father drink wine, and we will lie with him, that we may preserve seed of our father."*
> 33. *And they made their father drink wine that night: and the firstborn went in, and lay with her father; and he perceived not when she lay down, nor when she arose.*
> 34. *And it came to pass on the morrow, that the firstborn said unto the younger, "Behold, I lay yesternight with my*

> *father: let us make him drink wine this*
> *night also; and go thou in, and lie with*
> *him, that we may preserve seed of our*
> *father."*
> 35. *And they made their father drink wine*
> *that night also: and the younger arose,*
> *and lay with him; and he perceived not*
> *when she lay down, nor when she arose.*
> 36. *Thus were both the daughters of Lot*
> *with child by their father.*

Lot was a liar, she thought, anger kindling in her chest. She shook her head with disgust, reflecting that the history of incest was long indeed, as was the practice of pinning the blame on the daughters. Some things hadn't changed in thousands of years.

Well, she decided, maybe one thing had changed: Lot's wine-drinking defense wouldn't fly in Missouri courts. "Sorry, Lot; intoxication wouldn't be a defense to the crime in Missouri," she murmured.

Her mother gave her a sharp nudge, bringing Elsie back to the present. "Are you muttering to yourself in church? Stop it," she whispered, with a warning look.

Elsie flipped through the pages again. Skimming the chapters of Genesis, she looked again at the verses about Lot and his daughters, then closed the book. The text struck an uneasy chord, creating a mental picture of Taney and his daughters. Elsie felt a prickle at her neck and shuddered in the pew.

When the communion plates were passed, after a

moment's hesitation she took the tiny wafer and sipped her little plastic cup of grape juice. Though she closed her eyes, the image of the Taney daughters at the mercy of their father was locked in her head. With her eyes squeezed shut, she tried to block out the picture by thinking of something else, anything, but the vision persisted. In her mind's eye she saw Taney advance on Kristy, menacing, as the girl backed away to escape, her face a frozen mask of horror.

Elsie opened her eyes. When she raised her head, her jaw was set. She knew it was time to quit whining about the challenges of the Taney case. She needed to keep a sharp eye on Madeleine, to ensure that the prosecutor wouldn't abandon or fumble the prosecution. For the sake of the three Taney girls, she must fight the good fight in earnest. Bring it, she thought, and her spine stiffened.

When they rose to sing the closing hymn, Elsie stood by her mother's side, her eyes fixed on the open hymnbook without seeing it. *This story will have a different ending*, she told herself grimly. *Lot's daughters have an advocate this time.*

Chapter Eighteen

ELSIE SWIVELED IN her office chair on Monday morning, watching tiny balls of sleet bounce on the pavement of the street below. "I need sunshine," she whispered. "I hate sleet. I cannot handle sleet today."

Turning to her computer, she saw that the weather forecast on the computer screen didn't predict freezing precipitation. Stupid Weather Channel, she thought.

When her phone rang, she snatched it up, hoping to hear Breeon's voice, but it was Madeleine. In her usual frosty tone, Madeleine told her to come down to her office.

I wish I had the nerve to kick your ass, Elsie thought as she hung up the phone. She still nursed a grudge against Madeleine for deserting her at the Taney preliminary. Given the opportunity, she might have had the chutzpah to voice a complaint last week, when the offense was fresh. But by now too much time had passed to muster the courage for a confrontation.

Taking a moment to catch her breath, she strode down the hall to Madeleine's office, opened the door with a quick knock and stuck her head in. "What's up?" she asked, a shade of curtness in her tone.

Madeleine was examining a map of McCown County that depicted a breakdown of voter turnout at county polling places. She pushed a lock of lacquered hair behind one ear. "Sit," she said, and Elsie sat. "Did you bring it?"

Elsie gave her a blank look. "Bring what?"

"The file," Madeleine said with irritation. "Taney."

"No," she replied, wondering why she was supposed to read Madeleine's mind and anticipate her desires. "Did you want to see me about the Taney case?"

Madeleine pushed her leather chair back from the desk and crossed her legs. "Give me an update. What's the status of the case?"

Elsie related the events of the last week: Al Taney's failure to appear, the information gained from Kris Taney's wife and daughters, and the outcome of the court appearances. She made brief reference to Taney's abuse of her in the hallway, and the chicken parts that decorated her vehicle on Friday.

Madeleine toyed with a silver letter opener shaped like a dagger. "I know about that. Someone mentioned that chicken prank to me."

Exhaling with a sound that was a cross between a wail and a groan, Elsie said, "It was so nasty."

Madeleine tossed the silver dagger onto the desktop. "We don't know that it's connected." When Elsie sent her a dumbfounded look, Madeleine added, "To Taney."

"No," Elsie said slowly, "but we know it was connected to me."

In a superior tone, Madeleine said, "That kind of thing goes with the territory. You have to rise above it. In this job, there is a certain burden we bear."

Elsie clenched her jaw to keep her mouth shut, but she shouted inside her head: *Burden we bear? We? Are chicken guts on your car?*

"What else is being done?"

Elsie cleared her throat, and in as civil a tone as she could muster said, "Bob Ashlock is trying to run down outcry evidence, but there's not much to go on. Taney had his family under orders to keep their mouths shut about the abuse, and the household was so totally intimidated by him that they were afraid to talk about it."

"What about scientific evidence?"

"We have the girls scheduled for medical exams at the Victims' Center next week. Children's Services should have had exams done when Taney was taken into custody but they didn't. So that's about it."

"That's your whole case?"

Elsie looked at Madeleine with wonder. How could Madeleine be surprised at the scarcity of the evidence? It was supposed to be Madeleine's file.

As if explaining sex prosecution to an outsider, Elsie said, "That's pretty much how these sex cases go. At least in this case the girls can corroborate each other, because sometimes he did things in front of the family. We do have to clear up a problem with the state's main witness,

Charlene; apparently, she got into some kind of situation at school, and I need to get to the bottom of it."

"What situation?"

"Something about a sexual touching by some classmates. I don't know the details." She made a mental note to contact the school system.

"Well," Madeleine said, and to Elsie's amazement, her boss looked extremely uncomfortable. "I've been thinking. You seem to be handling the case in a competent way."

Though her eyes nearly bugged out of her head at the understatement, Elsie stayed mum.

Madeleine continued, "I've been tied up with some important schedule conflicts."

"Of course," she murmured, trying hard not to picture Madeleine in the stirrups.

"And I have a lot of pressing engagements coming up. I don't think I can give this case the attention it deserves. I'm assigning it to you."

The realization blossomed in Elsie's chest: Madeleine was bowing out, the Taney case was all hers. She exulted in the knowledge that she could proceed without the handicap of Madeleine's negligent oversight. She was glad to have the file to herself; she much preferred working solo to serving an incompetent master.

But it seemed like Madeleine felt guilty about something. Maybe, Elsie thought, her boss regretted unceremoniously dumping the case on her. Or maybe the case had grown too messy for Madeleine, with its chicken heads and hallway fights and angry evangelical Christians. When the going got tough, Madeleine generally got going—in the other direction.

But she was a warrior, Elsie reminded herself. Shrugging off her reservations, she sat straight in her chair and regarded her boss with a friendly expression.

"No problem, Madeleine. I feel like I've established good rapport with the witnesses. I'll be glad to see it through."

"Fine. Let me know how it progresses," Madeleine said as she picked up a copy of the *Barton Daily News* and began flipping through the pages, letting Elsie know she was dismissed.

Elsie stood up to go but then lingered in the doorway. "Anything else?" She wanted to make sure no hidden disasters would blow up in her face.

"Noooo . . . " said Madeleine, refusing to look up from the paper; clearly, she wanted her to leave.

As Elsie headed down the hallway back to her office, a dark thought lurked: Madeleine must think the Taney case was a total loser. Because Madeleine would buzz around a high profile case like a fly on shit, unless it looked weak. Her initial reaction of triumph faded as she realized that *State v. Taney* was a hot potato that had been tossed into her lap.

Oh, well, she thought as she sank into her office chair. Things could be worse. Much worse.

Now she was ready to begin her Monday morning in earnest. She checked her e-mail and saw a message from

Noah. He must be doing reports; otherwise he'd be more likely to text or call. She opened the message. It was short and sweet.

U R cute, it read.

Okay, she thought, he wasn't Shakespeare. But they'd had a pretty good time together on Sunday, though they tangled when he'd urged her to order salad for supper rather than ribs. Stung, she'd snapped at him, but he claimed she was overreacting, that he was only concerned with her health.

Staring at the e-mail, she resolved to keep the time spent with Noah on the happy side, so it could be an oasis in her life. She tried to think of something funny to send back, to keep it light. She mused on it for a minute, then typed,

U R hot.

He'll like that, she thought.

Another e-mail brought her back to business. Tina Peroni had sent a reminder that Donita Taney wanted to see her, that it was important. *Yikes, I almost forgot.*

A visit with Donita was not likely to kick off her week in a rosy fashion; Donita wouldn't be sharing good tidings. Moreover, the practical aspect of getting in touch with Donita was a pain; the apartment on High Street had no telephone, much less computer access, and Donita didn't have a cell phone. She would have to get in her car and drive over there.

Well, it was her baby now. A check of her calendar showed she had a couple of hours free. Resolving to get the meeting out of the way before other business required her attention, she put on her coat and dug her keys out of her purse.

On the way out of the office, she let Stacie know that she was going to see a witness.

"What if the people with the chicken heads come looking for you?" Stacie asked with uncharacteristic wit.

"Oh, that's funny," said Elsie. "Tell you what: they need to go over my head. You send them straight to the top."

"Now who's being funny," Stacie responded, but Elsie was already out the door.

Chapter Nineteen

Sleet coated the pavement leading to the apartment house on High Street. Elsie slipped on the ice and landed on her rear end. Cursing roundly, she picked herself up with care. Fortunately, she'd held tight to the file she was carrying, so her papers were not flung to the winds.

Donita Taney stared at her from the window of the apartment. Standing next to Donita was a man Elsie had never seen before.

Making her way on tiptoe to the front entrance, she took care not to slip a second time. Once inside, she knocked on the Taneys' apartment door. It didn't open right away. Geez, she thought, for someone who needed to see me ASAP, she's not moving very fast.

Finally the door opened. Donita stood in the doorway, looking over her shoulder at something in the apartment. She turned her head and gave a tentative nod in greeting to Elsie, who was unsettled by the reception.

"May I come in?" she asked, affecting an upbeat manner.

"Sure," Donita said. She smiled but seemed jumpy.

Elsie walked into the room. The unfamiliar man lounged on the couch, occupying Donita's customary spot. She didn't wait for an introduction but approached him and extended her hand.

"Elsie Arnold, McCown County Prosecutor's Office."

"Roy Mayfield." He gave her hand a perfunctory shake.

"Are you a friend of Donita's?" she asked.

"Friend of the family," Mayfield replied. He and Donita exchanged a look.

Elsie stood cooling her heels. She looked from Mayfield to Donita and felt a chill go down her spine. Josh Nixon's words fairly rang in her ears.

"Okay, Donita," she said, "clue me in to what I'm doing here. Didn't you tell Tina you needed to see me?"

Donita gestured toward the kitchen. "I got something to show you."

As Elsie followed, she saw Mayfield rise from the couch. Donita turned and flapped her hand at him. "Sit down, you silly old thing. You don't have to know everything."

Her tone with Mayfield, Elsie observed, was coquettish, like a Scarlett O'Hara impression. Mayfield took the hint, sat down and lit a cigarette.

Entering the kitchen, Elsie peered about the room with surprise. It was clean, in marked contrast to her last visit. All the plates and glasses were washed and stacked in the dish drainer, and the food was put away. A full dollar-brand bottle of green dish soap stood on the windowsill above the sink, and a dish towel hung on the oven door handle. The trash can had been emptied. Aside from the cardboard boxes set against one wall, the room was quite tidy.

Donita pointed at the boxes. "I boxed up Kris's things. Them is his boxes. I don't want them around. You can have them."

"What are they?" she asked.

"That's his stuff. All of it. His clothes, the stuff in his dresser drawer, everything. And JoLee's bidness, too. Mostly she took everything of hers. This is just what she left behind."

Elsie eyed the boxes with more interest. "Are you sure you want me to take these?"

"I want you to get rid of them. Take them, burn them, I don't care. I want it out, gone."

Donita dropped her voice to a whisper as she moved close, beside Elsie, and said, with a conspiratorial look, "Some people don't like to have nothing of Kris's around. It don't look right. Some people don't like to be bumping into another man's shit, you get my drift."

Donita peeked into the other room before she continued. "It's like his stink ain't gone, if his stuff ain't gone. JoLee's, too. I want ever' last bit of it gone. So we can have a fresh start."

" 'We'?" Elsie said. "Who's 'we'?"

Donita gave her a speculative look. After a moment, she said, "Me and the girls."

Tiffany, wearing faded pajama bottoms and a torn T-shirt, shuffled into the kitchen as the two women stood there looking at the boxes. She walked over to her mother and tugged on her sweatshirt. Donita put an arm around the child.

"Any better, hon?"

Tiffany didn't answer. Tendrils of curly hair hung in her flushed face. Donita smoothed the hair back and felt Tiffany's forehead with her hand.

"You feel like eating anything?" The little girl shrugged her shoulders. Donita gave her a little pat. "I'll make you something. Mama's gonna make you something *good*."

She took a slice of white bread from a loaf sitting on the counter and spread it with a layer of yellow margarine from a plastic butter dish. Then she pulled a bag of white sugar from an overhead cabinet, scooped a spoonful out and sprinkled it atop the oleo. She folded the bread in half and handed the sandwich to Tiffany. The girl bit into a corner of the bread with an expression of deep satisfaction.

Elsie moved to the open-flapped boxes, knelt and looked in. They were filled with wadded clothes and a hodgepodge of personal items. She reached into a box, picked up a shirtsleeve, then dropped it as if it had burnt her fingers. Four dead cockroaches clung to the fabric.

"There's some bugs in there," Donita said. "Landlord sprays once in a while but it don't even slow them down." She shrugged philosophically. "I guess everybody's got them. They're everywhere."

Elsie couldn't agree, but didn't want to argue. "Hard to get used to, huh."

"Oh," scoffed Donita, "me and the girls don't mind it so long as they keep out of our way. Roaches got nerve, though. I hate to see them on a toothbrush. When they get in the bathroom, I smash them with my fist." As if the thought just struck her, she added, "Our toilet's working. If you need it."

Elsie gave her best attempt at a smile. "No, thank you."

"Just saying."

The four boxes might contain nothing but trash, Elsie reflected, but it was possible that something inside them could support her case. It was worth a look. She pulled out her cell phone to consult with Ashlock about transporting the boxes but heard the answering machine recording of Patsy's voice, inviting her to leave a message.

"I'll take these to the police department, then," she said to Donita, and folded down the worn corrugated cardboard flaps. The prospect of waiting around in the High Street apartment until she raised someone at the P.D. held no appeal. Then again, it seemed that Donita was opening up to her; maybe she had forged a at the preliminary hearing. It might be an opportune time to open up a ticklish subject.

After a moment's hesitation, she said, "Donita, I've been worried about something, since the prelim. If you don't mind, I'd like you to shine a little light on this Charlene situation for me."

In the next room, Roy moved suddenly; Elsie saw his chin jerk toward the kitchen. Donita's voice was flat as she asked, "Just what is it you want to know about Char?"

Elsie took a deep breath. She didn't like to force a confidence, but it was vital that she know the facts behind what Nixon had said about Charlene.

"At the preliminary hearing, your husband's attorney brought up a situation Charlene faced at school. Something about boys touching her. They accused her of lying."

"Oh, that." Donita pushed one of the boxes with her foot.

"Yeah, that. What all happened with that?"

Donita pulled out a kitchen chair and sat in it sideways. "You know, that was partly her own fault."

"Tell me."

In a resigned voice, Donita said, "She had a crush on a boy when she was in eighth grade. What was his name? Carlos." She gave Elsie a knowing look. "*Mexican.* In trouble all the time. But she thought he was a looker."

Elsie nodded. Donita continued, "All the girls liked him, but he started giving Charlene the eye and was she excited. She'd have done anything for that boy." She dragged her chair closer to Elsie and whispered, "At lunch, he told her to meet him in the bathroom. The boy's bathroom. Like a fool, she did. I've taught her better than that."

Elsie blinked and swallowed back her response.

"He brung two friends with him. They wanted to see her titties. Little thing didn't hardly have nothing to show back then, but Carlos talked her into it."

"Oh Lord."

"Yes, ma'am. Then they wanted a feel, but she said only the one boy could, that Carlos, but they grabbed her and done felt her up anyway." Donita sat back. "And then a teacher come in and Charlene told."

Elsie shook her head sorrowfully. It was a classic scenario, a typical experience of a child who suffered abuse at home.

"Donita, she was a victim, actually," she said slowly. "She was under the age of consent, but she didn't go along, regardless; she said no, and they forced themselves on her. If a teacher can substantiate this, that's great. Why did the defense attorney say she was in trouble for it? That she lied?"

Donita looked away. "I don't know. Don't remember. I ain't never spent much time up at school."

Elsie pulled a piece of paper from her file and made rapid notes, summarizing what Donita had just told her. She would work with Charlene, prepare her for the cross-exam, and have the girl ready to explain exactly what transpired. She would explain to Charlene that she'd been on the receiving end of unwarranted sexual attention. Elsie knew the jury would buy it, if she played her cards right. Maybe.

Putting her pen and paper away, she said, "Well, I better get going." She bent over and hoisted one of the boxes of Taney's belongings, balancing her file on top. Donita led her out of the apartment to the front of the building and held the door open for her. It would have required four trips, but when Elsie returned to the kitchen for the third box, Donita offered to help, and carried the last box herself.

Meanwhile, Roy Mayfield remained on the couch, smoking. As they passed him the final time, Donita said,

"You keep an eye on Tiffany. I'm going out with the pros-ecutor for a minute."

He propped his feet up on the couch. With a grin, he said, "You bet. I'll stick to her like glue."

After the last of the boxes were loaded in her car, Elsie slammed the trunk down and turned to say goodbye. Donita lingered, leaning against the car.

"Is everything all right?" Elsie asked.

"Yeah, fine."

She persisted, "What about the girls? Are they okay?"

"Yeah, they're okay. Better than ever. We're going to have a good family now. There's good times ahead." Donita drummed her fingers against the car door, tap-ping out a rhythmic beat. She seemed preoccupied.

"Were they upset after the preliminary hearing? Did they understand what was happening?"

"Sure. You explained it real good. They was glad to get it over with, though. Hey, what do you think about Roy?"

Elsie stared blankly for a moment, until she associated the name with the man on Donita's couch.

"What, Donita, you mean your friend?" Josh Nixon's triumphant chuckle sounded in her imagination. "Is he a neighbor?"

"Not exactly."

"He's not your boyfriend or anything, right? Because you're still legally married, and it could give the defense attorney ammo to use against the state."

"Right. Hey, how about giving me a ride? I got to get

to the Lo-Cut market. It ain't that far, but it's awful cold out. And slick."

Hell, hell, hell. She would never get back to the office at this rate. "What about Tiffany?"

"Oh, she'll be fine with Roy. She knows him real good."

Donita ran back into the house for her purse. As Elsie waited, she glanced up and caught a glimpse of movement in a second-story window of the house. Startled, she squinted up at the figure, trying to see through the dirty pane of glass. It was Tiffany, and Elsie thought she saw a fearful look as the child pressed her face and small hands against the window and looked down at her. Elsie lifted her hand in a tentative greeting, but the gesture was aborted as Donita bustled down the sidewalk, purse in hand.

When she tugged at Elsie's elbow and offering to show her the short cut to the store, Elsie looked at her with a troubled expression. "Let's go in and get Tiffany," she urged. "We can bring her."

"No, let's get going. She's fine."

"I'd feel better if she came along with us."

Donita gave her an indignant look. "She's sick. You seen that. Why would I drag her out in the cold?"

Juggling her nagging fear for Tiffany against her reluctance to offend Donita, Elsie ventured, "After all she's been through, Donita, I think it's best that you keep her close, that's all. You shouldn't leave her in the care of a strange man."

Donita's eyes were hard as agates as she focused on Elsie. "Roy ain't no stranger. He's the best friend we got."

Her mouth formed a thin line. She looked down at the patchy ice covering on the street, shaking her head. "I ain't about to sashay in there and pull Tiffany out of that house. What would Roy think? It would look like I don't think he's fit to be around my girls."

Elsie opened her mouth to speak, but Donita cut her off. "You ain't her mama. That's me."

"I know," Elsie said, and fell silent.

It's not my call, she thought, unlocking the car with her key-chain remote. But something dark tickled the back of her mind, something dark and disturbing.

While they drove to the grocery, they sat in silence until Elsie asked why Tiffany was home sick.

"Little thing has the earache. She's got fever, so I kept her home with me today."

"That's too bad. Has she been to the doctor?"

Donita looked at her with wry disbelief. "We're Medicaid. Where we gonna go? I could stand in line at the downtown clinic, but that's pretty hard on a sick kid."

Chastened, Elsie held her tongue. Apparently, she was way too free with parenting advice this morning.

"I've got a couple tricks, though. I blew smoke in her ear; that always helps. I'm gonna get some eggs at the Lo-Cut, so I can boil one and wrap it in a towel, and that will feel good against a sore ear."

When Elsie pulled into the parking lot of the grocery, Donita invited her to come inside while she shopped. She just needed a couple of things, she said, and wondered aloud whether Elsie could provide a ride home. Sighing, Elsie agreed.

Finally, after dropping Donita back home, she headed for the police department. She pulled her phone from her purse to give Ashlock a heads-up: she could meet him at the P.D. and watch as he combed the contents of the boxes. It would be like a treasure hunt, she thought, her excitement mounting.

It wasn't yet noon, so she expected to catch him before he went to lunch. Her hopes sank when Patsy answered the phone and informed her that he was out.

"Out to lunch?"

"Out for two days, honey. It's that police conference at the Lake of the Ozarks. We won't see him until Wednesday."

"Oh," Elsie said in disappointment.

"Do you need me to get a message to him?"

"No," Elsie said, "no, I'll just talk to him when he gets back."

"Do you have his cell number?"

"Yeah, I've got it. Patsy, tell him I called when he checks in, okay? About the Taney case."

Nearing the police station, she had second thoughts about delivering the boxes to the P.D. Without Ashlock to examine and catalogue the contents, she knew that the evidence would end up in a dusty corner of the property room. She was seized by a fear that the evidence would be abandoned, forgotten, possibly misplaced or lost.

Sometimes, evidence that went into the property room was never seen again. One of her drug cases had to be reduced to a misdemeanor because the evidence mysteriously disappeared. When she reduced the drug charge, Madeleine had thrown a fit, as if the missing evidence was her fault.

She could prevail upon another officer to examine the evidence, but that didn't suit her. She only trusted Ashlock to do it right. No one but Ashlock would touch those boxes, she resolved.

Ashlock or her.

She could take the boxes up to her office, she thought, and go through them herself. Since Donita had handed them over to her, she was already a part of the chain of custody. She had secured evidence in her office before; she could lock it up tight.

Elsie felt a rush of enthusiasm as she hunted for a parking spot at the courthouse, wondering what the boxes contained. They might reveal nothing, nothing but junk. But they might hold a piece of the puzzle; something that would strengthen her case.

Chapter Twenty

THE TRASH CAN in Elsie's office was stationed between the four boxes from the Taney apartment. She squatted beside the boxes, removing the dirty garments and possessions one by one and shaking them over the wastebasket in an attempt to remove any vermin they contained. She worked her way through the first two boxes, accumulating a collection of dead cockroaches.

Ed Montee, of the janitorial staff, stuck his head in her office door.

"Heard you needed some help hauling boxes of evidence."

"Well I did, but when I couldn't find anyone I borrowed a dolly and brought them up myself."

"Okay," he said. Ed was a squat middle-aged man, and generally helpful. "I guess you don't need me, then."

"Nope," Elsie said as she continued shaking bugs into the wastebasket.

"What's that you're doing there?"

"I'm trying to clean out these boxes. They're full of dead cockroaches."

Ed scratched his head and walked over to take a look into the boxes of evidence. "There could be eggs in there. Cockroach can lay fifty eggs at a time. Some types can. You could have the place crawling if you don't watch out. You better let me burn those in the incinerator."

"Tell you what, Ed," Elsie said, maintaining a friendly tone as she rose and walked to the door, hoping he would take the hint and follow. She was glad to change her position; her knees were killing her, and the cheap nylon carpet had imprinted its pattern into her flesh. "Let me go through these boxes and see if anything valuable is in here. Then we'll figure out what to do with this stuff."

Ed followed her into the hallway outside her office door, but he was shaking his head in disgust. "I'm going to have to tell the county commissioners' office what you're up to, because we could have an infestation."

"Whatever you need to do." Elsie watched him walk away.

She needed a Diet Coke. She locked her office up so she could go grab a fountain drink from the coffee shop. When she came back, she decided to check her e-mail before returning to the vermin-filled boxes.

An e-mail from Noah was in her in-box. The message was short: *Can I come by tonight?* After glancing at the weekly calendar on her desk, Elsie typed *Sure* and sent it. She silently warned the computer screen that he better be in a good mood when he showed up. If he arrived with an attitude, she swore she would kick his ass out. Kick him out for good. Maybe.

Bree's footsteps sounded in the hallway outside. She stopped in the doorway of Elsie's office, gasping for breath.

"I've got exactly seven minutes to get to Taylor's school program," she said. "You still covering for me in Judge Carter's court?"

Elsie stood and took the files that Bree handed over to her. "I'll head right up there."

After the case load in Carter's division was exhausted, Elsie hurried back to her office, half afraid Ed Montee might have snatched the boxes before she had a chance to see what they contained.

Settled in her chair, she gingerly picked up a bundle and shook it out; it was a pair of Taney's dirty pants. She checked the pockets: nothing of interest. She sorted through a handful of overdue bills and a crumpled Bass Pro advertisement with some camping gear circled in pencil. It wasn't what she had hoped for.

Starting to feel discouraged, she sorted through JoLee's belongings in the third box. Beneath a collection of mildewed clothes and a few used-up dollar store cosmetics, she spied a small stack of cards. She picked them up and examined them, one by one. A birthday card, then a baby card containing a two dollar bill. The third card was a valentine.

Elsie handled it with care. A fuzzy red rose decorated the front of the card. She opened it gingerly; sure enough, a smashed reddish-brown cockroach was splayed inside.

After knocking it into the trash can with a decided shake, she read the card: it had a conventional sentiment, a printed jingle in fancy script, declaring true love.

A handwritten note was scrawled at the bottom. It read:

DON'T BE MAD what me and Char do don't mean nothing your my girl

"Oh my God," Elsie said aloud. She held the card gently, almost reverently. Opening a drawer in her desk, she rummaged for a plastic Baggie. Before she slipped the card inside, she opened it and read it again. Charlene, she thought, you are officially redeemed. With care, she locked the bag in her desk. It would go to the Barton P.D. tomorrow, to undergo handwriting and fingerprint analysis.

By the time she discovered the valentine in the third box, the sky outside had long been dark. The office was quiet as death; all of her coworkers had headed home. She decided to pack it up. A final examination of the first three boxes she'd dragged from the Taney apartment revealed no further evidence, just old clothes and trash. A collection of paper grocery bags in one, dirty shoes without mates in another, and in the last, a stiff mouse so long dead that it didn't stink.

The fourth box was as yet untouched, and she would go through it soon, but not tonight. She pushed it in the corner of her office and prayed that no cockroach eggs would hatch. She set out the other three boxes for the janitorial staff to dispose of. Ed would be glad to be rid of three-quarters of the vermin control danger, anyhow.

As she walked to her car, Elsie considered her evening plans. Since Noah was dropping by, pizza sounded practical. On her way home she dashed into a Jiffy Go to pick up a six-pack of Corona. Noah was generally more fun if she was drinking.

She made the pizza call as soon as she hit her apartment, took a quick shower, and sprayed her neck and wrists with cologne. There was always a chance that the visit would be a happy one.

After pulling on a clean sweater and a pair of jeans, she heard a knock at the door: the pizza. She tipped the delivery man and set the box in the kitchen. Within minutes she heard a knock at the door again.

Elsie checked through the peephole; it was Noah. He was off duty, wearing jeans and his leather jacket. She opened the door and he kissed her, a casual hello kiss.

"How are you?"

"Pretty good," she said. "Another crazy day. Would you like a beer?"

"Sure," he said. He took off his jacket and tossed it on a chair. His T-shirt revealed his magnificent arms. Lord, Lord, he looks like a Greek statue, she thought.

"I ordered a pizza, too. Would you like some?"

"Yeah, great," he said. He followed her into the kitchen, and Elsie opened two bottles of beer and put slices of pepperoni pizza on plates. She grabbed some paper napkins and they sat at her kitchen table.

"Hand tossed," she said.

"This is great," Noah said. "The high point of my day, I kid you not. What were you up to today?"

She launched into a description of her visit to the Taney apartment and the boxes she had taken to her office. Excitement crept into her voice as she told him about the valentine and the message.

"Yeah, that's pretty cool," he said. His hand wandered under the table; she felt its warm pressure on her leg.

Elsie wanted more of a reaction. Noah was also in law enforcement; how could he sound so casual about her evidentiary find?

"Pretty cool?" she repeated. "It's a fucking break-through. I'm going to nail him. Don't you care?"

"Elsie, don't jump on me the minute I walk through the door. You think I don't care about nailing criminals? I'm the one on patrol, doing the grunt work. And now I've got to get into a new schedule. I'm going on night shift next week."

She felt a twinge of remorse; she wasn't the only one who carried a burden at work. "How will that be?"

"It will be hell till I get used to it. It messes up your sleep routine, messes your body up, really. Then just about when you get in the swing of it, they switch you back to days."

"I know you all alternate," she said. "I bet that's rough."

"Yeah, it's supposed to be fair. But it just keeps every-body messed up all of the time."

He took her hand and turned it over on the tabletop,

running his fingers lightly over the lines of her palm. It tingled, giving such a pleasurable sensation that she visibly relaxed.

"That feels good," she said with a sigh of pleasure. "If I get you more pizza, will you do it again?"

"No more pizza; I'm good." He slapped his belly. "Don't want to get fat."

"That's not likely," she said, unhappily registering that he'd worked body fat into the conversation. Unable to stop herself, she blurted in a rush, "Do you think I'm attractive?"

He leaned away with a bemused look. "What the fuck?"

Blushing, Elsie fortified herself with a swig of beer. "You're always talking about getting fat, and eating salad, and exercise. Do you find me appealing? Physically?"

"Hell yeah. Of course. Where's this coming from?"

Elsie wondered the same thing, now ashamed that she was showing her belly in such a fashion. "I just wondered. If maybe you prefer someone little. Petite. Like Paige."

Noah rolled his eyes. "Didn't I tell you not to worry about her? She's just a friend."

Trying to suppress a vision of Noah and Paige bent over the pool table, Elsie asked a question that had been eating at her: "Have you ever slept with her?"

He cursed under his breath and looked away. When he looked back, he gave her a rueful half smile. "Is this the way this is going down? Do you want me to ask you who all you've slept with?"

His response did nothing to help allay the jealousy that nagged at her; but he was right, She was not interested in a game of True Confessions. "I guess I get your point."

"Now you're being reasonable," he said, his voice becoming warm again. "You know I think you're hot. And it doesn't matter what happened before we met. What's important is what we've got now." He tipped back in his chair. "Think I could have another one of those beers?"

"Sure," she said, and she jumped up to get one from the refrigerator. When she handed it to him, he pulled her down on his lap and kissed her, lingeringly this time. "Everything straight now?" he asked.

"Yeah, I think so," she replied as she ran her fingers down the contour of his arm.

He pulled her close and whispered, "You're the one I want."

As she nestled up to him, she couldn't help wondering, What do I want?

But that train of thought stopped when he unzipped her jeans. While he teased her with his hand in her pants, she remembered what she liked about him. When they stood to move into the bedroom, he picked her up and carried her inside. They fell into bed, pulling at each other's clothes, and Elsie was finally able to shut her thoughts down and lose herself in Noah's embrace.

When they were done, he rolled over on his back.

She watched him as he lay there after a gymnastic round of lovemaking, his chest rising and falling as his breathing returned to normal. Maybe she was too hard on Noah. "Do you want to sleep here?" she asked, kissing his bare shoulder.

"Oh, honey, that's sweet," he said. "But I'd just be in your way tomorrow. You'll be getting to the office, and I'm working, too." He groaned and hauled himself out of bed. "I'd better get going."

She looked at her clock. It was 10:42. "Well, okay. It was nice to see you."

She watched him as he quickly dressed. Then she got out of bed and said, "Just a sec, I'll get my robe and walk you to the door." Feeling resentful of his abrupt departure, she added, "You better hurry. Paige is probably waiting at the pool hall."

He smacked her on her bottom, hard, and said, "I don't want to hear any more about that." She gasped and took a step back.

He took her by the waist and pulled her back to him. "Hey, honey, I'm just fooling. Just kidding around." He kissed her ear and whispered, "Gotta teach you to behave."

"That's a joke?"

He kissed her and gave her a little squeeze. "See you soon," he said. He left while she was putting on her robe. She went into the living room after he was gone and turned the dead-bolt lock.

When she went back to the bedroom she inspected her stinging behind in the mirror and saw a red hand print. She was furious. Was that really some kind of joke? Or was he a Stanley Kowalski throwback: a guy who'd smack a girl on the butt to show he was the boss of her?

"Son of a bitch," she said out loud.

Chapter Twenty-One

KRISTY TANEY WALKED with her head bent against the wind as she made her way home on High Street. Tiffany followed a couple of paces behind, stumbling a little in her big coat. As Kristy neared the peeling white house, Charlene jumped from behind a ragged bush and grabbed her.

"Gotcha," Charlene hissed.

"Stop it," Kristy said, twisting away from Charlene's grip on her arm. "That's creepy."

Charlene laughed, but kept her hold on Kristy. "Come on. This way."

"No. It's cold. I'm going home. I got homework." Kristy tried to free herself from her sister's grip, kicking at Charlene's legs.

"Don't go in there. Mama's out."

"I got a key." Kristy fumbled in her coat pocket and pulled out a key, fastened to the inside of the pocket by a safety pin. "I can let myself in."

Tiffany stood in the street, hanging back. Charlene released Kristy from her grasp. Walking over to Tiffany, she knelt and gave her a hug. Over the child's head she told Kristy, "Fine, then. Do what you want. But you ain't gone be alone, Miss Goody Shoes."

Kristy paused, key in hand. "Is he in there?"

"Yep."

Charlene whispered something into Tiffany's ear that made the little girl smile. Taking her hand, Charlene said, "Let's run."

The two of them ran down the street, away from the house. Loose gravel flew underfoot as they dodged the muddy puddles in the road.

After a moment, Kristy followed. "Wait!" she called in a fierce whisper. "Hold up!"

At the end up of the block, Charlene paused and looked back, with Tiffany clutching her hand. Kristy joined them, panting.

"Where you going?" Kristy asked.

"Gas station."

"How come?"

"Get candy and pop."

Kristy scoffed. "What with? You ain't got no money."

"Oh yes I do."

"Oh no you don't."

Charlene crossed the street with a swagger, pulling Tiffany along with her. Kristy looked deliberately to the left and right before crossing, then hurried to join them.

"You ain't got no money," Kristy insisted when she caught up to them.

"Fine. Think what you want."

After a moment's silence Kristy said, "You lie. You lie all the time. Everybody says."

Charlene didn't respond. She lifted her chin and walked faster, dragging Tiffany along.

They turned a corner. The dowdy convenience store with its two gas pumps came into view. A plastic grocery bag shrouded one of the gas nozzles with a hand-printed sign reading: NO GAS.

Kristy tugged the back of Charlene's jacket. "Okay, then, let me see."

Charlene shook her head. Eyes narrowed, she said to Kristy, "Take it back."

"What?"

"Take it back."

Kristy sighed and looked at her feet; she was standing in an oily spot on the parking lot, so she shifted to the side a step. "I take it back. You ain't either."

"Ain't what?"

"A liar."

Tiffany watched her sisters' exchange anxiously, her lips pressed together in an unhappy line. She reached out and took Kristy's wrist with her free hand. Kristy shook her off.

"Your fingers is freezing, Tiffany. Hey, Charlene," and her voice took a wheedling tone, "let me see."

Charlene glanced around, taking care to look over her shoulder. She dug into the pocket of her thin nylon jacket and pulled out a handful of change.

Kristy gasped, and Tiffany covered her mouth with

her arm. "God," Kristy whispered, "where'd you get all that?"

"From my teacher."

"Huh? How'd that happen?"

"They made me sit at detention table at lunch."

"How come?"

"We had a test today. I told the teacher I didn't have no pen, and she said it was my third strike. I'd like to give her three strikes. Stuck-up bitch."

"They give you money for sitting at detention table?"

"Ha ha. Very funny. No. But the detention teacher sent us back to class before the English class got back from lunch. So I figured I'd just get a pen out of her desk. Smart, right?"

Kristy looked suspicious. "And?"

"And when I opened the desk drawer, she had like a million dollars in quarters in there. I didn't stop to think, just grabbed some."

"That's stealing."

"Serves her right." Charlene clutched the coins in her fist and shoved them back into her pocket. "She treats me like shit. Thinks she's better than me."

She turned on her heel and marched toward the convenience store entrance, then stopped short. "I was so flipped out by the money, I forgot to take her pen. Guess I can buy one now, if I feel like it."

Inside the warm store, Kristy trailed her sisters with a troubled expression. "You gonna get caught."

"Not me," Charlene said. "I'm gonna eat the evidence."

She and Tiffany roamed the snack aisle. Charlene ran her fingers over the candy bars, picked up the Snickers and the Butterfinger and hefted them in her hands, assessing the size and weight. She picked up a beef jerky stick and sniffed it, then shook it at Tiffany and said, "Them is good."

Tiffany nodded sagely and followed along.

Kristy picked up a can of barbecue-flavored Pringles and looked at it with longing, but set it back down.

The clerk at the counter—a gaunt woman in her thirties with sallow skin and a sparse head of dyed blond hair—eyed the girls with a frown. "You'uns buying?"

"Yeah, we are. We're just taking our time."

Charlene stepped over to the refrigerated drink display. To her sisters, she said, "Root beer or Dr Pepper?"

"Dr Pepper," Kristy cried, in spite of herself.

Charlene nodded with satisfaction, and plucked a twenty-ounce plastic bottle from the rack. "We can share this," she said.

With Tiffany and Kristy at her heels, she selected a Slim Jim beef stick, a package of Skittles, and, with a glance at Kristy, the can of Pringles.

As Charlene counted out the change on the counter, the clerk tried to make amends.

"I didn't mean to ride you, sweetie. It's just that you would not believe how many people come in here to rip me off." Smiling, the clerk revealed a mouthful of jacked-up teeth, with molars missing on both sides.

"Yeah?" said Charlene as Tiffany fingered the energy shots by the cash register.

"Mercy, yes. And kids. I hate to say it. Kids stealing, too."

Charlene shook her head. "That's a sight. Don't they know? It's a sin to steal."

"And then who ends up in trouble over it? Me. Well. You'uns have a good day. Stay warm and take care of that little bitty thing."

"Yep, we will."

Charlene twisted the cap off the Dr Pepper and handed it first to Tiffany, who raised it to her lips for a greedy swallow.

"I'm taking care of this Little Bit. Someday soon, I'm gonna get my own place so she can be with me. Nothing's going to happen to her if I can help it."

With a dubious expression, Kristy popped the top off the Pringles can. "How you gonna move out? You ain't but fifteen years old."

Charlene lifted her chin, smirking at Kristy. "I got plans. I got somebody to get me out."

"Who?" Kristy asked, but Charlene just shrugged in reply.

Kristy turned to Tiffany. "Quit hogging that pop. It's my turn."

Tiffany wiped the Dr Pepper off her chin with her coat sleeve. "Lord, that's good," she whispered.

Chapter Twenty-Two

JUDGE CARTER DECLARED a five minute recess and left the bench, and Elsie flung herself to the door. She'd juggled a furious docket in court that morning with cases called one after another, and the judge had not seen fit to take a break. Clearly, he did not care to use the bathroom facility, but she desperately needed to go. She ran around the rotunda to the third floor women's room, half afraid she wouldn't make it on time.

She heard footsteps echoing behind her and thought someone might be calling her name, but she didn't pause. She tore through the door and into one of the pink metal stalls, tremendously thankful that there had been no line.

Afterward, washing her hands at the restroom sink, Elsie checked her hair in the mirror and sighed. She looked pretty doggone terrible, she thought, but she tried to be philosophical about it. It was a Wednesday, and she'd overslept, and so had done a slapdash job of getting ready. She'd twisted her hair into a claw comb, thrown on an old suit of some drab permapress fabric, and run out the door with a naked face. But she was only doing garden-variety associate court business today, and didn't expect to be much in the public eye. She also didn't anticipate seeing Noah, fortunately. He might be foolhardy enough to comment on her appearance.

When she exited the bathroom, Josh Nixon was waiting for her.

"Hey, didn't you hear me calling you?" he asked.

"Sorry," she replied. "I was trying to get to the restroom before I peed my pants."

He looked somewhat taken aback. "Okay. No problem. Well, I need to talk to you about discovery in the Taney case."

She checked her watch. The time for the recess was nearly up. "Sure. I only have a minute, though. We're in recess in Associate Division 3."

With a nod, he said pleasantly, "You look really nice today."

She stared at him with disbelief. She had checked her miserable reflection a half minute earlier, and it wasn't at all nice. She wondered whether he was mocking her. Or working her.

Hastily, he amended, "I like your suit. It's got a nice shape. Cut."

She laughed out loud, in spite of herself, but her antennas were buzzing. This was a marked change from their combative relationship. It might be a trick, some new strategy. But two could play that game. With a toothy grin, she said in rejoinder, "Your new haircut looks great."

Running his hand through his unshorn locks, he said, "I haven't cut it in a while."

"Really?"

Giving her a look of reproach, he said, "Cheap shot."

Despite her skepticism, Elsie warmed to him a notch. She was amenable to friendly fencing with Nixon. As long as it didn't undermine her case, it made life easier to regard the defense attorney as a friend rather than a foe. She leaned against the rotunda railing, willing to prolong the conversation, until Judge Carter's bailiff stuck his head out the courtroom door and bellowed, "Elsie Arnold, EL-seee Arnold, you're wanted in Associate Division 3."

As she hurried back in the direction of Judge Carter's courtroom, she asked Josh whether he'd picked up his discovery yet. She had watched Nedra reproduce the file, so she knew it was ready for him.

"Yeah," he said. "Not much to it. I wondered if you were holding out on me. There's no statement from Al. Is he still out of pocket?"

"Yeah. Terribly inconvenient."

"Terribly *suspicious*, I'd say. So the stuff in that file is all you've got."

"About that," she began, and told him about the boxes from the Taney household. "I wasn't sure about it from a discovery angle, whether there would be anything in that box I could use, honestly. It's mostly trash and dirty clothes. But I found what looks like an admission. I'm going to need handwriting samples from your client so that the handwriting guy at Barton P.D. can compare them to the handwriting on the card."

"What exactly is it that you found?"

"It's a valentine. I think we can prove that it's an admission of sorts."

"What does it say?"

"You'll need to see it. I'll show it to you."

"That's a coincidence. I've got something to show you, too." He opened his briefcase, but she waved him away.

"I'm tied up in court right now." She opened the courtroom door, then stopped and called to his retreating back. "Stop by my office at noon and you can see. Hey, Josh, that's not all: I think I'm going to have some more witness statements this week in the Taney case."

He swung around and looked at her quizzically. "When are you going to finish your investigation?"

Good question, she thought, but she didn't respond. As the door swung shut, she heard him shout, "You're supposed to investigate *before* you file."

IT WAS PAST twelve when Judge Carter declared they could break for lunch. As Elsie hurried to her office to meet Josh, she passed Stacie, eating a Banquet microwave enchilada at her desk.

"That smells pretty good," she said as she walked by.

"Hey, Elsie."

"What?"

"There's a witness trying to get in touch with you."

Elsie paused and turned to face the receptionist, who was sawing the tortilla with a flimsy plastic fork. "Who?" she asked.

"Some guy."

"What name?"

"Didn't leave a name."

"What case?"

"Didn't say."

"That's helpful."

"Are you trying to be sarcastic?" Stacie asked with a frown.

Elsie shook her head as she walked through the doorway that led to the long hall of offices. Stacie called after her, "He said to tell you he called. And don't worry about missing him, because he'll call back."

When Elsie reached her office, Josh was waiting outside the door. She turned the key in the lock and pointed out the remaining box of Taney's effects.

"So you found your big admissions in there?" he asked.

"Pretty much."

"Aren't you making yourself a witness by supplying all this do-it-yourself investigation?"

She flipped open a file on her desk and removed stapled pages bearing a photostatic copy of the valentine. Handing it over to him, she said, "Don't give me a hard time."

"Yeah. When can I have total access to this exhibit? I want to see the original. This is unsigned. My client probably never saw it before."

"Hmm." She put on her bargaining face. "If I can get the handwriting samples I need from Taney, you can have access by the end of the week."

"Okay," he said, and they stood up. "Nice flowers."

They both looked at the bouquet sitting on the corner of her desk, a dozen yellow roses arranged with lush greenery in a big glass vase.

"Why, thank you."

"From someone at the jail?"

She tried to keep a straight face. "Oh, shut up."

He dug into his briefcase and pulled out a couple sheets of paper. "Told you I've got something for you. We'll take it up Friday morning." He tossed them on her desk.

She scanned the documents as he refastened the buckle on his bag. No surprise, she thought. He'd filed Taney's Motion to Reduce Bond and called it up for hearing before Judge Rountree on Friday. Apparently Taney wanted to be released from jail pending trial.

"When pigs fly," she said, sitting at her desk.

"How's little Miss Charlene?"

Elsie grew wary. "Fine. I guess."

"Making lots of nice friends at school?"

Her eyes narrowed. Maybe she didn't like Josh Nixon after all. "You've got Charlene all wrong. If you try to beat her up on the stand, I'll make you look like the bad guy."

"You think? She's got quite a reputation."

"That school thing didn't go down like you think. She's a victim."

He laughed incredulously. "Where do you get your information? She recanted. She lied. She *admitted* it."

Elsie swallowed, silent for once.

"That's not all. There's more."

"What?" she asked.

"It's a bombshell."

"What kind?"

"About your witness."

"Who?"

"Mom," he answered with a sardonic grin. "The lovely Donita."

"Why can't you leave that poor woman alone?"

"You will find that your witness isn't exactly Miss Lily White. You'll see."

"Oh, fine. Smear the mother next. You're like a broken record."

"I've got a subpoena." He pulled a pink subpoena from the file folder he was holding and dangled it in front of her. Suspicious, Elsie lunged from her chair and made a grab for it, but he stuffed it in his pocket.

"What the hell?" she snapped. "If you had anything, you'd come out with it. You're bluffing."

In a huff, she sat back down.

"As it turns out," Nixon said, "Donita is a business-woman. An entrepreneur. She's in manufacturing."

Elsie looked blank.

"Can't guess?" he asked.

She shook her head.

"Meth. Hillbilly heroin."

Her jaw dropped like a ventriloquist's dummy.

Nixon continued, "Donita's in the methamphetamine manufacturing line. I'm subpoenaing the pharmacy records of her ephedrine purchases. Because you know what they're going to show?"

Elsie was speechless. Nixon prepared to leave, but he was clearly enjoying himself. Before he walked out, he paused and said, "You ever see anyone that skinny who *wasn't* on meth? Hell, this ain't California."

Chapter Twenty-Three

As soon as Nixon cleared the doorway, Elsie grabbed the office phone, dialing Ashlock's cell phone so fast that she pushed the wrong numbers and was rewarded by the blare of the misdial tone.

"Fuck," she whispered, dialing again, squeezing her eyes shut as it rang. "Fuckfuckfuck."

"What is this?" Ashlock demanded through the receiver.

"Oh Lordamighty, Ashlock, it's me. How do we get the information on pseudoephedrine purchases?"

"Elsie? Why do you need it?"

"Josh Nixon is calling Donita Taney a drug lord now. He says she's making meth. So we've got to try to prove the negative."

Ashlock's voice was calm, even. "I can get the records. If she's been buying over-the-counter ephedrine, we can track it. If she hasn't, her name won't come up."

There was a moment of silence, which was broken by Ashlock's observation: "She is awful skinny."

"Goddamn it, I know she's skinny. Maybe she's got a fast metabolism," she said irritably, though Elsie doubted that such a condition existed. She rubbed her eyes while she held the phone. "Do you think it's possible?"

"Hey, we're the capital," he said.

"I know. I read that."

"Missouri is the meth capital of the United States."

"Yep."

"We're number one."

She laughed a little, despite her anxiety. "My mom always says Missouri is number one. Now I can tell her she's right."

Ashlock suggested they ask Donita up front. He was taking JoLee's statement at four and could bring Donita in as well to see what she had to say.

"I want to be there. Where can I meet you?" Elsie knew that JoLee's testimony could be vitally important, and she was desperate to hear a denial from Donita regarding the meth accusation.

"I'll interrogate her at the department. Detective Division."

"Okay, I'll come on over. Four o'clock?"

"Yep."

"See you then."

She hung up and stared at the roses on her desk. When the florist delivered them to the front office, there was a buzz of excitement. Stacie had called her to the reception area to receive them, and she felt a thrill of pleasure as she pulled the little florist card from its envelope amidst the green foliage. The card was printed with script that read: THINKING OF YOU. Under the script was scrawled, *Love ya! Noah.*

Elsie had borne the flowers back to her office like a trophy; people expected that. But now, as she set the bouquet on the corner of her desk, she regarded it with a jaded eye. In her experience, flowers signified three things: love, lust, or a guilty conscience. Was Noah apologizing for his high-handed departure smack the other night? Or was it something else?

Her reverie was interrupted when Bree walked in.

"Got a minute?" she asked.

"Sure."

Bree shut the door before she sat down. Elsie eyed her with surprise. "Closed door conference, huh? This must be super secret. What's cooking?"

"I just overheard something pretty interesting."

"What?"

"Madeleine tried to pull Ashlock off the Taney case."

Elsie shook her head. "No, Bree, that can't be right. He's still on the case. He's taking a witness statement today."

"That's what makes it such a good story." Bree didn't try to disguise her glee. "She told him that she needed his help on the trial she's got coming up; she told him to take himself off the Taney case, to hand it off to someone else. She said—this is a quote, 'Taney is not a priority.'"

"Backstabber." Elsie snatched up a pen from her desk and twisted it, fighting the urge to confront Madeleine. "So what happened then?"

"He said he was seeing Taney through to the end. That Madeleine didn't make the case assignments at the Barton P.D."

"I bet that blew her away," Elsie said with awe. "Where did you hear this?"

"The chief assistant was talking about it in Rountree's courtroom, giving a friend of his the blow by blow. I was in the jury room, looking up a statute, so they thought they were alone. I was quiet as the tomb."

"Bet it absolutely curled her hair. Wouldn't you have loved to see her face?"

"I'll just have to imagine it," Bree said, rising from her chair with a blissful sigh. "Guess old Madeleine learned that Detective Ashlock won't be kicking our Elsie to the curb." She reached out and touched the petals of the roses on Elsie's desk as she turned to go.

FOUR O'CLOCK FOUND Elsie at the police department. She hurried up the short flight of stairs to the Detective Division on the second floor, eager to finally get a look at JoLee. Patsy, manning the front desk at the investigative unit, pointed toward the interrogation room in the northeast corner. Elsie headed to the door and knocked.

Ashlock let her in. A girlish looking woman in her mid-twenties sat quietly at a metal table with her hands clenched in her lap, out of sight.

Elsie glanced at Ashlock. "Will we be taking two statements?" she asked.

He returned the look. "A minor complication with the other statement. I'll explain later." She nodded.

"JoLee," he said, "this is Elsie Arnold. She's handling the case against Kris Taney."

"I know who she is." The woman fixed a hostile eye on Elsie. She returned the gaze, surprised to observe that JoLee was rather pretty, despite her Goodwill castoffs and ragged haircut. When JoLee brought a hand up to rub her eye, Elsie saw dark blue polish on fingernails that had been chewed painfully short.

She tried to sound friendly. "I'm really glad to meet you, JoLee," sitting down at the table across from her, a few feet from Ashlock. "Thanks for agreeing to talk to us today."

"I ain't agreed to talk to nobody," she said. Her eyes had a hunted look. "Is she going to read me my rights? You ain't read me my rights."

Ashlock spoke in a soothing tone. "JoLee, you're not a suspect. This is an interview for the investigation. We just want to talk to you, ask you about Kris Taney."

"Plus, this isn't custodial interrogation," Elsie blurted. Ashlock turned on her with a look and she shut up. Her mother had an old Missouri saying that Elsie now repeated to herself: *Jesse, who's robbing this train?* She needed to let Bob do his job.

Ashlock turned back to JoLee. "You don't mind if I record this, do you?" he asked in a voice that would melt butter while gesturing at the tabletop record. "I'm just doing it so there will be no chance, no way, anyone could put words in your mouth or claim you said something you didn't say."

"Like her?" JoLee demanded, jabbing a stubby blue-tipped finger in Elsie's direction.

Elsie opened her mouth to speak, but Ashlock laid a warning hand on her arm.

"Like anyone," he said in a soothing voice. He continued, "So I'm going to record this, right?" When JoLee didn't voice an objection, he turned on the machine.

Ashlock started the interview with some preliminary questions, which she answered readily enough: her name, age, address, education, occupation. So far she had not been asked to reveal anything damning, so her responses about failing to finish high school and intermittent employment in food service should have been easy to provide. Still, she seemed edgy. Elsie watched JoLee fidget with the zipper on her hoodie jacket, her leg restless under the table, her heel tapping on the floor in a continuous dance.

When Ashlock asked JoLee whether she knew Kris Taney, the process became choppy.

"Yeah."

"Yes, what?"

"I know him."

"Have you lived with him?" When she didn't respond, he added, "Under the same roof?"

JoLee didn't answer. She turned her head and studied the cinder-block wall, as if an answer could be found in its rough surface.

Ashlock came at the subject from another angle, and asked whether she had any children. After a moment's consideration, JoLee's demeanor relaxed.

"I got a little boy."

"How old is he?"

"Nine months."

"What's his name?"

"Kris."

"Who's the father?"

She fixed Ashlock with a defiant stare. She did not speak.

Patiently, he asked whether she knew Donita Taney. After a period of silence, JoLee nodded. Ashlock told her that she would have to speak, that the machine could not record a nod, and JoLee said, "Yes. I know Donita."

Ashlock followed up and asked her whether she had ever met Charlene, Kristy, or Tiffany. JoLee admitted that she had. He inquired whether she had ever been at their home on High Street in Barton. After a prolonged silence, during which JoLee stared at her lap as she ran the zipper up and down a dozen times, she allowed that she had been to the residence before.

"And I can tell you something about that Charlene," she added, looking up. "She's no good. She's a liar and a whore. Biggest slut in town."

"Tell us about that," Ashlock said smoothly.

JoLee gave him a sly look before she added, "Should've seen how she carried on with Al. You would've thought he was her boyfriend instead of her uncle. Said she could be a movie star." JoLee scoffed. "Yeah, right."

Elsie shifted in her chair, suddenly uncomfortable, anxious about things JoLee might reveal that the family had hidden thus far.

Warming to the topic, JoLee said, "I know Donita's been feeding you horseshit. That whole house is a pack of liars. It's an outfit, is what it is."

She fell silent, fiddling with her zipper. Ashlock waited for her to begin again. When she didn't, he resumed his questions: "Were you at the house in November—"

She cut him off. Looking straight into Ashlock's eyes, she said, "That Kristy plays like she's Miss Goody-goody, but she ain't. I swear. She's mean. I seen her knock the snot out of Tiffany before. Then lie about it."

As Elsie digested the statement, Ashlock asked, "Did Tiffany ever tell you anything about her relationship with her father?"

JoLee hooted in disbelief. Looking from Ashlock to Elsie and back again, she said incredulously, "Tiffany? Tell me anything? Ain't you seen her with your own eyes? Tiffany's a half-wit. Can't hardly talk."

The denouncement stirred something in Elsie, forcibly reminded of the silent child and her Barbie. She fought the urge to lash out at the woman sitting across from her.

Ashlock asked, "What is your relationship with Tiffany?"

"I ain't got no relationship with Tiffany. Or Kristy. Or Charlene. I wouldn't sit in the same room with that Charlene, if I didn't have to. She's the devil."

"Why do you say that?"

"Because she's a lying, stealing, dirty whore. With the filthiest mouth in town. If it wasn't for her daddy keeping her in line, she'd be in jail." JoLee caught herself. She froze and fell silent, looking fearful, as if she'd said too much. She cast her gaze down.

Trying to keep a neutral face, Elsie pondered JoLee's violent dislike of Charlene. It seemed an extreme reaction. But the only explanation followed from Kris Taney's valentine: Charlene was JoLee's sexual rival.

While JoLee sat, looking at her lap, Ashlock waited. The woman looked up again, a flash of inspiration in her eyes. "Donita ever tell you about the time she wore Charlene out with an extension cord?"

Elsie leaned back in her seat as far as she could, her throat tightening. The woman's voice had the ring of truth.

"Striped her up so bad, they had to keep her home from school for a week. She tell you about that?"

Frowning, Ashlock asked, "Did you witness the event? Personally?"

JoLee regarded him with a knowing smile. But when Ashlock pressed her to expound on her statement, JoLee shrugged, shook her head. "Nothing more to say."

Ashlock then asked whether Kris Taney had been present at the time.

No answer.

He asked whether she was Taney's girlfriend. She picked at her nails. When he asked whether she'd had sexual relations with Taney, she was nonresponsive.

"Does he whip you?" he asked.

Her head jerked up; JoLee looked at Ashlock with apprehension. Ashlock and Elsie saw that he'd touched a nerve. He pursued it.

"Is it true that he hits you when you talk back to him? Gives you a whipping?"

She started to shake, but did not speak.

"You don't have to put up with that kind of treatment," he said gently. "It's against the law, JoLee. A pretty young woman like you should have a good guy, somebody who treats you right."

Tears ran down JoLee's cheeks. She squeezed her eyes shut to stop them. When Ashlock offered her a Kleenex box, she knocked it away and dried her eyes with the back of her hand.

"You don't know what you're doing," she said finally in a grim voice. "You got no clue. Nobody hits me. Somebody's spreading lies."

"He's in jail, JoLee," Ashlock urged in a comforting tone. "He's locked up, behind bars. He's not going anywhere. Right, Ms. Arnold?"

"Right," said Elsie, trying not to think about the bond reduction motion on her desk.

Rigid, JoLee sat in her plastic chair, fists clenched, her voice shaky but determined. "You can't make me say nothing about him. You can beat my head in and I won't do it. Besides, I know the law. You can't make me say nothing. Not a word. I'll take the Fifth."

Ashlock played his trump card. "I know you love your baby, JoLee. Social Services lets you see him, what, once a week?"

She eyed him murderously. "Every other week," she spat.

"They were real encouraged at Social Services to hear that you were talking to us. They'll be taking it hard over there to hear you won't cooperate. Don't know what they'll think about that."

JoLee's face was mottled with suppressed rage. "Dirty stinking pig," she whispered. "Cheesedick cocksucker."

Ashlock pretended not to hear. "Well, if that's it, I'll get a patrolman to drive you back home. You think about it." He clicked off the tape recorder and departed abruptly.

The tension in the room was palpable. Elsie watched JoLee covertly as the woman stared into her lap while tears rolled down her face and dropped on her clothes, making little wet dots. Elsie was uncertain of her role in the proceedings, now that Ashlock had departed. Was the interview over, or was she supposed to worm some information out of JoLee?

The silence grew increasingly uncomfortable for Elsie. Finally, she was moved to ask: "JoLee, why won't you testify? Don't you want him locked up?"

JoLee regarded her with frank dislike. She said, "You don't know nothing about "He clicked the tape recorder off and departed abruptly love. You're so dumb."

Aside from a skeptical glance, Elsie didn't respond. When JoLee saw the expression, she scooted her chair back from the table, looking Elsie up and down.

"You think you're so smart, think you're hot shit. You ain't. You ain't no better than me."

The words sent a guilty shock through Elsie.

"You're dumber than a dog," JoLee hissed, but Elsie scarcely heard her. Noah's angry face flashed into her mind and she shuddered. The very idea that a parallel could exist between her and the woman across the table struck an uneasy chord; resolutely, she resisted it.

I'm nothing like you, Elsie thought. Nothing like you at all.

Chapter Twenty-Four

A UNIFORMED OFFICER reported to the interrogation room to escort JoLee back home. Elsie waited for Ashlock to return; when he didn't appear, she left the room in search of him. She felt a little put out with him for deserting her. When she spied him at the end of a corridor, in deep discussion with another detective, she called, "Hey, Ashlock!"

He swung around, a shocked expression on his face. Elsie jerked both palms up. "Where the hell did you go?" she hollered, in a tone of voice that she had not picked up at charm school.

"Quit shouting and come on over here," he said. "I've got someone I want to introduce you to."

She approached the men, still perturbed. "Sorry," she said. "But it was no picnic in there alone with Lady Macbeth."

Ashlock shook his head, struggling to suppress a

smile. When his companion gave him a quizzical look, Ashlock explained that they had just concluded an unsuccessful witness interview.

"The witness called Ash 'cheesedick,'" Elsie added.

"Thank you, Miss Arnold, for sharing that information with the lieutenant here. Elsie, do you know Lieutenant Tomlin? He works a lot of the property offenses."

She extended a hand. "We haven't met. Nice to know you. Any friend of Ashlock's is a friend of mine; those are the words I live by."

"Oh, I've seen you around," Tomlin said.

"Around the courthouse, I expect. Ash, when you're done, I need to talk with you."

"Yeah," Tomlin said with a look on his face that she could not mistake. "And I've seen you on the town, too. Weren't you getting drunk over at Noah Strong's place?"

Taken aback, Elsie said, "I don't know what you're talking about."

Tomlin insisted, "I know it was you—you and Strong. Getting drunk as a skunk, slopping liquor all over the place."

She could feel the color suffusing her face. Maybe she'd met Tomlin on New Year's Eve. Noah had a rowdy party at his place, and she'd celebrated with tequila shots. The night was pretty much a blank. Elsie answered, "Goodness sakes, I remember now. We were just acting silly." Ashlock was watching her with a keen eye, and it made her nervous.

Grinning, Tomlin went on, "You're a party girl. I heard you were knee walking at Baldknobbers."

Pulling herself to her full height, Elsie gave the lieutenant a cool stare, though she could feel her cheeks flush. Then she reached out and tapped Ashlock on the arm with her file. "I'll wait for you in the lobby," she said, turning on her heel and walking away.

Damn it to hell, she thought, wishing that the floor would open up and swallow her. It was too much to hope for, in a town the size of Barton, that her indiscretions would go unnoticed. She dodged into the first floor restroom to see if her blush was very obvious. A glimpse in the mirror confirmed her fears; she was positively scarlet. Fervently wishing she'd made time that morning to cover her complexion with makeup, she doused a paper towel with cold water and patted her face. It didn't help: rubbing her face only made it redder.

Examining herself in the mirror, she shook her head. Why did she do reckless things? The notion of the Barton police force comparing notes on her follies made her wince.

She left the restroom thinking dark thoughts, and collided with Detective Ashlock. He grabbed her to keep her from falling.

"Shit, Ashlock," Elsie squealed. Regaining her balance, she wheeled on him. "I can't believe you ratted me out. About Baldknobbers."

Ashlock shook his head. "You know me better than that. I wouldn't diss you, Elsie—I'm your biggest fan."

Marginally satisfied and unwilling to dwell on the topic, she asked about Donita. Ashlock said that when he stopped by the house on High Street and asked her to come to the P.D., she begged off, telling him she had to be home for the kids.

Elsie wanted to talk to Donita without delay; the meth allegation was bothering her. "I'll borrow trouble about this until it's resolved. I need to hear what her reaction is."

"You want to see her tonight?"

"If you don't mind."

"Well, if we're going to do this, I've got to get back upstairs first," he said. "Where's your car?"

"It's across the street at the courthouse."

"Want to drive to the Taneys' together?"

"No. I'll just meet you over there."

Ashlock headed back to the second floor and Elsie departed through the front door. As she buttoned up her coat against the cold, a squad car pulled up with a familiar driver at the wheel.

She walked up to the driver's side as the window rolled down. Raising a brow, Noah asked in an offhand tone, "Anything delivered to your office lately?"

She had resolved to mention her displeasure about his swat, but as she stood by the patrol car, she decided against starting an ugly conversation. After all, the flowers were probably an apology. "The roses are beautiful. Thanks."

"Glad you like them. I got the yellow ones, because of your hair." He jerked his head to the passenger side. "Take you for a ride, baby?"

"Sure. Take me across the street, to the courthouse." She walked around to the passenger side and got in the car.

The radio yammered information at them; Noah pressed the receiver with his right hand and responded, then said to her, "I've been looking all over the place for you. I tried to run you down at the courthouse, but they said you were at the Detective Division. I've been cruising around, waiting for you to come out."

"That's sweet. I've been sitting in on a witness statement with Bob Ashlock." As he pulled up to the side entrance, she said, "Ugh, I'm not ready to go back yet. Take me for a ride around the block?"

Nodding, he reached over and stroked her cheek. "You've got a pretty mouth," he observed, before returning his attention to handling the squad car.

Now, that's what I like to hear, Elsie thought, turning in the seat to face him. If he would make free with sweet talk, she could ride around with him all day long. She asked, "So what's your schedule this week?"

"I'm working from ten at night to seven in the morning, starting tomorrow. It's a hell of a deal. I'm going to be all messed up. I hate it, honey, but I don't know when we're going to get together."

"Well, hell. That's disappointing. Breeon's having a party Saturday, I was going to see if you wanted to go."

He frowned as he stared through the windshield. "Why is Breeon having a party? Doesn't she have a kid?"

"She had a jury trial set for Monday that just pled out, and she's throwing confetti in the air. Plus, her daughter will be at a weekend volleyball camp. She's ready to cut loose."

"Well, I can't go." His face wore a sulky look. "I might

not want to anyway. I don't think Breeon likes me too much."

Lightly, Elsie asked, "What makes you think that?"

"I don't know. She always gives me an attitude." He shifted in his seat and asked, "You sure you want to go?"

Incredulous, she replied, "Hell yeah. I wouldn't miss it."

"I'm just thinking that people will think it's funny, you showing up alone, when everybody knows we're together."

Elsie didn't know how to respond to something so ridiculous. Why was he trying to deprive her of a good time?

After a moment's silence, he added, "Don't you have too much fun without me."

"No promises," she quipped, but when she saw his face take on a hurt look, she backpedaled to keep the peace. "Just kidding. Nothing is as much fun without you," she said. She leaned over and kissed his earlobe, nearly injuring herself with the seat belt in the process.

They had circled the courthouse twice, and Noah pulled back into the side lot. When he pulled up next to Elsie's car, she unbuckled her seat belt and scooted close to him. As they kissed, savoring the taste and smell and feel of him worked its customary magic. He's not so bad, she reflected. A guy who could kiss like Noah had a lot to recommend him. I could do worse.

With regret, she pulled away, and reached for her bag. "You call me when you get free."

"Don't go yet," he said, and hit the lock button.

"Don't you have to go back on patrol?"

"Not this second." He paused, stroking her leg, giving her a look that was part entreaty, part devilment. "We could spend some time together right here."

She gaped at him. "You want to do it here? In the squad car?"

He raised his brows but didn't speak.

She sputtered, "You mean in the backseat? That's where criminals ride! That's filthy."

"No, honey, we don't have to get back there; no way," he said persuasively. "We can stay right here." His voice dropped to a whisper. "You could make me feel so good."

He unzipped his pants.

"Well, I'll be damned," she said flatly. "You want me to blow you in the front seat of a police car here in the fucking courthouse parking lot."

"Damn, baby, don't cuss like that; it sounds terrible."

"I am not believing this," Elsie said as she struggled with the door handle. "Let me out of this fucking car."

"I don't see what you're going on about. We're not going to see each other all week. Why wouldn't you want to be with me?"

"Don't you understand how offensive this is to me?"

"No," he said shortly. "Why don't you want to make me feel good?"

She turned away for a moment and rubbed her nose with her scarf; she feared that her anger would turn to tears at any moment. "What woman wants to have oral sex in a car? In a public place?"

"We don't have to do that," he whispered, taking her

hand. At his touch, she relaxed a trifle, until he pulled her hand into the opening of his pants.

She snatched her hand away, saying, "Oh, shit, this is ridiculous." Still fumbling with the locked door, she said, "I gotta go."

"Now? Just like that?"

"Yes, now. Ashlock's waiting for me."

His expression was sullen. "I tell you I can't see you for a week, and you won't touch me, and then you want to run off. Makes me feel real important."

"Noah, I've got to go talk to Donita Taney."

"Okay, then," he said, his voice frosty. He reached across her and unlatched her door. "Later."

The hell with you, she thought. "Later," she said, and slammed the door without looking back.

Chapter Twenty-Five

ELSIE'S STOMACH GROWLED as she drove down the rutted street leading to Donita Taney's apartment house. Though she didn't believe in fasting, she had missed two meals so far that day, and suppertime was fast approaching. Had she not taken time to drive around and fuss with Noah, she could have grabbed a burger, she thought with resentment.

The Taneys' block of High Street looked forlorn, as always. A few splintered trees dotted the yards, reminders of a recent ice storm that had taken its toll on the pin oaks and maples. Smashed soda cans and plastic cups and bags, still visible in the waning light, littered the gutters and blew around the yards. Parking her car on High, Elsie shook her head. Winter is double ugly this year, she thought, and January is going to last forever.

Bob Ashlock's shiny car outside the apartment house was the lone bright spot. Elsie hustled up to the house and through the door, left slightly ajar for her.

In the front room, Ashlock tested his recorder. Donita stood against the cracked plaster wall as if she faced a firing squad. Tiffany's face was buried in her mother's side; the child's body shook as she wrapped her arms around Donita's waist.

"Hey, guys," Elsie said, forcing a cheery tone. "Everybody ready to go?"

"She wants some reassurances, I think," Ashlock said without looking up.

Elsie locked eyes with the older woman, whose closed face could not mask her fear. "What are you thinking, Donita?"

"I'm thinking I don't want to go to prison," Donita choked out. "I'm thinking I don't know who's gonna take care of my kids if you've got both me and Kris locked up."

Raising both hands in a gesture of protest, Elsie said, "Whoa, settle down, Donita, you've got the wrong idea. This is not investigative. We're not interrogating you about a crime we're trying to charge you with. I just want to be prepared for anything the defense attorney might try to do to you."

Donita jerked her head at the detective. "How come he's got that recorder?"

Elsie looked at Ashlock. He settled back on the threadbare couch, regarding the women with a disgruntled expression. She walked up to Donita and laid an arm on her shoulder. "You don't want the recorder?"

Donita hesitated, as if she anticipated a trick. "No," she said.

"Okay then, no recording. I can take some notes on

paper, if I need to. It will work out better anyway; that's my protected work product." Privately, Elsie agreed with Donita. She didn't want hard evidence of the interview that she would have to hand over to Nixon. Her personal notes were not subject to discovery by the defense.

"Why am I here?" asked Ashlock.

"You just make the place look so good." When he didn't smile, she said, "How about you ask the questions, Bob."

Tiffany regarded Elsie with enormous eyes. Squatting to the child's eye level, Elsie said, "Miss Tiffany, everything's A-okay here. I see that you're upset, but there's no need to be. Can you go upstairs and play?"

Tiffany squeezed her mother tighter. Donita disengaged the child's arms, saying, "You heard her. Go on."

When Tiffany didn't move, Donita gave her a little shove. "Get."

The three adults took their seats in the room, Elsie joining Ashlock on the couch, Donita in the plastic chair. Ashlock locked up his recorder and was ready to commence with questions, but Elsie stopped him.

"Donita, I need to ask you something before we get going. Did you tell me everything I need to know about Charlene and those boys at school?"

"Huh?" Donita said.

"The defense attorney said something today, about Charlene taking back the accusation, admitting that it didn't happen. Why would he say that?"

Donita pulled her cigarettes out of a black vinyl purse resting at her feet. "Yeah, Kris probably told him so. He made her do it."

"What do you mean? I don't follow."

"Because there was a big stink when it all came out; school made me come up there, and everything. And I had to tell Kris about it. Lord, he was mad."

"Really?" Elsie asked, surprised to hear that Taney would rally to his daughter's defense.

"Mad at Char."

"Oh."

"Called her a whore. Troublemaking whore. Whipped her good. And told her she'd go back the next day and say she made it up."

"Donita, why?" she asked, struggling to comprehend how a parent could make his child confess a wrong she did not commit.

"Because he didn't want anybody looking at us too close, I guess." She looked at Elsie through hooded eyes. "He never worried too much about explaining himself to me."

Elsie turned to Ashlock, who regarded her impassively. "I'll contact the school," she said, nodding. "The teacher who came into the bathroom can back her up."

"You want me to call?" asked Ashlock.

"No, I'll do it. I need to hear this account myself."

"Okay, then, let's get down to business," Ashlock said, turning to Donita. "You know why we're here, Donita, what we want to know. Did you or your husband manufacture methamphetamine?"

She sniffed and folded her hands. "Yes and no."

Elsie braced herself. How bad would it be? Was Donita about to reveal matters that would take down her case?

Ashlock frowned. "That's not an answer."

"It's true. We tried to, but it didn't work out. It didn't make."

Elsie scrawled on the notepad: *Didn't work out!* She silently thanked the heavens as her visions of Donita's drug enterprise faded.

Ashlock relaxed a bit; when he did, Donita eased a little as well. "Tell us about that," he said.

She rubbed her eye as she said, "It's been a while back. It was Kris's big idea. He said we'd get rich off it. Said we could take two hundred dollars and turn it into, oh Lord, I don't remember how much money. Of course," she said ruefully, "two hundred dollars is hard to come by."

"How did you get the money together?"

"It took some doing. We sold plasma, all of us, me and JoLee and Al, even Kris done it. Sold anything we had that was worth anything. Sold our food stamps."

White trash, Elsie thought. Taking government assistance meant for your kids, and letting your man use it for drugs. She tried to hide her disdain but couldn't keep it from showing on her face.

Donita paused, looking at her and Ashlock defiantly. "It was bad, I know. The kids went hungry. We done without. But we scraped that money together."

Elsie shook her head and said, "I'll sure hate for the jury to hear that. About the food stamps. That's taxpayer money."

Donita turned on her. "The taxpayer? You're feeling bad for the *taxpayer*? How about hearing your kids cry because they's hungry? Them going to bed with nothing to eat and I'm thanking God the next day's a school day so they can eat there. Or making supper for six from a box of mac and cheese, and mix it up with water, not no margarine or no milk."

Elsie was silent. Bob continued with the questioning.

"What did you do with the money?"

"Bought the stuff. The drain cleaner, the lye, acetone, the Coleman fuel, the tubing. The pills was the hard part."

"That right?"

"Yeah, because they'll only sell you so many, and you have to sign a paper. Kris said me and JoLee should do it, we should always tell that we had a sick kid. He said it would look funny for him or Al to do it. A man wouldn't be taking care of a sick kid."

Soberly, Elsie made a star on the pad. So Nixon was right; there was a paper trail that connected Donita, but not Kris, to the meth production. Nixon would be sure to use it on cross-examination.

"So you got the ephedrine at the local drugstores."

"Yeah. Took a while, but we done it. And Kris was so excited. He treated me real nice, like old times. Al wasn't sold on the idea. He said there was easier ways to make money."

Donita paused, looking as if she might say more, when Kristy appeared in the kitchen door.

"Mom, I got to have a spiral notebook for school."

Donita rose halfway out of her chair. "You get upstairs." The girl disappeared instantly and clattered up the back stairway.

Ashlock continued, "How did you know how to make it?"

"He had a friend who told him. Somebody he knows, who said he got it off the computer. Kris had wrote it down on paper."

With a nervous gesture, she grabbed another cigarette and lit it. "I was to cook it. Rest of them can't cook nothing. Kris put me in charge. I made it on the stove." She examined her cigarette. "I followed the directions on the paper, did it exactly like he said. Cooked it and strained it and dried it. *Exactly.*"

She tapped the ash in the ashtray, rolled the cherry of the lit end around to remove any remaining fragments. "It didn't turn out right. It was supposed to make crystal, but it didn't. Didn't turn. Lord, did it stink, though. Made the kids sick."

Donita began to tremble. Elsie softened toward her, finding that she was caught up in the story in spite of her disapproval. She glanced over at Ashlock, but his face was stern. Donita's tale of woe made no impression on him.

Shaking, Donita jumped up from her chair and walked to the window. With her back to them, she said, "God, he was mad. He blamed me. It wasn't my fault."

Elsie echoed her in a sympathetic voice. "Well of course it wasn't." She stopped short when she saw Ashlock eyeball her as if she'd taken leave of her senses.

"He must have wrote it down wrong, left something out. He said it was all my fault."

She realized that Donita was crying. She shifted in her seat, wondering whether she should go over to her.

Would Donita want her to comfort her, or would she prefer to pull herself together? "Donita?"

"He beat me so bad I can't even remember it. I was in bad shape for a while. Messed my jaw up pretty good. I couldn't eat for a long time. That's when I got so skinny."

She paused. Turning to look at them, she smiled a little, showing her stained teeth. "Guess that's a good thing, anyhow."

The comment left Elsie speechless. Staring at the woman's gaunt face and the skeletal figure under her T-shirt, she nodded, mute.

As LUCK WOULD have it, Elsie's cell phone rang just as the girl at the Sonic Drive-In walked up to the car with her order on a tray. She looked at the phone; it was Ashlock. She answered, "Hi, Ash," as the Sonic waitress announced, "Extra long Coney with mustard and onion; regular onion ring; extra large Route 66 diet cherry lime-ade."

Ashlock said, "What was that? I can't understand you."

"That's my grub, dude," Elsie replied, paying the girl gratefully before taking the warm fragrant bag into her car. "Just looking at poor old Donita's collarbone makes me hungry."

"Where are you?"

"The Sonic on the highway. I would've invited you, but you took off like a bat out of hell."

"Yeah, well, that woman gives me the creeps."

"Hey, I'm feeling pretty good about this interview, considering." She poked her straw in the cherry limeade and took a long pull. "She's not a drug lord. She didn't even do it right."

"It's still an attempt. Could've been worse, though."

"Ashlock," she said in a pleading voice, "you're not going to do anything with this, are you?"

He was silent for a long moment before he answered. "Guess not. Can't make a drug case without physical evidence. No corpus delicti. What do you tell the defense about it?"

"Nothing. I didn't make an offer of immunity I'd have to disclose. We'll just be prepared when he attacks Donita with it, and we can throw it back on Taney."

"And what about Tina Peroni?"

"Yeah, I'll tell her."

"Think she'll remove the kids?"

"If they took every kid away from parents with a seedy past, the Ozarks would look like a ghost town. Besides, this meth thing is ancient history."

She could hear a dog barking on Ashlock's end of the line. "Get down, girl," he said. To Elsie, he went on, "I didn't ask her about that licking with the extension cord, the one JoLee talked about. I thought you'd want to broach that yourself."

Elsie tried to block out the image his words created. After a pause, she said, "JoLee's not credible."

The silence on the other end of the line made her uncomfortable. Finally, he asked, "You not worried about the kids?"

"Oh, Ash," she said quietly. "I'm worried about them. I worry about them all the goddamned time."

"I know that, Elsie. I didn't mean it like that."

Grasping for a positive topic, she asked, "What do you think about that valentine I found?"

"Now that's really something. Can't hardly believe you uncovered that. You're a regular Nancy Drew."

Elsie smiled with satisfaction. She squirted a packet of ketchup onto an onion ring then licked it off.

Ashlock asked, "You worried about a Fourth Amendment issue?"

"No search and seizure problems with this stuff. She gave it to me voluntarily. I've got my ammo ready with a consent argument: *U.S. v. Moon.*"

"Didn't you say there's another box of stuff from the house?"

"Yes. I'm keeping it locked up in my office."

"Do you think that's wise? What about chain of custody?"

"I have a closet in there. I've got it under lock and key."

"Is it secure in there?"

Was it? Concern nagged at her. "There's probably nothing else to find in there, anyway." She should have burrowed through the last box, but she'd been busy and put it off. And tonight she was dead tired, but if Ashlock was willing to take a look with her, she would forge ahead. "Want to meet me over at the courthouse tonight? We could go through it together."

"No. Can't tonight."

She waited, expecting him to offer an explanation. When none was forthcoming, she shrugged it off. Ashlock was not at her beck and call. "No problem." I can do it myself. Later, she thought.

Elsie crunched into an onion ring. Ashlock asked, "What are you doing?"

"I'm eating, fool." She dug in the bag for the salt packet. "Jealous?"

"I don't know. What are you eating?"

"I'm about to bite into a foot-long wiener," she said. "You want one?"

"Got one," he replied, and she was still howling with laughter as he hung up.

Chapter Twenty-Six

ELSIE TRUDGED UP the stairs to her apartment, clutching the banister. She shivered in her coat. It wasn't that late, but wrangling with JoLee and Donita had worn her slick.

The second floor landing, which led to her apartment door, was pitch-dark, the overhead light burned out. "Son of a bitch," she groused aloud, mentally adding to the long tally of her landlord's shortcomings. She had to dig for her keys, no small feat as she juggled her purse and briefcase. When at last she grasped the key ring at the bottom of her purse, she fumbled with it, trying to locate her apartment key by touch, and dropped the keys to the floor.

"Damn. Son of a bitch," she whispered as she knelt and scoured the dirty carpet with her hands.

She found the keys. They lay beside a cardboard container, about the size of a boot box, blocking her door.

Elsie leaned back on her knees. "What on earth?" she murmured. She wasn't expecting a package, and it didn't look like it came from UPS or the postal service. But it might be a present. A surprise from Noah, to make up for their unfriendly parting. Sometimes he substituted a gift for an apology. In the early days of their relationship she found the practice endearing, but had long since tired of it. He once left a Victoria's Secret bag hanging on her doorknob after an ugly spat. The memory still stuck in her craw. She would far rather receive a few sincere words of remorse than a lace thong and a push-up bra.

So it would be typical Noah to dodge an apology by dropping off merchandise. Still, she approached the box with caution. She had recently received a hank of poultry parts, after all. Elsie stood, brushing dirt from her knees, and unlocked the door to her apartment. Reaching inside, she flipped on her living room light switch. It illuminated the hallway.

In the indirect light, she knelt again, examining the box. It was a shoe box, but a good-sized one; probably it had contained men's boots or shoes. She pushed the apartment door open wider; the light revealed a product name: TOMMY'S WESTERN WEAR.

Why would Noah be bringing me shoes? She was almost inclined to laugh. Her grandfather wore that brand of boots. Built for comfort. Not too hip.

She nudged the box with her hand. Something inside squeaked.

"What on earth," she breathed again, and curiosity overrode caution. With a tentative hand, she lifted the box lid. Inside, she saw two bright eyes and a furry coat, with tiny babies nestled to the belly.

"Kittens?" she muttered unhappily. If Noah was trying to win her with a box of cats, he'd missed the mark, because she could not keep a family of cats in her small apartment. She was about to secure the lid, tempted to leave the offering where it lay, when the sight of a long hairless tail brought her up short.

The beast bared its sharp teeth and hissed at her: a wicked, ugly hiss. Elsie stumbled backward and fell on her backside, scurrying away in her fright.

"Goddamn possum," she said. "I hate possums!"

The animal escaped the confines of the box with remarkable speed and shot into Elsie's apartment, its offspring still clinging to its belly.

"No," she wailed, but it was too late. She jumped to her feet and stood in the doorway of her apartment.

The possum was nowhere to be seen. Elsie leaned against the doorway, tempted to scream with frustration. She was not up to a showdown with a feral rodent. Especially a rodent with teeth like an alien in a horror movie.

Sometimes, having a cop as a boyfriend was a tremendous advantage. Still standing in the open doorway, she found her cell phone and dialed Noah's number.

He answered promptly. "Officer Strong."

"Hey, Noah, it's Elsie. Oh, honey, I'm all shook up." She laughed, her voice tinny.

"What's the matter?"

"A possum ran into my apartment and I'm totally freaked out."

Silence met her comment. She waited, wondering if the connection had been cut off.

"Noah?"

"Yeah. Maybe it's your imagination. I don't see how a possum could get into your apartment."

Elsie paused. He sounded like he still had an attitude problem. "What?"

"Maybe you saw a mouse."

"You think I don't know the difference between a possum and a mouse?"

"Well, I don't get how a possum would be in there."

"I know a possum when I see one," she said, her dander rising.

"Okay."

"Some creep left it in a box for me to find."

"And you took it into your apartment."

"No!" She looked over her shoulder, peering into the dark, worried that the possum's procurer was still nearby. "It ran into my apartment."

"Okay."

"There's nothing nastier than a possum. I hate possums."

"Okay."

The line fell silent again. Elsie spoke first, saying, "So what do you think?"

"I think you ought to call animal control."

It was reasonable advice, but her temper flared nonetheless. Why wouldn't he come to her aid? Why wouldn't he want to?

"Fine," she said. "Fine. I will. 'Bye."

She broke off the call. With her phone in hand, she looked furtively about her. She felt exposed in the dark hallway but didn't want to be locked inside with the possum. She pulled her door shut with a jerk, then bolted down the stairs and took refuge in her car. Before she hit the lock button, she twisted around, peering into the backseat to ensure that no one was there. This is like a horror movie, she thought, shaking.

She began to dial information, to get the number for animal control, when she had an idea. She might try Ashlock instead.

She dialed his cell phone and was relieved when he answered on the second ring. "Elsie?"

"Oh, Ash," she said, "I'm so glad I caught you. You are not going to believe this."

"What is it?" he asked. As Elsie was about to launch into the story, she heard a woman's voice in the background. Ashlock said, "Just a second, Elsie." Then the sound disappeared, as if his hand were over the phone.

She felt a pang, though she couldn't justify it. Ashlock was certainly entitled to have female company. It was no concern of hers.

But it gave her a sinking sensation, and she realized that she had taken comfort in the idea that Ashlock would always be available for her. Even though she was tied to Noah, she had privately relished the thought that Ashlock might carry a secret longing for her.

When he came back on the phone a second later, he said, "Sorry about that. What's the problem?"

"Nothing," Elsie said. "I'm sorry to bother you. Talk to you later."

She slumped in the car seat, ashamed of herself. She had no right to call on Ashlock to save the day whenever she had a personal crisis. She looked at her phone again, and punched in the number to dial information.

AN HOUR LATER, when the animal control officer emerged from her apartment, cage in hand, Elsie was huddled on the stained green carpet of the second floor landing.

"Got it," he said.

"Oh, thank the Lord," Elsie moaned, pulling herself up to a stand, picking up her purse and briefcase.

"We'll test her for rabies," the man said. "Possums carry rabies, you know."

"Yeah, I think I've heard that."

"Did she bite you?"

"No." Scooting inside her apartment, she dropped her belongings onto the floor with a groan.

He juggled the cage, handing her a clipboard. "Can you sign that?"

"Sure." She leaned over and fished a pen from her purse.

"We'll bill you at this address."

Her jaw dropped. "You mean I have to pay?"

"Sorry. It will run about ninety-five dollars."

Elsie tried to calculate the dent that ninety-five dollars would make in her budget, but she was too tired to do the math. "Whatever."

"She had some offspring."

"Yeah, I saw that." Elsie nodded, leaning against the wall.

"I found three."

She paused as she pulled off her coat. Had she seen more?

The man continued, "Sometimes there's four or five. So keep an eye out." He winked. "You got our number."

The man left, pulling her door shut. Elsie spun around, half expecting to see possums in every corner. She got down on her hands and knees to check under the couch and coffee table. After peeking in the bathroom, she proceeded to the bedroom, where she lifted the dust ruffle and peered under the bed.

She finally went to bed with the lights on, fully clothed. As she lay under the blankets and quilt, she thought, Someone is fucking with me.

It was all about the Taney case. Of that she was certain.

Putting a pillow her over face to blot out the overhead light. *If they think they can scare me away from Taney with a possum, they're crazy.*

She turned over on her side, so the pillow wouldn't suffocate her. Another thought occurred to her, one that kept her awake for a long time.

Fuck. Me. Running. Now I've got to get that teacher to back up Charlene's story about the boys in the bathroom. If I don't, my case is shot.

Chapter Twenty-Seven

ON FRIDAY MORNING, as Elsie walked up to the court-house, she saw a crowd loitering in front of the main en-trance. They were organizing a protest of some kind, with signs and placards. When she drew near enough to get a better look, a wave of uneasiness struck her. The crowd bore a frightening resemblance to the Our Earthly Fa-thers group. Watching them as they milled around, dis-tributing their poster boards, her intuition clicked. With sudden clarity she knew who sent the possums and the chicken heads: it was the Earthly Fathers of the Westside Apostolic Church. They were targeting her. She was filled with apprehension. What was their next play?

Stopping in her tracks on the sidewalk, Elsie wanted to turn and run, to enter the courthouse through another route. Though she knew it was unlikely she'd be attacked in public view, she wanted to avoid the protesters; she was not eager to see what they were capable of doing. Poised to make a getaway, she saw it was too late. They had spied her.

One of the men pointed, saying something she couldn't make out. A dozen people clustered on the sidewalk; all of them turned to look at her, their countenances stony.

Buck up, girl, she thought. She resolved that she would not run away, as if she had done something to be ashamed of. In the case of *State v. Taney*, she was in the right. Looking into the throng of men and women, she slowly advanced toward them.

Though her heart pounded, she held herself very erect as she entered the fray. At her approach, they waved the signs, and a couple of them began to chant. The signs were a blur to Elsie, something about Christians and fatherhood. The protesters surrounded her, brushing against her, their voices a babble of noise. She set her jaw and strode up the stone courthouse steps. A couple of the protesters followed her, shouting in her ear.

One of the men at her heels had a head of snow-white hair. His shirt was secured with a horsehair bolo tie. "Jezebel! Whore of Babylon!" he cried.

Wearing a scowl, Elsie played deaf, fervently hoping she looked formidable enough to discourage them. A hand on her arm restrained her. She turned, looking into a young man's face that was twisted with anger. He sneered, said, "Dirty leg." Leaning in close to her, he taunted, "You ain't nothing but a dirty leg. Big old slut with your legs open wide."

Pulling her arm away with a jerk, Elsie blindly made her way to the door. Beneath her brave façade, she was deeply shaken. The man's ugly words injured her. An insult so personal and degrading could not be brushed off. The words were corrosive, and made something shrivel deep inside of her.

Once she reached the courthouse door, the protesters dropped back. The security personnel waved her through. Elsie ran for the elevator and rode up two floors on shaking knees.

Fumbling for the key to her office, she was struggling to regain her composure when she saw Madeleine storm down the corridor toward her.

In desperation, Elsie reached out to her boss. "You would not believe what someone just said to me."

Madeleine acted as though she hadn't heard. "I demand an explanation."

Elsie turned the key in the lock and opened her office door. She tossed her purse and briefcase in a corner and dropped into her chair. Madeleine followed.

When she saw Madeleine's expression, she knew she could not look to her for comfort. She must have been crazy to think otherwise. Steeling herself, she said, "Have a seat."

Madeleine ignored the invitation. "Did you see that display?" she demanded. She had a smear of bright lipstick on her front teeth.

"Yeah." Elsie tried to keep her eyes off of Madeleine's teeth, but it required too much energy. She was exhausted, and her day had only begun.

"Can you offer any explanation for this?" When Elsie didn't reply immediately, Madeleine repeated the question, her voice shrill.

"They're protesting the Taney case," she finally said. "We have a hearing this morning."

"But why?"

She longed to tell Madeleine to shut up and get out, but she didn't dare. "Exercising their First Amendment rights, looks like. They are engaging in a protest."

"I know what they're doing. What I want to know is *why* they're doing it. What have you done to upset these people?"

A surge of righteous indignation swept over Elsie. She longed to snarl and say, *Madeleine, you just buzz on out there and ask them what their fucking problem is.*

But she controlled the urge. Instead, she said, with a shade of petulance, "I can't explain those people, Madeleine. Can't even begin to do it. I don't understand their reasoning."

She hoped Madeleine would offer some word of agreement, but she was disappointed. With a warning look over her reading glasses, Madeleine said, "I don't like the way you're handling this case. You're drawing terrible attention. You're making the whole office look bad. This reflects on me. I'm the elected official." Then she disappeared.

After she departed, Elsie whispered, "You were never elected." Then she dropped her head onto her desk. "Dear God, just get me through this day," she moaned.

Chapter Twenty-Eight

ELSIE SPENT THE next hour licking her wounds in Bree's office. After fortifying herself with three cups of coffee and a long pep talk with Bree, she regained her composure. Shortly before ten she walked into court, carrying her file.

Josh Nixon was already there, sorting through documents. He handed Elsie some printed pages. "These are my suggestions in support of the motion."

"Geez, you briefed it and everything," she said, flipping through the pages and noting the thread of the argument. "Missouri citations, Supreme Court cases, the whole nine yards."

"You bet."

Scornfully, Elsie tossed the papers on the counsel table. "Why are you spinning your wheels with this? You're going to lose this motion. Rountree is not letting that perv out on bond."

"Just doing my job," Nixon said, flashing a smile, but he dropped the friendly demeanor when Taney's supporters entered through the courtroom door. Elsie shot a challenging look at the group, then abruptly turned her back to them.

When Merle entered with Taney, the Our Earthly Fathers and their few female companions broke into applause. A couple of them rose to their feet and repeated their chant, an uneven declaration of support for parents' rights. Nixon glanced at Elsie and she rolled her eyes. She saw him suppress a smile as the bailiff unshackled his client and settled him into the chair next to Nixon.

In the midst of the noisy display, the door to the judge's chambers flew open and Judge Rountree stormed out, still in his shirtsleeves. "I'll clear this courtroom," he cried. "There will be order in here or you'll all by God land in jail."

The chanting stopped. Elsie could hear a pin drop. The judge then announced in a milder tone, "Bond hearing in this cause will be held in five minutes, and I expect everyone to comport themselves appropriately, or there'll be the dickens to pay." He glowered under a furrowed brow, turned around and limped back into his office on his crippled knees.

When the door shut behind him, Elsie, emboldened by the judge's admonition, turned to gaze on the assembly with a superior air. Troublemakers, she thought. You can't pull your bullshit on Judge Rountree.

The judge reappeared in exactly five minutes, garbed in his black robe and exhibiting his usual calm demeanor.

Taking up defendant's motions, he said, "Counsel for defendant has filed a Motion to Reduce Bond and a Motion to Shorten Time. What is the position of the state on these motions?"

Elsie stood and said, "The state opposes both motions, your honor."

"You object to the Motion to Shorten Time?"

"Yes, your honor, I do. I'd like to speak to it if I may."

"You may not. Your objection is overruled. The Motion to Shorten Time is granted."

As if on cue, Taney's supporters burst into another round of applause and cheers. The judge's eyes popped like a pair of novelty store glasses.

"This is not a sporting event," he bellowed. "You do not cheer because you think your side scored. If I hear another whisper out of any of you, I'll clear the courtroom."

The dark-haired leader of the group leaned forward and quietly mouthed something in the ear of the man sitting in front of him.

"That's it. Out." The judge slammed his gavel. When no one moved, Judge Rountree turned to his bailiff. "Merle, everybody out. We won't proceed until the courtroom is empty."

Delighted, Elsie turned and stretched in her chair, folding her hands behind her head, as she watched the support group depart. "Good riddance to bad rubbish," she said, but she spoke so softly that it was only the barest whisper. As the last spectator exited, she caught a glimpse of Taney out of her peripheral vision. He twisted

in his seat, appeared agitated at the group's departure.
He exchanged a look with the dark-haired leader of the
Earthly Fathers and then turned his angry countenance
to the judge.

Judge Rountree waited for Merle to close the door on
the empty gallery and take his chair behind the bailiff's
desk. The room was silent. The judge nodded at Nixon.
"Proceed."

As Josh launched into his argument, Elsie drew a
vertical line down the center of her yellow legal pad. She
made notations of his arguments on the left side of the
line and jotted her rebuttals and counterarguments on
the right. The points he raised were nothing new; she
had heard it all before, in other cases. Nixon recited the
Constitutional prohibition against excessive bail or fine.
He turned up the volume dial on his voice as he declared
that a bond amount of $250,000 was totally out of line,
considering the defendant's means. Nixon reminded the
court that the purpose of bail was to ensure appearance
at trial, not to keep defendant behind bars. He paced up
and down before the bench as he talked, pushing back
stray locks of hair that fell over his brow.

Nixon stopped pacing and stood behind his client. He
made an offer of proof that Taney was no flight risk because he had no money to travel and nowhere to go. As
Nixon concluded, he placed a sympathetic hand on the
shoulder of his client. Taney shrugged his hand off with
an abrupt jerk.

Elsie wrote furiously while Nixon made his argument;
then sat quietly, waiting for her turn. When the judge

nodded, she jumped to her feet and rebutted the defense arguments one by one: that defendant's bail was far from excessive, considering the nature of the offense; that defendant was most assuredly a flight risk, as he had no job, no property, no home, and no intact family relationships; in short, he had no reason to remain and every reason to flee. She reminded the judge that Taney faced the possibility of life imprisonment, which was, she argued, a most pressing motive for a criminal defendant to run. In addition, she urged, he was a threat to the safety of the state's witnesses.

Pausing, she checked her notes, but didn't find anything she'd missed. She wrapped it up then, urging the court to overrule the defendant's motion.

The judge turned his gaze back to the defense table. "Anything further in support of your motion, Mr. Nixon?"

"Yes, your honor. The prosecution just said that defendant's motion should be overruled because Mr. Taney is not employed. I'm prepared to call a witness who will testify that he will offer Mr. Taney employment if he's let out on bond."

"Where is this witness, Mr. Nixon?" the judge asked.

"He's in the hallway, I think. He's one of the people that, ah, that left the courtroom earlier."

The judge looked skeptical. He tossed his pen down on the docket sheet. "Call him," he said shortly.

Nixon called Martin Webster to the witness stand. Webster entered the courtroom with the tentative step of a person who had previously been thrown out. The judge beckoned to him to come forward and be sworn. After taking the oath, the man took his seat in the witness box.

Elsie watched him closely as he answered Nixon's questions. Webster was an unremarkable fellow, ordinary in appearance, and if she encountered him on the street, she would not look twice. His short cropped hair and dark suit were certainly not exceptional in outstate Missouri. But something was wrong, she knew. It didn't make sense that this evangelical Christian would be so fervent in his support of Taney.

His demeanor on the witness stand was smug, sanctimonious. When Nixon asked him his occupation, he responded that he owned his own business. Nixon then asked him to describe his business, and Webster loftily said that it was a Christian plumbing business. He then claimed that he was willing to hire Taney to work for him.

Nixon asked, "How soon can you put him to work?"

"As soon as he can get there. We're always in need of a good hand."

"No further questions."

Elsie rose. "May I inquire, your honor?"

The judge nodded.

"Mr. Webster," she began in a conversational tone, "what is the nature of your Christian plumbing business?"

"Just what it sounds like." He spoke with scorn, as if he addressed someone with limited understanding. "We do plumbing services in homes and businesses."

"What background does Mr. Taney have in the plumbing business?"

Webster paused before he answered. "We have employees who aren't plumbers. Someone has to answer the phone, deal with the public. The plumbers need helpers on some jobs."

"So you can't put him to work as a plumber—-because he isn't a plumber." She smiled at the witness. "Correct?"

"Yes."

"So you see the defendant as your receptionist? To 'deal with the public,' I think you said?"

Webster colored and became visibly angry. "We can train him. We'll find work for him to do."

Elsie advanced on him; she needed to show him who was boss.

"Please answer yes or no: will he be your receptionist, employed to deal with the public?"

Webster glared at her, refusing to answer.

Glancing at Judge Rountree, she said, "Your honor?"

"Answer the question, Mr. Webster."

"No. I don't know." Webster said shortly.

"Did you investigate his employment background before you made this generous offer? Are you aware that he has not had gainful employment for several years?"

"I don't put any stock in anything you say," Webster said, and he rose from his seat as if he meant to depart.

Judge Rountree swiveled in his hair and addressed him. "You're not done quite yet," he told the witness, not unkindly. "We'll let you know when you can step down."

Webster reddened as he sat back down.

Elsie said, "I'll repeat the question. Are you aware that he hasn't had gainful employment for several years?"

"I don't know. We haven't talked about that."

"So you have a plumbing business—a Christian plumbing business. And you're going to hire the defendant to work for you. But he doesn't have training or skill as a plumber, and you haven't talked about his employment history. Is that right?"

"Right."

In an incredulous tone, she asked, "Mr. Webster, would you tell the court why on earth you would make this generous offer."

Mulishly, Webster spoke. "Because that's what family does."

Elsie paused, surveying Webster with a wrinkled brow. "Family? You mean church family?"

"Family." Webster's chin was up; he looked combative, resentful.

She spoke slowly as realization dawned. "Mr. Webster, are you and the defendant related? Kin?"

Webster turned to the defense table, as if waiting for an objection, or instruction of some kind. When none came, he said, "We're cousins."

Elsie shook her head in amazement. Nixon threw his pen on the counsel table and looked daggers at his client. The judge eyeballed Webster, then Taney, then back again, as if looking for the family resemblance.

"How close? First cousins?"

When Webster nodded, she said, "You'll have to answer. The court reporter can't record a nod."

Webster said, "We're first cousins. His mother and my father was brother and sister."

"Well," said Elsie in a congenial tone, "that explains a lot." Finally, it made sense to her. The witness was unmasked.

Nixon barked irritably: "Is the prosecutor up there to testify, judge? I believe she's supposed to ask questions, not make a commentary."

"Miss Arnold, ask a question," the judge said mildly.

"Is the defendant related by blood or marriage to any other members of your group out there? The church, the Earthly Fathers?"

"My wife's out there."

"Anyone else?"

"No. My folks were members, but they're in the nursing home now. And Kris is from the Bootheel."

"Ah." *The Bootheel. Wouldn't you know.* She ruffled through her notes for a minute, then said in a friendly tone, "No further questions." Webster continued to glower as the judge released him and he took a seat in the courtroom behind Taney.

Nixon declined to produce further evidence in support of his motion, and the judge summarily overruled it, announcing that the defendant's bond would remain at $250,000. Elsie exhaled with relief, although she hadn't even been aware that she was sweating the judge's decision; she could not believe that Judge Rountree would be so foolish as to inflict Kris Taney on the public pending trial. She felt positively jolly about connecting the dots between Taney and the Pentecostal Our Earthly Fathers. At least the support made some sense to her now: families were notoriously blind.

She capped her pen and shuffled her notes into an untidy pile. The deputies entered to put additional constraints on Taney for his walk back to jail. The courtroom was silent but for the clank of metal when Elsie heard Martin Webster speak again.

"Your honor?"

She twisted in her seat to look at him. Webster stood, flagging his arm. "Judge. Your honor, sir?"

Judge Rountree was on his feet, a pace away from the door to his chambers, but he paused and squinted over his glasses at the gallery. "Mr. Webster?"

"I've got to get my cousin released somehow. It's shameful to leave family locked up in jail."

"I've already ruled, Mr. Webster," the judge said, with a hand on the doorknob.

"There's a farm."

Elsie stared at Martin Webster, momentarily confused. When his meaning struck home, she blanched. Jumping to her feet, she cried, "Don't even think about it!"

She bounded to the bench to protest Webster's implicit proposal. "Your honor, this is not a proper case for a property bond. The state objects, I absolutely positively object."

Nixon followed on her heels. "Judge, if a relative is willing to post property as surety, it's the court's duty to permit it."

Glancing over her shoulder, she saw Taney rise from his chair, facing Webster, who had walked up to the defense table. Webster draped a supportive arm around the defendant as the two men talked in low voices. She heard

Taney say, "If you can just get me out of here, I know I can clear this whole dang mess up."

Elsie turned back to the bench, fighting to keep the panic from her voice. She said, "Judge, if you want to assure the defendant's appearance at trial, a property bond won't do the trick. Who will go after him if he fails to appear? There won't be a bail bondsman in the picture, to find him and bring him in."

Judge Rountree addressed Martin Webster. "Mr. Webster, if you post a property bond, you'll forfeit that farm in the event your cousin fails to appear. Do you understand that?"

"I do."

"Now Mr. Webster, I see you're willing to make a sacrifice on your cousin's behalf. But wouldn't it make more sense for you to work with a bail bondsman? Then you wouldn't risk your property."

Webster's nose wrinkled, as if he detected a mighty stink. "We don't need no bail bondsman. I'll not do business with anyone who profits from another man's sin and iniquity. So the Book says."

Elsie's mind was racing. "Judge, this is all hogwash anyway. The bond amount is $250,000. Where in these parts can you find a farm that's worth a quarter of a million dollars?"

"I'll inquire. Attorneys and defendant will be seated. Mr. Webster, approach the bench, if you please, sir. What manner of farm are we talking about?"

"Livestock operation. It's been in the family a long time. About ninety years."

Livestock, Elsie jotted on her pad, thinking they were raising some chickens out on the farm, too. *Not hard to find a possum.*

"Who owns the property?"

"Me, your honor. It was passed down to me by my daddy, and to him by his."

"Where is it located?"

"Douglas County."

Oh, Lord: not Booger County. Douglas County was infamous in the Ozarks for its hostile treatment of outsiders. Historically, if someone in Douglas County mysteriously disappeared, the local explanation was "the Booger Man got him."

"How many acres?"

"Two hundred."

Nixon jumped up. "Your honor, a farm of that size should be worth close to a quarter of a million dollars. I'd like the court to commence proceedings for approval of defendant's property bond."

Elsie stood, scoffing. "We're in the middle of an economic recession, last I heard. And we haven't even seen this property, or conclusive evidence of ownership, or its condition, or anything else, for that matter. Defense counsel is getting way ahead of himself."

Nixon brushed off her argument. "We can get all the information online, through the recorder's office. It won't take twenty minutes."

Her palms grew clammy as the possibility of Taney's release hit home. She left the counsel table and marched up to the bench without asking leave.

"Flight risk! Judge Rountree, stop and think, a bond must effectively deter the defendant from running off. This property bond, which for some reason the court seems to actually be considering, it's the pledge of some *cousin's* farm. And it's property outside the county, property in which defendant has no ownership interest. What's that to Kris Taney? What power, what hold, could it possibly have on him?"

"Family pride," declared Webster, stepping over to stand hip-to-hip with Elsie at the bench.

"Will you please move?" she asked with irritation, shoving Webster with her shoulder before returning her focus to Judge Rountree. "Judge, this is a dangerous discussion. Perilous. Setting the defendant free will disrupt the state's case. Our witnesses will feel threatened."

"We'll agree to bond conditions," Nixon offered.

Making a scornful face, she demanded, "Why should we believe that the defendant will comply with bond conditions when he doesn't comply with the Missouri Criminal Code?"

"Allegedly," Nixon said.

The judge studied them in silence. After a moment, he shook his head. "I'll have to give this some thought," he said. "I'll take the matter under advisement while defendant gets his paperwork in order."

Elsie had a flash of inspiration. "I'll need to request an appraisal."

The judge nodded. "That's reasonable."

"And a survey of the property," she added, wracking

her brain. "And a title search. And an environmental audit to make sure the property's not contaminated."

"Oh, come on," Nixon protested. "The state is just trying to create unnecessary delay."

Judge Rountree sighed as he pushed his chair back from the bench. "We'll see. In a case of this type, it seems wise to approach the request for property bond with caution. Make your recommendations in writing and see that it's filed before the end of the day."

"Yes, your honor."

"And Mr. Nixon, I'll need to see an amended motion from you."

"Yes, sir."

The judge exited through his chambers door. As the door shut, Taney demanded, in an aggrieved tone, "So am I getting out of here today or not?"

"*Hell*, no," Elsie muttered at the prosecution table. She sneaked a look at the counsel table to see whether she'd been overheard.

Nixon was huddled in consultation with Martin Webster, but Kris Taney returned her stare. Taney made a kissing noise at her, then stuck out his tongue and flicked it back and forth. As the deputies hastened to take him away, Taney puckered his lips and whistled a tune. Elsie placed it after a moment; it was "Ding, Dong, the Witch is Dead" from *The Wizard of Oz*.

"You wish," she said aloud, but he had disappeared.

As she left the courtroom, she saw that the Taney group still waited in the wings. They clustered on the benches that lined the walls of the courthouse rotunda.

As she walked by, trying in vain to act as if she didn't notice them, she was fleetingly reminded of Suzanne Pleshette and Tippy Hedren fearfully eyeing Alfred Hitchcock's birds, watching from the telephone wires.

The high heels of her shoes clicked and clacked on the marble floor, and as she passed the men and women perched on the benches, Martin Webster began to stomp his feet. Following his lead, all the men and women who occupied the benches rapidly stomped their feet on the marble floor in unison. After halting a moment in confusion, she strode purposefully for her office door. She was well aware that they were making fun of her, but she put on a brave face. The stomping continued until she passed into the protection of the Prosecutor's Office. Once inside, her shoulders dropped and she exhaled, unaware that she had been holding her breath as she walked through the stomping crowd.

"Madeleine said she wants to see you when you're done with that hearing," Stacie told her.

"Thanks," said Elsie, who had no intention of heading down the hallway to Madeleine's office door. She entered her own office and sat down abruptly, breathing out like a deflating balloon.

She closed her eyes, drawing strength from the quiet, when Josh Nixon stuck his head in the door. "Can I have that exhibit yet?" he asked.

She nearly jumped out of her skin.

"Sorry," he said. "Did I wake you up? You sleeping on the job?"

"No," she said irritably, "I have never slept at work," which was not quite true. "What do you want?"

"I said I want the original of that valentine card. And whatever else you found in my client's property. And I want your ridiculous demands for the property bond, just as soon as you give it to the judge."

She fought the urge to lash out at him, to blame him for the behavior of his client and the people on the court-house benches. She was curt as she told him that she couldn't give it to him because she hadn't gone through it all yet.

"You know what, Elsie, this is bullshit. That's my client's property and you're depriving him of it. I gave you the damned handwriting samples, like you asked. I don't want to fight this out in front of Judge Rountree, but if you jerk me around, I'm going to have to. You said I could have the stuff today."

"You're a total whiner," she countered, "and Judge Rountree isn't going to want to hear it. Besides, you don't have anything to complain about. I didn't snatch this property from him; his wife gave it to me. She demanded that I take it. I don't need a warrant to take what someone hands to me."

They glared at each other. For a long moment neither of them spoke. The silence gave her time to reflect; she was obligated, ethically bound, to give him the evidence he sought. Fighting a losing discovery battle in court, when she needed Judge Rountree to rule in her favor on the property bond, was unwise.

"Tell you what," she proposed in a more reasonable tone. "I can't hand it all over today, because I haven't seen it all. How about if I hand over the valentine? You can show it to your client; I'm certain he'll have a perfectly plausible explanation. If I uncover anything else, you can have it on Monday."

He digested the offer. "Are you giving me the original?"

"Hell no. How about a color copy? It's at the crime lab across town, with the officer who does the handwriting analysis. We can go make the copy there."

"Well," he said, "I guess so."

"Good. I'll even drive."

"Okay, you drive."

"I'm at the very end of the parking lot. Story of my life."

Nixon loosened up, adopting a friendlier manner. "Ooh, long walk. Bracing. On second thought, maybe you could see whether Madeleine brought her golf cart from the country club, and we could ride in it."

The mention of Madeleine brought her up short. Madeleine wanted to see her, and after their morning exchange, the meeting would not be a happy one. She shook her head to banish the worry. Later, she thought as she dug her keys out of her purse, then headed to the parking lot with Josh Nixon.

Outside, Elsie was glad to leave the courthouse behind. The sun shone bright and warm, a January day that teased people with the notion that winter was over, when in fact spring was many cold weeks away. Her mood improved as she and Nixon strolled through the lines of vehicles to her car. When they reached it, she stared at it without recognition for a moment. The car was where she left it, but its appearance had markedly changed. It had been pelted with dozens of eggs. Crushed brown and white shells speckled the vehicle, and it dripped a thick layer of egg white and broken yolks. The vile stench of sulfur assaulted her. The eggs were rotten.

In the gelatinous mess on the hood of the car, someone had written a message, using the eggs like finger paint. It read, *Deut. 22:5.*

Elsie closed her eyes, as if blotting out the image would make it disappear. "Again," she whispered, more to herself than to Nixon, "they got me again." Fear rushed over her in a wave, and blinking her eyes open, she jerked her head from left to right, as if the vandals were all around. She covered her nose to block the sulfur smell, but bile rose in her throat and she couldn't swallow it back. She leaned over beside the car and vomited.

As she retched, she felt Josh Nixon's hand, patting her on the back. "It's okay," he said. Gently, he pulled her hair out of the way, so she wouldn't heave on it. "Everything's okay." But his troubled tone belied the words.

Chapter Twenty-Nine

JUDGE ROUNTREE SAT in his chambers in the old rolling chair that he had occupied for thirty years. It tilted at a dangerous angle, and he leaned back as he stared out the window at Elsie's vandalized car. She and Josh Nixon sat across from him, waiting for him to speak.

Sitting before the judge, she wished she'd dared to bring a cold drink into chambers with her. Though she had rinsed her mouth at the water fountain in the courthouse hallway, the acrid taste of vomit remained, and her throat burned from the caustic bile.

The bitter taste matched her mood, but she tried to mask her feeling of violation as she kept her eye trained on the judge.

"So this is the second incident, you say," he said, swiveling around to address her.

"It's the second incident at the courthouse. After the arraignment, my car was vandalized with chicken heads.

Today it was eggs. And two nights ago someone left a possum on my doorstep . . . " She paused, wondering whether invoking the possum sounded frivolous. But she felt certain that the same villain had inflicted all of the damage.

"Have you talked this over with Mrs. Thompson?"

Like Madeleine would care, she thought, but she answered, "A while back, when it first happened."

"What did she say?"

"She didn't think too much of it."

A look of disapproval crossed the judge's face as he brought his chair back to floor level. "How's discovery going, Mr. Nixon?"

"We're working on it." He stole a sidelong glance at Elsie. "The prosecutor has some stuff I haven't seen, but Elsie says I'll have it all on Monday. And we're waiting on a handwriting report."

"I'll turn the heat up on that, Judge."

"See that you do." He wore thick glasses, and his expression as he looked through them was stern. "This case is starting to get out of control. I think we need a special setting. Mr. Taney is entitled to a speedy trial, and I'm inclined to give him one."

Shifting in his chair, Nixon looked uncertain. "What do you mean, Judge?"

"I have a jury coming in on a civil case a week from Monday. It was specially set; they're coming to try the wrongful death case from the car wash explosion on Cherry Street in '08. I hear that the plaintiff and defendant are talking seriously about settlement. I think," and he took the glasses off and rubbed his eyes, "I think *State v. Taney* will be my backup case."

Elsie and Josh were struck dumb. Judges occasionally placed cases on a fast track, but generally the opposite was true; cases languished as they crept their way up crowded dockets, dogged by continuances and delays.

As she grasped the notion that the Taney case might possibly be disposed of in a couple of weeks, a weight rolled off her. Taking a deep breath, she sat up straighter in her chair. "The state is always ready for trial, your honor," she said, with a shade of the old ring in her voice.

The judge turned to Nixon; he appeared to be deep in thought. He glanced at Elsie. "Do you anticipate any further medical evidence?"

"No." She had received the reports of the girls' medical exams a week ago; they held no surprises. The results were consistent with the claims that the two older girls had intercourse, but the state could not pursue DNA evidence.

She asked Nixon, "Did you see the statement of JoLee? It's in the file, but I attached it to an e-mail so you'd be sure to notice." Nixon nodded.

The judge instructed Elsie to disclose her witness list. "I want it in defendant's hands by five today."

"Yes, your honor," she said. She nudged Nixon's leg with the toe of her shoe. "Any alibi to disclose?"

"Please."

"What?"

"You know."

"What, for heaven's sake?"

"Don't make me crazy." His hair fell over his forehead. "If you haven't even disclosed your whole case to me, how can I be expected to know whether I have an alibi defense? If we come up with one, *after* you do your job, I'll let you know."

"Well, both of you better figure out your strategies," Judge Rountree said, "because you're set number two for a week from Monday. In light of the special setting, I believe I'll overrule the request for a property bond in this case. No need to prepare those suggestions after all."

His decision made, the judge's humor improved. "That's it for now, I guess. You young folks need to get to work. Miss Arnold," he added, "you'd best head to the car wash. Eggs are hard to get off when they dry. That's why pranksters like them."

As they rose, a large book on the judge's shelf caught Elsie's eye. "Judge Rountree, is that a Bible?"

"It is." The judge rose from his chair and limped over to the bookshelf. He pulled a worn black leather-bound Bible out of the shelf and examined it. "This is the one my father used back in the old days, when people had to swear the oath to tell the truth with their hand on the Bible."

Elsie said, "There was a message smeared in the egg mess on my car. It was a Bible verse, I'm pretty sure. May I look it up in your Bible? Would you mind?"

He handed her the book and she flipped to Deuteronomy. Verse five of chapter twenty-two was short, and she read it aloud.

"'A woman shall not wear a man's apparel, nor shall a man put on a woman's garment; for whoever does such things is an abomination to the Lord your God.'"

"You have pants on," the judge said kindly, as if she needed him to explain. "Some conservative sects don't hold with women wearing pants."

Staring at the text on the page, her vision blurred. The idea of her foes using the Bible to condemn her injured something deep inside her. "I guess I'm not their feminine ideal," she said, trying in vain to keep her voice level. She handed the book back to him.

The judge patted her shoulder. "Keep a watch out, for now."

"I wish I knew how to do that. I don't know much about self-defense; always did my fighting in the courtroom." In a troubled voice, she said, "I don't want to get a gun."

The judge shook his head as Elsie continued, thinking aloud, "Lord knows I'm antigun. I hate guns. But should I be armed, if there's a threat?"

Judge Rountree dismissed the notion with a wave of his hand. "Don't be fooling with a gun. Guns are dangerous in the hands of people who don't know how to use them." Sighing, he added, "What you need, Miss Arnold, is a husband."

Her temper flared and she couldn't hold her tongue. "Why don't you tell Nixon to get a wife?"

The judge looked taken aback. "I meant no offense, Miss Arnold."

She stood, still affronted; how dare he attribute her vulnerability to her marital status? Stiffly, she said, "If that's all, I need to go."

He nodded, and did not try to pat her again. "Let's get this one tied up. Then we'll all sleep better."

As Elsie and Nixon left the judge's office, Nixon whispered, "God damn! They think you're an abomination."

"Back off, Nixon," Elsie snapped.

Chapter Thirty

ELSIE TUGGED AT the bottom drawer of the file cabinet behind the receptionist's desk. "Stacie, I need blank subpoenas, and I need them right now. Please don't tell me we don't have any."

Stacie spun her chair around and regarded Elsie with an anxious face. "I need to tell you something weird."

Elsie knelt before the cabinet with a room temperature can of Diet Coke, a remnant from an earlier day. Though it was flat and hot, she drank it in a desperate bid to clear the taste from her mouth. She took a swig, swished it around in her mouth and swallowed as she flipped through a folder that contained, to her relief, a handful of pink subpoena forms behind a stack of criminal background check forms. "Okay, Stacie, so what's weird?"

"You have a mystery witness. He keeps calling. He called while you were in court."

Elsie straightened to a stand, holding tight to her subpoenas. Eyes trained on Stacie, she took another sip of flat soda before asking, "Who called?"

"He didn't leave a name. He won't tell me who he is." Adopting a defensive tone, Stacie said, "I can't help it if people won't leave a name. It's not like I can make them."

Wary, she asked, "What did he say?"

"He said he knew you'd want to hear from him. He said, 'Tell the little lady I want to talk to her.' That's what he called you. 'Little lady.'"

The message started a chill up Elsie's spine. This man was not one of the egg-throwing rabble; he represented a different problem.

"Did he have a hick accent?"

"Yeah. I mean, most people do. But this guy creeps me out. It's the Taney case, isn't it?" Stacie demanded, in a voice that held an accusatory note.

"If I had to guess right or die."

Stacie's face was unhappy. Standing up behind her desk, she leaned over and peered through the glass doorway. "That Taney case is spooky. It's pulling in a bunch of weirdos. I'm afraid something will happen here. I'm the one at the front door of the office. I'm like a sitting duck."

For once, Elsie felt a bond with the receptionist. "Stacie, I hear you. I really do," she said. "I'm in the same boat. All of a sudden, I'm looking over my shoulder all the time."

"At least you've got a boyfriend who's a cop. He'll watch out for you."

"Guess you're right," Elsie said as she made her way past Stacie's desk. I'm a liar, she thought. She knew that she couldn't trust Noah to be there for her.

Before unlocking her office, she stopped to examine a message Stacie had taped to the door, a pink memo bearing the receptionist's handwritten addendums: *IMPORTANT!!! CRAZY CALL!!!!* It was punctuated with stars and exclamation points. The caller line was filled with a big question mark. Underneath, the message read: *Said he'll call back at two!!*

Inside, sitting in her chair, as Elsie logged onto her computer she felt compelled to peer out the window at the street below. Nothing was amiss; she only saw a trickle of traffic and a pedestrian making her way into the courthouse. Satisfied, she turned back to the computer screen.

With a possible trial date fast approaching, her worries about Charlene's school controversy needed to be put to rest; it was time to make an important call. A quick computer search turned up the phone number of the school Charlene attended in eighth grade.

She picked up the phone at her desk and dialed. The line was picked up and a woman said, "Osage Middle School."

Elsie sat up straight and readied her pen. "Afternoon," she said in a cordial tone. "This is Elsie Arnold at the county prosecutor's office, and I need some information regarding a criminal case."

"The guidance counselor is at a meeting."

"Well, fortunately, I don't need to speak with the counselor. I need to talk to a teacher who witnessed an assault at school last year, or it may have been the year before. An assault involving an eighth grade student named Charlene Taney. Can you help me out?"

"I wasn't here last year."

Closing her eyes, she counted to ten.

"Put me through to the principal, please."

"He's at a meeting."

A flush washed over her face. "Would you give him a message, please?"

"I'll put you through to his voice mail," and with that the woman was gone. Elsie listened to the recorded voice of the Osage Middle School principal, directing her to leave her name, her student's name, her number, and the reason for the call.

Working hard to keep the impatience from her voice, she related the particulars of the court case and explained the information she sought. She barely recited the digits of her return phone number when a buzz terminated the message.

Slamming the phone receiver into the cradle, she told the phone, "I'll subpoena your ass down here if you don't get back with me pretty damned quick."

A glance at the clock revealed that it was almost two. Elsie muttered, "Let's talk, Brother Taney."

Since the day Ashlock had stormed the county jail on her behalf and learned that Kris Taney was not her anonymous caller, she'd figured out who the caller must be. She hoped it was Al Taney resurfacing, and that he would come forward and testify. She could use him.

The insistent ring of the phone on her desk interrupted her thoughts. Before reaching for the receiver, she paused for just a moment to don her mental armor.

"Elsie Arnold," she said in a smooth voice.

Silence greeted her. She waited it out, refusing to speak again before the caller did. Finally he broke the silence. "You ready to talk, little lady?"

Elsie wrote *ready to talk?* on her notepad as she answered, "Sure."

She heard the man cough into the receiver, a phlegm-filled retch. When he recovered, he said, "I got something you need."

"Tell me what that might be."

"Information. Testimony. You got a case you need me on."

"What case?"

"Taney."

She leaned back in her chair, studying the stained ceiling without seeing it. "What information can you provide about the Taney case?"

"I'm the dude who busted the whole case wide-open. Wouldn't be no case if it wasn't for me."

"Right. Al Taney."

"You got it." He spoke with a note of satisfaction. "Guilty as charged."

Al Taney was already getting under her skin, but she tried to keep her voice neutral. "You were subpoenaed to come testify at the preliminary hearing in your brother's case, Mr. Taney. You didn't appear."

"That's right. Guilty as charged."

Though the repetition grated on her, she hid it; he might supply something she needed.

"I'd like to have a chance to meet you," she said. "The case may be going to trial soon."

"You'll need me at that trial, I bet."

"Well, I'd like to hear what you might contribute."

"What did the girls say?"

Elsie paused, her brows drawing together. "I beg your pardon?"

"The little gals: Kris's girls. What they done told you?"

Smoothly, she responded, "What we need to discuss is your testimony, Mr. Taney, not the testimony of other witnesses. From the reports, it sounds like you personally observed some of the abuse. Were you present at the Taney home on Thanksgiving Day? Because—"

He cut her off. "You talk to Tiffany? Bet she ain't said nothing. Tiffany don't hardly never talk."

Elsie didn't answer. Drawing stars on the legal pad, she said, "Can I have your updated contact information? I need an address and phone where you can be reached. And when can we meet?"

"You tell me what the girls said and I'll tell you where I'm staying."

She hardened her tone. "Mr. Taney, I realize you don't know me very well, but I'm not going to bargain or barter with you. We're not going to play any little games. I'm going to ask questions about this case, and you're going to provide information."

"Yes, ma'am."

"You understand me?"

"Yes indeed, yes ma'am."

"So you will help with the case and testify at trial?"

"Oh, I will, all right. What I'm gonna say is gonna be real helpful."

She hesitated; she still didn't like his tone. "And just what is it that you'll be saying at trial?"

"Whatever you want."

"What I want, Mr. Taney, is for you to tell the truth. You'll be under oath."

"Sure, you do. I'm your man."

A look of exasperation crossed her face. She had no strength to put up with Al Taney's antics, after all that had gone on that day. She tossed her pen across her desk; it rolled off onto the floor. "So what specific recollections about your brother's behavior with his daughters can you share with me?"

"I mean it. You tell me what you want me to say, and I'll say it."

"Mr. Taney, you're just messing with me."

"Oh no I ain't."

"You certainly are."

"Hey, little lady, don't go off on me. I wasn't trying to piss you off, honest. I want to help you out." His voice dropped to a whisper. "And you can help me out."

"What are you talking about? How do you want me to help you out?"

"There's something called immunity, ain't there? Something like witness immunity?"

An unhappy connection was forming in her head. "Immunity? Are you charged with something? Some other county?"

"No! Not me. Nothing I know of."

"Then what do you need immunity for?"

He sighed softly into the phone. "Well now, let's see. Anything you think of. Whatever you say."

Elsie hung up without further comment. She dialed Stacie's extension and told her that the nameless caller was Al Taney and his calls were not to be put through in the future.

"What did he say?" Stacie asked. "Will he come over here?"

"I don't think he will, Stacie. He's been dodging us so far." She knew that it was impossible to predict what a Taney might do, but she wondered what Al Taney was up to. Her heart started beating faster as she tore the top sheet from the notepad and threw it in the trash. *Block it out*, she told herself sternly. *Forget Al Taney. He's history.*

It was barely mid-afternoon, but she wanted a drink in the worst way. She sighed and turned her attention to the blank subpoena forms.

She filled one out for Donita and one for each of the Taney daughters. As she checked the calendar to ensure that she had the correct date, her office phone rang again and she checked the caller ID: GEORGE ARNOLD.

"Oh, thank God," she said with a ragged breath. Picking up the receiver gratefully, she said, "Mom?" To her dismay, tears came into her voice.

"What is it? What's the matter?" her mother demanded.

Though she struggled to get her voice under control, it was hopeless. She could hide her belly from Madeleine and the Our Earthly Fathers and Taney and the judge, but not from her mother.

"It's been a bad day, Mom. Really bad."

When Marge Arnold insisted that she relate all of her problems, Elsie found that recounting them in detail was more than she could bear at the moment. So she just said, "There was a protest at the courthouse, about the Taney case. And they got my car with rotten eggs. And—" Then her voice broke.

"What, baby? What is it?"

Elsie rubbed her nose, hard. She wanted to tell her mother about the name-calling, to confide the terrible things the man had said on the courthouse steps. But she had to collect herself before she could say it out loud.

"Tell me," her mother urged.

"A protester. He called me a slut. Dirty leg slut, with my legs—"

She couldn't finish; Marge exploded on the other end of the line. "Son of a bitch! How dare he?"

Her mother's anger was a panacea. Elsie's distress eased as she heard Marge rant into the telephone, cursing the Our Earthly Fathers in particular and evil-minded men in general. When her mother demanded that she come home to stay with them for the weekend, Elsie caved without a fight.

"Okay, Mom. See you tonight," she said, drawing strength from the prospect.

"I'll bake a ham!" her mother declared.

Chapter Thirty-One

I AM NOT driving Donita Taney around today, Elsie swore as she headed to High Street in her dripping car. Two run-throughs at the Jiffy Go automatic carwash rinsed a fair amount of the shells and the muck, but a coating remained that seemed to be stuck there for good. She could read the reference to the verse in Deuteronomy. People gonna think I'm born again, she reflected, cracking a humorless smile.

When she parked in front of the Taneys' apartment house, she glanced in the front window. Someone was home; she could see bodies moving around inside. She was relieved to know that her drive was not a waste of time. Now that the trial could be just around the bend, it was imperative that she connect with the family.

Donita looked curious as she opened the door in response to her knock. "Did something happen?" she inquired.

"Actually, yes, you could say that," Elsie hedged. "May I come in?"

Donita nodded. Elsie followed her into the front room, where the family was gathered around a recent acquisition: a television. Obviously a secondhand set with major picture and sound problems, it was not providing much entertainment. The girls watched anxiously as Roy Mayfield fiddled with the knobs and dials.

"Just look at that," Donita whispered with awe, nodding in the direction of the television. "I never in my life had a man who could bring something like that home, and make it work. That Roy's something."

She looked at Elsie as if she expected a response. Staring at the woman's blithe expression, Elsie's gut clenched and she tasted bile. But she swallowed back her response. Working hard to keep her face neutral, she said, "That's sure something."

"Roy has a head for that fancy stuff. He's got a computer. And a cell phone. Of his own."

"Well, that's handy."

"Yes it is. So if you want to get ahold of me, you could call Roy's phone. Ain't that right," Donita said, turning to Roy, who was manipulating a screwdriver. "Ain't you got a cell phone and a computer?"

Roy looked up from his task, regarding Elsie and Donita with a flat expression. "Nobody touches my computer. Or my phone."

"We ain't bothering it, I'm just telling Elsie. How's the TV coming?"

He gave an inarticulate grunt, which could be interpreted as either good or bad news.

Donita smiled. "That Roy. He'll get it working in two

shakes of a tail. We got a good daddy to take care of us now."

Elsie looked at Donita with a sinking feeling in her stomach.

"Maybe we should go to the kitchen. I need to talk to you about something important," she said to her in a quiet voice.

Mayfield looked up from the TV as she spoke. "No need to go anywhere," he said firmly. Donita looked uncertain as she glanced from Elsie to Mayfield.

"We don't want to disturb you all," Elsie said reassuringly. "We'll just be a minute." With that, she started toward the kitchen, willing Donita to follow. She needed to assert leadership. At this point in the proceedings, she couldn't let Roy Mayfield create an impediment.

But Mayfield stood and laid a hand on Donita's shoulder. "You ain't got nothing to say to Donita I can't hear," he said. "I'm head of the house here. Everything goes through me." He gave Donita a shove. "Sit down, Donita."

Donita did as she was told. Elsie surveyed the situation with concern. Donita sat on the edge of the couch, regarding her with an apologetic smile, waiting for her to speak. Kristy and Tiffany also had their eyes on Elsie, while Charlene kept her gaze doggedly fixed on the fuzzy television screen.

Elsie felt a chill, despite her heavy coat. This was what Josh Nixon predicted when he revealed that Donita had another man. What else, she wondered, was he right about?

She wanted to slap Mayfield down but stopped herself.

Maybe she should proceed as though he wasn't creating a problem.

"Okay," she said, walking over to the couch and taking a seat next to Donita. "Well, here's the news. Kris's lawyer filed a motion to reduce bond, and the hearing was held today."

"So he's getting out," Mayfield said accusingly, turning away from the set and fixing Elsie with an angry glare. "I knew it."

Kristy, with an expression of horror, said, "Lord, Lord, he's gonna be mad. We're all gonna get it." Donita's hand involuntarily went to her jaw, as if to deflect a blow. Tiffany jumped up and ran to Elsie and clutched her hand. She squeezed it, looking at her with urgency in every muscle of her small face.

Elsie gently detached herself from the child's grip. "He's not going anywhere," she said. "The judge overruled the motion; he said he would *not* lower Kris's bond, so he's staying in jail while he waits for trial."

The relief in the room was palpable. The girls relaxed. Tiffany returned to her spot. Picking up her Barbie where she'd dropped it a moment before, she kissed the doll's nylon head, though she kept her gaze trained on Elsie. Kristy's head dropped to her knees and she exhaled audibly.

"So that's good," Elsie continued, cheerfully. "And the other big news is that the judge set our case as the backup to a big civil case the week after next. And that civil case is looking like it could settle. So it's just possible that we may go to trial in ten days." The room was silent.

"Wouldn't that be great? We can put all this behind us when it's done."

She examined the faces that turned toward her in the Taneys' front room. They wore uniform expressions of dismay. She wasn't surprised; going to trial wouldn't be a treat for any of them.

"But we just had a trial," Kristy said.

"Now, honey, remember, that was the preliminary hearing before the judge upstairs."

"You bet I remember. It made me sick. I puked. Two times."

"But you'll be an old hand now, Kristy. This time it's the real trial, in the big courtroom with Judge Rountree and a jury in the jury box. You'll testify, and Charlene will, and your mom, and Dr. Petrus, and Tina Peroni, and some police officers. And I'll be in the courtroom every minute." Elsie spoke with false enthusiasm, trying to dispel the air of dread that hung over the room.

"I don't want to do it again," Kristy said. "I don't like it at the court. It scares me to death." She hid her face on her knees, covering her head with both arms.

Elsie sat in silence for a few moments. She wanted to offer comfort, but she could not deny the painful challenge that awaited the girl. "It's going to be all right, Kristy."

A muffled voice came from Kristy, whose head remained buried in her arms.

"I can't. I can't do it." Kristy lifted her head. "Roy, I don't want to." Jumping up from the floor, the girl ran to Roy and wrapped her arms around his waist. "Roy, say I don't have to. Please," she begged in a wheedling tone.

Elsie said, "You have to, honey. You don't have any choice." She found it disconcerting to see the child snuggled up to Roy Mayfield. Turning her head away, she rummaged in her purse for a pen and smoothed down the top sheet of a pad of paper.

Mayfield advanced on her. "Just a minute here," he said, his chest thrust out. "These girls don't want to fool with this no more. They want to move on, go on with their lives, put what their daddy done in the past. You get him to plead guilty. That's your job."

She'd lost her patience with his interference. The reach of his attempted domination extended beyond the Taney family circle; he was trying to shut down her case.

In a sharp voice she said, "I can't get him to do anything. That's not how it works. We have to be ready for trial, to prove our case in court. The girls are the state's witnesses; they have to appear."

"This is a free country, man. Nobody in this family has to do anything unless I say so. I know the law," he added. "Maybe we'll drop the charges. You make him a deal that, if Kris leaves town, we'll drop the criminal thing."

Drop the criminal thing? she thought, dumbfounded. Who the fuck do you think you are, cracker? Mayfield's demands were setting alarms off in her head.

Elsie decided to change tactics, not eager to discuss legal theory with him. Maybe if she pretended Mayfield was invisible, he would actually disappear. She turned back to Donita and gave her arm a friendly pat.

"Donita, I won't tell you that testifying in a criminal case is easy, because it's not, and I'm not going to be anything but straight with you." Donita locked eyes with her and seemed focused on what she was saying. "But it's the truth: it's out of your hands at this point. People get the mistaken notion," she continued, intentionally refusing to look at Mayfield, "that when they are the complaining witness in a criminal case, they can just drop the charge and make it disappear. That's not how it works."

She had the attention of everyone in the room, except for Charlene, who turned her head so Elsie could only see her ponytail. Kristy shook her head and stretched out on the floor. Tiffany came over and sat on her mother's lap, staring at Elsie, and Mayfield glowered by the TV set.

"I always thought you could. Drop it. I seen it on TV a hundred times," Donita said lamely. She ran her hand gently through Tiffany's red curls, combing out tangles with her fingers.

"Yeah, well, it's not like that in real life. This may sound weird, but it's the state of Missouri's case, and only the state gets to decide to drop the charge. See?"

Looking around the room, she hoped to see comprehension. Donita and her daughters focused on Mayfield, waiting for his reaction. He looked angry, like he was itching to fight.

When Elsie directed an unwavering gaze toward him, he turned abruptly and walked to the kitchen. She heard the faucet as he poured a glass of water. He returned a moment later and stood in the doorway.

Mayfield announced, "It ain't good for them girls to

be in court against their daddy like that, talking about that family business in front of the whole town. Don't you know it shames them?"

"Don't be ridiculous," Elsie replied matter-of-factly. "These girls are agents of justice." As she opened her folder and pulled out four pink subpoenas, she silently vowed that if Roy got in her way, she'd make him sorry he was ever born. After tearing off the originals, she handed them to Donita, then tucked the copies back into her file. "It's official now," she said, affecting a cheerful voice. "You've been served."

Donita examined the documents. "Tiffany, too?"

"Yeah, we better have her there. You never know."

From the kitchen, Mayfield said, "You can throw that one for Tiffany in the trash. Tiffany got nothing to say." Returning to the main room, he reached for Tiffany. "Ain't that right, baby? Come give Uncle Roy some sugar."

With a look of horror, the child shied away from him, clinging to her mother like a spider monkey.

Without a look at anyone, Charlene rose from the floor and dusted off her knees. She headed to the doorway.

"Charlene," Donita said, "where you going?"

Elsie spoke up. "Charlene? Can we go somewhere private? I need to talk to you. I need the name of a teacher from middle school."

Charlene didn't respond. She picked a jacket up off of the floor and put it on without looking back.

"Charlene!" Donita said again.

"Your mama is talking to you," Mayfield said in a warning tone.

Donita turned back to Elsie with Tiffany in her arms and spoke confidingly. "We think Charlene's got a boyfriend. We can't hardly keep her to home these days. Char," she repeated as the door opened, "when you coming back?"

Charlene looked over her left shoulder. Her face was stony. "Later," she replied shortly.

She had a black eye.

Startled, Elsie asked, "What happened to Charlene's eye?"

Donita laughed pleasantly, shaking her head. "That girl. She walked into a cabinet. She never looks where she's going."

Elsie looked at the others in the room, but no one would meet her eye. On impulse, she jumped up and ran out in the front yard, calling Charlene's name.

She caught a glimpse of the girl's black hair as Charlene rounded a corner and disappeared from view.

She wanted to curse. If she didn't find that middle school teacher, this house of cards could fall. But the glimpse of Charlene's black eye brought new worries. With Kris Taney in jail, who was using Charlene as a punching bag?

Chapter Thirty-Two

WHEN ELSIE ARRIVED at Breeon's party on Saturday night, she didn't bother to knock. Hearing music and revelry inside, she pushed the door open and walked right in. She was ready to cut loose in a big way. Since leaving Donita Taney's apartment on Friday, anxiety had dogged her. Spooked by Mayfield's ominous presence, the resistance of her witnesses, and the signs of abuse in the household, her head was about to explode.

A night under her parent's roof had provided a measure of relief. She'd rested soundly, lulled into sleep by a bellyful of ham and scalloped potatoes and the knowledge that her mother and father were watching over her. But when she awoke on Saturday morning, her problems remained: Our Earthly Fathers might be plotting their next move; trial was fast approaching; and Charlene's reputation for truthfulness was still an issue. She also feared that Charlene was at risk.

Because Elsie was a mandated reporter under Missouri statute, she was obliged to report the signs of abuse to Social Services, and she had done so the day before. Tina assured her that they would investigate, but Elsie felt a personal responsibility for the girl's safety. Maybe if she had confronted Donita about JoLee's revelations, the black eye would not have been inflicted.

Elsie spent the daytime hours on Saturday working out of her parents' house, combing the Taney file and preparing for other felony hearings she would handle in the coming week. But now it was Saturday night. She decided that taking a few hours off would do her good; she couldn't solve all the world's ills in one night anyway.

It was time to pour some alcohol on her problems. Armed with a bottle of red wine, she would drown out the Taneys and the chickens and the trial and Charlene's bruised face.

Elsie squeezed through the mass of party guests in Breeon's living room, exchanging shouts of greeting. It looked like the whole courthouse had turned out. Stacie and some women from the Circuit Clerk's office were packed like sardines onto the sofa. When Stacie leaned over to shout something to the girls next to her, they screamed with mirth as Stacie collapsed on the shoulder of the closest woman.

The crowd parted just enough for Elsie to push her way through to the kitchen. She needed a corkscrew and a glass without delay, because everyone was way ahead of her. In the kitchen, she found Breeon pulling a tray of hot wings out of the oven.

"Hand me that platter," Bree ordered. As Elsie found the dish for her friend, Bree shouted over the din, "Where have you been?"

"Working like a dog. Glad to be here, I promise you."

"Can you give me a hand with the food? They're eating like they've never seen a cocktail wienie before." She pointed out the pretzels and chips. Elsie swigged wine from a plastic cup while she poured the chips in a bowl.

As she leaned over to filch a chip for herself, someone grabbed Elsie's rear end. She shrieked, turning on her heel to see Doug, a young assistant prosecutor fresh out of law school. He obviously had too much to drink; his eyes were nearly crossed.

"Doug, that's not funny," she warned. "Don't mess with me. I'll snatch you bald, son." He was so out of it that she felt a little sorry for him. "You go sit down somewhere. Maybe someone should take you home." She was relieved to see him stumble into an available chair and close his eyes.

Ashlock appeared at her shoulder. "Is that guy bothering you?"

"Oh, Bob, he's just a drunk kid," she said. Ashlock gave Doug the evil eye as the boy nodded in the chair. Elsie gave the detective an impulsive hug. "I am so glad to see you here. You don't generally make it to these wild Hollywood parties. Hey, what's up with my valentine?"

"Only partial prints, but the handwriting matches the samples given by the defendant."

"Great! That's wonderful news. Thanks for elbowing your way over here to tell me."

He took her arm and led her to a corner of the kitchen where they could talk without shouting. "I want to talk to you. Why didn't you tell me about the trouble you've been having?"

She was perplexed for a moment; she'd been juggling so many problems lately that she wasn't sure which one he referred to. "What didn't I tell you?" she asked.

"Good God, girl, how about those church people heckling you and protesting and vandalizing your car? Why did I have to hear about that secondhand?"

"Oh," she said, leaning against the counter and taking a sip from her cup. "I didn't want to sound stupid."

He looked like he hadn't heard her correctly. "Stupid?"

"You know. Chicken." She laughed at the irony of her word choice. "Ha ha. A pun." When he shook his head in disagreement, she reached over and squeezed his shoulder. "I wanted to handle things myself. I didn't want to look like I was afraid."

"Did it occur to you that I might be able to help you?"

"Lord, Ashlock, you're a most fabulous friend, but I can't expect you to serve as my constant protector, like a bodyguard or something."

"Yeah, well, I can help you call off the dogs. With that church group, those 'dads' rights' people."

He had her complete attention. She even set her cup down on the kitchen counter. "How?"

Ashlock had a relative who worked in the Pentecostal church who was familiar with the congregation in Barton whose members had rallied around Taney. "He says they're not bad people, they're just mistaken about the facts on this one. That guy, Webster, who's hooked up with the Earthly Fathers thing, he's a member of the church, and he's fed them a bunch of baloney about Taney being the victim of a plot cooked up by an unfaithful wife. Did you know Webster's related to Taney?"

"Yeah, they're cousins: I stumbled onto that. Still, it's strange to me that Webster would throw all that public support to Taney. Webster looks pretty clean."

"Well, they're blood kin: it's the code of the hills. And since he's a leader in that little Pentecostal church, he's managed to get everyone worked up over this case. It's not that hard to convince people of a big bad government conspiracy these days."

"You know, I'm Missouri Ozarks born and bred, and all my life I've heard people talk about the 'code of the hills,' but no one has ever outlined it for me."

"Miss Elsie," Ashlock drawled, "if you don't know the code of the hills, I don't believe I can explain it to you."

Elsie gave him a little shove. "But the church people. What's your buddy say we should do?"

"My uncle. It's a done deal. The church has lay clergy that preaches most Sundays, because they're so small. But they have a traveling preacher who comes in once a month. It's a guy my uncle knows. He's talked to him about it, and the preacher is going to try to shut the Taney stuff down. Tomorrow."

Jubilant, Elsie flung her arms around Ashlock's neck and gave him a hearty squeeze. "You're the best, Ash. The best." She gave him a resounding kiss on the cheek before she let him go. She backed away with regret—Ashlock was built like a brick shithouse. "Let me get you a drink. We should celebrate that piece of news. You don't know how those people have been flipping me out."

He stopped her before she could go in search of refreshment. "One more thing. He thinks we should be there."

Her smile dimmed as she asked, "Be where?"

"At the church. Tomorrow morning. He thinks it would help."

"Go to church? Tomorrow? Their church?"

He locked his eyes with hers. "Do you want to put this to rest or not?"

She made a face, but nodded.

"Okay," he said. "I'll pick you up at ten-thirty."

A woman appeared at Ashlock's shoulder. "There you are," she said. "I thought I'd lost you."

He smiled at her. "We've been talking business. The Taney case."

"Oh, Taney," she said, slipping her hand around Ashlock's arm. "I read about that in the paper."

Scrutinizing the woman, Elsie recognized her. She was a family law attorney from Lawrence County, down the highway from Barton. Elsie stuck out her hand. "Elsie Arnold."

Ashlock looked sheepish. "I should've introduced you. Elsie, this is Caroline Applegate."

Politely, Elsie said, "Nice to meet you," as she tried to scope her out without being obvious.

"You, too. Bob's told me all about your case. Thank goodness you all are locking that man up. I do a lot of guardian ad litem work, so I know how tough those cases are."

Ashlock's date was nice, Elsie admitted to herself grudgingly. She was attractive, too, with dark eyes and an impressive rack.

The woman tugged at Ashlock's arm. "You promised me dinner."

"I'm ready," he agreed. To Elsie, he said, "Tomorrow morning, don't forget. I'll pick you up."

"I'm staying at my mom and dad's," she said, feeling absolutely infantile.

But Ashlock nodded with satisfaction. "I'm glad to hear it. I'll see you there."

As they walked away, she assessed Caroline Applegate's butt, glad to see it was no smaller than her own. Instantly, she chided herself; she was competing with Ashlock's date when she had no right, like the classic dog in the manger.

Well, shit, she thought, I think I'm going to get drunk. She took a massive swig from the plastic cup.

Trying to make her way back into the living room, she bumped into Bree, who responded by grabbing her in a fierce hug and kissing her on the forehead.

Bree said, "I just want to say, you're a great friend, and I love you. I just wanted to say that."

"Honey, I know that," Elsie replied.

"I know you do. How do you like my party?"

"Great."

"Where's the jackass?"

Though Elsie felt she should rise to Noah's defense, she laughed. "Night shift."

"Good. Bet you're having more fun without him."

She couldn't deny it.

Bree went on, "What do you need? Your glass is low. Let me get you some more wine."

Bree scooted through guests and made her way to the kitchen counter, where she found Elsie's wine bottle and poured her a brimming refill. "Here you go," she said, and then stopped short. "What's that?" she asked, looking around her.

Bree pushed her way into the living room, demanding, "Who's smoking in here?"

On the sofa, Stacie was cozied up to a man holding a cigarette.

"I told him I didn't see any ashtrays," Stacie said. She gave the man a little smack on the knee as he dropped the cigarette into an empty beer bottle. The smoke wafted up the bottle and out the neck. "Maybe next time you'll listen to me."

Breeon announced that she did not allow smoking in her home, reminding those within earshot that she had a young daughter and she did not intend for her child to sniff residual cigarette smoke.

"Sorry about that," the man said, rising from the couch cushions with a grunt and a chastened expression. "I'll take it outside."

The smoker headed out the front door with Stacie in tow, and Elsie followed. It would be nice to get out of the crowded rooms for a minute. Outside, she joined them as they sat on the front steps.

"Elsie, this is Scott," Stacie said, giving the man an adoring look. "I brought him to the Christmas party at Madeleine's house. We went to high school together in Sparta."

Elsie didn't remember him, but she said, "Nice to see you again, Scott."

"Yeah. Nice to meet someone who's not psycho about cigarette smoke. People are crazy these days. I can't even smoke in my own office since they passed that city law." He lit a fresh cigarette with a Bic lighter. With a look at Elsie, he extended the pack of Marlboros. "Want one?"

She hesitated, then took it. Sometimes she smoked a cigarette in a party setting, just for the heck of it. It seemed racy and daring. Tonight she was in a reckless mood.

Stacie gaped at her. "I cannot believe you smoke."

"I don't. Not really. I smoked some in undergrad, when I was drinking. Which was frequently," she confessed with a grimace. "But I haven't smoked in years," she assured them, which was a lie.

Shivering on the steps, she inhaled the smoke. It burned her throat like a hot poker and tasted terrible. She took a slug of wine to mask the lingering flavor. "Scott, this is vile. Don't be mad if I pitch it. I don't want Phillip Morris to get their hooks in me."

Scott winked at Elsie and blew a smoke ring. She laughed, the alcohol kicking in, and said, "I can do that."

Stacie gasped. "You cannot."

"Watch me," Elsie said. Her first attempt was unsuccessful; it had been a while since she'd done the trick. But she took another stab at it by coaxing the smoke over a curved tongue, and a cloud of smoke emerged in a relatively circular shape.

"Better," Scott said as he blew a series of rings, one after another.

Laughing out loud, she said, "Stacie, your friend is a show-off." This is fun she thought as she took another drag and tried to inhale again. It still tasted awful, but she was starting to get a nicotine buzz in addition to her alcohol glow.

"What the fuck do you think you're doing?" demanded a voice from the street.

Startled, she looked up to see Noah bearing down on her from the front walk. Feeling instantly guilty, she dropped the cigarette and ground it out with her shoe, before she thought to question her reaction. Why would she need to act like smoking a Marlboro was a hanging offense?

Stacie, failing to register Noah's demeanor, said, "Elsie, your man's here. Yay for you."

Elsie regarded him with caution. His face was like a thundercloud. Taking a sip from her cup, she tried to appear nonchalant. "What are you doing here?"

He took on an expression of disbelief and responded, "That's great. What a really sweet way to say hello."

She backpedaled to avoid a fuss. "I thought you weren't coming."

"I went to a shitload of trouble to get here tonight." She could see his anger rising. "I knew it. I fucking knew it."

He was so keyed up, he was scaring her. "Knew what?" she asked. She was a little muddled, but still, he wasn't making any sense.

He snatched the cup from her hand and flung it into the yard. "I knew I needed to check up on you tonight."

Checking up on me, she thought, aghast. She nearly spat as she exclaimed, "What is your fucking problem?"

"You're drunk again. Your tongue is purple. And you're smoking, for Christ's sake. If I don't watch you like a hawk, you'll act out. You are a full-time fucking job."

His audacity infuriated her. She cocked her head and said, "I ain't your job, bitch."

He grasped her upper arm and jerked her to a stand. "We're out of here," he said, pulling her down the sidewalk.

Cursing, Elsie twisted away from him to escape his grip, but she couldn't free herself. He had dragged her most of the way to the street when Bree came tearing out of the house. She ran up to Noah and grabbed him by the collar of his shirt. "Let her go or I swear I'll kick your ass."

"Fuck you," he said.

Elsie quit struggling with Noah; she needed to put a stop to the madness. "Let's all settle down," she said.

But Bree took her by the hand, trying to pull her back toward the house. "Come on back inside," she said.

"She's going home," Noah barked. "She's drunk. You both are."

Bree faced him down with fury. "You get off my property before I call the cops. You're not welcome here."

"Call the cops?" he jeered. "You're the one who's in for trouble. Drunk and disorderly. I could report a noise complaint right now and shut your shitty little party down."

"Stop it. Stop," Elsie entreated him. She was desperate to defuse the situation. She would let him take her home, to get him out of there. The night was ruined for her anyway. "I'll go on; I'm ready, anyhow. Just let me grab my purse. It's there on the front steps." She hurried back to the porch and snatched up her purse, horrified to see that Stacie and her friend Scott had witnessed the whole episode.

"Everything okay?" Scott asked.

"Yeah, fine," Elsie said, turning her back to them. She rushed back to the pair on the street, giving Bree a hug as she told her good-night.

But Bree kept her eye trained on Noah. "I've got your number," she said.

Without waiting for Noah to lead the way, Elsie started toward his car. "Let's head out," she said over her shoulder.

As they drove away, she slid low in the seat, angry and humiliated. They sat without speaking for several blocks, until Noah broke the silence.

"Want to go to my place?"

Elsie looked at him with incredulity; she knew what the invitation implied. He must be crazy to think she would be willing to have sex with him after he'd man-handled her.

But she swallowed back a sharp reply and said, "Take me to my parents' house. I'm staying with them this weekend."

He exhaled an injured breath. "So after I went to all that trouble to get off tonight, I'm just supposed to chauffeur you to your folks' house."

Looking out the car window, she nodded. "Yeah. That's what you're going to do."

Staring through the windshield, he clutched the steering wheel convulsively, pressing his fingers into the vinyl cover. "I'd think you'd be ashamed to let them see you like this. I would never let my folks see me drinking. Never," he repeated with conviction.

Wearily, Elsie closed her eyes, rubbing her eyelids so hard she saw colors. She wished him a million miles away. "Well, I suppose that's because of your moral superiority."

They came to a four-way stop and he hit the brakes so hard that her body jerked against the seat belt. He turned to her and said, "You got a smart mouth. You know it?"

When she didn't respond, he said, "Answer me when I'm talking to you. How come you've got such a goddamn smart mouth?"

Weary of his tirade, she snapped, "It comes with the smart brain."

He threw the car in park. Reaching over, he grasped her around the neck with one hand. With the other, he swung back and slapped her hard across the mouth.

She covered her mouth in a reflexive gesture as blood spurted through her fingers. The blow was so vicious, her front teeth cut into the soft tissue inside of her lip.

He released her neck, shaking his head at the sight of the blood dripping down her hand and onto her arm. "That's your own fault. You've been pushing me all week. That smart mouth was bound to get you in trouble."

Reeling from pain and shock, she stared at him as he put the car back in Drive. Glancing at her again, he said, "You can't go to your parents' house looking like that. I'm taking you to my place."

Like hell you will, she thought, unbuckling the seat belt with her bloody hands. She opened the door and shot out of the car. She stumbled as her feet met the pavement, then righted herself and ran blindly down the street into a residential neighborhood.

Elsie could hear him curse and a car door slam behind her. She knew he could outrun her, so she dodged into an unfenced yard where the house was still lit up and people inside were awake. Taking refuge in the bushes beside a patio door, she saw a couple watching television in the family room. She pulled out her phone, prepared to call for help, and decided that if he came into the yard after her, she would pound on the glass door and beg for assistance.

Her heart pounding like a kettle drum, she heard Noah call her name in the distance, but as the seconds slowly passed, the sound grew fainter, then stopped altogether. Maybe he gave up, she thought. Maybe got himself under control. He surely wouldn't want to have a bloody confrontation with his girlfriend in the public eye.

As she huddled in the bushes, pressed against the aluminum siding of some stranger's house, she pressed her shirt against her bleeding mouth and wept, wondering how she could possibly have wound up in this position.

Chapter Thirty-Three

EARLY THE NEXT morning, Elsie awoke at her apartment with a start. Looking around, she was confused to see that she was sleeping on her living room couch, tangled in a quilt. When the memory of the prior night came to her, she lay back on the cushions with a shudder.

The night before, when she finally dared to emerge from the bushes, she'd been so distraught she hardly knew where to turn. Certainly her parents would rush to her aid, but she couldn't bring herself to make the call; she couldn't let her mother and father see her in that condition.

She wouldn't go back to Bree's house, either. If she did, everyone from the courthouse would see what had happened. So she stumbled to the street corner, called a cab, and then sat on the curb under the street light and waited, pressing her shirtsleeve against her mouth to stem the flow of blood. Shivering in misery, she wished she hadn't left her coat at Bree's house.

When the cab finally came and ferried her to her apartment, she trudged to the bathroom to check the damage in the mirror. She had shed so much blood, she was afraid her mouth would need stitches, and she could not contemplate a trip to the emergency room. Lifting her lip to examine the wound, she could see where her teeth cut into the inner flesh of her mouth. To her relief, the wound was not gaping.

No stitches. She didn't want to seek medical attention unless it was absolutely necessary. She didn't want to answer questions about how it happened.

So she spent the night curled into a corner of her sofa, nursing her wound with an ice bag and reliving the fight with Noah, involuntarily experiencing the blow in her mind over and over again, even when she shut her eyes.

On the sofa on Sunday morning, something nagged at the back of her mind. She tried to shrug it off and sleep but there was something she was supposed to remember, something she couldn't quite place. When recollection struck, her mental fog cleared instantly: she had promised to go to the Westside Apostolic Church for morning services, and Ashlock was picking her up. At her parents' house.

She vaulted off the couch and flew to her phone, digging it out of her purse in a flash. *Please please please pick up,* she prayed as his cell phone rang. When he answered, she exhaled with relief.

"Elsie?" he said.

"Hey, Ash, I'm so glad I caught you. I'm not at my folks; I'm home. At my apartment," she added, to ensure that she was totally clear about her whereabouts.

"Are you okay? You sound funny."

She did. Her fat lip made it difficult to enunciate. "Yeah, I'm fine. Well, actually," she amended, "I'm not feeling so hot. I think I'm coming down with something. You ought to go on without me this morning."

She fancied she could sense his disapproval through the telephone. "That's not the deal. You need to be there, so we can put this to rest. These people have done you wrong, and we need to put a stop to it. Together."

In frustration, she groaned, "Ash, I'm not up to it."

"You were up to it—what? Twelve hours ago? So you've either got a case of cold feet or the cocktail flu. I'll pick you up in twenty minutes. 'Bye." And he hung up.

Elsie wanted to howl. Treading into the bathroom, she surveyed herself in the mirror again. It was as bad as she feared. She turned on the faucet and went to work.

Though she painted her face with skill, there was no hiding her swollen mouth. Awaiting Ashlock on the cold steps outside her apartment building, she pulled her scarf over her head, hoping to hide her appearance when he picked her up. But as she slipped into the passenger seat, he eyed her with shock.

"What happened?" he asked.

"Nothing. I mean, I took a tumble. Again." She tried to make a comical face but it hurt.

He looked away from her. Staring out the window, he said, "Who did it? Noah?"

She shook her head. "Ash, don't make a dramatic thing out of this. It was an accident, really." Her sense of shame was profound. She could not bring herself to admit to anyone that she'd been assaulted, least of all Ashlock.

He sat in grim silence for a minute. "You need to report it."

"Nothing to report," she said adamantly.

Ashlock put the car in gear. "Son of a bitch," he spat.

As he drove across town, neither of them spoke. When she ventured a glance his way, the fury in his countenance was almost frightening; his eyes were narrowed and the muscle in his jaw twitched repeatedly.

Turning away, she stared out the window. They had entered a neighborhood of aging strip centers serving residential blocks of ranch-style houses. Most of the homes suffered neglect, with buckled exterior siding and crooked plastic miniblinds hanging askew inside the windows.

One such house had been converted to a church. A hand-stenciled sign stood in the front yard, pronouncing it the Westside Apostolic Pentecostal Church. Next to the sign, a large cross was rooted in the yard. It was painted white except for three bright splashes of red, placed where large nails symbolized the crucifixion.

"That's just creepy," Elsie observed, taking in the bloody cross.

Ashlock didn't acknowledge the comment. Without looking at her, he said, "I'm going to kick his ass."

Facing him with a jerk of the head, she almost repeated her denial of Noah's involvement. Thinking better of it, she asked, "Who? Martin Webster or the preacher?"

Ashlock put the car in Park and said, "Well, we're here." He looked out the windshield for a long moment, then shook his head. "Let's get in there and turn these folks around. Ready?"

"Yeah," she said, nodding. "Let's beard the lion in his den."

They entered a converted garage that served as the church sanctuary. With only a few portable area heaters evident, the temperature inside was frigid. Congregants sat on the four rows of folding chairs set on the concrete floor, with a center aisle dividing them into two sections. Ashlock led Elsie to two empty seats in the back.

Settling in her chair, she felt the shock that her arrival created and grew unnerved as the congregants turned to stare. Her presence, especially as she was sporting a battered face, provoked gawking and whispering. Martin Webster and the Earthly Fathers were present, sitting front and center. Pointing at Elsie and Ashlock, a couple of men got up to consult with Webster. She recognized a man who came in carrying a stack of collection plates as the white-haired man who had called her Jezebel, wearing a leather bolo tie with a rodeo clasp. Upon closer inspection, she saw that he was younger than she had originally thought, maybe in his late forties; the shock of white hair was deceptive. And he was big as a mountain, at least as tall as Noah Strong. She looked around for the young protester who had called her a dirty leg slut, but he was nowhere to be seen.

Fortunately, the preacher appeared quickly. He walked up to Ashlock and offered his hand. "I'll take a shot and guess you're an Ashlock," the pastor said.

"Yessir, pastor."

"You and your cousin Frank look enough alike to be brothers."

"Oh, don't be telling him that. He'll say it's an insult."

The pastor laughed, a booming sound that rang in the confined space. Martin Webster approached, grasped the preacher's arm and began to speak. The preacher silenced him with a look. Rebuffed, Martin returned to the front row.

"We're ready to begin the service. Welcome to the house of the Lord," the preacher said, and proceeded down the aisle.

Men with pressed shirtsleeves passed out worn maroon hymnbooks as the preacher lifted a wooden lectern and set it on a folding table. The chairs and table made up the only furnishings in the makeshift church, apart from a large galvanized metal tub, the kind that farm supply stores sold for watering cattle. Elsie knew without being told that it was used as a baptistery. She craned her neck to see whether it held any water but couldn't tell. A terrible thought intruded; it occurred to her that the tub was deep enough to drown her. Ashlock won't let it happen, she thought, and scooted her chair a little closer to his.

The congregation stood as a woman pushed a button on a small CD player located next to the lectern, then they all began to sing "Onward Christian Soldiers" in harmony with the recorded music. When the last chorus was sung, the pastor pushed the Stop button on the CD player and launched into an exhortation, inviting the Spirit to enter.

"But first," the preacher said, "let us begin by embracing the stranger in our midst. Are there any visitors present today?"

Elsie and Ashlock looked at one another. Ashlock paused for a beat, then raised a hand.

"Welcome, brother," the preacher said heartily. "Introduce yourself."

"I'm Bob," Ashlock began, but the preacher interrupted him, encouraging him to stand. Ashlock set his hymnbook on the floor and stood. "My name is Bob Ashlock, and I'm a visitor here. I brought a friend of mine with me." Elsie gave a tentative wave from her seat. Ashlock tugged on her arm and she stood beside him. "Her name is Elsie. Elsie Arnold."

An angry buzz sounded in the garage, but the pastor's voice projected over it. "Welcome to you; it's a privilege to welcome all children of God into the Lord's house. Be sure to stop in the kitchen for coffee and refreshments after the service. Now, do we have any prayer requests?"

As petitions were offered on behalf of the sick and the infirm, Elsie relaxed a little. Maybe she wouldn't be tarred and feathered by the angry mob. She thanked her stars for the benevolent protection of the preacher. When other heads bowed in prayer, she didn't have to fake a prayerful attitude. She offered up a fervent plea: *Dear God, please let us get out of here alive.* After a moment's thought, she added, *And please let Kris Taney be convicted and sentenced to the maximum penalty under law. And don't let his conviction be overturned on appeal.* There, she thought with satisfaction. Good prayer.

A second hymn was sung, invoking hand clapping and arm waving from the congregation. Elsie tried not to stare as a man took to the aisle and engaged in an uneven jig, stomping and dancing to a rhythm all his own. Others in the church were nonplussed, and the preacher applauded him, announcing that while sinners danced in nightclubs and bars, Christians danced for joy in the house of the Lord.

A long sermon followed, in which the pastor exhorted his flock to avoid specific temptations: the evils of strong drink and lusts of the flesh. Then he began telling them to resist conformity to the secular world, but soon zeroed in on the particular sin he wanted to focus on: violation of the Seventh Commandment. He roundly condemned adultery and those who engaged in it; even the contemplation, he reminded them, was sin. The preacher built momentum as he called for their consensus.

"Did David sin when he lay with Bathsheba?"

"Yes he did," a man in the first row shouted, and arms lifted in agreement.

"Did Amnon sin when he lay with his sister Tamar?"

"Yes!" rang out the voices in the church.

The pastor's face was red and sweat dripped from his brow as he called out, "Did Noah sin when he lay with his daughters?"

"Yes!"

The pastor leaned over the lectern and roared, "Did

that man, Taney—the one at the county jail—sin when he lay with *his* daughters?"

One or two voices said "Yes," but the response was patchy; people looked about in confusion.

Martin Webster raised his hand. "Pastor, I'd like to speak to that, if you don't mind."

"Speak to that?" Pastor Tom's sweat made a wet ring around the collar of his shirt. "Speak to *what*? Are you arguing with the book of Genesis? Second Samuel? The Seventh Commandment? Will you speak to whether a man laying with his daughter is a sin and an abomination?"

"Pastor, the government, the prosecutor, they trump up charges, they make up lies about people, to take their kids away. Like in Texas," he added feebly.

"You mean those Texas Mormons?"

"Well, Fundamentalist LDS, yes, pastor."

"Is this Taney a Mormon?"

"No. A Mormon? Land, no."

"Well, what is he?"

Webster's voice was defensive as he said, "He's my kin. And the head of his household."

Clearing his throat, the preacher pointed at Webster. "Cut that Taney away like a cancer. I'll tell you what Taney is. He's worse than a pagan. He has sacrificed his little children on the altar of his own evil lust!"

The congregation recoiled as the preacher recited a litany of Taney's crimes. Elsie had to credit Pastor Tom for his thorough account. His blow-by-blow description of the crimes committed by Taney were more detailed than the police reports and media coverage, and more vivid than the courtroom testimony. One by one the congregation seemed to be swayed by the preacher's account; men shook their heads in disgust, while women covered their mouths with their hands. Only Martin Webster and a few other stalwarts remained unmoved, sitting very straight in their chairs, showing no sign of sympathy or remorse.

Ashlock stole a glance at Elsie and gave her the barest wink. She took his hand in hers and gave it a squeeze. A blissful feeling washed over her as she realized that her courtroom critics' corner had been dispelled.

After the benediction, Elsie desperately wanted to make a quick getaway, but Ashlock led her into the kitchen, where they were serving pink grapefruit juice and some hard gingersnap cookies. The men made pleasant conversation with Bob, but Elsie was generally ignored.

Crunching the cookie, she was surreptitiously seeking a trash can to dump the uneaten portion when a young woman approached. She leaned in close to Elsie and whispered, "Your dress is pretty."

Surprised by the contact, Elsie surveyed the girl. She was a remarkably pretty woman of about twenty, with a scrubbed face, arched eyebrows, and a long braid of shiny brown hair. But when she smiled, she revealed prominent front teeth.

Elsie glanced at the girl's dress, eager to return the compliment; she wore a long smock in a blue print. "I love that pattern," Elsie said. "So nice."

The girl's eyes darted around the room. "I need to talk to you for a minute," she whispered.

"Sure. What can I do for you?"

"Not here. In the restroom." Looking over her shoulder, as if afraid they'd be overheard, she jerked her head to a hallway. "Follow me."

She followed the woman's rapid steps. They ducked into a small bathroom fitted with a toilet and a sink. The girl latched the door with a hook and eye lock.

Reaching behind Elsie, she turned both faucets on the sink then sat on the toilet with a nervous laugh. "That's what me and my sis do at home when we don't want Daddy or Mama to hear. I'm Naomi."

Elsie nodded. She was growing uncomfortable.

Naomi said, "I saw you at the courthouse. I was one of the ones with the signs."

Elsie immediately reached for the lock and flipped it up, thinking, I'm out of here. But Naomi grabbed her hand.

"I just went because Daddy said to. He hates you like poison, but I don't. I think you're brave."

Elsie caught a glimpse of her swollen mouth in the bathroom mirror. Turning away from the reflection, she asked, "Why does he hate me?'

"He says you're a Jezebel. Tempting believers to stray from the family."

Jezebel. "Does your father have white hair?"

Naomi smiled. "That's my daddy. Luke Morrison. You remember him."

Elsie shuddered, an involuntary twitch. "What do you want from me?"

Naomi reached into her smock and pulled out a piece

of paper folded into a small square. "I want you to give this to my sis."

Elsie's brow wrinkled. "Do I know her?"

"Goodness sakes no, you wouldn't. But she's in that place where women run away to, to get away from their husbands."

"Oh, okay," Elsie said, as understanding dawned. "Your sister is at the Battered Women's Center."

Nodding, Naomi said, "She told me she'd be running off for sure, the next time he wore her out. He's awful mean; it's just how he is. You saw him at the courthouse, he called you nasty names."

Elsie knew exactly who Naomi referred to. She held out her hand and the girl pressed the paper into her palm. "You'll take it? You promise?"

"I'll do it. Anything you want me to tell her?"

Rising, Naomi flushed the toilet. The water in the tank made a furious sound.

"Tell her it don't matter to me what she did. Tell her I love her anyway." She scooted in front of Elsie and peeked out. "Me first," she whispered. "You wait a minute."

The door clicked shut and Elsie waited, turning off the faucets and watching the water circle down the drain.

Returning to the kitchen, she made a beeline for Ashlock and clutched his arm. Giving him a look he could not mistake, she sent him a mental message: *Let's blow this firetrap.* With a nod to the preacher, Ashlock took her by the elbow and they made their way out.

In the sanctuary of Ashlock's car Elsie moaned with relief. "Oh my God, that was a killer."

Ashlock smiled. "Was it worth it?"

"Yes, absolutely. You were right. But now I have to go to the Battered Women's Center of the Ozarks. Take me over to Bree's; my car is there."

"Why are you heading to the BWO?"

"I have to deliver a message from one of our Pentecostal pals."

"So that's where you went off to. I saw that girl whispering at you."

"She's scared as a rabbit. We had to hide in the bathroom so Big Daddy wouldn't hear." Rooting in her purse for her car keys, she found the note and put it in her wallet. "I felt sorry for her. She was nice. Pretty little thing."

Ash turned onto Bree's street. "I thought so until she smiled. That girl could eat corn through a picket fence."

In spite of herself, Elsie laughed. "You're terrible."

His mouth twitched. "You look beat. How about I take that note for you? You go home, get some rest."

"Thanks, Ash, but I said I'd do it. It shouldn't take long, I'm just dropping it off." As she opened the car door, a battered blue pickup whizzed by, startling her. "What the hell?" she said.

Ashlock was frowning. "He's going way too fast for a residential street."

"Crazy son of a bitch could've run me down. Well, I'm heading, thanks. See you at the courthouse, okay?"

But Ashlock didn't respond. He was squinting, looking through the windshield as the blue pickup turned a corner and vanished from sight.

Chapter Thirty-Four

ELSIE PULLED HER Ford Escort up to a red brick hotel in the old section of town not far from the Taneys' apartment house on High Street. The hotel sat near the railroad tracks, on a commercial block that fell from use when the town moved south in the 1970s.

As she sat in her car, she examined the hotel, certain she had the right place, though the building bore no name. The location of the Battered Women's Center of the Ozarks was not a secret in a community the size of Barton, Missouri.

She grabbed her purse and headed inside. The place looked deserted. She walked up to the front desk and took in her surroundings while waiting for someone to appear. The lobby bore signs of former grandeur. The floor was covered in octagonal tile in geometric designs, and the room was paneled in dark walnut trim, with a grand staircase leading to the second floor. Time and neglect had left their mark, however; water-stained plaster and faded wallpaper stood in jarring contrast to the building's original features, like a grand old lady in a tattered dress.

A woman with long gray hair plaited into a braid appeared from a back room and took her place at the front desk. She asked, "What can I do for you?" eyeing her with sympathy, as if she assumed Elsie was in need of refuge.

Standing up very straight, Elsie spoke in a business-like manner. "I'm here to deliver a message." Pulling the note from her wallet, she placed it on the counter where the gray-haired woman could examine it.

"That's for Ruth. She's here, all right." The woman scrutinized her, wondering whether she posed a threat. "She don't want to see nobody."

"I don't want to disturb her," Elsie said, raising a hand to dispel the suggestion. "Her sister gave me this note and asked me to deliver it. And said to say that she loves her."

"I'll see she gets it." She locked Elsie in a steely gaze. "Anything else I can do? To help you?"

"Nope," Elsie said resolutely, "that's it." A stack of flyers lay on the desk. To break eye contact, she turned her attention to them. "What's this?"

"It's a list of things we could use around here. Some groups give us donations, so we put down the things we need the most."

Elsie scanned the list: shampoo, soap, toothpaste and brushes, gently used clothing.

"I'll hang onto this," she said brightly. "When I have

the chance, I'll pick some things up and bring them out here to you."

The woman nodded, her face knowing. "You do that."

Elsie ducked out of the building in a hurry. She wanted to go home and make an ice pack. Her mouth hurt.

But she was only a stone's throw from the Taneys'. It was high time to sit Charlene down for a talk. Standing on the sidewalk, she struggled with the decision. Looking up, she saw that the sky threatened rain. She was sick to death of foul weather. And she was worn-out, and her bed was calling to her like a siren.

But she needed to seize the opportunity to get Charlene alone, if she could. I'll just drive by, she decided. They may not even be home.

When she reached High Street, rain was pelting the windshield. Shivering in the driver's seat, she took a moment to gird herself for battle. Roy was probably inside, and she'd have to fight her way through him to get to Charlene.

But she was determined to talk to her, outside of Roy and Donita's presence. With the trial approaching, there were too many unsettled issues with Charlene for her to proceed with confidence.

She was still framing an excuse for her surprise visit when a figure appeared on foot at the end of the block. Elsie sat up straight, peering through the windshield at the girl, her dark head ducked against the rain, fists thrust into the pockets of a thin jacket: Charlene. Elsie shivered, with a combination of relief and trepidation.

Starting the engine, she crept down the street until she and Charlene were almost abreast.

"Hey, girl," Elsie called in a cheery tone, resting her elbow in the open window. "What you doing?"

Charlene flicked a bare glance at her and kept walking.

"Charlene, it's Elsie. Hold on a minute; I want to talk to you."

Charlene walked on for several paces before stopping. It was easy to see that she was not pleased to run into her. Slowly, she crossed the street and walked up to the car. "What you doing around here?"

"Hanging. Waiting for you."

Charlene leaned in the driver's window and stared into Elsie's face with curiosity. "Who slapped the shit out of you?"

Elsie opened her mouth to lie, then snapped it shut. Studying Charlene's black eye, she said, "I was going to ask you the same thing."

Charlene backed away from the car. "Didn't you hear? Walked into a door. Wasn't looking where I was going."

Elsie gave her a glum smile. "Yeah. Yeah, me too." With a jerk of her head, she asked, "Want to get in?"

"What for?"

"I'm going to Sonic. You hungry? Thirsty?"

The rain ran down Charlene's face in rivulets as she eyed Elsie with a wary look.

"Come on," Elsie said. "You're getting wet."

After a second of silent consideration, Charlene shrugged and walked to the passenger side. As she slid into the seat, Elsie said, "Buckle up."

Charlene ignored her, looking toward the old white house. "Why didn't you go inside? How come you're waiting out here?"

"I just need to see you. So we can talk."

Charlene's eyes were hooded. "So talk."

"Let's get to Sonic first. I need a big drink."

"I don't know. Maybe I should go inside. I got to see Tiffany."

"We can get something for you to bring back to Tiffany. You know what she likes. Kristy, too."

"I don't care nothing about bringing Kristy stuff. She can take care of herself."

Elsie headed for the Sonic Drive-In. The car was silent; now that she had Charlene at her side, she wasn't sure how to proceed. Pulling into the parking slot, she let Charlene study the menu items on the display board for a minute before asking, "What do you want? I'm buying."

"What you getting?"

Elsie rolled down the car window and pushed the red speaker button. "Diet cherry limeade. My favorite."

"I like Coke."

"Okay." Feeling nervous, she pushed the button a second time. "You want diet?"

"What for?"

With a glance at the girl's bony frame, Elsie didn't answer. *Lord yes—what for indeed?*

When the curb waitress brought the drinks to the car, Charlene gaped at the size of the cups. Elsie made a face. "I know, it's embarrassing. I drink this stuff by the gallon. Looks like they're bringing it in a bucket, doesn't it?"

"I don't mind," Charlene said in a warmer tone, jamming the straw into the lid.

"You want to play the radio? Pick a station."

"I don't know none. You pick."

Elsie turned to a country station, noting with satisfaction that Charlene's face had lost its hostile aspect.

Charlene said, "That's Brad Paisley. Mama likes him. She thinks he's good looking."

"What about you? Who's your favorite?"

"I don't know nothing about it." But after a moment she said, "I like Toby Keith."

Elsie unbuckled her seat belt and turned to face Charlene. "Because he's good looking?"

"Because he's tough. He ain't afraid of nobody. Don't put up with nobody's shit."

Elsie digested the statement. "That's how I'd describe you."

Charlene's head jerked up in surprise. "Huh?"

"What you said about Toby Keith, it's how you seem to me. Lord knows you're tough."

Charlene looked pleased by the comparison, though she ducked her head to hide it. She sucked on her straw.

"So," Elsie said, treading carefully, "there's something I've been needing to talk with you about."

The guarded look dropped down like a curtain. "What?"

"About the deal in middle school. When the boys were after you in the bathroom."

"I done told you already."

"Yeah, back at the courthouse? You wouldn't talk about it. Didn't you say 'maybe later, maybe never'?"

Charlene rubbed her nose but didn't speak. Turning to face Elsie, she shot her a challenging glare.

Elsie sighed. "Oh, hon. Don't you know I'm on your side? This isn't morbid curiosity. I want to be able to protect you in court."

Chewing the straw, Charlene appeared to think it over. She said, "Nobody protects anybody. You got to take care of yourself."

Elsie laughed. "That sure sounds like Toby Keith. But he'd write a song about it."

Charlene looked out the window, rubbing condensation off the glass. "I want tater tots," she said.

"Okay. Ketchup and salt?" Elsie asked, rolling her window down.

"Yeah," Charlene said. After Elsie placed the order, Charlene spoke abruptly, words tumbling out.

"I shouldn't of believed nothing he said. Nothing. He went on like he liked me, but I should've knowed better. A man will do anything to get in your britches. Mama always told me."

"So who was the boy? Carlos?"

"Yeah." She smiled, an ironic twist of her mouth. "He played basketball, so he was a big deal, big somebody. And God, he was so hot."

Groaning, Elsie nodded. "What is it about the handsome ones? Why do strong women turn to mush when they come along?"

She saw that Charlene was studying her swollen lip. Elsie was glad when the waitress arrived with the tater tots and she could turn away to pay. She handed them to Charlene.

Popping a tot, Carlene chewed as she spoke. "That's the goddamned truth. When he said to meet him in the bathroom, I was so dumb. I was happy to do it, like it was going to be fun, breaking the rules, just him and me."

"And then?"

"I was hiding in a stall, waiting. And them other boys come in with him, and he bragged that he could make me show my tits or do anything. Anything he said."

"I bet that broke your heart."

"Pissed me off. I told him, 'Go fuck yourself,' and tried to light out of there. But there were three of them. They held me on the toilet while they felt me up."

"Oh, sweetheart. I'm so sorry. How'd the teacher find out?"

"I was shouting my fool head off."

"So the teacher heard you and came to the rescue?"

"Ha." Charlene's eyes hardened and she bent to suck on her straw.

"Didn't he help you? What did he see?"

Charlene looked out the window. "I don't know what all he seen. But he seen a girl in the boy's room where she ain't supposed to be. That's what he said, anyhow, when he took me to the principal's office."

"But you set him straight."

"I tried. But I said one thing and them boys lied."

Righteous anger rose in Elsie's chest. "That's so

unfair." She banged the steering wheel with the flat of her hand. "The teachers and the principal are supposed to protect you. I can't believe they didn't support you."

"Yeah? Well, it don't surprise me none. You got to look out for yourself. Can't wait around for someone to fix it. Do what you got to do." Shifting in the seat, she pulled something from the pocket of her jacket. It was a square of blue denim fabric, with two small holes cut through it. Smoothing the remnant on her knee, Charlene asked, "Are we getting something for Tiff? I need to get back."

"Sure." Elsie leaned out the window and pushed the button a final time. When she turned to face Charlene again, the girl was shaking her head.

"I can't believe you got slapped around. Wouldn't have figured."

Elsie opened her mouth to respond, then clamped it shut. She couldn't lie to Charlene about Noah. But she was not about to tell her the truth.

ON SUNDAY NIGHT Elsie spent the evening poring over the case of *State v. Taney*. By midnight, as she sat with the file at her kitchen table, pressing a dripping ice bag against her mouth, she was sick of thinking about it. But she couldn't call it quits yet; she had to dig through the remaining box of Taney's belongings. She had agreed to give the defense access to the materials Monday morning, and she couldn't go to sleep until she was aware of the contents. With a groan, she sat back on the padded vinyl seat of her kitchen chair, rolling her head on her neck, listening to the little cracking noises it made. "I'm popping and crackling like an old lady," she said, speaking aloud to keep herself awake.

Elsie got up to pour a refill from her Mr. Coffee and then sat cross-legged on the floor to examine the contents of the box. She sipped the coffee with the corner of her mouth as she cautiously flipped up the cardboard flaps. Peering inside, she confronted more of his unwashed clothes. Though she hated to touch the garments, she was loath to discard them without a thorough examination. So she rummaged through the grab bag of Taney's worldly goods, reaching into pockets, opening bags, and reading paper scraps.

A man's canvas jacket was wadded near the bottom of the box. As she lifted it out, the grit on it dirtied her hands. It gave her an uneasy feeling; a red flag came up in her mind, but she couldn't put a finger on it.

Elsie shook the jacket out. As she patted the fabric, she felt something flat in the front pocket: a package, maybe. She reached in and pulled out an envelope: plain white, letter-sized. Her heart fluttered and a shiver ran down her back. Someone is walking on my grave, she thought.

With care, she opened the envelope and looked at the contents. It held a short stack of Polaroids; just three. Holding them by the edges to avoid making a print, she looked at the top photograph. It was a picture of Charlene. Unsmiling. Naked.

"Oh, shit," she whispered. "Jesus." With the gentlest care, she looked at the second. It was a back view of the girl's body. Her horror growing, she examined the third: a picture of Charlene lifting her shirt, exposing her breasts.

She almost dropped the pictures, her hands were shaking so violently. While it was hard to hear the child relate her abuse on the stand, stumbling onto pictorial evidence of her victimization was devastating. Elsie closed her eyes, absorbing the enormity of Charlene's suffering. She meticulously transferred the photos and the white envelope that had held them to a plastic bag and placed it back into the cardboard box. She folded the canvas jacket into a clean trash bag and placed it inside as well.

She stared at the box without seeing it. The pornographic photos of Charlene were burned into her mind's eye. Though she thought she was all cried out, her tears began to flow again. The graphic evidence of Charlene's exploitation made her heartsick.

The tears ran onto her sore lip, stinging. She wiped them away with a jerk, thinking, I've got him. The enormity of the realization took a moment to sink in. "Got him, got him, got him," she whispered. She would bet a hundred dollar bill that the Polaroids bore fingerprints, and those fingerprints would belong to Kris Taney. Moreover, she was confident that his hair, his DNA, would be on the jacket that had held the photos. Her bare-bones incest case had just become very solid. Most scientific.

"We're going to nail him to the wall, Charlene," she vowed. She had pornographic pictures of her witness, which she could use to corroborate the girls' testimony regarding the defendant's conduct with his daughters. Maybe they would bring new charges based on the pictures. The possibilities filled her head as she took a swig of coffee from her cup. Elsie winced. "This is vile," she said aloud. A cup of tea was in order, she thought.

With renewed energy, she turned on the faucet to heat water in a saucepan, and stood by the stove waiting for it to boil. She needed another dose of caffeine, because the advent of the new evidence meant she needed to draft a Motion for Continuance. Much as she hated to delay the case, she knew that DNA analysis was beyond the abilities of local law enforcement. The jacket must be sent to the state lab at the Missouri State Highway Patrol, and the testing would take time. It would be worth it, though. To show the jury a pocket full of naked pictures bearing Kris Taney's fingerprints from a pocket of Kris Taney's coat was an evidentiary gold mine.

She turned and checked the digital clock on her stove: 12:45 A.M. She opened her laptop and set to work.

As she hoped, she was in bed by 2:00 A.M., but the discovery of the new evidence was so exciting that she couldn't get to sleep. Her head spun with the things she needed to do: talk to Charlene about the pictures, find out whether he photographed the other girls, and see what Donita knew about it. She watched as the bedside clock clicked to 3:00 A.M., then to 4:00 A.M. When it hit four-thirty, she decided that in a minute or so she would get out of bed and get an early start on the day.

With that, she dropped off to sleep.

Chapter Thirty-Five

ELSIE TRUNDLED OFF the courthouse elevator with difficulty on Monday morning, juggling the cardboard box of Taney's possessions in addition to her usual burdens. She had managed to convey the double armload from her car to the courthouse without dropping anything onto the wet pavement, but only by luck. She was reminded of her mother, who would ask her to bring in the groceries and then reprimand her for attempting to bring all of the bags in at once. "Make two trips," Marge would cry shrilly as canned goods rolled out of the bags and onto the kitchen floor.

Nothing hit the floor until she reached her own office, where the Taney file slipped from her grasp and papers scattered. She set the battered box of Taney's belongings carefully on the floor, between her file cabinet and the trash can. The contents were neatly folded and labeled, with the bag bearing the canvas jacket on top. The clear plastic bag containing the Polaroids of Charlene and the white envelope was tucked securely inside the box for safekeeping. She took the pictures out with a cautious hand and made a single copy of each one on the office copy machine, then slipped them back in the plastic bag and into the cardboard box, folding down the dirty cardboard flaps. She then knelt on the floor, swiftly gathering her scattered paperwork into a neat stack.

She paused to check her reflection in the office mirror. Assessing the swelling on her mouth, she considered whether she should volunteer an explanation or wait for people to ask. Best to let others broach it, she decided. Just act like it's no big deal.

A blinking light on her office phone indicated voice mail. She picked up the receiver and pushed a button and a man's voice came over the line: "This is Mitchell Holmes. I teach science at Osage Middle School . . . "

Elsie picked up a pen, prepared to scribble down any particulars.

"The principal gave me your message—the one about Charlene Taney. I'm the teacher who walked in on Charlene and three boys in the bathroom. I'd be glad to come down to the courthouse and tell you what I know, but it isn't much. I didn't see anything."

She dropped the pen, deflated.

"They were in a stall. I heard a commotion, but I didn't see an assault with my own eyes. That's why the school wasn't sure how to handle it; we had the boys saying one thing and Charlene saying another, and I couldn't tell them exactly what went on.

"It's been a while, but I think Charlene went to the principal at some point and said she made it up. Seems like that's what happened. So, I don't know what else to tell you. Awful sorry." The message cut off.

Elsie hung up the receiver. "Damn," she said aloud. "Good thing I've got those Polaroids. I couldn't salvage Charlene otherwise."

Nedra leaned in the open doorway. "I have correspondence for you," she said.

"What is it?" Elsie asked, puzzled. Nedra never delivered mail. Stacie generally sorted the correspondence and dropped it on the attorneys' desks.

Nedra handed an envelope to her without comment. The return address was Missouri Supreme Court, Office of Disciplinary Counsel, and it was addressed to Elsie Arnold, Attorney at Law and marked "Personal and Confidential."

"Hey, Nedra," she called, hopping out of her chair and addressing Nedra's retreating figure. "This has been opened."

Nedra answered over her shoulder. "It came on Friday when you were in court. Madeleine wanted to take a look at it."

Elsie pulled the two sheets of paper out of the envelope. The cover letter, sent by the ethics counsel of the bar, stated that an ethics complaint had been lodged against her; a copy was attached. It directed her to respond to the complaint in writing within thirty days. "What the hell," she said aloud, as a wave of anxiety rolled over her. She flipped to the second page. It was a copy of a document claiming that on January 13, Elsie Arnold had violated the Missouri Rules of Professional Conduct: specifically, Rule 4–3.8(f), which prohibits prosecuting attorneys from commenting on pending cases. The complaint said, "Ms. Elsie Arnold made extrajudicial comments that heightened public condemnation of the accused, when she made statements to reporters following the preliminary hearing in *State v. Taney*." The Public Defender's Office had signed the complaint.

Elsie looked up and around, hoping someone could explain it away. Letter in hand, she walked to Madeleine's office and was about to knock on the door when Nedra said from her cubicle, "Don't bother. She's meeting with the County Commission."

"When will she be back?"

"Dunno."

Elsie ran to Breeon's office then, and not finding her there, kept going, searching the courts for her. She wanted someone to share her dismay.

As she rounded the corner to the second floor stairway, she nearly collided with Josh Nixon.

"You!" she said hotly. "How dare you?"

"What?" he asked, backing away as he sensed the anger radiating off of her. "What's wrong?" With a curious look, he added, "What happened to your face?"

"Don't change the subject. And don't act so innocent. You're trying to destroy my professional standing." Her voice was shrill and cracked as she spoke. She was so agitated that she felt a little dizzy. She reached out for the brass handrail for support.

"Elsie," Nixon said, the picture of sincerity, "I don't have a clue what you mean."

When she told him about the letter from the ethics counsel, he winced and looked away. To her it was an admission, but he denied lodging the complaint against her. It had come from his office, but not from him.

"So you knew it was coming; you knew it was in the works."

"No, honest to God, I only knew they talked about it after the preliminary hearing. The Defender's Office is tired of people in the Prosecutor's Office working the press. Madeleine is forever calling some damn press conference where she wants to convict a guy without the benefit of a trial. Her predecessor played that game, too. The public defender has been planning to make an example of someone in the Prosecutor's Office who shoots his mouth off about a pending case."

"You told them! You told your office that I commented about the Taney case."

Josh looked at her as if she had taken leave of her senses.

"Elsie, I didn't have to tell them. It was on the evening news. They got a copy of the newscast from the television station the next day."

"Oh. Huh." He was right about that. Her statements were hardly secret.

He had the good grace to look embarrassed. "Can I get you a cup of coffee?"

She didn't answer immediately. Still dizzy, she sat down on the marble step and looked up at him. After a moment she said, "Hell, no. I wouldn't take anything from you."

Regretfully, Nixon said, "I hate this, I really do. I'm going to get you that coffee. I'll bring it up here. Wait for me."

Elsie didn't reply. She stared at the letter in her hands and thought about the work involved in three years of law school, passing the bar examination, all so she could receive a license to practice law in Missouri. A license that could be revoked, if the bar association wished.

Elsie buried her head in her hands. Since she was nineteen years old, all she'd wanted to do was practice law. She wanted to fight injustice, stand up for the underdog, and change things for the better. Her goal was the guiding force throughout her education, spurring her to study criminology and political science in college, to burn the midnight oil in law school. She wasn't qualified to do anything else. And yet, her profession could disappear with the stroke of a pen.

After a while her breathing returned to normal. Her perch on the marble steps blocking traffic, people looked at her askance as they stepped around her. With an effort, Elsie rose and made her way to a hallway bench on the third floor.

She sat alone on the bench until Nixon, bearing a cup of coffee, managed to find her.

"Here," he said, offering it to her.

She shook her head.

"Okay. You don't have to take the coffee. But we've got

to talk. You haven't made me a plea bargain offer yet on Taney."

"I don't intend to. Especially now. The backstabbing public defender is getting no buddy treatment from me today. Besides, I don't have any reason to give you a break. My case is airtight. I'm holding out for the maximum penalty."

With her confidence returning, she told him about her discovery of the photos.

"If it even *is* his jacket," Nixon argued, lifting the lid from the coffee he'd brought for her and taking a swig. "She could have thrown her boyfriend's jacket in that box, for all we know. Anyone could have taken the photos." Despite his protests, Elsie could tell he was rattled by the discovery.

"So we'll send it to the state lab," she said. "They'll tell if it's his jacket. Their hotdog fingerprint man can look at the photos and that envelope. But we can't get all that done by Monday. I'll need a continuance."

"Great."

"So now you can think about your other hundreds of clients," she said, rising from the bench. She knew that overload at the Public Defender's Office in Missouri had reached crisis level. "Come down to my office for copies of my new motion and the Polaroids. I want you to take them right now. I don't want you filing an ethics complaint against me for failing to disclose evidence."

When they reached Elsie's office, the Taney file, along with the copies she'd made for Nixon, rested where she'd set it on her desk that morning. The box of Taney's possessions was missing.

"Well, that's weird," Elsie muttered, looking under her desk. "It was right here."

"I'm going to take my copies."

"Yeah, sure," she said as she searched. She poked around her office and looked in the reception area; it was a big enough box that it wouldn't be easy to overlook, but she couldn't find it.

"Someone took it," she said, but only to herself. She stalked down the hallway, panic and indignation driving her. "Nedra," she hollered, "where the hell is that Taney stuff?"

The door to Madeleine's office flew open, and she stood in the doorway, a look of cold displeasure on her face.

"I need to talk to you," Madeleine said.

"Later, Madeleine, okay? I'm looking for my evidence."

"What evidence?"

"My Taney evidence. It was sitting in my office and now it's gone." She poked her head in an empty office across the hall but it was not there.

"Why would anyone take it? Was it in a file folder?"

Elsie blanched. "It was in a box. A cardboard box."

"Was it secure? Was your office locked?"

"I always lock it up. But I dropped my file on the floor. Then I got this letter," she finished lamely, holding the letter out where Madeleine could see it.

Madeleine shot her a frigid look. "The letter. We need to talk about that."

"After I find my box. It has crucial evidence inside, my smoking gun."

Shouldering Elsie out of the way, Madeleine walked down to the reception area. Elsie followed, her breathing shallow. "Stacie," Madeleine said, "did you see anyone go into Elsie's office?"

"No."

Elsie shook her head with confusion; how could it disappear into thin air? Who would even want it, other than her and Josh Nixon?

"Just Ed Montee."

Elsie gasped. Ed Montee was the janitor. Running into her office, she picked up her waste basket. Earlier that morning it held a brown apple core and empty soda cups. Now it was empty. "He took it," she wailed. "He took it out with the trash."

Madeleine appeared at her shoulder. "Was it marked?"

"No," Elsie said, shaking her head with horror. "It was in a cardboard box, from the Taney house." Wildly, she made for the door. "I've got to find Montee. I've got to stop him."

"Come to my office; I'll call," Madeleine ordered, turning on her heel and walking down the hall with a military step. Elsie had no choice but to follow.

Picking up her office land line, Madeleine dialed the McCown County operator. "LaDonna, connect me with the custodial office."

Standing beside Madeleine's desk, Elsie waited to hear the fate of the evidence box, twisting her hands as Madeleine waited on the line. Closing her eyes, she offered up a frantic prayer. *Dear God, please let me get the evidence back. I'll do anything, just let me get it back.*

Elsie opened her eyes when she heard Madeleine say, "That's it, then. There's nothing to be done about it."

She hung up the phone with a click. Fixing Elsie with an accusatory glare, she said, "Monday is trash day."

"Oh?" Elsie croaked.

"The trash from the second floor has already been incinerated. Checking her watch, she added, "Fifteen minutes ago."

At the word "incinerated," Elsie nearly blacked out. She heard Madeleine's voice as if it were coming from a tunnel, asking, "What did you lose?"

She whispered, "Pictures. Polaroids of one of the Taney victims. Naked." In a shaking voice, she said, "I guess I should've taken it to the property room at the P.D."

"You think?" Madeleine responded with venom. Leaning back in her chair, she said, "Close the door."

Uh-oh. Even through her fog of dismay, she smelled trouble. She walked to the door, gave it a push, and walked away without waiting for it to click shut.

When she took a seat, Madeleine was staring at her. "What's wrong with your face?"

"Nothing. I ran into a cabinet." Elsie stopped as soon as the words were spoken, realizing she had borrowed Donita Taney's excuse.

Madeleine surveyed her over crimson reading glasses studded with little crystals. "When I tell you to do something, I expect you to do it."

Elsie didn't respond immediately. The women stared at each other. Finally, Elsie broke the silence. "Madeleine, I'm not getting you——maybe because all I can think about is losing that evidence. I don't know what you're talking about."

"I sent word on Friday that you were to come see me, and you never showed. That's insubordination."

Elsie rubbed her forehead with her fingers. She had a dull ache that threatened to grow severe. "Friday was a pretty crazy day, Madeleine. I had that bond hearing in Circuit Court, and a conference in chambers with Rountree, and I ran over to the Taneys' to serve subpoenas. I didn't really have an opportunity to come and see you."

Madeleine folded her hands together on the desk, and Elsie studied her boss's pale pink manicure and the eye-popping diamond adorning her left hand. When Madeleine cleared her throat, it struck Elsie that this conversation had been rehearsed in Madeleine's head in advance.

"Your explanation doesn't wash. I don't buy it. But this is only one of a long list of complaints I have. For example, the Disciplinary Committee of the Missouri Bar has commenced an ethics investigation of you."

Elsie fidgeted in her chair. "Hey, Madeleine, I don't mean to be overly sensitive, but wasn't that marked 'Personal and Confidential'? I'm not sure I understand why you opened it Friday."

"Friday, when you were too busy to talk to me," Madeleine said in a mocking tone, then turned on a voice that was deadly serious. "It came to the Prosecutor's Office. I am the Prosecuting Attorney of McCown County."

"Well, I got to the bottom of that whole ethics thing this morning. The public defender is trying to make an example of me, to shut us up in the Prosecutor's Office. They're tired of us talking to the press; they hate it when you call press conferences. This is as much about you as it is about me."

Madeleine waved away her attempt to explain. "*I* am not the subject of an ethics charge. But apart from all that, you have the community in an uproar over this case of yours. That protest on Friday was an embarrassment."

"That's not my fault—" Elsie began, but Madeleine interrupted her.

"And just this morning, you intentionally left sensitive evidence in your office instead of turning it over to the police department. And now it's gone."

"I kept it locked up the whole time. Until this morning. I guess I got distracted when I saw that letter."

Madeleine barked out a short laugh. "Distracted? I'd call it gross negligence. You should have been more responsible. If it was crucial evidence, why didn't you mark it? Lock it up? Why did you keep it in that cardboard box? Everything you do leads to disaster. And embarrassment for me."

Elsie was afraid she was going to be sick. She wanted desperately to return to the sanctuary of her own office, to sit in her chair and think. She stood and said, "I'm not feeling so great. I need to go sit down."

"I'm not finished with you."

Elsie sat back down. Poised on the edge of the seat, she thought, I've got to get out of here.

"We have another problem to discuss. Aside from your professional shortcomings." Madeleine placed her palms on her desk and leaned toward Elsie. "Your activities outside the office."

Elsie cocked her head; she didn't follow, until Madeleine went on: "Do you actually think people don't inform me of your ridiculous public behavior? This is a small town, Elsie. A fishbowl." As Madeleine served up her reproof, Elsie felt surprisingly numb. Madeleine was "appalled and disgusted" that she would engage in "rowdy drunken debauchery" in a public place, a "filthy bar where everyone in town might view your antics." What kind of example was she setting in the community, falling onto the floor, making a scene with a group of law enforcement officers?

"Ridiculous behavior. Scandalous. Unbelievable, for a woman your age and a public official."

Elsie shrunk into her seat as the assault continued. So, she thought, this is how it feels to suffer total humiliation. She concentrated on Madeleine's lipsticked mouth, watching her lips reveal chemically whitened teeth, and found that she was able to block out a good measure of what was being said. *Remain expressionless*, she told herself. *Don't speak.*

At last Madeleine paused, picking up a dainty handkerchief and polishing her reading glasses. Avoiding Elsie's eyes, she said, "I'm afraid I've about reached my limit with you."

Elsie clutched her hands together in her lap, dreading the words Madeleine was about to speak.

Madeleine said, "You've bumbled this Taney case until it's turned into a nasty mess. And now you've allowed your evidence to be destroyed. If you lose the jury trial, you're done here. Do you understand?"

Elsie nodded, her throat closing. "I think I've got a shot at convicting him."

"Well, that's it, then. If you win, I'll think about letting you stay on. Questions?"

Shaking her head, Elsie bolted for the door.

Chapter Thirty-Six

THE BOX OF evidence was reduced to ash, Ed Montee assured Elsie when she went downstairs, grasping at the minute possibility that the box had been spared. Though the janitor offered to demonstrate the effectiveness of the destruction, she didn't linger. As she walked away, tears burned behind her eyes. Her case was crippled without the evidence, and her career was hanging in the balance.

Just as she returned to the second floor, Stacie flagged her down to report that Judge Rountree had summoned her to his courtroom. Elsie guessed that the summons meant her case was advancing to the number one position on the court docket.

She and the judge sat in silence, waiting for Josh Nixon to arrive. The judge fixed her with a quizzical look. She imagined he was curious about her injured mouth but was too polite to inquire.

When Nixon appeared, Rountree invited him to sit.

"You're number one," he said with a smile as he regarded them across his desk. "The parties in the car wash case came to terms this morning. So I guess this counts as our pretrial conference. Any outstanding issues?"

Elsie's blood pressure increased by double digits as soon as the judge announced their imminent trial status. "Judge, I have a problem," she said. "I found evidence that incriminates the defendant when I was going through his personal effects. Naked pictures of the victim."

"Finding that kind of evidence doesn't sound like a problem for the prosecution," Judge Rountree observed.

"This is a total setup," Nixon said. "She got this box of stuff from the defendant's wife, the woman we believe has coerced all the testimony against my client. That woman could easily have taken the photos and put them in that box."

"Ah," Elsie said with an involuntary groan. "The county janitorial staff disposed of the box with the evidence, the photos, and the jacket. Incinerated it."

"You had it this morning," Nixon said in disbelief.

"I know," she said.

"Is this some kind of trick?" he asked.

"I think I'll ignore that," she said. "Judge, the defense has copies of the photos. I'll need to have access to those so I can offer them in lieu of the originals."

Nixon jumped to his feet as if he were in court. "She is attempting to violate the best evidence rule."

"You know that's wrong," Elsie barked back. Once the original document was lost, properly authenticated copies could be received into evidence.

"But you can't tie the photos to my client. Without the originals, you can't get prints, and you burned up all the DNA evidence. You can't get the copies into evidence."

"I can ask Charlene if he took pictures of her, idiot."

"That's enough. Brief it," said Judge Rountree shortly. "Next issue."

"I don't suppose my juvenile witnesses could testify by video," Elsie offered with a hopeful air.

Josh Nixon's explosive response was interrupted by Judge Rountree's abrupt rejection of the suggestion. "I know they fiddle with that two-way video testimony in federal court, but it doesn't fly in my courtroom. I don't want any Sixth Amendment Right of Confrontation issues being kicked around on appeal. What else?"

Her mind raced. She wasn't quite prepared to hash out all of the pretrial issues, so she had to think on her feet. She ran through her witness list in her head: Charlene, Kristy, Donita, Tina Peroni, Bob Ashlock, Officer Maggard to testify about the handwriting, Dr. Petrus.

"It would be nice if the defense would stipulate to the physician's report."

"What report?" asked the judge.

Nixon looked sulky.

Elsie said, "The physical exams of the complaining witnesses. Nothing dramatic like DNA evidence, but we do have gynecological exams that show that neither child is a virgin. It would be a professional courtesy to stipulate to the reports so that the doctor doesn't have to spend the day waiting in the hallway of the courthouse."

"Mr. Nixon?"

"Not gonna happen. Defendant won't stipulate to anything." Nixon toyed with a button on his jacket. "I thought about having an evidentiary hearing. To look into a witness's reputation for truthfulness. Now I won't have time."

The judge dismissed his concern. "You don't need a special hearing for that. The proper place for character evidence is at trial. Be prepared to proceed."

Elsie didn't comment, knowing that she would be unable to rebut the attack on Charlene.

The judge picked up the list of his prospective jurors and examined it. "Is there a plea bargain in the works? I've got a jury panel of eighty citizens coming in, and if you're working on a last minute settlement, I don't want all these people inconvenienced."

"Elsie hasn't made a plea bargain offer," Nixon said. "She told me this morning that she doesn't intend to."

The judge looked surprised. "Miss Arnold?"

She met his look squarely. "Judge, if the defendant wants to stand up and plead, that would be great."

"So cut me a deal," Nixon said.

"Like what?" she asked.

"Time served," Nixon proposed.

Resolutely, she shook her head. "You know the kind of allegations we're dealing with in this case. I can't possibly offer some cheap deal, knowing what I know about defendant's crimes. This one will have to rest solely with a jury. We'll let the community decide what is just in this action."

Josh Nixon gave a contemptuous snort. "Save the speeches for Channel 7."

Elsie turned on him, eyes ablaze. "Funny advice coming from you, my *good pal*."

The judge waved a restraining hand. "That's enough. How many days will it take to try this case?"

Josh Nixon shrugged. Elsie was silent for a moment, reflecting, looking at the gray clouds outside the north window as she calculated. "Two to three, depending. It's hard to be exact, at this point."

The judge nodded in agreement.

She continued, "Judge, it's a good thing you have eighty folks coming in for the jury panel, because I expect we'll need that many, in this kind of case. When we question the prospective jurors, some of them are bound to say they can't be impartial when a man is charged with child molesting."

She glanced at the inside of her file. "But the presentation of the state's case will be straightforward. Of course," she said, with an unfriendly squint in Nixon's direction, "I have no idea what the defendant's case will be."

"Well," the judge said congenially, "the element of surprise keeps our blood pumping, wouldn't you say?" He flipped the paper file closed and tossed it to the side. "I reckon we're good to go here. If you have any motions, get them filed. We're counting down."

Elsie and Nixon withdrew from the office. "Josh," she implored as they walked into the courthouse hallway, "I've got to have those copies I gave you of the pictures of Charlene. Please. I need to reproduce them for my own file."

"File a motion," he said, walking away with a strut. Over his shoulder, he added, "Brief it."

She stood in the hallway for a long moment, uncertain which one of a dozen tasks she should undertake first. Turning, she bounded back to the Prosecutor's Office, calling out to Stacie, "The Taney case is number one on Monday in Rountree's court."

"I'll get the subpoenas right out," Stacie said.

"The Taney girls and their mom are already served," Elsie told her.

"Got it."

"Thanks," Elsie said as she dashed back to her office.

The heady realization that the case would commence in six days was enough to make her a little crazy. She sat down at her desk, moving deliberately to avoid a manic episode. She needed to proceed calmly. She had done this all before; she simply had to take it one step at a time. Opening the bottom drawer of her desk, she pulled out an old accordion file and a fistful of manila folders and neatly labeled them in black ink: *Motions, Jury Instructions, Voir Dire, Opening Statement, Direct Exams, Cross-Ex, Closing Argument.*

See, she told herself, *that's not so hard. I can do that.* She wheeled her chair over to the filing cabinet and opened the drawer that held her standard voir dire questions, the basic presentation she always made during the jury selection process. *There. I've already begun. This is going to be okay.*

She reached for the phone and dialed Tina Peroni's number. Tina answered on the second ring. Elsie tried to stay positive as she informed the Social Service worker that they would be going to trial on Monday. Tina didn't respond. As the silence extended from one moment into two, Elsie wondered whether she had lost her phone connection.

"Tina," she said loudly into the receiver, "are you there?"

"Yeah," Tina said in a desolate voice. "Oh Lord, Elsie, I'm so sorry."

"About what?" she asked, her head suddenly pounding.

Tina paused before she answered. "Charlene's gone. I was just there this morning. She's run away."

Chapter Thirty-Seven

ELSIE AND TINA walked shoulder-to-shoulder down the cracked sidewalk that led to the door of the Taneys' apartment building on High Street. Their expressions were grim. Elsie opened the door and stood aside for Tina to enter first. Tina gave her a conspiratorial wink behind her tortoiseshell glasses.

"Elsie, we are going to see this through."

"Hell, yes," Elsie responded, thinking, We don't have any choice.

Donita answered the door, greeting them with a somber face. Roy Mayfield was in his customary seat. It appeared that he had coaxed the television set into a minimal performance level, because the volume was blaring. A battered laptop computer was open on his lap, but when the women entered the room, he snapped it shut and turned his attention to the TV screen.

Elsie gave Donita a hug, inhaling the scent of unwashed hair as she did so. "Donita, I'm so sorry to hear about Charlene. Has there been any word?"

"Nothing," Donita said. "I was afraid of this. Been worrying and worrying it would happen. Just didn't know when." She nodded in the direction of the kitchen. "Let's go set in here. Roy's watching Maury."

Troubled by her attitude of resignation, Elsie asked, "What did the police say?"

Donita turned on her with an impatient look. "You know I got no phone," she said. "Got no phone, no car, now how am I gonna get to the police station? Tina says they'll come out here. She called them."

"You could have called on Roy's phone," Elsie said.

"I asked him, but he's got to charge it up. He says it has to be plugged into the electrical, and he don't have his special plug on him."

Elsie looked at Tina, who said, "I called this morning. They should come by to take the report today."

"Donita," Elsie said, speaking more abruptly than she might have, to counter her rising panic, "do you have any idea where Charlene might have gone?"

"Run off with her boyfriend, I bet. Said she wanted to get out of this town. Roy seen it coming. She wouldn't mind him, talked back to him, she was in trouble with him all the time. That boyfriend was probably putting her up to it."

"Donita, listen to me," Elsie said, taking her hands and looking intently into her face, "we have to do everything in our power to get Charlene back, because she has to testify next week. We're going to trial on Monday. The judge told me this morning that our case is set number one."

As she spoke, Donita's face grew closed and hard. She pulled her hands away as she said, "That's the reason you're worried about Char for. You're just worried about her not being there for your trial. That's all you care about."

Taken aback, Elsie responded, "And her safety, of course. Primarily her safety."

"If you're just thinking about her safety, then it don't matter too much whether she makes it to that trial." Donita picked up a plastic bag of corn flakes from the table and folded the top shut. She stood to find the box; when she located it, she shoved the bag of cereal inside and set it back down on the counter.

Speaking urgently, Elsie said, "But Donita, we knew from the start that if we were going to put Kris in prison, it would be a jury that would do it, and we've got to put on evidence that your husband committed those crimes. I mean, we can't just wave a magic wand, and poof!—he's convicted."

Donita took a glass from the cabinet and filled it from the faucet at the sink. She walked leisurely to the refrigerator, pulled out a plastic ice cube tray and twisted it, popping out four or five ice cubes. She dropped them into the water. Raised her glass, surveyed Elsie over the rim and said, "Kristy don't want to testify no more."

"Donita, we went over this. It's just not a matter of choice. This is a criminal case. She's under subpoena."

Donita didn't respond immediately. Leaning against the kitchen sink, she took a drink and rattled the cubes in the glass. She appeared to be debating whether to speak. "I been thinking. I got a idea."

"What's that?" Elsie asked warily.

"I done told you about the meth. That's against the law. Do your trial about that."

Elsie realized she was open-mouthed. *"What?"*

"Put him in jail for the meth."

Unable to keep sarcasm from her tone, Elsie said, "Do you hear what you're saying? Donita, you *made* it. You cooked the meth. If we wanted to do a drug prosecution, we'd charge *you.*"

Tina let out a short laugh, and Donita looked from one woman to the other. Setting her water glass on the counter with a clink, she said, "You're turning on me. I know what you're up to; I ain't no fool. Roy warned me about you; he was right. Well, I'm done with this. I've had it with both of you. I know what you been up to. You been backstabbing me with that whore, JoLee."

"What?" Elsie demanded.

"You think I wouldn't hear about that? About you and JoLee and that detective talking stink about me?"

Elsie sat back, squarely meeting her angry stare. "Donita, Detective Ashlock took JoLee's statement. This is a felony investigation, we have to talk to people who can provide information. And JoLee did say something you need to explain. She said you beat Charlene with an extension cord."

Donita's eyes grew wild as she cried, "That was Kris! That was all Kris and JoLee knows it. That woman is poison!"

Tina's voice was unrelenting as she said, "You need to come clean on this. If the girls are at risk here, we'll have to take action."

Donita swung around to Roy, looking for direction, but he was glued to the television. Her face was frantic as she said to Elsie and Tina, "Kris made me. I only done it because he made me."

With disgust written on her face, Elsie said, "I don't see how someone can make you beat your child."

Donita snatched a dirty dish towel and twisted it, so distraught that spittle sprayed from her mouth as she answered, "He said if I didn't, he do it hisself, and it would go worse on her. A hundred times worse. I knowed he would. So I done it. But I held back." When the women didn't respond, she cried, "You'uns don't know him. You ain't seen how he can be."

Donita spread the dish towel on the counter and smoothed it with her hands. "I ain't going to no trial. Ain't none of us going."

Elsie said wearily, "You're under subpoena, Donita."

"You can shove that subpoena up your ass."

Elsie's eyes flashed and she spoke in a tone she reserved for cross-examination. "Are you aware that I'm trying to help you out? Protect you?"

"You're trying to help yourself," Donita spat. "Nobody's helped me all these years. Putting up with Kris for sixteen years, I got no help from nobody. I finally got someone to stand between me and Kris Taney, and it ain't you. And he says I'm not going to be at your trial."

"The sheriff will get you on the stand. Is that how it's going to be?"

It was Donita's turn to laugh. "Who knows what I'll say when I get up there? Maybe I won't be able to remember. Or I could take the Fifth, isn't that right? Isn't that right?"

"Donita, you'll be under an oath to tell the truth."

Donita tossed the dish towel into the sink. "I'm not fucking around anymore. Here's the real story: it's all horseshit. A big old lie. Me and the girls made it up because we was mad at Kris. Tired of his meanness. We wanted him out of here, so we cooked up a story for you."

Elsie's heart froze in her chest. She looked at Tina with panic in her eyes. A pernicious seed had been planted in her head. *What is the truth here? What really went on in this house?*

Mayfield deserted his television program to watch the altercation in the kitchen. He leaned in the doorway, regarding Elsie with a gap-toothed smile.

Tina was nonplussed. "Not so fast, Donita," she said. "What the hell is up with you? You've given sworn statements; we've got it under oath that your daughters were raped by your husband under this roof."

"I'm wore out with it, that's what. Wore out with the whole business. Done."

Tina grabbed at Donita's arm but broke off the contact and took a half step back. In a dangerous tone, she said, "You don't understand the consequence of saying you're done."

"I don't care."

"I bet you do. Why do you think we didn't take custody of your children when the reports were substantiated? You swore to us that you wanted to get your girls away from their abusive father. I believed you."

Donita didn't speak. She looked at Tina with snake eyes, her face stony.

"So if you refuse to testify at trial, to make good on your promises, I'll assume I can't believe anything you say. Including your statements that the girls are your chief concern." She paused, locked in a staring war. "You'll lose them. The girls. And the government assistance, the money, the food stamps for them. You understand that."

Donita didn't respond.

Tina raised her voice. "You understand that?"

With a slight jerk of her head, Donita nodded.

Tina's shoulders relaxed. "So you will participate at trial?"

Donita looked like she'd swallowed brown iodine. "Yeah. I'll do the trial."

Elsie released a relieved breath, but she was still uncomfortable. She needed to think; she wanted desperately to get out of Donita's kitchen, out of the house. Her case was falling apart: Charlene was gone, her evidence was destroyed, and Kristy and Donita were wavering. In a week she could kiss the Prosecutor's Office goodbye.

"Tina," she said, "I gotta go."

Tina looked at her in surprise. "Sure, of course."

Elsie wanted out of the house so badly that it made her skin crawl. She tore out of the apartment and made her exit into the street, Tina following her, and gulped the fresh air as if she had come out of a house afire.

"Tina," she said, grabbing her friend's coat sleeve, "I need to talk to Tiffany."

Chapter Thirty-Eight

MARK TWAIN ELEMENTARY School was a sturdy Depression-era structure built of brown brick and granite. Air-conditioner units jutted out of various windows like warts. The grounds were neglected, and the outdated playground equipment looked utilitarian and forlorn. Still, the old brick schoolhouse conveyed a certain dignity, an ability to weather the passing years.

Approaching the entryway, Elsie wondered what the hell she was doing chasing down a mute kindergartener and grasping at straws. Her work situation was so snarled, she hadn't even had time to think about her abusive boyfriend. Ex-boyfriend, she amended.

Holding the heavy oak door for her, Tina asked, "Elsie, how are you going to handle the interview?"

"Been thinking about that. My voice is loud enough to call the hogs; maybe I need to turn my volume down." Inside the school entryway, she paused to pull off her gloves. "Charlene knows how to communicate with Tiffany. I've seen Charlene whisper in her ear before. I ought to try that. Like we're telling secrets."

They identified themselves at the front office and asked for the principal, Ms. Horner. After a hurried consultation with the receptionist, Ms. Horner led them to the nurse's office. "You won't be disturbed in here," she said. "The nurse went home sick today." She instructed them to wait inside and went to fetch Tiffany.

The nurse's office was oppressively bare, even spartan. A metal desk and two chairs sat in the far corner; a small Igloo cooler containing ice rested in a puddle upon the desk. A cot was pushed against the opposite wall.

As they waited, Tina inspected Elsie's face with an expert eye. "You look like somebody popped you in the mouth."

Elsie shook her head, saying with a sigh, "God, I'm a total klutz. It's such a stupid story, I'm embarrassed to tell you how it happened." She stopped without further comment. She would not offer the phony cabinet explanation. She knew Tina had heard that one before.

Tina said, "Okay," and fell silent.

Ms. Horner appeared in the doorway, holding Tiffany by the hand. Tiffany eyed Elsie and Tina with trepidation.

"You can take Tiffany back to class when you're done," the principal told them. She gave Tiffany's shoulder a pat and left, closing the door behind her. The three stood uncertainly for a moment.

"Let's sit down and get comfortable," Elsie said.

She settled into one of the chairs and asked Tiffany to

take the other. The little girl obeyed, eyes downcast. Tina eased onto the little cot, brushing a Band-Aid wrapper to the floor as she sat.

For a minute or two the three sat quietly in the small office. Tina perched on the cot, waiting for Elsie to begin. Tiffany slid back into the adult-sized chair and hung her head.

Elsie struggled desperately for an icebreaker. She wished she had a cookie to offer, a doughnut, a dozen doughnuts. She rummaged in her purse, hoping to find a stick of gum. All she managed to uncover was a box of Tic Tacs.

She set the Tic Tac container on the desktop. Tiffany continued to look down. Elsie shook the little box, rattling the green pellets of candy. Tiffany glanced at the box. Elsie flipped it open and shook out two.

"Want one?" she asked. "They're spearmint."

Tiffany eyeballed the candy but didn't reach for it. Elsie popped one in her own mouth and placed the other in her palm; she offered it to Tiffany. "They're good. Try it." She spoke softly, her words almost a whisper.

Tiffany hesitated, but reached out and took the green candy from Elsie's palm with her thumb and forefinger. She inspected it for a moment and popped it into her mouth.

Elsie raised a brow. "Okay?" Tiffany nodded. "Not too strong? Too minty?" Tiffany shook her head.

Quietly, she scooted her chair closer to Tiffany's. She leaned in close, so close that their heads were almost touching.

"We have to talk about your daddy, Tiffany."

Tiffany squeezed her eyes shut and shook her head emphatically. Elsie spoke in a whisper, right next to the child's ear. "I know it's hard to talk about. It'll just take a minute. Like when you got your kindergarten shots. It was scary, but it was over in a second."

Tiffany didn't respond. Elsie shook out another Tic Tac. She placed it in Tiffany's palm. The girl put it back on the desk.

Elsie sat back and took a breath. She leaned forward to whisper again. "Can't you tell me about it?"

The child shook her head no.

"Did he tell you not to talk about it?"

Sliding farther into the chair, Tiffany hung her head.

Scooting a trifle closer, Elsie whispered, "How about just telling me about your sisters. About what happened to them." When Tiffany didn't respond, Elsie pondered for a moment, then added, "If you just talk to me today, I promise I'll never ask again. You'll never have to talk to me about it again. Ever."

Tiffany stole a glance at Elsie and looked away.

Elsie pressed on. "Did you ever see your dad doing things with Charlene or Kristy?"

The child placed her head on the desk and covered it with her arms. Elsie could see that she was breathing hard, her small chest heaving under her sweatshirt.

"What did you see?"

The child clutched her hands together at the back of her neck, shaking her head back and forth. With frustration, Elsie shot a look at Tina, but Tina just shrugged.

Desperate to crack the child's wall of silence, Elsie forgot to whisper. "Tiffany, did you see how Charlene got that black eye?"

Scrambling out of the chair, Tiffany slid under the desk, where she huddled with her face on her knees, her back to Elsie.

Elsie got off the chair and crouched down beside the girl, pressing on: "Tiffany? What did you see?"

Tina broke in. "Elsie."

Elsie ignored her. "Tell me, Tiffany. Tell me so you can help Charlene."

Louder, Tina said, "Elsie!"

Turning on Tina with a flash of anger, Elsie snapped, "What?"

"She doesn't want to talk to you."

Elsie leaned back on her knees, frustration washing over her. "Okay."

"You're done."

"You're right." With a groan, Elsie stood. "Any ideas?"

Ruefully, Tina shook her head.

Tiffany was still huddled under the desk. Elsie bent down and spoke to her, quietly. "Hey, Tiffany. Want to go back to your class?"

Lifting her head from her knees, Tiffany nodded emphatically, still refusing to look at her.

"Come on out of there, hon. Can you show me where it is? The teacher will be missing you," Elsie coaxed. She extended her hand but Tiffany ignored it.

Slowly, with tension in every muscle of her small form, the child crawled out of her hiding place under the desk.

On impulse, Elsie picked up the mints and held them out to Tiffany as a peace offering. Giving the candy an appraising glance, Tiffany put the box in the small pocket of her worn corduroy pants. She then let Elsie take her by the hand, and together they walked down the hall to the kindergarten class.

Chapter Thirty-Nine

On Friday, Elsie was waiting in the Taneys' apartment. .When Donita had let her in, she made little effort to mask her hostility. The women sat on the tattered couch in uncomfortable silence until shortly before three, when Kristy rattled the knob of the front door and came inside, bringing a gust of cold wind with her. They sat down at the kitchen table and Elsie handed Kristy a stapled sheaf of papers. The apartment reeked of pesticide and Elsie's eyes were watering.

"Kristy, this is your preliminary hearing testimony. You'll want to read it over as kind of a review before the trial."

Kristy pushed the papers aside, refusing to meet her eyes. Elsie regarded her silently for a moment before pulling out her secret weapon: a bag from the Jiffy Go.

"I'm parched, absolutely dying of thirst. When I'm working, I always like to have a Diet Coke." Cold water beaded the sides of the can as she popped the tab.

Kristy's eyes cut to the silver can. Reaching into the bag a second time, Elsie said, "Someone told me—maybe Charlene or Tina—you like Dr Pepper."

The brown can glistened with moisture. "Thirsty?" Elsie asked.

She could see that Kristy was tempted. Nodding, the girl accepted the can from Elsie, popped the tab and took a healthy swig. A little grin played around her mouth at the unexpected treat.

Elsie tapped the papers with her pen. "So—you'll review your preliminary hearing testimony before you go to court."

Finally, Kristy spoke up. "I don't see why."

"Because it's under oath, sworn testimony. So we need to be careful not to say anything inconsistent, anything that doesn't match with it. It's kind of like studying for a quiz. I bet you do that for school. Your mom says you're a good student."

"I don't want to read it. Because I don't want to go. To the court."

"Well, that just means you're normal. Nobody likes it. Nobody wants to go to court, Kristy—and not just kids, but grown men and women, too."

"Then why do I have to?"

"It's the only way we can see to it that your dad goes to prison."

Kristy slumped in her seat, her chin touching her chest. Elsie wished she'd brought a candy bar along, and a big bag of chips.

Reaching out and giving Kristy's shoulder a gentle

shake, she said, "It's just one of those things. You don't have a choice. You have to do this."

Kristy's nose turned pink and she started to cry. Elsie watched anxiously for a minute before asking, "What are you thinking, hon?"

"I ain't never had a choice." Her voice wavered. "Nobody never lets me pick what to do. You was gonna make things better, but it ain't. It just goes on and on."

"What we need to do to make it better is go to court and tell the judge and jury what your father did. So he can go to prison, and you won't have to be scared anymore."

In a forlorn voice, Kristy said, "I don't know. I don't know what to do."

Elsie took her hand. "Look at me." When Kristy looked away, Elsie repeated it, her voice insistent. "Look at me."

Finally Kristy turned to face her, her nose and eyes wet.

"You are not alone. You won't be alone in that courtroom. I've got your back. I'm doing this for you."

Kristy snuffled, sucking snot back into her nose. Elsie dug a paper napkin from the Jiffy Go bag and handed it to her.

While Kristy wiped her nose, Elsie pressed on. "This is about you, Kristy. You were done wrong, and he's going to have to pay. The state will make him pay. But for that to happen, you have to show up and tell your story in court." Elsie pressed her hand hard, trying to communicate the urgency of their mission. "Do you understand?"

Kristy blinked. Drops of water clung to her eyelashes. Elsie took it as a yes. She nudged the Dr Pepper can toward her. "Take a drink to clear your throat, and we'll run through your direct exam. Just like we'll be doing it in court."

A cockroach climbed up the table leg and scampered across the table. Elsie jumped up, nearly knocking over the soda cans.

With a nervous laugh, she said, "Guess that one survived the bug killer."

Kristy snorted. "Fool landlord. The spraying just riles them up. They'll settle down in a day or so."

AN HOUR LATER Elsie pulled into the visitor parking lot directly in front of a sign announcing: BARTON HIGH— HOME OF THE MOUNTAINEERS! She was relieved to see Ashlock's car several spots down; she was afraid she had missed the interview.

Walking with shoulders hunched against the cold, she made her way to the front door. It had been thirteen years since she'd walked the halls as a student, but she didn't need to ask directions. She went straight to the front office and began filling out a visitor name tag, noticing that a new secretary manned the desk.

"You need to put a time of arrival on that name tag." The woman was brusque, all business.

"Oh, okay. I'm here from the Prosecutor's Office, to meet with Detective Ashlock. Is he in the counselor's office?"

"I'll see if you can come on back." The woman picked up a phone. Swiveling her chair, she turned her back to Elsie.

Elsie's eyes narrowed. "Ma'am?" When the secretary didn't turn around, Elsie checked her name plate and raised her voice. "Ms. Rice, this is my rodeo." She walked around the counter and flashed her badge. "Just tell me where Ashlock is and I'll get out of your hair. Please," she added with a tight smile.

The secretary made a show of inspecting the badge. Elsie would have found it funny if it wasn't so maddening. "They're in Room 102," she said, handing the badge back to Elsie.

When she reached 102, the door was shut; she rapped before she entered. Ashlock and a teenage girl were seated at the back of the room, which looked to be an English classroom, judging from the posters of Mark Twain and Harper Lee on the walls. Battered copies of *To Kill a Mockingbird* lined a small bookcase near the desk where Ashlock sat, facing the girl.

They looked up at the interruption. Elsie whispered, "Hey, Ashlock." Beginning to unbutton her coat, she turned a smile on the interview witness.

The girl was about Charlene's age and height, but at least forty pounds heavier, with fuzzy hair dyed pale pink, and a gold hoop through one nostril. She wore a scoop-necked T-shirt with a picture of a banana split that read, "Want a cherry?"

"Shawna, this is Ms. Arnold from the prosecutor's office." Ashlock gave Elsie an inquiring look. "I was expecting you earlier."

"Had to see a witness over on High Street." She pulled up a chair and gave Shawna a bright smile. "Can you all bring me up to speed on your conference? It's Shawna, right?"

The girl nodded. She showed no sign that she was intimidated by the presence of Ashlock or Elsie. "The cop was asking about Charlene Taney."

Elsie pulled out her legal pad. "Yes, we are so concerned about her. Did she confide in you?"

Ashlock said, "Shawna was telling me that Charlene and Roy didn't get along."

"Yeah. She couldn't stand him. Said he was a piece of shit."

Elsie asked, "Did she talk about any specific fights? Any abuse?"

"He was pretty much riding her all the time. Wouldn't get off her back."

"But how, exactly? Can you be specific?" Elsie still wanted to pin down the black eye.

Shawna reached for a battered purple backpack. "Just what I said. Is that clock right? I got someplace I got to be."

Elsie scooted her chair closer to Shawna. "Not quite yet, please. Did Charlene tell you her plans? I hope you can help us locate her."

With a shrug, the girl said, "Sorry. She didn't say nothing about where she was going." She unzipped the backpack and groped inside it.

Ashlock spoke up. "But she did mention some plans she had in mind. Would you tell Ms. Arnold what you told me?"

"Yeah, she's got a fiancé."

Elsie thought she'd misunderstood. "Beg pardon?"

"A fiancé. She's getting married. I'm real happy for

her, I told her so. I can't wait to get married and get out. But my boyfriend is a total dumbass, he won't pull the trigger. He don't want to move out yet."

"Shawna, Charlene is only fifteen. She can't get married until she's eighteen years old. Who is this boy?" Elsie had her pen out, poised to write down the answer.

"Her fiancé? I never met him. But they're getting a place. I guess they'll get married as soon as they can do it."

"How long have you known Charlene?"

"Since fourth grade. That's when me and my mom moved here."

"But you don't know her boyfriend? Is he someone at Barton High?"

"He's not a kid. Older. Char don't give a shit about guys our age. Not even interested."

Elsie digested the answer. She asked, "Did she ever say his name?"

Shawna picked at her blue mascara before she answered. "Darren."

"Darren what?"

Shawna tipped back in her chair. "The cop already asked me. She never said, I don't think."

"How did she meet this guy, if it wasn't at school?"

"He was cruising the square on a Saturday night a while back. Char said it was cool that he got his own car. Got a real job."

Eagerly, Elsie asked, "Where? Where does he work?"

"Chicken plant. Processing."

Elsie turned to Ashlock. "We can surely find a 'Darren' working at the plant."

Ashlock pulled his phone from his pocket as Shawna interrupted. "I don't think it's the one in Barton. Maybe Monett. Maybe even Springfield."

Deflated, Elsie frowned as her lead dissolved. "We'll still try to follow up." Ashlock rose and walked away to place the call.

Elsie said, "Tell me what he looked like."

Shawna yawned. "I never met him, man."

Elsie tapped her pen on the pad of paper, thinking. "What about a picture? Or a note? Did you ever see his photo, or anything he sent her, in her bedroom at home?"

The girl looked alarmed. "No way. I never been to her house."

Elsie looked up in surprise. "Never? I thought you and Charlene were friends."

"Yeah, we are."

"For how long?"

"Forever. Since fourth grade. We were both scrubs, so we stuck together."

"That's six years. In all that time, you never once set foot in her house?"

"Lord, no. My mom would skin me."

"Why?"

The girl looked at Elsie as if the answer was too obvious to state. "You know why. Nobody at school could go to the Taney house. Because of what was going on."

"You knew?"

The girl rolled her eyes. "Duh. It was just one of those things. Everybody knew."

Chapter Forty

AT FIVE-THIRTY THAT evening, Elsie walked into the Kinfolks diner near the courthouse, bringing the cold air with her. Tina sat in a booth in the corner, away from the wintry blast that blew each time a customer entered.

Elsie stomped her feet on a rubber-backed rug spread on the tiled floor and made a beeline to Tina's booth. Sinking gratefully into the seat and struggling out of her coat, she eyed the plate in front of Tina. It was the fried chicken special, as yet untouched.

"Damn, that looks good."

"Are you eating?" Tina asked.

"I'll wait for Ashlock," Elsie replied. "I just left him at the high school; he'll be by any time. You go ahead."

"So," Tina said, picking up a chicken leg, "where are we?"

Elsie answered carefully. Two days of trial preparation had passed since she'd last updated Tina. Things were shaky, she told her, but could be worse.

"Well, I don't see how," Tina said with a frown. "We've lost four out of five counts with Charlene gone. Will you be able to find her?"

With a stubborn set to her mouth, Elsie shook her head. "No, but all's not lost with Charlene. Maybe. I've got her preliminary hearing testimony. It's under oath. The court reporter is transcribing it right now. I'm pretty sure I'll get it into evidence since she's unavailable."

Tina asked whether the jury would convict on the evidence of an absent witness. "If she doesn't care enough to show up, why would the jury care?"

"Yeah, well. Reading the transcript at trial doesn't have the same impact that Charlene would have had; you're right about that. Hell, they may throw it out; I can't say that they won't. But I'm not waving the white flag yet. I had a 'come to Jesus' talk with Kristy, and she's back in the fold. And she can substantiate some of the allegations involving Charlene."

Tina buttered her roll. "So you've got Kristy, you've got the valentine. But you've lost Charlene, and you've lost the photos."

"The originals of the photos," Elsie corrected her.

"What do you think a jury will do with this?"

She sat back in the booth and sighed. "Lord, I don't know."

"Who makes the call on punishment in this case? The judge?"

"Taney's not a persistent offender, so the jury will recommend the sentence."

"I didn't think juries got to do sentencing anymore."

"We're one of the last states that lets a jury weigh in on punishment. Unless he waives it, anyway. Taney can make a written request that the judge decide his punishment."

"Why would he do that?"

Elsie shrugged. "Maybe he's worried the jury will go after him with torches and pitchforks."

Ashlock appeared in a snowy jacket. He hung it on the back of the booth and scooted in beside Elsie. "Who's got a pitchfork?" he asked.

She caught him up on their discussion about the sentencing. "It's a bifurcated trial process," she told Tina. "We put on our case in chief—sorry, present our evidence of the crime—for the guilt phase. Then, if the jury finds Taney guilty, we have the second stage of the trial for the jury to determine punishment."

Turning over the empty coffee cup on the table, Ashlock looked around for a waitress, to no avail. He turned to Elsie. "Have you got any evidence for the punishment stage?"

She rolled her head back, exhausted. "I haven't even had time to think about that yet. I get to offer evidence of the impact of the crime on the victims and the family. I might talk to Tiffany's teacher. She may have some testimony I could use, about how the kid won't talk. Tina, I may put you on in the punishment phase to give your assessment of the home life."

Tina swallowed a bite of mashed potatoes and said, "I'm all yours."

Ashlock said, "How about putting the little sister on the stand in your case in chief? Tiffany?"

Simultaneously, both women groaned. Elsie said, "No. No! Oh, Ash, it would be a disaster. You can't get her to say boo to a goose. I've tried."

Ashlock offered, "Would there be any benefit to letting the jury just get a look at her? To see the impact Taney has had on her?"

"I'm telling you, she'll flip out. She'll hide under the chair."

"Maybe they should see that. It might paint a picture."

Elsie couldn't bear to see Tiffany's fear in a courtroom. "Ashlock, it would be such a gamble. Plus, I think to force her onto the stand could damage her emotionally in a big way. Tina, am I exaggerating?"

"No," Tina said, then continued slowly. "But I know you'll do what you have to do, to get the defendant behind bars. Because, sweetie, you've got a lot riding on this. Personally."

Elsie rubbed her face with her hand. She was so tired that she was about to drop. She wished that Tina would back off; maybe she shouldn't have confided in her about Madeleine's threat. She didn't need to be reminded that her case was going to hell, and with it, her job.

"I'll do anything to win this case," she said. "But there's no point in calling that poor screwed-up kid to the stand."

She looked at Ashlock and gave him a wan smile. He patted her shoulder. "I'm going to the counter to get you a sandwich," he said. "If we wait for service, it will be breakfast time. How about ham and cheese? With a Diet Coke?"

"Ashlock, you're the best," Elsie said.

As he walked away to order, she closed her eyes for a second and nearly fell asleep.

She'd stayed up the better part of the night before, doing research and drafting a brief in support of her motion to submit photostatic copies of the nude Polaroids of Charlene, in lieu of the originals. She also prepared her suggestions in support of submitting preliminary hearing testimony at trial, so that Charlene's testimony could be heard. Then, after only a couple of hours' sleep, she'd spent a full day chasing down the court reporter who was working on Charlene's transcript, running down the handwriting expert who could tie the valentine to Kris Taney, and persuading Kristy to testify, in addition to their fruitless mission at the high school. Between her witness conferences, she'd prepared the final versions of her direct examinations for trial. She still had a big task ahead; she needed to anticipate Nixon's argument against submission of the valentine, so she'd be ready to combat it. She felt like she was pulling a heavy load from Kansas City to St. Louis.

Tina gave her a little kick under the table that awoke her with a start. "What does Madeleine think about all this?"

Elsie gave a short laugh. "Can you believe it? She came to my office today, not to see if I needed anything, not to offer any help, but to remind me that my job is on the line. Like I'd forget."

Tina didn't respond. She fixed Elsie with a worried look. "So what did you say?"

Elsie laughed again, a tired, mirthless sound. "Oh, I told her, I'll win this one. Guaranteed. One hundred percent." She wadded a napkin in her fist. "Maybe I should've said I'm guaranteed to lose. Closer to the truth."

Ashlock set a sandwich and a plastic tumbler of Diet Coke in front of Elsie. "Better eat something," he said.

As she bit into her sandwich, he recounted the status of the investigation into Charlene's disappearance. After talking to Charlene's friend, he believed Donita's theory might have been right; Charlene had in fact talked about running off. Shawna had confirmed that a boyfriend was in the picture, and that the conflict between Charlene and Roy had escalated.

"Probably physical abuse," Tina said.

"Sounds like it," Ashlock agreed.

"She had a black eye the last time I saw her," Elsie said.

Tina sighed and shook her head. "After Elsie reported the black eye, we never got the chance to investigate it; Charlene disappeared. Of course, Donita and Roy said it was an accident."

"Could've been an accident, could've been a boyfriend. Most likely, though, it was Mayfield," Ashlock reasoned.

"But do you think," Elsie ventured, afraid to say it aloud, "it's at all possible that Mayfield was abusing her sexually as well? Or her uncle? Like Kris Taney says?"

Ashlock looked at her. "What do you think?"

She was quiet for a moment. "I think," she said in a firm voice, "I *believe*, that Charlene was raped and beaten by her father. She may also have been knocked around by

Roy Mayfield after he became head of the household; it's possible that she was also abused by her uncle. Shoot, it's even possible that she gets the same treatment from her boyfriend. But the guy who's going on trial next week is Kris Taney, and my gut tells me he's good for it."

There was silence around the table.

"Charlene. That poor kid," said Elsie, shaking her head. A tear collected in the corner of one eye, and she didn't blink it back fast enough. She needed to steel herself; this was no time to become emotional. It was time to don the armor.

Ashlock handed her a paper napkin and she used it to wipe her nose. "How's the case holding up?" he asked.

"Going to pieces," Tina murmured.

Wearily, Elsie laid her cheek on her hand as she surveyed Ashlock. "I've got a live victim and a written admission of the defendant," she said. "I'm going to see this through."

"Are you putting the mother on?" he asked dubiously.

"Lord, I wish I didn't have to call her. I wish her at the bottom of the sea. Donita and I aren't getting along so hot these days. She and her boy Roy are giving me the evil eye. But I've got to put her on the stand to get my valentine in, and the photos. Chain of custody. Other than that, I won't ask her a blessed thing. Lying snake."

"Aren't you afraid of what she'll say under cross-examination?"

"Sure. Hell yes. If I didn't need to get that valentine into evidence, I'd skip her altogether." Her voice took on a hopeful note. "But she's a wild card. She's like Pandora's box. Nixon could easily open something up in his cross-ex that would hurt the defense."

"The way your luck is going—" Tina began, then stopped. Two pairs of steely eyes silenced her.

Ashlock pushed the sandwich closer to Elsie. She'd put it back on the plate after one bite. "You going to eat something?" he asked.

"Maybe in a minute. I'm so tired," she said, and her eyes closed in spite of her.

Tina clucked sympathetically. "She's been working herself to death on this case. I've got to watch my pessimistic remarks. She could snap."

"I'm not asleep. I can hear you," Elsie said, eyes still shut.

"Do they want to plead? Have you offered him a deal?" Tina asked her. Elsie didn't respond. Her chin dropped.

"I think she's out," Tina said. "What should we do?"

Ashlock appraised Elsie as she nodded in the booth. "You go on. I'll sit with her for a minute. I'll make sure she wakes up."

Tina hesitated, then nodded and said, "Okay. I'll see you in court on Monday." She grasped her heavy coat and slipped out of the booth.

Elsie slumped in the booth and Ashlock caught her. He gently eased her back against the seat, cushioning her head with his jacket. Then he reached out and stroked her cheek, and her face relaxed.

Chapter Forty-One

On Monday morning Elsie was ready to go. The weekend had been hellish. She'd worked nonstop on her trial preparation, had suffered insomnia and fought panic. But now that the time for trial had actually arrived, she felt relatively sane.

Before jury selection, Josh Nixon began with a move that took Elsie by surprise. Approaching the bench, he handed the judge a sheet of paper.

"Judge Rountree, my client has decided to waive jury sentencing."

Raising his eyebrows, the judge inspected the document, as Elsie hurried up to the bench to get a look at it. She knew that it was the defendant's choice to have punishment determined by the judge rather than the jury, but she'd never seen it done.

Turning to Nixon in astonishment, she whispered, "Why doesn't he want the jury to decide punishment?"

Nixon shot her a sidelong glance. "I don't think it's appropriate for me to share my client's confidential communications with the prosecution."

She fell silent, but remained perplexed. Generally, defense attorneys found it far easier to fool a jury than a judge. If Nixon and Taney were afraid of what a jury might do in this case, it was a good sign for her. She warmed at the thought.

After the judge took notice of Taney's waiver, jury selection began. Elsie, Josh Nixon, and Judge Rountree would whittle the panel of eighty-three prospective jurors down to an even dozen.

Judge Rountree crowded the prospective jurors into the courtroom and placed them under oath. After the judge commenced the voir dire with general questions to establish bias, Elsie and Josh had their chance.

Elsie's voir dire presentation was tried and true; she made the same general pitch in every case to introduce herself to the jury, adapting the questions to the crime.

When she was done, Josh took the podium. With a solemn face, he said, "Ladies and gentlemen, my client doesn't have to prove anything. He is presumed to be innocent. You all understand that, don't you?"

Elsie watched their faces intently as she pulled a chart of the jury panel in front of her at the counsel table. A woman in her forties with elaborately coiffured hair smiled at Nixon and nodded vigorously. Elsie took her pen and marked the woman's name with an X.

You're out of here, sis, she thought. The woman was

already trying too hard to please the handsome defense attorney.

"Is there anyone on this jury panel who believes my client must be guilty of something just because he's been charged with a crime?"

Elsie saw a man in the front row shift in his seat, his eyes darting away from Nixon. Yesss, she thought, drawing stars by his name. She checked his employment: he was a farmer who worked construction on the side. *Perfect. Just what I need.*

"Raise your hands, please. This is important, ladies and gentlemen."

Keep your hand down, she silently begged the construction worker/farmer. I need you on this jury.

A hand shot up. An old salt in weathered overalls spoke up and said, "Don't seem like the court would go to all this trouble if the man hadn't done nothing."

Nixon raised a hand to cut him off. "Thank you for your candor, sir."

Elsie went ahead and marked off the old guy. Nixon would get rid of him with a challenge for cause.

When Nixon completed his questions, both attorneys approached the bench and argued their strikes for cause. Nixon persuaded the judge to strike the old citizen in overalls, as well as half a dozen citizens who had said that hanging was too good for a man who had sex with a child; and Elsie managed to convince him to dismiss a juror who claimed that false rape accusations were a common occurrence. When the judge told the man he was excused, Elsie had to exercise control to keep from shooting him a triumphant farewell smirk.

"Miss Arnold, Mr. Nixon," the judge said, "we'll take number one through twenty-four of the remaining panel. I'm giving you each six peremptory strikes; you may each remove six jurors of your choice from the panel."

The attorneys sat at their respective tables as the judge declared a recess. Josh Nixon pored over the list with Kris Taney at his side.

Elsie took her pen and drew an X over two young men in their twenties, got rid of the woman who already had a crush on Josh Nixon, and then struck three women whose faces she couldn't read. Though she was a staunch feminist, she'd learned the hard way that men made the best jurors for a prosecutor. Blue collar men in particular weren't afraid to convict; they didn't quail from sending someone to prison. Young men were the exception. In sex cases, they might identify with the defendant, and be skeptical of the complaining witness.

Elsie had a complicated relationship with female jurors in sex cases. Although plenty of women wanted to avenge violent crimes committed against their gender, there were others who wanted to blame the victim, and she couldn't always tell them apart on sight.

The peremptory strikes reduced the final group of twenty-four to twelve, and they had their jury for the Taney case. As she sat at the prosecution table, Elsie studied the faces of the twelve jurors seated in the jury box. She was pretty well satisfied with the makeup of the group. It contained the farming construction worker, and the females on the jury either had some higher education or had children. A couple of the jurors might be wild cards, but she felt the Taney case was in good hands. It was a strange thing to know that this jury held her own fate in their hands as well.

Turning in her seat, Elsie inspected the courtroom gallery to see if any representatives of the Earthly Fathers were lurking, and was relieved to see that they were markedly absent. A glimpse of the hallway outside showed that they weren't occupying seats in the rotunda either. She was delighted to see that Ashlock was right and the plug had been pulled on the group.

Her adrenaline was running high; any minute, the judge would instruct her to make her opening statement. She uncapped a pen and, turning through the pages of her handwritten opening statement, struck out all references to the photos of Charlene. Judge Rountree had made a split ruling on the evidence; he'd let the valentine in, but Elsie would not be permitted to offer the photos in her case in chief without Charlene present in court to identify them, or some forensic evidence tying the originals to the defendant.

Finally, the judge cleared his throat and inclined his head toward Elsie. She was poised on the edge of her chair, her muscles tensed, as she waited for him to speak.

"Is the state ready to make Opening Statement?"

She stood, drawing up to her full height. This was no time to slouch. "If it please the court."

"Proceed."

She walked to the jury box with a determined stride. Facing the twelve men and women, she scanned their faces before focusing on juror six, the construction worker, her primary favorite. "Ladies and gentlemen of the jury, this is what the evidence will show."

Juror six returned her gaze with a neutral expression. He wasn't in her pocket yet; she would have to win him over.

"The state of Missouri will present evidence that this man," and she swung around, pointing an accusatory index finger at Taney, "this man, Kristopher Eugene Taney, committed five counts of the crime of statutory rape in the first degree."

For the jury's benefit, she gave Taney a hard glare as he sat at the defense table. He glanced away and scratched his nose. Pointing the finger of guilt at the accused was a procedure she used in every jury trial. She'd read it in a novel by Scott Turow, or maybe Grisham: if the prosecutor won't confront the defendant, why should the jury do it? So she always stared the defendant down as a way to set the stage.

Back to the jury, she presented a grave face. "We will call the defendant's daughter, Kristy Taney, to the witness stand. Kristy is twelve years old. She will testify that on the twenty-fifth of November of last year, her father forced her to have sexual intercourse with him in the family's home, here in Barton, Missouri."

A young woman on the front row with light brown hair pulled back in a ponytail gave her a slight nod. Elsie almost broke into a grin as the tightness in her chest eased. She hadn't counted on that particular juror to be in the prosecution's camp.

Her voice held a hint of warning as she said, "You'll also hear the testimony of Kristy's sister, Charlene. Charlene, the defendant's oldest daughter, is fifteen. She will provide sworn testimony that her father has been having sexual intercourse and performing deviant acts with her since she was nine. Nine years old." She added smoothly, as if it were an inconsequential detail, "You'll hear these facts from Charlene Taney's preliminary hearing transcript. Unfortunately, Charlene is not available to be here and testify in person." At this, a motherly woman who had been listening with rapt attention looked away.

Aw shit. This wasn't going to be easy.

Standing straight, Elsie launched into a summary of the remaining evidence: her doctor, the valentine, and the handwriting evidence.

When she concluded and sat down, the judge asked the defense to proceed. Nixon briefly took the podium, taking shots at the state's case, her medical evidence and the relevance of the valentine, without revealing any evidence that the defense intended to produce. That nettled her a little; clearly, he didn't want to reveal his hand.

The judge called for the state to present its evidence, and Elsie called Kristy Taney to the witness stand.

Kristy entered the courtroom wearing an expression of dread on her face. The girl settled into the witness chair, her lank black hair tucked behind her ears. It appeared that she had not shampooed it in advance of the trial, and Elsie felt a twinge of irritation with Donita; why, she wondered, wouldn't a mother get the girl cleaned up before coming to the courthouse?

"State your name for the record, please," Elsie asked the girl in an encouraging tone.

"Kristy Taney," the girl said. "Kristine, I mean." She shot a nervous glance at her father, and looked back at Elsie.

Elsie directed Kristy through the events of Thanksgiving Day the year before. Kristy provided the necessary facts, though she spoke so softly that the judge had to instruct her to speak up.

When Kristy concluded her description of her father's abuse, Elsie asked her to identify the man who had committed the act. Kristy hung her head in silence; Elsie feared that she wouldn't carry on. Just as she was about to repeat the question, Kristy spoke up. Staring at the floor, the child said, "It's him. Dad. He done it."

"Is he in the courtroom today?"

"Yeah."

"Could you point him out to the jury, please."

It was a tense moment. Kristy lifted a hesitant finger and pointed, stealing a glance at Taney. When the daughter's eyes met her father's, she jerked, as if she'd been shocked with a wire.

Elsie broke the spell, saying, "May the record reflect that the witness has identified the defendant, Kris Taney."

"It will so reflect."

"Kristy," she continued, "tell us who lived with you in the apartment on High Street."

"You mean before Dad went to jail?"

"Yes."

"Mom and Dad and Charlene and Tiffany. And for a while, JoLee and her baby. And sometimes Uncle Al."

"Charlene and Tiffany are your sisters."

"Yeah."

"Who is JoLee?"

"Objection: irrelevant," Nixon snapped.

"Sustained."

Elsie had to regroup; she was determined that the jury should know about Taney's harem, but she would try again later.

"Kristy, did you ever see your father touch Charlene—"

"Objection!" Nixon jumped to his feet this time. "May we approach?"

Elsie walked to the bench, pausing to give the jury a knowing smile as she did so. Once the lawyers stood before the judge, Nixon said, "She's trying to introduce evidence of crimes the defendant's not charged with."

"Section 566.025, Revised Statutes of Missouri, specifically provides that evidence of other sex crimes with a victim under the age of fourteen is admissible to prove propensity to commit the offense," Elsie rattled off handily. Turning to Nixon, she added, "This your first sex case, junior?"

"No, Ms. Arnold, it is not. Judge, the evidence is admissible *unless* its probative value is outweighed by prejudicial impact. The prosecutor is trying to bootstrap testimony that hasn't even been offered. Defendant objects; this is highly prejudicial, highly damaging."

"You bet it's damaging," she retorted. "Judge, she's going to corroborate Charlene. This is the purpose for which the statute was enacted."

The judge studied the carved handle of his wooden gavel. "I believe I'll allow it. Miss Arnold, see you don't go too far afield with this."

"Yes, your honor. Thank you," she said, feeling a surge of triumph for the first time that day. As she walked away from the bench, she smiled and nodded at Kristy, then repeated the question.

Kristy looked at her, frowning. "You know what he done."

"Kristy, you need to tell the jury."

"Which time? Which time you talking about?"

"Objection—"

"Ms. Arnold, narrow your inquiry."

Elsie was growing flustered. Kristy had been thoroughly prepared; the examination should be going more smoothly. She took a breath and continued.

"Kristy, I want to direct your attention to December sixth of last year. What happened at your home?"

"I was outside when it happened. I didn't see nothing."

"Well, Kristy, have you ever seen—"

"Objection. Your honor, may we approach—"

The judge cut them both off. "I'm going to shut this line of questioning down. Objection sustained."

Elsie couldn't contain a little huff of irritation, and the judge shot her a warning look. "Proceed, ma'am."

"But judge—"

"Proceed."

She felt herself blushing. "Kristy, can you describe any physical relations between your father and your sister Charlene—"

"Judge, I object! She's disregarding the court's ruling."

"Miss Arnold?"

Elsie shot the defense a look. "No further questions."

She returned to the counsel table and perched on the edge of her chair, apprehensive about the damage that might be done in cross-ex. To her surprise, Nixon's examination was brief and quite pleasant. He did not harangue the witness; he spoke to Kristy respectfully. The questions were so nonconfrontational that she was almost caught off guard when he asked, "Who sleeps in your mother's bedroom now that your dad is gone?"

"Objection, irrelevant," Elsie spat, just in time to cut off the child's answer.

"Sustained," the judge said, and she exhaled a relieved breath.

Nixon smiled at Kristy. "No further questions."

"May this witness be released from her subpoena?" the judge inquired.

"No, your honor," Nixon said. "I may need to inquire further, later on."

Elsie saw Nixon and Taney exchange a look before Taney turned his head away, covering his mouth with his hand. Elsie was dumbfounded; it looked like Taney was grinning.

Chapter Forty-Two

AFTER KRISTY STEPPED down, a juror asked for a bathroom break. Judge Rountree declared a five-minute recess and left the bench. Elsie readied the direct examination of her next witness, then glanced out the courtroom door at the jurors lined up behind Merle, waiting to be escorted down the hall.

In the hallway, across from the courtroom door, stood Noah. He was holding a bouquet of flowers wrapped in colored tissue paper.

This is insane, she thought. Having him pop up at trial was a nightmare. She needed to be focused, not looking over her shoulder to avoid her volatile ex-lover. Maybe she could ignore him.

He walked up to the courtroom door but didn't enter. Stationed just outside the door frame, he blocked the doorway, staring at her.

Elsie picked up her pen and tried to write. When her

hand began to tremble, she put it down again. As much as she wanted to delay the confrontation, it was inevitable. With a mighty shove, she pushed her chair away from the counsel table and walked directly up to Noah.

"Hey, girl," he said, beaming, "I've been missing you. I came to wish you luck. Brought you something to brighten up your office."

She whispered, "You can take those flowers and give them to someone who doesn't mind getting knocked around." She glanced around the courtroom, not wanting to be overheard. She would not make a scene.

In a level voice, he said, "You know, it takes two to fight. But what happened in the car was totally out of character. That's not really me. I was pushed over my limit."

So it was my fault that you hit me? His implicit accusation stirred a fire in her chest. Still speaking quietly, she said, "Your limit's not my problem. We're through."

He looked away with a hurt expression.

"It's over."

His eyes narrowed. "You don't get to say when it's over," he said.

Elsie watched him storm to the nearest trash can and jam the flowers inside. Without another look, he was gone.

Block it out, she told herself. She couldn't think about it, not at that moment. Her work here was far more important. Her performance was crucial. She returned to the courtroom and took her seat. As she sat, she smoothed her skirt with her hands, trying to erase every wrinkle in the fabric.

But she was shaken, despite her best efforts to resist it. Don't just sit here, she thought. She had a few minutes left. She should print a copy of the Missouri statute she'd cited earlier, in case the issue arose again.

She headed for her office at a speedy clip. Midway along the rotunda, though, she paused, her hand on the wooden railing. A book would be better. Juries liked to see a law book on the counsel table. It made the attorney appear learned and studious.

Turning, she made a beeline for the old law library in a dim corner of the second floor. It had originally been a resource for judges and local lawyers, though it was rarely used anymore for its original purpose. Missouri statutes and case law and law review articles were available online at the touch of a computer screen and printed in an instant.

But the law books remained, lining the walls of the room in glassed walnut cases: sets of the Southwestern Reporter and Missouri Revised Statutes, along with federal statutes and case law. She pulled the RSMo volume containing the criminal code, and as an afterthought, a random volume of Southwestern 3d, just for show, and hurried back to the counsel table in Judge Rountree's courtroom.

A muted buzz sounded as Merle shepherded the jurors back to the jury box. When everyone was in place, Judge Rountree gave Elsie the sign to begin.

Charlene's preliminary hearing testimony was read into the record. Elsie then called Dr. Petrus to the witness stand. She believed that juries liked to hear from expert witnesses, particularly in cases that involved a swearing match. The witness was a pleasant family practitioner in his mid-thirties who would make a good impression on the jury.

"Dr. Petrus," she said, "did you have occasion to perform a physical examination of Kristy Taney in January of this year?"

The doctor said, "I did."

"Did your physical include a pelvic exam?"

"It did," he replied with a somber expression.

"What did the exam reveal?"

"Objection: unless the witness can tie the results of his exam to the defendant, then his answer is irrelevant and immaterial," Nixon said.

"Overruled," Judge Rountree said shortly. "Answer, Dr. Petrus."

"The hymen was not intact on Kristy Taney."

"In your opinion, is that finding consistent with sexual activity?"

"It could be."

Elsie asked about his examination of Charlene, and the doctor testified that the hymen was not intact on Charlene either.

"Additionally," he added, "the exam revealed inflammation in the vaginal area."

"In your opinion, would that be consistent with sexual activity?'

"In my opinion, yes."

"No further questions."

She covertly checked out the jury's reaction; she

sensed that she was making progress with them. Several jurors were growing markedly sympathetic, providing Elsie with significant eye contact. That was a good sign.

Nixon was battering the doctor with a predictable line of questioning.

"Isn't it possible, Doctor, that a girl's hymen can rupture in any number of ways?"

"It is."

"Riding a horse? A bicycle?"

"That's true."

"So you're telling the jury that it's entirely possible that these girls have never had sexual intercourse."

"That's possible."

"And even assuming that they have had intercourse, you have no scientific evidence as to who the sex partner might be, isn't that correct?"

"That's true."

"It could be anyone: a boyfriend, or another male living in the household, isn't that right?"

Elsie jerked into action, objecting that the question called for speculation, but the doctor had already answered the question in the affirmative. The judge told the jury to disregard the answer, but it was cold comfort to Elsie.

Can't unring a bell, she thought.

Nixon asked the witness, "Why didn't you take samples and send them to the crime lab for DNA testing?"

Damn, Elsie thought, She should have cleared that up.

"The father had been in custody for weeks. The samples have to be taken closer in time to the act."

"But if you'd taken samples, they might have revealed the presence of another partner, correct?"

Elsie shut the question down on grounds of speculation again, but Nixon had planted a seed, and the jury got the message. In redirect, she scored a point or two by asking whether children with no bicycles and no access to horses were likely to lose their virginity through those activities. Still, she worried that her damage control was incomplete. When the doctor was dismissed, a couple of jurors exchanged quizzical glances.

Elsie didn't like that. Not a bit.

Chapter Forty-Three

ON TUESDAY MORNING, before trial commenced for the day, Elsie sucked down a cup of weak coffee in her office. Donita sat opposite her, hugging her black vinyl handbag and regarding her with a resigned expression.

"It's showtime, Donita," Elsie said with a counterfeit grin. The women walked to the courtroom side by side.

When court convened, Elsie called Donita Taney to the witness stand. Donita walked in with a hangdog expression, still clutching the black purse. Acts like she's got a stash in there, Elsie thought impatiently, before she restrained her thoughts with a jerk. She extended a welcoming hand to her witness.

"Donita, come on over here and be sworn," she said in a voice that radiated goodwill.

Donita took the oath and sat in the witness chair. She settled the purse on her lap, then as an afterthought, set it on the floor beside her. She tucked her hands, palms together, between her knees.

Elsie walked over to the jury box to ask the questions so Donita's face would be turned toward the jury.

"Donita, direct your attention to January eighteenth of this year: what happened on that date?"

"That was the day you come to the house to pick up them boxes."

"What house are you referring to?"

"Our house over on High."

"What were the boxes?"

"I'd packed up Kris's stuff. To get it out. I didn't want it around no more. And JoLee's stuff she left behind."

"Who is JoLee?"

"JoLee Stokes. She'd been living with us ever since Kris knocked her up."

"Objection!" Nixon was on his feet. "Irrelevant. Judge, may we approach?"

Rountree shook his head. "No need. Sustained. Jury will disregard the last statement."

But checking the jury's reaction with her peripheral vision, Elsie was pleased to see a woman bristle at Donita's revelation.

She then took the valentine from its bag and handed it to the court reporter, instructing her to mark it as an exhibit.

"Donita, I'm handing you what has been marked as State's Exhibit Number One. Could you examine it, please?"

Donita opened the card without expression, looked at it, and handed it back to Elsie.

"What is it?"

"It's a valentine card."

"Addressed to whom?"

"JoLee." For the first time, Donita looked directly at the jury box, and as an aside, said to them, "My husband's common law."

"Objection!"

"Sustained."

Elsie's mouth twitched but she kept a straight face.

"Donita, did you have the opportunity to examine the handwriting on that card?"

Yeah."

"Is it familiar?"

"Yep."

"Whose handwriting is it?"

"Objection: is this witness a handwriting expert?"

The judge peered at Elsie through his glasses. "Qualify the witness, Ms. Arnold."

"How long have you known the defendant, Kris Taney?"

"Been married fifteen years. Knowed him a while before that."

"During your marriage and acquaintance, did you have occasion to see his handwriting?"

"Sure. Lots of times."

"Please read the writing on the card."

Donita did, reading aloud in a voice that conveyed

deep sadness. Elsie thought that her problem witness was performing much better than anticipated.

"Do you recognize that handwriting?"

"Oh yeah."

"Whose is it?"

"Kris. Kris wrote it."

"Donita, please examine State's Exhibit Number One again. Is it in the same or similar condition today as it was when you handed it over to the state?"

Donita looked at it with contempt. "Yep. Sure is."

Elsie smiled a beatific smile. "No further questions."

Nixon glowered as he rose from the chair. He descended upon Donita with a barrage of questions attacking her veracity, her mothering, her lifestyle. He flatly accused her of forging the valentine and planting it in the box for the state to find. She hunched her shoulders and suffered the questions, setting her jaw like a bulldog and answering in short phrases.

"Is there a new member of your household?"

Elsie quickly objected but was overruled.

Donita hesitated. "No."

"What about Roy Mayfield?"

Elsie stood this time. "Objection, your honor, irrelevant."

"I'll tie it up, Judge." When the judge nodded, Nixon said, "Donita, tell us about Roy Mayfield."

"Roy's a friend."

"Is he spending his days at your house?"

"He's there some."

"Spending the night there, Mrs. Taney?"

"No."

"Oh, come on: he's your lover, isn't he, your new romance?"

"Objection," Elsie interjected.

"Overruled."

When Donita remained silent, Nixon added, "Want me to repeat the question?" Donita shook her head, and Nixon added, "Need I remind you that you are under oath?"

"Roy's been a good friend to me. To all of us."

"What about Al Taney? Is he your good friend, too?"

"He's Kris's brother."

"Haven't you had sexual relations with Al Taney during your marriage to his brother, Kris?"

Elsie objected loudly, but her objection was overruled again.

Nixon moved closer to the witness stand. "Isn't it true that you and Al Taney plotted to remove Kris Taney from his home?"

Donita pressed her right hand against the side of her abdomen. "It's true I've wished Kris Taney gone lots of times, I tell you that much. Wished him gone to the devil."

"Didn't you and Al and Roy all cook this allegation up to get my client out of the way?"

"No."

"Didn't you convince your girls to lie about their father so that you and Roy could live happily ever after?"

"That's not right." Donita was clutching her side with both hands, pressing her lips together; she was pale as death.

Nixon said, "You nervous, Mrs. Taney? Is talking about this giving you a pain?"

She shook her head. "It's my side. My ribs. Kris broke my ribs when he beat me with a axe handle last year, and they didn't heal up good."

As a juror gasped, Elsie saw fireworks; a colorful spray of roman candles burst forth in her brain.

Nixon hurled toward the bench. "Objection, your honor! Instruct the jury to disregard!"

Elsie, on her feet, hooted with scorn. "Objection to what, Judge? He asked the question; he's got to live with the answer."

While Nixon hotly contested the point, Elsie glimpsed Kris Taney. The defendant, his gaze focused on Donita, looked demonic, his eyes glinting malice. His wife met the look, but then shook her head and stared off into space.

Elsie stole another glance at the jury box. The jurors were noting the defendant's demeanor. One man nudged his seatmate and nodded in Taney's direction. Elsie caught the juror's attention and widened her eyes. The man nodded and looked away.

Now we're getting somewhere, she thought with satisfaction.

Chapter Forty-Four

AFTER SHE RESTED the state's case, Elsie felt blissfully confident. The handwriting expert from the police department had corroborated Donita's testimony regarding the defendant's handwriting on the valentine, but the expert testimony proved anticlimactic; Donita's unexpected revelation about the axe handle, and Taney's reaction to her, carried the day.

Sorry, Madeleine, but I won't be looking for a new job, after all, she exulted.

During the recess that followed, Josh Nixon announced to the judge that he needed to make a record. Elsie perked up; she had a pretty good guess as to what that request signified.

Kris Taney was not going to testify in his own defense.

Sure enough, while the jury was outside of the courtroom, Nixon put Taney on the stand and ran him through a short examination, to make a record about his decision.

The big man dwarfed the wooden witness chair. He was mulish as he acknowledged that, yes, he understood that he had the right to testify; his attorney had advised him that it was in his own best interest to testify; and that it was his own decision, freely made, to stay off the stand in his case.

Elsie watched the exchange, baffled, though it was a common enough occurrence. Defendants often opted to stay off the witness stand and rely on their right to silence. The witness stand was an intimidating place to be.

But in the Taney case, she thought the decision to stand silent was foolhardy. She pushed her chair away from the table and crossed her legs, tapping the pen on the counsel table as she assessed the impact of that decision. How could a defendant in a case like this consider staying off the stand? This was a "he said–she said" type trial, and Taney's refusal to testify meant that he wouldn't have a chance to deny the charge, explain away the accusations, point the finger another direction.

She flipped a file open to double-check Taney's rap sheet. His criminal record showed a number of priors: a misdemeanor marijuana, a couple of DWIs, and two third-degree assault convictions, along with numerous domestic dispute arrests that hadn't resulted in convictions. If he didn't testify, his criminal history would not be revealed to the jury; it could only be raised in cross-examination. Still, she was surprised that a misdemeanor record would keep him off the stand in a felony case. Maybe Taney was too stupid to realize he needed to testify. Or maybe his attorney thought the combination of his offenses would offend the jury. Or maybe Nixon was disgusted by his client. Maybe he was ready to let Taney hang himself.

Nixon concluded his record, and the men returned to the defense table. *Why is Nixon making my life so easy, all of a sudden?* she asked herself, then shrugged inwardly. Whatever the reason, it was fine with her, and she smiled at the defense attorney.

A thought nagged at her, however: if Taney didn't testify, she couldn't bring out the nude shots. When Rountree granted Nixon's motion to block the Polaroids from the prosecution's case in chief, the judge hinted that Elsie might use them to cross-examine Taney when he took the stand. Now she wouldn't have the opportunity. She brushed the thought away. *We're looking good,* she thought. *What could go wrong?* The jury didn't even need to see the photos.

The judge signaled the bailiff bring the jury back. Merle knocked on the door to jury room and told the twelve men and women inside that court was reconvening. They filed back into their seats in the jury box.

"Call your first witness, Mr. Nixon," the judge ordered.

Nixon stood, casting a sidelong glance at Elsie, as if anticipating a reaction.

"The defense calls Kristy Taney, your honor."

Elsie gasped audibly. She jumped to her feet, and for one terrible moment she couldn't articulate a response. "Objection," she choked.

Without looking in Elsie's direction, Nixon said smoothly, "We ask leave to treat her as a hostile witness."

"May we approach the bench?" Elsie asked. The judge nodded, and she stormed to meet Nixon at the bench, her face turning scarlet.

"What is going on?" she demanded.

"You're about to find out."

The judge interrupted. "Do you have a legal argument to make, Ms. Arnold?"

In fact, she did not. "I'm working on it."

Nixon, the cat who swallowed the canary, cut his eyes at her. "Well?"

"Unfair surprise," said Elsie, speaking very rapidly. "The defense didn't disclose this witness to me, Mr. Nixon never said he'd be calling her."

Nixon snorted and shook his head. "Since when do we have to disclose a witness list to you? And why on earth would we have to apprise you of your own witness? Judge—"

"Objection overruled. Defendant will proceed."

The bailiff called for Kristy in the courthouse hallway, and she walked into the courtroom hesitantly, looking confused and reluctant to return. Nixon grinned broadly at her and indicated the witness chair with his right hand.

"Please come and take a seat, Kristy."

She looked at the judge, who smiled and nodded, adding, "You're still under oath, Miss Taney."

Kristy shot a look at Elsie, who she responded with a weak smile.

As Kristy settled into the chair, Nixon approached her in a manner that seemed positively chummy to Elsie.

"Kristy," he said, "I want to show you something. I

warn you that it's shocking to see, but you need to look and tell me what it is."

Nixon had the court reporter mark one of the copies of the photo of Charlene, and handed it to the girl.

"What is that?" he asked her.

"It's a picture of Charlene. A naked picture."

"By Charlene, you are referring to your sister, isn't that right?"

Kristy said yes.

With a herculean effort, Elsie kept her face impassive, waiting for the next move. The jurors shifted in their seats, intent on the witness.

"Did your father take that picture?"

"Nope," she answered, matter-of-fact.

"How do you know?"

"Daddy don't never let us be in a dirty picture."

Kris Taney beamed and nodded, the proud father.

"Who do you suppose took that picture, then?" Nixon asked.

"Objection," Elsie said, her voice like a rifleshot. "Calls for speculation."

"Sustained."

"If she knows, Judge," Nixon argued. "I'm not asking her to guess. I just want her to say it if she knows."

"All right, then. Watch how you frame the question, sir."

Smiling sadly, Nixon leaned against the jury box, close to Kristy, and asked in a confiding tone, "Kristy, look at Defendant's Exhibit Number One—who took the picture?"

Kristy looked at it, made a face. Wrinkling her nose, she said, "Uncle Al, I expect."

Elsie's heart sank to her stomach. With her mouth suddenly dry, she said, "Objection. Witness is speculating."

"Because it's with a instant camera, see?" Kristy said, holding the exhibit up toward Elsie. "That's how Al takes them pictures. Roy takes our pictures with his phone."

As the courtroom erupted, the jurors turned to one another and to Elsie, looking at her with confusion and disbelief. Her mind formed a single thought: *Reasonable doubt.*

Chapter Forty-Five

THE COURTROOM WAS bedlam after Kristy's revelation. Recovering, Elsie jumped to her feet, shouting objections on every ground she could think of—nonresponsive, irrelevant, hearsay—while Taney slapped his knee and tipped backward in his chair, grinning to beat the band. The buzzing from the jurors in the jury box and the spectators in the gallery rose to such a level that Judge Rountree finally had to bang the gavel three times before there was silence.

"Order!" he called. Pointing the gavel at Elsie, he said, "Objection overruled. Mr. Nixon, you may continue."

Josh Nixon shook his head with a cocky air. "No further questions."

It was Elsie's turn. Her ears were ringing; she needed time to collect her wits, but she didn't have the luxury.

She tried, in her cross-examination, to go over safe ground, walking the witness through her prior allegations against her father, until Josh shut it down as outside the scope of direct examination. Elsie faltered a moment, uncertain what to do next. She couldn't risk asking anything about Roy or Al, or how the pictures came to be taken, because she didn't have all the facts; every trial lawyer knew that proceeding blindly, asking questions when you didn't know the answer, was suicide.

But she couldn't give up. The jury was looking at her askance, and Elsie knew what that foretold. Nixon didn't have to prove his client innocent. The defense only had to raise a reasonable doubt to obtain a Not Guilty verdict. Nixon accomplished that with Kristy's testimony; any juror who wasn't scratching his head at this point wasn't paying attention.

Elsie made a stab at damage control. She drew close to the girl, and addressing her with gravity, said, "Kristy, you know that you have sworn to tell the truth in this trial, haven't you?"

Kristy nodded. "Yes."

"It's a sacred oath. You understand that."

"Yes."

From his chair, Nixon said, "Judge, I'm going to object to this line of questioning. She's trying to bootstrap the credibility of her witness."

"Our mutual witness," Elsie replied without looking his way. "Defense can't logically object to that."

"Miss Arnold's right. Overruled."

Staring eyeball-to-eyeball with Kristy, she said, "Think hard, Kristy. Is everything, every single word that you've said in this courtroom true?"

"Yes."

"I mean today, and yesterday. All true?"

"Objection. Asked and answered."

"Sustained."

Shut down. She couldn't reinforce Kristy's earlier testimony. Elsie stared intently at the girl, nodding, then nodded at the jury, before she told the judge, "No further questions."

When the judge declared a recess, Elsie raced out the door. She headed for the last stall in the women's room, and bolting the door, braced herself; she thought she might vomit. Thought she'd feel better if she did.

Nothing happened. She was so dry she couldn't even spit.

She sat on the toilet and buried her face in her hands. It was over. She had blown it. How did she fail to pick up on such a terrible crime occurring right under her nose? How could she have been blind to it? Remorse sat on her chest like an elephant: she should have realized what Roy and Al were up to. Certainly, there had been signs. Looking back, she wondered fleetingly whether she'd been afraid to see the whole picture.

She looked at her watch. She had about three minutes to pull herself together.

She left the stall and scrubbed her hands at the sink, ran a comb through her hair, applied a swipe of lipstick. She shook her head to clear it, squared her shoulders and headed down the hallway. As she turned the corner, she spied Ashlock. He walked up to her, and she asked, in a near whisper, whether he'd heard about Kristy's testimony. He nodded.

"They should be picked up, Ash," she said. "Roy May-field and Al. Questioned about child porn activities."

"I sent an officer out to find them about five minutes ago."

"Thank God. What do we do with Donita?"

"I've got her shut up in the conference room across the way. As soon as Patsy gets here with the recording equipment, me and Donita gonna have a talk."

Elsie nodded, silent. Ashlock put an arm around her and gave her a squeeze. "But what about our case against Kris Taney? How does it look in there?"

Elsie let herself lean into him for a moment. "I've lost it, Ash."

"What about rebuttal evidence?"

Closing her eyes in a bid to control her panic, she said, "I got nothing. Not a goddamned thing."

"Tiffany is under subpoena."

Her eyes popped open. "Fuck, Ash, the girl can't talk."

"I think you're going to have to take another shot."

Their eyes locked, she debated the possibility. After a pause she said, "Meet me by my office with her in a minute. I'll get Rountree to extend the recess."

A few minutes later she sat in her office surveying Tiffany, dwarfed in an office chair with her favorite Barbie. The child twisted the doll's head back and forth; Elsie thought it might split in two from the punishment.

Rising from her chair, she walked over to Tiffany and stood at her side, studying the Barbie with interest. It was naked, except for a makeshift denim jacket, a blue square of fabric from which her plastic arms protruded. With a start, Elsie recognized the remnant of fabric Charlene had toyed with in the car at Sonic. "Your Barbie is so darned pretty; almost as pretty as you," she said. Looking at Tiffany with a friendly smile, she asked, "Is she your best friend?"

Adamantly, Tiffany shook her head.

"Oh, okay," Elsie said, nodding thoughtfully. "I should've thought: I bet I know who your best friend really is." *Be careful*, Elsie warned herself; *don't spook her.* "Bet it's Charlene."

Tiffany ducked her head, but Elsie saw a flash of pain cross the girl's face. "Is it Charlene?"

After a moment the child nodded, a slight movement of her head.

Elsie touched the Barbie's blue jacket with a gentle finger. "Did Charlene make that for your Barbie? Before she left?" Tiffany pressed her lips together, but she stroked the jacket on the doll's back.

Quiet, gotta be quiet. In a whisper, Elsie said, "Charlene's my friend, too."

Though Tiffany's head was bent, Elsie could see a skeptical expression; but she forged on. "We were helping each other before she left. Tiffany, she'd want you to help me, too."

Elsie knelt before the child and peered into her face. "Charlene would want you to tell me about it, Tiffany."

Tiffany pressed her lips tightly together, lifting the Barbie to block her face. In desperation, Elsie tried another tactic.

"Maybe Barbie could tell me. She's a big girl, all grown

up." Elsie scooted closer and said, "Show me on Barbie, please, Tiffany. Did your daddy touch Charlene? Just show me where, on your Barbie."

Though it seemed that the child wasn't listening, Elsie waited for a long moment, holding her breath. Finally, Tiffany's hand moved, hesitantly grazing Barbie's groin.

Elsie's scalp prickled with excitement, but she suppressed her reaction and spoke quietly. "Where else? Where else did your dad touch Charlene?"

Tiffany put a finger on Barbie's breast.

"Did you see it, with your own eyes? Tell me, Tiffany: what did you see?"

The child sat, silent. Trying not to press her too hard, Elsie urged, "Tell Barbie what you saw."

A whisper came out as soft as the rustling of a leaf. Focused on the doll's face, Tiffany said, "I seen it. His worm."

Elsie's breath caught. At long last the child had spoken. Carefully, lest her excitement scare the girl, she said, "Tell me. What did he do with his worm?"

"He put it in they tootie."

Bending close to her ear, Elsie asked, "What about you?"

Tiffany made a face and shook her head. "When I'm bigger."

Elsie's eyes stung; she turned away, so the child couldn't see. When she composed herself, she said, "Tiffany, what would you think of coming into the courtroom with me, you and Barbie? Could you say just what you told me?"

A violent change came over the girl; she jumped from

her chair and fled to a corner, huddling with her head buried. Elsie watched her in silence for a moment, before stepping over to the child and laying a firm hand on her shoulder.

Soothingly, she said, "It's all right, Tiffany; don't worry. Everything will be all right."

Watching the child shaking in misery, she knew that there was no way she could extract testimony from her in court. The sight of Tiffany in the corner rekindled her fighting spirit; the man who had crippled his child in such fashion should pay.

The trial wasn't over yet, she thought. She still had closing argument.

Taking a deep breath, she said, "Don't you worry, Tiffany. I'll do the talking for both of us."

THE PALMS OF Elsie's hands were clammy as she held onto the wooden bar of the jury box and looked into the faces of the twelve jurors. Midway into closing argument she had summarized her evidence and explained how it applied to the jury instructions.

The valentine, she thought. Time to drive that home.

She had to be careful; she couldn't comment on the defendant's failure to testify. It could be reversible error because he had the right to remain silent.

She said, "Remember the valentine card. You heard about it—saw it—held it in your hands when it was passed around the jury box. What did the defendant say on that card? What were his exact words?"

She focused on a mustached juror with savvy eyes. He should get the point: the card contained the only statement that Taney had provided at the trial.

"That card, addressed to JoLee Stokes, said 'what me and Char do don't mean nothing. You're my girl.'

"Think about the significance of those words. 'What me and Char do.' Ladies and gentlemen, you know what he's talking about. You heard the transcript of Charlene Taney's preliminary hearing testimony—sworn testimony—where she described exactly what it was that Kris Taney and his daughter 'do,' the sexual and perverse acts he made her perform. You heard that in the transcript."

At the word "transcript," a middle-aged woman in a knit pantsuit cut her eyes away. A negative jolt went through Elsie; she was rejecting the point. Maybe she didn't like a transcript substituted for live testimony. Or maybe she found Charlene's descriptions off-putting.

Without a pause, Elsie moved her focus to the young woman with the ponytail. She had been extremely attentive throughout the trial. "He says in the valentine, 'You're my girl.' Why does he say that? What does it mean? Ladies and gentlemen, we get his point, don't we? The defendant is reassuring JoLee that she has the position of girlfriend rather than his daughter Charlene."

The juror with the mustache nodded, just a fractional movement of his head. Elsie breathed out; she needed the mustache juror and the construction worker in her pocket in the jury room.

Nixon stood. "Objection. Calls for speculation."

Rountree's brow wrinkled. "Overruled."

Elsie was heating up, feeling the endorphin rush that sometimes came to her during argument.

"So—we have the Taney family in Barton, Missouri. On High Street, the defendant lives with his battered and beaten wife, a woman he has crushed in countless ways. You remember the axe handle. And in that home, the defendant has his 'girl' JoLee. And he has his daughters. Kristy Taney sat in this courtroom and told you under oath that her father has raped her. You heard the testimony of her sister Charlene describing the sexual abuse the defendant inflicted on her since she was nine years old."

A juror in her fifties with salt and pepper hair looked bored or skeptical or both. Elsie zeroed in on her; the woman held one of twelve votes.

"Remember the testimony of Dr. Petrus. He examined Kris Taney's daughters. He told you that neither Kristy nor Charlene has the hymen intact. Ladies and gentlemen, we are adults, we know what a broken hymen signifies."

"Objection. The witness did not tie the examination to my client."

Judge Rountree said, "Sit down, Mr. Nixon; the jury recalls what the doctor said."

Elsie continued, "What the doctor told us is a part of the picture, a picture of a household in McCown County where women and children are subjected to the abuse and the tyranny and the sexual whims of the defendant."

Nixon jumped up again. With an ironic tone, he

asked, "Is tyranny a violation of the Missouri criminal code?"

Turning on Nixon with ire, Elsie said, "You want to make jokes? Is this funny to you?"

Judge Rountree raised a restraining hand. "Overruled, Mr. Nixon; this is argument. Miss Arnold, you have one minute remaining."

She returned her focus to the jury. "We have proved in this trial, beyond a reasonable doubt—that this man," and she pointed at Taney again, "this man committed the felony offense of statutory rape of his daughter Kristy on November twenty-fifth. And we have proven that defendant committed the felony of statutory rape in the first degree on multiple occasions with his daughter Charlene."

"Ladies and gentlemen, the defendant believes: what he and his daughters do sexually '*don't mean nothing.*'

"It is your job to prove him wrong. To prove that what he has done to his daughters is a horrific and significant violation of the criminal law of this state. The way to prove this—to Kris Taney and to our community—is to find the defendant guilty of counts one through five."

After a final look over the twelve faces, she sat down, a pulse pounding in her throat.

While Josh Nixon delivered his closing argument, Elsie sat in her seat, composed, wearing a skeptical expression on her face. She held a pen and wrote rapidly, almost illegibly, as she prepared to have the final say. She would have five minutes for rebuttal when Nixon was done.

Nixon was having a field day, waving the pictures of Charlene, calling Donita a liar, and painting the police as bunglers and fools. He wove a conspiracy theory in which Donita, Roy, and Al made Kris Taney the fall guy, whose objection to their child pornography enterprise was silenced by having him thrown in jail.

"But you don't need to believe me," Nixon said, "you don't have to take my word for it. The facts were revealed by the state's witness. Kristy Taney told you who the real criminals are in this scenario."

Nixon turned and gestured scornfully at Elsie. "The prosecutor, in her argument, wanted to talk about the testimony of the handwriting expert and the doctor. She even dared to refer you to the testimony of that sainted 'Mother of the Year,' Donita Taney. These investigators are so misguided, they didn't discover a child porn operation going on right under their noses. They couldn't see through the gossamer web of lies spun by Donita Taney. If they had, Roy Mayfield would be in jail, not Kris Taney. Come to think of it, why isn't Roy Mayfield in jail? Or Al Taney? Or Donita? And why didn't the state get some DNA evidence from those children? Sure would be interesting to see who it matched up with in this household, don't you think?

"You know, the defendant in a criminal case doesn't have to prove anything. That's the prosecution's job: they have the burden of proof. But in this case, the defense has proven that the evidence is unreliable and unbelievable. That the state has bungled this investigation and failed to do their job. If ever a case had a reasonable doubt, this is it. For these reasons, ladies and gentlemen, I ask that you find the defendant Not Guilty."

Elsie rose and walked to the jury box with a steely glint in her eyes.

"Ladies and gentlemen of the jury, we need to focus: what is this case about? Who is on trial here? The *defendant*, the man who has been charged with rape, is sitting in this courtroom, in that chair; it is Kris Taney." At that, Elsie turned to point at him, and they locked eyes for a second. He made a malevolent squint in her direction, but she turned away from him and faced the jury again.

"You have sworn an oath to do a job in this trial. You must make a decision. Is *this man, Kris Taney*, guilty of the sex acts with his young daughters, Kristy and Charlene? That is your job. That must be your focus.

"Now, Mr. Nixon has a different job: his job is to distract you with smoke and mirrors, to confuse you."

"Objection!"

"Sustained. Jury will disregard the last statement."

Elsie continued, unwavering in her intensity. "Don't let the defense distract you from your duty. Think of the victims, recall the facts they gave you. Listen to Kristy Taney, and remember what she told you: that on Thanksgiving Day, a day that should be special, a happy family time, *that man*, her own father, held her down and raped her in his bed. Remember the transcript of Charlene, how her father raped and sodomized her from her early childhood on.

"Mr. Nixon doesn't want you to focus on that. He wants you to reject the state's case because he introduced testimony that the girls were victimized by other people as well—by Roy, by their Uncle Al. What kind of twisted logic is that? What kind of argument is he force-feeding you? The defense is trying to tell you that, because these children were abused by others, then it's okay, what their father did to them! That because other, terrible, evil men photographed Kristy or Charlene, you should just overlook the fact that Kristy's own father had sexual intercourse with her, a twelve-year-old child, and with her sister. That's crazy! How does the abuse of other predators make what *Kris Taney* did okay? Do you intend to close your eyes to Kris Taney's crimes? Can you live with that?

"You, the twelve of you sitting in this jury box, you set the standards for our community. In McCown County, Missouri, here in the Ozarks, what will we tolerate? The twelve of you determine what kind of actions *will be* tolerated and what acts *won't be* tolerated. Ladies and gentlemen, do we condone rape and incest and child molestation in McCown County, or do we not? Do we turn a blind eye to the suffering of our children in this community? Do we protect our children here, or don't we?"

Elsie gripped the wooden banister of the jury box, leaning toward the jurors, looking them in the eye.

"I want you to send a message with your verdict. I want you to send the message, that down here in McCown County, a man can't violate his daughters like Kris Taney did, then just walk away. You tell everyone that we will not permit it.

"I have faith in you, ladies and gentlemen. I ask that

you find the defendant, Kris Taney, guilty on all counts. Thank you."

As Elsie sat at the counsel table, the bailiff shepherded the jury into the jury room to deliberate. Elsie checked her notes, rustling through pages of argument to make sure she hadn't missed anything she'd meant to say, before she realized the futility of the effort: it was over, one way or the other.

The deputies shackled Taney up for his walk back to the county jail to await the verdict, and after they hustled him into the hallway, Nixon turned to her.

"Well . . ." he said, and paused.

She grimaced and raised her brows. "It's in the hands of the gods now, Nixon."

"Yep, I guess so." Grudgingly, he added, "Good argument."

"You, too." She started stuffing her papers into the accordion file on the counsel table, but before the job was done, Merle received a knock from the jury on the other side of the jury room door.

Both Elsie and Josh Nixon froze as they waited to see what the jury had to say. After a whispered consultation between the bailiff and a juror, Merle called to the judge, who was standing in the doorway of his chambers, waiting to hear.

"Judge, they want to eat."

Elsie and Nixon both groaned. "This is going to take a while," Elsie said.

Chapter Forty-Six

WHILE THE JURY deliberated, Elsie had time to kill. On the left side of her untidy desk sat a stack of files that needed attention, containing motions from defense attorneys in other cases. She picked up the top file, but tossed it back without opening it. She was too distracted to accomplish any real work. She wasn't even up to answering her e-mail.

The volumes she had borrowed from the judges' law library sat on a chair where she dropped them the day before. She should return them to the conference room. She could muster the energy to do that.

The hallways of the second floor were deserted and dark. It was so quiet she could hear the click of her heels on the tile floor. The courthouse always emptied out at five o'clock, so only the people invested in the Taney trial remained. Judge Rountree was ensconced in chambers and the jury was shut up in the jury room with Merle standing guard outside the door. Even Nixon had stepped out for a sandwich. Elsie wished Ashlock had stayed to await the verdict with her, but he had catch-up work to do at the P.D. He'd told her to text him when the verdict came in.

She opened the oak door of the library. It had a pane of frosted glass embedded with chicken wire, but no light shone in from the darkened hallways. Elsie groped along the wall for the light switch and flipped on the overhead light, a fluorescent fixture that shed a greenish glare. She set the volumes on the massive conference table, scarred with cigarette burns from decades before smoking bans were imposed.

A coffee cup on the table held a collection of freshly sharpened pencils. She leaned over and rummaged through them. Maybe she'd nab one for her office.

Behind her, she heard the door slam shut with a bang, just as the light clicked off.

With a gasp, she turned. Without the overhead light, she couldn't see. The room had no window other than the frosted panel. "Noah," she said, spitting his name with fury. She'd been tensed for this confrontation ever since she rejected his flowers in the courtroom. "What is your fucking problem?"

A body made contact, pressing her back against the table and covering her mouth with his hand. She felt the callused pads of his fingers along her cheek. It wasn't Noah.

In her ear, he whispered, "If thy hand offend thee, cut it off."

He smelled faintly of sweat, and his breath had a sharp odor, emanating from a nervous gut.

She raised her hands to his chest, trying to push him away with a tremendous shove. Her right hand brushed the metal tip of a bolo tie beneath a wad of rough fabric. She instantly knew —it was Luke Morrison, the man from the Pentecostal church who had called her Jezebel. He wrested her right hand and twisted it behind her back, whispering, "Cut it off and cast it from thee."

Her heart pounding like a drum, she struggled against him, kicking at his legs with the pointed toes of her shoes, but he pinned her against the table with his pelvis and gave her arm a wicked twist. She could feel his penis under his pants. It was hard.

"And if thy right eye offend thee, pluck it out."

He released her hand. She prayed it was over, that he had delivered his message and was done with her. But in an instant his hands were on her face, slapping something sticky over her mouth. Her hands flew to her face faster than he could restrain them. It felt like duct tape.

Desperate to gain a step ahead of her attacker, Elsie reached for his neck and found the bolo tie. With a frantic jerk, she twisted it as tightly as she could. If she pulled it taut, hopefully she could strangle him.

He gagged against it, taking a step back. Even in the darkness, she was able to make out the shape of his head. He was wearing a mask: a horned mask with holes for the eyes and a gaping mouth. A Baldknobbers mask.

Elsie lunged away from the table, but he caught her around the waist and dragged her back, struggling to grasp her wrists. She heard a ripping sound from the roll of tape; he'd use it to tie her hands together. She fought, lashing out with her fists. He managed to pin her against the table again and caught her right hand. Twisting it behind her, he said, "I've been watching you. You've caused sin and destruction."

She panted against the tape on her mouth, struggling to keep her left hand free.

He said, "You won't stop with Taney. You want to bust up my family. Like the Bible says, you tempt the little ones to stray. The believers to fall away."

Frantic, she shook her head back and forth in denial. He pinned her tighter with his body.

"My daughter run off, left her husband, and you went down to see her at that place. I followed you there on Sunday. You ought to have a millstone around your neck and be drowned."

He pushed her down onto the surface of the table on her back. "No," she screamed, but the sound was garbled by the duct tape. The Baldknobbers mask looming over her looked demonic. She punched at his head with her free hand and he tried to grab it. Stars danced before her eyes, but she couldn't pass out; she must not.

He reached into his coat and pulled out an object, displaying it for a moment before he set it on the table. She thought it was a hunting knife; it had a jagged edge.

Her left hand scrambled along the varnished top of the wooden table, trying to gain a grip to pull herself away, and scattered the cup of pencils. The freshly sharpened pencils.

Her fingers curled around the length of one of the wooden pencils. Her eyes were growing accustomed to the dark; she could make out his eyes through the holes in his mask. As the man whispered, "Pluck it out, cut it off and cast it from thee," she raised the pencil and plunged it into his eye with all her strength.

Elsie was left-handed.

With a roar he staggered back, releasing her, and she flung herself to the door. The man was a step behind, still howling, but she was too fast for him; she got out the door and fled into the hallway.

Ed Montee, the courthouse janitor, was standing in the open door of the men's bathroom with a mop in his hand. Elsie ran toward him and into the men's room. She ripped the duct tape off her mouth, shrieking as it came off.

"A man attacked me!" Slumping against the tiled wall, she pointed with a shaky hand. "In the library."

Montee dropped the mop, and its wooden handle clattered on the floor. "Is he armed? He got a gun?"

"Lord, I don't know. He's got a knife. I don't know if he's got a gun."

Ed and Elsie peered out into the hall. There was no movement by the library. "He has to be in there. There's no way out," she said.

Merle, the bailiff, rounded the corner, wearing an expression of righteous anger. "Judge wants to know what the ruckus is. Don't you know the jury can hear this carrying on?"

Elsie ran to Merle and clutched his arm. "I was attacked by a man in the library. He's still in there, he must be." Her wrist began to throb with a vengeance, as if providing proof of her claim.

Merle started to fumble for his gun but began walking away from the library rather than toward it. "We better get the sheriff over here." He handed his cell phone to Elsie, and she saw he was shaking as badly as she was. "You make the call so I can keep my eye on the situation."

She could barely push the buttons. When a deputy answered, she begged him to come without delay.

"Are there injuries?" the man asked.

"No," Elsie said, before she amended her answer. "There's an asshole with a pencil sticking out of his eye."

Chapter Forty-Seven

AFTER LUKE MORRISON was taken to jail, Elsie had to make a statement at the sheriff's office. By the time she returned to her office, thoroughly shaken but still waiting on the jury's decision, she was exhausted. She put her head on her desk and managed to fall asleep still clutching the claw hammer she'd borrowed from Montee after the incident, determined to have a defense weapon.

An hour later she was still dozing when Merle rapped on the door frame. "Jury's got a question Elsie," he said.

She awoke with a jerk, sitting up so quickly that her chair rocked to one side. Her hand clutched the hammer in her lap

"Who's there?" she babbled, then seeing the bailiff, gave a short laugh, shaking her head. "Sorry, Merle. I'll be right there."

Merle nodded and moved on.

When Elsie reached the courtroom, Taney was being

released from his handcuffs, after what had obviously been a contentious argument between the deputies and Josh Nixon.

"The judge has already decided this point; I don't know why you make us battle it out every damn time the defendant comes and goes," Nixon declared, the blood high in his face. "The defendant has to have his hands free to assist with his defense."

The deputy hooked the cuffs on his belt. "Feet stay shackled," he said shortly as he and the other escort turned to go.

Elsie stared at the empty jury box, wondering what question the jury would ask. They had to make decisions on five separate counts; they could be confused about the verdict forms, or the instructions, or the evidence.

Or they could be sending out for another snack.

As the door to the judge's chambers opened, a knock sounded from the inside the jury room. Merle hurried over and opened the door a crack. In a moment he swung around to address the judge.

"Your honor, they said to forget about the message."

Elsie shrugged and prepared to go back to her office.

"They say they've reached a verdict."

She froze. Though to her it felt like days since her closing argument, the jury had only been deliberating for three hours, and part of that time involved selecting a foreman, making the dinner order, eating, and filling out the verdict forms. She didn't think they could reach a guilty verdict in a five-count criminal case in three hours.

The jurors filed into the jury box. Elsie generally tried

to read the jury at this point, but this time she was too nervous. She concentrated on her pen, twisting the lid, but when she saw that her hands were shaking, she set the pen aside and folded her fingers together before her on the table.

"Have you reached a verdict, Mr. Foreman?"

"We have, Judge," the foreman answered.

The judge reached out his hand. Merle took the papers from the foreman and handed them to the judge. Judge Rountree rustled through the pages before he began to read.

"'As to count one, we, the jury, find the defendant Kristopher Eugene Taney Not Guilty.'"

Elsie's heart plummeted in her chest. She pressed her lips together, but didn't permit herself any other outward reaction.

"'As to count two, we, the jury, find the defendant Kristopher Thomas Taney Not Guilty.'"

Kris Taney hooted and slapped Nixon on the back. Judge Rountree shot the defense table a reproving glare.

"'As to count three, we, the jury, find the defendant Kristopher Eugene Taney Not Guilty.'"

"Yesssss," Nixon hissed in a whisper, while Taney grinned from ear to ear, like a man with a winning lottery ticket.

"'As to count four, we, the jury, find the defendant Kristopher Eugene Taney Not Guilty.'"

Taney had his arm around Nixon at this point, extending the other hand to him in an exuberant handshake.

The judge read the last verdict form. "'As to count five, we, the jury, find the defendant Kristopher Eugene Taney guilty of statutory rape in the first degree, as submitted in instruction number seven.'"

Elsie jerked to attention, and the jollity at the defense table came abruptly to a halt. He was only found guilty of one count. But that one count was enough to get a sentence of life imprisonment.

After a stunned moment, Taney roared, "Son of a bitch!" With the arm that he had thrown around Nixon's shoulder moments ago in a gesture of goodwill, he jerked the attorney into a neck hold.

"You done sold me out!" Taney cried, while Josh Nixon choked and flailed in a futile attempt to escape the big man's hold. Taney tightened his grasp, cutting off Nixon's windpipe; Elsie jumped to her feet as the attorney's complexion changed color. Taney abruptly dropped the neck hold, and as Nixon stumbled, trying to catch his breath, he grabbed his attorney by the hair on the front of his head and savagely punched him in the mouth.

Nixon went down like a carnival game target. As the courtroom erupted in chaos, two county deputies burst back into court at a run. Taney tried to lunge over the defense table, but because of his shackled feet, he landed on his back and the county deputies pounced. Struggling with the big man, they tried to roll him onto his stomach, but Taney fought so violently they couldn't control him. He flailed at the deputies with both fists, while the bailiff, Merle, watched from a safe distance. As the deputies labored to pin Taney, unsuccessfully attempting to get his hands into cuffs, he roared and shouted incomprehensible epithets.

The jurors cowered in the jury box, eyes glued to the unfolding confrontation. Elsie remained on her feet behind her counsel table, watching the scene as if it were happening to someone else in a movie or a television show.

One of the deputies pulled the Taser from its holder on his belt and jammed it into Taney's neck. Taney's body gave a mighty jerk, and the battle was done.

As the deputies moved to handcuff the incapacitated man, Rountree pounded his gavel with a resounding bang. Once he had the attention of the court, he barked, "Sentencing in this cause will be set for Friday, February seven. Defendant Kristopher Eugene Taney to remain in custody. The court orders defendant remanded to the McCown County jail." He also ordered a presentence investigation, to be prepared by the Probation and Parole Office. The office would examine Taney, look at his background and the severity of the offense, and make a recommendation regarding his sentence.

Turning to the jury, gawking in the jury box, Rountree paused, taking a moment to moderate his demeanor. "Ladies and gentlemen of the jury, I thank you for your service. You are dismissed, but please remain seated until the defendant is removed from the courtroom."

Elsie knew she should sit down, too, but first she leaned over the counsel table to watch as Merle and the deputies prepared to drag Taney from the courtroom. As Taney lay on the floor, twitching, she saw his eyes focus on her, fixing her with a look of pure hatred. She shivered and sat back quickly.

After the jury filed out of the courtroom, Elsie followed with a spring in her step. Walking down the corridor, she saw Madeleine speeding to her office at a near gallop. With a burst of elation, Elsie followed. This is it, she thought; it's time for me to dance my victory dance right on the carpet in front of her desk.

The door nearly shut in Elsie's face, but she caught it before it latched. Poking her head inside and regarding Madeleine with a jubilant grin, she said, "What do you say, Madeleine? Did you come back to the courthouse to hear the verdict?"

Madeleine had just popped the top on a can of Slim-Fast; at the sound of Elsie's voice, she sloshed the contents onto her desktop.

"Oh, shoot," Elsie said, stepping inside, "didn't mean to startle you. I just wanted to make sure you heard about the Taney verdict."

With a pinched look on her face, Madeleine nodded as she mopped at the spill with a wad of Kleenex.

Waiting for a word of congratulations, Elsie tensed, thinking, Come on Madeleine, give it up to me.

The silence dragged as Madeleine pulled more tissues from the box with an angry twist.

Elsie took a breath and said, "I guess we're good then? Everything between you and me?"

Madeleine replied sourly, "I guess we are."

You're fucking with my buzz, hateful thing, Elsie thought, and couldn't refrain from adding, "It wouldn't kill you to tell me I did a good job."

Madeleine shot her a look of resentment. "You got lucky."

Chapter Forty-Eight

FOUR WEEKS HAD passed since the Taney trial. On the Saturday morning after Taney was sentenced in Rountree's court, Elsie unlocked her apartment and walked inside, toting a bulky Wal-Mart bag. Making her way to the sofa, she pulled a newspaper from the bag: the *Barton Daily News*. The top news story carried a bold headline: TANEY GETS LIFE SENTENCE.

Leaning back against the sofa cushions, she stared at the headline and relished the moment. Over twenty-four hours had passed since Rountree handed down the sentence, and she was still absorbing and savoring her triumph.

But when she unfolded the front page, she beheld an image that nearly jolted her from her seat. The article carried a large photograph of Madeleine Thompson. Smiling.

Claiming victory.

Outrage washed over her as she stared at the photo in disbelief. In a fit of temper, she crumpled the paper and flung it across the room.

A minute passed as she sat and fumed, stewing over the enormity of Madeleine's hubris. But finally she reined in her hurt pride—she didn't go to trial in the Taney case to get her picture in the paper.

Rising from the couch, she picked the wadded newspaper off the floor and carried it into the kitchen, smoothing it on the counter as she prepared a pot of coffee.

She was still reading the article when she heard a knock. She opened the door beaming after spying her visitor through the peephole.

"Ashlock!" she cried. "You're a welcome sight; I've been wanting to talk to you all day."

"That's mighty nice to hear."

"Well, get on in here. Where the hell were you yesterday? I thought you'd be at the sentencing."

"I hated to miss it," he said, then broke into a smile as she held up the wrinkled newspaper like a trophy. "That's a heck of a win. You made us proud."

"It's our win, Ashlock. We're a team," she said, adding with a hint of acid, "Of course, the real credit should go to the fabulous Madeleine Thompson."

Ashlock dismissed the comment with a wave of his hand. "Everybody knows who won that case."

She flashed him a grateful smile. "Have a seat, Ash. What can I get for you? Diet Coke? I've got coffee made."

"Sure, I'll take a cup." As she moved into the kitchen to pour the coffee, he said, "I should've called before I came over. Not polite to come by unexpected like this. You'll think I was raised in a barn."

"Ash, you are welcome anytime. Drop by whenever you get the notion," she said, handing him a steaming mug. "Now sit down and tell me what was so important that you missed out on the sentencing yesterday."

She sat on the couch and patted the spot next to her. As Ashlock joined her, he said, "We found Al Taney."

"No!" She groaned with relief. "How did you run him down?"

"Roy Mayfield tipped us off to a couple of his regular hangouts, and sure enough we nailed him."

"Roy's talking?" she asked. Scooting sideways on the couch to face him, she sat cross-legged on the cushions.

"Singing like a bird."

"Ah, confession is good for the soul," she said with a sardonic nod.

Ashlock settled into the couch a little. "Roy would like to lay everything off on Al. But we've got Roy's cell phone, and his computer."

"So Roy was photographing the girls."

"All three."

"Oh, don't tell me that. Tiffany." Elsie sank back onto the sofa and looked away from Ashlock.

He continued, "Roy was just starting out. He and Al were drinking buddies at a dive on Frisco Street. Al had shown Roy some Polaroids, but Roy wanted to take it into cyberspace. He liked to hang out in those porn chat rooms, and he got the idea they could make big money off the girls. He took stills with the phone, or snippets of video, then uploaded it onto his computer. He'd accessed some Web sites that show kid porn and was offering to provide the product."

Outraged, Elsie shook her head. "Horrible. Oh my God. And what did Donita think about the enterprise?"

"Oh, you know Donita. Didn't know nothin' about nothin'. But she knew more than she's letting on. Because she helped Roy plant the Polaroids in the box of Kris Taney's personal stuff and pass it on to you."

Elsie gave a huff of disgust and rose to grab a plate of cookies from the kitchen. Sitting back down, she asked, "So didn't Kris Taney want in on the porn thing?"

"No."

"Why do you suppose?"

"Roy told us that Kris didn't want strangers to see the girls naked. Now, whether his aim was to minimize his chance of being caught, or he was just keeping them for himself, we just don't know."

"Because he ain't talking."

"Nope. Worthless son of a bitch."

Elsie shook her head. "I keep beating myself up for not seeing what was going on at the Taneys'. I always sensed something was rotten. From now on I listen to my gut."

She took a meditative sip of coffee. "Tina says the girls are doing okay in foster care. She found a placement that took them both, thank God. But Ash . . . " she said with a sigh.

"What?"

"I wish I knew about Charlene. Wish I knew she was okay."

"That's the other news I had for you. We've got a lead. We think she's in Poplar Bluff, down by the Bootheel. Poplar Bluff police are checking it out. I'll let you know."

"Good, I'm so glad. Get that girl out of the Bootheel. You know what they say about the Bootheel."

"What?"

"They say, if you took the Bootheel of Missouri and gave it to Arkansas, it would raise the IQ of both states."

Ashlock groaned and shook his head.

With a hint of irony, Elsie said, "Noah grew up in the Bootheel."

Ashlock shot her a look. "Anything new with him?" he asked in an offhand manner.

"That shithead. He texted a couple of weeks ago to tell me that we were through—like it wasn't over till he decreed it. He's FBO with Paige, lucky girl."

They fell silent for a moment. Elsie sighed and said, "Hey, Ash."

"What?"

"I wasn't honest with you about me and Noah. That day we went to the Apostolic church."

"I know."

"I feel bad about lying to you. It seems stupid now."

He shook his head. "You don't need to go into it. I dealt with it."

Surprised, she said, "What? What happened?"

"I reported it to Internal Affairs."

"At the police department? But you didn't have any information. I didn't tell you anything."

"Breeon came to see me the Monday after the party.

She gave a statement, and I put in my observations. It's confidential; can't talk about what went on at the disciplinary proceedings. But it needed to be done."

"Huh. Okay, then. So what will happen? They won't fire him."

"Can't go into it. He's on the night shift. He'll be on nights for a long time."

Elsie hid a smile. Noah hated the night shift. She was lost in her own thoughts until Ashlock tapped her knee and asked, "Have you had lunch yet?"

"No," she said, adding, "Lord, I don't think I'm fit to be seen. Look at me, in my Saturday rags."

She thought she saw a flash of emotion play over his features, but he turned his head away. He said, "I think you look terrific. How about a burger?"

Setting her coffee carefully on the table, Elsie studied him: something about his manner indicated that he might want their friendship to head in a new direction. "I don't know. I've got someplace I need to go this afternoon."

"I won't keep you out all afternoon. We'll just get a burger at the chili place on the North Side."

She faced him and said earnestly, "I don't mean to sound like an idiot. But is this lunch? Or is it a lunch date?"

He didn't smile. He looked back at her and asked, "Would you like that?"

"What about that woman you've been seeing? Caroline Applegate?'

Ashlock looked a little sheepish as he said, "I broke it off. Didn't seem fair to take up her time."

"It didn't?"

"Not when it's you I want to be with." He gave her a direct look; she felt it all the way to her toes. "So what do you say? Would you like that? If it's more than just lunch?"

She didn't need time to think it over. "Yeah," she said, breaking into a smile. "I'd like it a lot."

Pulling on her coat, she headed out the door with Ashlock. She couldn't remember the last time she'd felt so light of heart.

Chapter Forty-Nine

WEAK AFTERNOON SUNLIGHT cast a glow on the red brick hotel that housed the Battered Women's Center of the Ozarks. Elsie pulled her car up to the front door.

She hefted a box of clothes from the backseat along with her Wal-Mart bag, then entered the hotel and walked into the lobby. The woman with the long gray braid sat in an ancient rolling chair behind the front desk. She looked at Elise for a moment, as if trying to recall where she might have seen her before, then good-naturedly asked, "What can I do for you?"

Elsie set her box on the counter. "I heard you could use clothing donations."

"Mercy, yes. Sometimes women come in here with just the clothes on their backs." Peering into the box, the woman said, "These is nice."

"Oh," Elsie said modestly, "they're used, all of them. I went through my closet and boxed up things I don't wear. Mostly because they're too small," she confided ruefully.

"We'll find someone who can wear them," the woman assured her.

Opening the Wal-Mart bag, Elsie said, "I got some toiletries and stuff, too. You need toothpaste and shampoo and Tide, right?"

Taking in the contents of the bag, the woman rolled her eyes in ecstasy. "This is a gold mine. Heavenly days. You know what we need. Now, let me get you a tax receipt."

As the woman sorted through a file folder in search of a form, Elsie leaned on the wooden counter and said, "This is nothing; I'm glad to help. It's little enough I can do."

"What's your name, ma'am," the woman asked, with pen in hand.

"Elsie Arnold."

The woman scrutinized her, as recognition dawned on her face. "You're the prosecutor. The Taney prosecutor."

Elsie nodded, privately pleased at the acknowledgment.

The woman crossed her arms and beamed at her. "That was something, what you did."

"Thank you," Elsie said. "It wasn't just me. A lot of people worked together to make that happen."

Nodding, the woman agreed. "It takes a mess of people to do anything worth doing. You know," she said, as inspiration washed over her face, "we're so shorthanded here, it's a struggle staying open. We have to have someone at the desk day and night, and I'm having a time trying to cover it with volunteers."

Elsie's glow faded as the woman's meaning struck home. She could see where this was headed. "I don't think I can help you. I work full-time."

The woman persisted. "The weekends is the toughest. Lots of my help has to be home with their kids, and the college girls who volunteer won't sign on for a weekend time. Could you ever help us out on Saturday or Sunday? Just to fill in?"

Inwardly, Elsie fought against the suggestion; avoiding the woman's eyes, she shouldered her purse and backed away a step, determined to escape. After living with the Taney case night and day for weeks, she didn't want to take on more suffering. She was tired, worn-out. She needed to recoup.

"I'm so busy. I work on weekends a lot of the time."

"You could bring work here," the woman suggested. "Mostly you just sit and wait for someone to come in, or the phone to ring."

"No," Elsie said firmly. "I can't."

The woman sighed with regret. "Well, it was worth a try." Over her shoulder, she called into the back room. "Britney? You still back there?"

The door opened and a young woman appeared. Clearly, she was a recent arrival; her battered face was healing, both eyes still ringed with bruises.

The gray-haired woman gestured toward Elsie's donations. "Honey, will you carry that stuff upstairs? It needs to go to the storage room on the second floor. Ruth can show you."

Silently, the young woman did as she was bid. As she

picked up the box of clothes and balanced the Wal-Mart bag on top, Elsie turned her head away, taking care to avoid staring at the woman's injured face.

The older woman leaned over the counter and called up the stairs. "Ruth, you hear me? Give Britney a hand with the donations."

Elsie looked up the stairway, where a girl with uncut hair appeared. She wore the long skirt of a Pentecostal. As she helped Britney carry the box of clothes, Elsie realized that Ruth must be the sister of Naomi, the girl who had given her the note to deliver here.

The gray-haired woman initialed the tax form and offered it to Elsie. Looking at her curiously, the woman asked, "Have we met somewhere?"

"Not sure. Maybe." Grasping the paper, Elsie fled the building. As she slipped into her car, she let out a breath, grateful for her getaway. Reaching into her purse, she found her keys without looking and started the ignition.

I can't do it. I'm too busy.

But something pricked at her, a whisper in her head.

I don't want to, she insisted to herself. *I don't want to be in there.* And a thought took shape: *I don't belong in there.*

While the engine idled, she caught sight of herself in the rearview mirror, and her eyes narrowed. *Liar. Hypocrite.*

As the reality and shame of the truth washed over her, Elsie's nose stung and her eyes brimmed over. She covered her face, fiercely ordering herself to stop. Crying in public mortified her.

But she knew the reason for her dismay. It was the knowledge that the women inside the shelter were no different than she was. She'd been on the receiving end of an abusive attack, ignored the signs leading up to it, and lied to cover it up. The ignominy of her victimization and the duplicity of her attempt to distance herself from it cut deep.

Popping open the glove compartment in search of a Kleenex, she only turned up a McDonald's napkin. She seized it gratefully and blew her nose.

Resting her forehead against the steering wheel, she had a moment of clarity.

This isn't about me. It isn't about me at all.

She turned off the ignition. It took some courage to walk back into the lobby after her hasty departure.

Approaching the woman who still stood behind the desk, Elsie spoke in an offhand manner, to counter her red eyes and swollen nose. "You know, Sunday mornings are actually good for me. Maybe once or twice a month."

The woman grinned. "Really?"

"Yeah," Elsie said, meeting the woman's smile. "Sign me up."

Acknowledgments

TAKING THIS NOVEL from the seed of an idea to publication has been a long journey, but I received much-needed assistance along the way. I want to thank my editor, Trish Daly, for her vision as we crafted the story into its final form, and for liking Elsie's shortcomings as well as her strengths. My agent, Jill Marr of the Sandra Dijkstra Literary agency, is an angel with a halo; thanks go to her for taking on an Ozarks hillbilly and shaping the manuscript with her sharp editorial eye. I want to thank Andrea Hackett for help with publicity, and Peter Weissman for excellent copyediting.

Showers of thanks go to friends who were early readers of the book and who rooted for me along the way: Lisa, Patti, Julie, Kathy, Amy, Laura and the neighborhood pals; Laura and Louise at NACC; my wonderful students at Missouri State, especially my advisees in AKPsi. And Alan, who taught me the meaning of hashtag.

My family has provided support in countless ways, from the legal expertise given by my brother John and sister Susie, to the editorial suggestions and encouragement from sisters Carol and Janice.

But above all, I must thank the three people who mean more to me than words can express: my beloved husband Randy, my precious Ben, my darling Martha. You are my rock and my salvation.

About the Author

NANCY ALLEN practiced law for fifteen years, serving as Assistant Missouri Attorney General and as Assistant Prosecutor in her native Ozarks (the second woman in Southwest Missouri to serve in that capacity). During her years in prosecution, she tried over thirty jury trials, including murder and sexual offenses, and is now a law instructor at Missouri State University. *The Code of the Hills* is her first novel.

@TheNancyAllen

Facebook.com/NancyAllenAuthor